OUT OF THE EMBERS OF HELL

Book III in the Coalition/Orthodoxy Universe

J. E. Bruce

BooksForABuck.com

2016

Dedicated to my muses: Miles, Mandy, Buck, Oliver, Indigo, Red, Wally and Gromit

Earlier in the Series

They are the Elkanasu's beloved A'tuu'shahn'i. To everyone else they are the enigmatic and feared Hahtooshan Orthodoxy, believed by many to be organic machines, rumored by others to be the remnants of a once powerful alien civilization and capable of shapeshifting.

They now make their living as the mercenaries of choice, and their services are in constant demand as the known galaxy's hegemonies, the Matarran Star Empire and the human-dominated Rim Coalition, have found it impossible to co-exist. The Orthodoxy has grown wealthy on the avarice of others, but its success has engendered universal enmity. And now the Orthodoxy has finally met its match, confronted not only with the enemy from without, but the enemy within when it becomes widely known that Hahtooshans, bio-engineered humans themselves, have no resistance to many common human illnesses.

Faced with the genocide of his people, one Hahtooshan, Khusaaq, risks all and loses almost all in an attempt to save his kind, and in the process finds allies in the most unexpected of places: the very members of the crew of the Coalition patrol ship, *Baidarka*, which had taken him prisoner.

Through these unlikely allies, an alliance is forged, but the nascent compact between the Coalition and Orthodoxy is fragile, with many on either side willing to do anything they can to destroy it before it can fully take root. One such group, spurred on by radical Coalition colonists, kidnaps Khusaaq's human bond-mate, Ensign Sirin Corsali and her friend, Lieutenant Drakin, as bait to entrap him. Another abducts Khusaaq's closest kin, Qar'qaah, with the same intent. Both parties flee with their hostages to a non-aligned planet, Poonda Five, with Khusaaq and the *Baidarka* hot on their heels.

Temporarily escaping captivity, Sirin and Qar'qaah bump into each other in the deserted streets of Poonda Five's space port, The Gorgon's Lair, and unhappily join forces in hopes of eluding their respective captors. Believing they have found freedom, Sirin and Qar'qaah take refuge for the night in a hostel, only to find that their kidnappers are far more cunning, and persistent than they'd assumed.

Cast of Main Characters

Crew of the Coalition Expeditionary Forces patrol ship,
Baidarka:
Ensign Sirin Corsali, human, captain's adjutant
Commander Robert Aquila, human, captain
Doctor William Amalfitano, human, chief medical officer
Lieutenant Zarijan Izraad, human, intelligence officer and
chempath
Crewman Xosé Tasende, human, ship's pathologist
Doctor Jenna Fleming, human, medical officer
Lieutenant Drakin, Eltannian, nurse/surgeon
Ensign Tace Pardix, human, former chief navigator, now
renegade
Lieutenant Edwin Teague, human, exec
Ensign Ife Lesedi, human, chief weapons officer
Lieutenant Alain Perou, chief engineer

Hahtooshans:
Chercjengh'khusaaq Abhijit'tischinjgra, Sha'ashahn (rank
equivalent to commander); goes by his use name, Khusaaq
Sarhah'matoosh Abhijit'tischinjgra, Ruh'ta'aq (rank equivalent
to lieutenant); goes by his use name, Matoosh
A'uha-larkahn'qar'qaah Abhijit'tischinjgra, Kon'ta'aq (rank
equivalent to corporal); goes by his use name, Qar'qaah
Teq'tu'narbrooi ket Tashar'anhi, Hahtra'tzrhi (rank equivalent
to fleet admiral) of the Orthodoxy destroyer, *Faridour*; goes by
his use name, Narbrooi
Pashna'gaalan ket Tashar'anhi , Nahru'tzhri (rank equivalent to
captain), Khusaaq's former commanding officer; goes by her
use name, Gaalan.

Other characters:
Jonathan Urbat, human ringleader of the group who kidnapped
Ensign Corsali and Lieutenant Drakin in order to entrap
Khusaaq
Syr, human, one of Urbat's accomplices

Pava, Matarran, one of Urbat's accomplices
Mathoc, Looper, one of Urbat's accomplices
Seitakap, President of the High Council of the planet Tuli

Chapter 1

Poonda Five. Just before dawn, planetary time.

"Wakey-wakey..."

Ensign Sirin Corsali reluctantly opened her eyes at the whispered voice. It took her groggy mind a moment to realize that she was staring into Qar'qaah's filthy, robe-shrouded back—and more critically, the voice not only wasn't Qar'qaah's but came from behind her.

She turned her head and looked up.

Jonathan Urbat, one of her kidnappers she thought she'd eluded, loomed over her, his blaster pointed at her face. As their eyes locked, he grinned and stepped back. "Up—and keep your hands where we can see 'em."

She did as she was told, leaving Qar'qaah's pistol under the pillow where she'd hidden it earlier, and peeled the blanket back slowly. As she levered herself up to a seated position at Urbat's urgent motioning, she noticed he wasn't alone. The Poondian landlady stood nearby, bracketed by a Matarran and a Looper.

It took Sirin only an instant to recognize the two aliens as the very same pair from the café the day before. *Gods...!*

"Now you've got what you want," the Poondian said as she started to back step towards the doorway, "you'll be leaving, just as you agreed?"

The Matarran clamped his hand on her shoulder, stopping in her tracks and growled, *"Not so fast."*

The Poondian, her swarthy face turning a shade paler, glanced wide-eyed at his restraining fingers, then at Urbat.

"No need to dash off, is there?" Urbat replied sweetly, to which the woman visibly swallowed. "We haven't thanked you properly for assisting us in retrieving these two... *ship jumpers.*" He nodded to the Looper.

The Poondian, clearly thinking the worst, stammered, "N-n-no n-n-need to to t-t-thank m-m-me, I w-was..." but her frightened voice abruptly trailed off as the Looper offered her a handful of tokens. She stared at them, tempted but hesitant then at the Looper's prodding gesture, snatched them from his furry palm.

"I hope it goes without saying," Urbat continued in the same affable tone, "we'd rather you not mention this to anyone else who might come asking—wanna keep this matter from our captain's ears you see—he's not a man who is as... *forgiving* as we are."

"Of course! I run a respectable establishment here—don't want no trouble from no one." She eyed Sirin as the Matarran released his hold, then she hurried from the room, closing the door behind her.

Urbat chuckled, then, using his free hand, pulled his tac-pac from a pocket and brought it to his mouth. "Tace? Lock onto our coordinates. And you—" he again motioned to Sirin with his blaster. "Up."

Sirin did as she was told and slowly rose from the bed.

"Now move aside." Urbat again gestured with the weapon.

She remained where she was. "Why?"

"Whaddaya think?"

"So you can shoot him in the back while he's sleeping? He can't—"

"Shoot him in the back? Why would I want to do that? He's worth a fortune alive—not much at all dead."

Out of the corner of her eye, Sirin noticed Qar'qaah start to slide his hand under the pillow and to his pistol. *So not in fact asleep...* The Matarran noticed too, and was just a split second faster than Qar'qaah: he fired his shocker. The beam hit Qar'qaah square between the shoulder blades.

Sirin screamed, *"NO!"* as Qar'qaah convulsed. Then, before she could grab him, he rolled lifelessly forward, tumbling off the narrow bed to land face first in a tangle of blanket and robe. She started for him, but Urbat grabbed her arm and jerked her back. "Oh no you don't!"

"But he—"

"Don't worry, your lover boy there isn't dead."

Sirin started to open her mouth, her eyes darting between the inert heap that was Qar'qaah and Urbat. Then she thought better of it. If they believed Qar'qaah was Khusaaq then he did indeed have value. Enough, she hoped, to get him the medical attention he so desperately needed—she'd worry about the consequences of the deception later—assuming there was a later. If Urbat knew the truth, he'd likely kill him—and her too for wasting his time. Ensign Tace Pardix, Urbat's partner in crime she noted, was noticeably absent and that left her wondering about his fate. His absence, though, did mean that no one present had ever actually seen Khusaaq up close....

Urbat, still holding her arm in a painful grip, motioned irritably to the Matarran with his blaster. "What are you waiting for, Pava?—we haven't got all day. *Go on!*"

The alien unhappily and warily walked around the bed, in the process tossing the pillow aside and revealing the pistol. He favored Sirin with a smirking look, then at Urbat's prodding dip of the chin and keeping his shocker pointed at Qar'qaah's head, he grabbed the pistol and stuffed it in his belt. With a nod to his Looper companion, who stepped closer, his blaster now covering the Matarran, the alien yanked the blanket free of Qar'qaah's limp body, then began patting him down for more weapons.

Qar'qaah's utility knife was yanked from its sheath and placed on the bed but, in a display of an abundance of caution by the Matarran, well out of Qar'qaah's ready reach, followed a minute later by his weapons belt. The Matarran then shoved Qar'qaah onto his back and placing a knee on Qar'qaah's stomach, began roughly frisking him, sparing no part of his body, with little of the expected aversion to touching a Hahtooshan, much less Qar'qaah's slowly morphing trousers. In the process of his very thorough search, the alien found a tiny locator clipped to a fold of his robe's cowl.

He held it up for the others to see and grasp its significance then the Matarran placed it on the floor not far from Qar'qaah's head and with more force than was necessary, smashed it with the butt of his shocker.

Satisfied, he grabbed the utility knife, then rose and slipped it into his belt as well. At Urbat's nod, the Matarran slung Qar'qaah's weapons belt over his shoulder, and as the alien stepped away, he eagerly fingered his undisputed reward for doing the hands-on frisking: Qar'qaah's maser pistol.

Urbat let Sirin go, walked over to Qar'qaah and knelt down, then pulled out a small, spatula-shaped device from his hip pocket, shoved it into Qar'qaah's gaping mouth and scraped it across his blistered tongue; a moment later tiny machine bleated softly.

Urbat grinned at his confederates. "Perfect match, down to the very last short tandem repeat." He patted Qar'qaah on his barely moving chest. "This is our boy all right." He got back to his feet and turned to Sirin. "I knew you'd lead us to him. All we had to do was let you *think* you'd escaped, then follow you."

"What...?"

He stepped closer, tapped the collar of her jumpsuit. "Another imbedded tracking device. Granted, we lost you due to this planet's damned jamming, but then you decided to find a place to hole up in 'til morning and in a case of pure dumb luck, we just happened to pass by this marvelous establishment and reacquired the tracker's signal. Lucky for us that is—not so much for you and your lover boy here."

Sirin scowled at Urbat as she slipped around him then she knelt beside Qar'qaah and felt for a pulse, satisfying herself he was in fact still alive as Urbat brought his tac-pac back to his lips and said,

"Syr... it's go time. Agreed upon rendezvous."

Sirin fixed him with a baffled look.

Urbat grinned, said, "Just in case your friends who were following," he motioned to the shattered locator, "are listening."

A moment later and feeling the familiar tingle of a flicker, Sirin grabbed Qar'qaah's shoulders and barely had time to draw him tightly against her before the five of them were whisked away.

Chapter 2

Poonda Five, shortly before dawn.

"Sha'ashahn?"

Khusaaq glanced sidelong at a clearly flagging Nihaal as they continued to make their way up yet another street, suspecting the young soldier, frustrated and exhausted, had finally reached the point where he could no longer continue. The trooper's telltale distortion, which should have read as an eeling bright cyan, was now little more than a sluggishly flickering watery green and getting dimmer by the minute.

So far it had been a long, so far utterly fruitless night for everyone. The locator Matoosh had attached to Qar'qaah's clothing had proven to be worthless, and worse, Tejat, working in close concert with the sensor officers aboard the two koursans had been unable to pick up Qar'qaah's personal identifier after the first few sporadic pulses, compelling Khusaaq's reluctant decision to request twelve attentional crew from *Illuyanka* and *Kashkuh* to assist in the ground search as well as break up the two groups from *Jirah* into smaller teams, all to cover more ground.

Together they'd thoroughly reconnoitered the southern and eastern landing fields and searched a goodly portion of the industrial district—an astonishing amount of ground covered by such a small number and in such a short period of time. Now, the Gorgon's Lair showed distinct signs of waking up. Streets, which they'd had largely to themselves aside from the occasional cargo crawler, were beginning to fill with creatures of all descriptions, rapidly increasing their risk of detection.

He'd been pushing everyone, not that he needed to as everyone was keenly aware that this was their last chance to find Qar'qaah alive. And Nihaal, along with the other three from Rasal Ghul, were paying the price, willingly giving more than their weakened bodies could deliver without one word of complaint.

Perhaps it's time to recall everyone, regroup, rethink... and yes, accept. "Yes, Ha'tat?"

"Tejat Ruh'ta'aq reports that a Coalition vessel has just entered orbit," Nihaal replied, adding with audible astonishment: "It's hailing *Jirah...* on an A'tuu'shahn-only frequency."

That totally unexpected news stopped Khusaaq in his tracks. He'd been so preoccupied with looking for any sign of Qar'qaah he'd left everything else, including monitoring feeds from the foldboat and koursans and communications with the other widely dispersed teams to Nihaal.

"Jirah identifies it as…" Nihaal paused as he listened to the continuing stream of information before he continued, "the Coalition Patrol Ship, *Baidarka*? Tejat Ruh'ta'aq is requesting orders."

Khusaaq looked upwards and the multitude of sensors contained within his helmet shifted their focus to search for the unexpected visitor. A moment later a telltale lit up and he murmured, *"There you are…"*

Nihaal, for his part, warily looked around him as he audibly caught his breath.

Khusaaq tapped his chin on his visor's tac-net. "Tejat…"

"Yes, ta'ahn?"

"Tell the others to keep searching."

"Ta'ahn…?"

"Tell the others to keep searching," Khusaaq repeated with a trace of annoyance.

"Yes... ta'ahn. Of course." Tejat relayed the seemingly unnecessary order to the others and had no sooner confirmed acknowledgement from each team when Khusaaq said, "Can you patch the Coalition vessel's hail directly to me without it being detected?"

"Yes, ta'ahn—there may be some noticeable artifact, but—"

"Do it." He paused, heard the confirming echoing click of a connection, smiled a relieved smile and said, *"Baidarka?"*

There was a faint crackle of static then a familiar male voice replied, *"This is* Baidarka, *Sha'ashahn. How may we be of assistance?"*

"It's a bit complicated, Commander Aquila—perhaps it would be best if I explained in person?"

"Of course," Aquila replied.

"Stand by." He motioned for Nihaal to follow him as he hurried into a side alley, stopping only after they were well away from its mouth, next to what at one time had been a shipping container and now clearly served as a trash dump. He glanced back at the street and muttered, "It will have to do."

"Do, ta'ahn?" Nihaal said an instant before Khusaaq grabbed his arm and drew him into the concealing gap between the container and the alley wall.

"Transmitting locator identifiers... now," Khusaaq said.

There was a momentary pause then the disembodied voice said, *"Received, Sha'ashahn."*

"Ready on your order, Commander."

"Just you, or—"

"Both." Khusaaq barely had time to notice Nihaal's wan distortion quiver as the trooper's helmeted head snapped towards him before the flicker effect washed over both of them.

A moment later, a rapidly enlarging beige wall rushed towards them, but just before it would have made impact, it stopped and solidified into the ubiquitous interior door of a Coalition flicker mechanism.

The door slipped open and Khusaaq found himself staring at a familiar trio of faces: Doctor William Amalfitano, Lieutenant Zarijan Izraad and Commander Robert Aquila, all of whom were standing not far away and within yet another familiar sight: the *Baidarka's* main flicker chamber—scene of his bloody escape only a few weeks before. To his young companion, though, these Rimmers were still the enemy, a long hated and deeply distrusted enemy. Even more disconcerting for Nihaal was that he found himself confronted, to his obvious shock going by his sharp intake of breath, by three A'tuu'shahn'i. His hand instinctively reached for the grip of his maser pistol.

The three bodyguards assigned to Amalfitano instantly mirrored Nihaal's reaction while shielding the doctor with their own armored bodies.

"No," Khusaaq warned over the link.

Nihaal obediently, but unhappily dropped his hand to his side and the three soldiers reacted accordingly, to some extent relaxing their own tense posture. Their watchful stares never wavered from the fully armored Nihaal—or his pistol hand.

Amalfitano sharp-elbowed his way through the burly A'tuu'shahn troopers, his eyes searching the new arrivals' expressionless blast visors. "Khusaaq...?"

Khusaaq unclipped and slipped off his helmet. Tucking it under his arm and smiling, he stepped out of the flicker chamber. "Doctor!"

Amalfitano grinned a decidedly relieved grin, clapped him on his armored back and said, "Gods, I'm so happy to see you!" then he looked past him to Nihaal and gave him a quick once over with his eyes. He turned to Khusaaq. "Not Matoosh."

"No. One of those left behind on Rasal Ghul."

"Narbrooi's been keeping us informed—said you'd managed to rescue all of them,' Amalfitano added as he turned his smiling attention back to Nihaal. "Good job!"

Khusaaq impatiently motioned to Nihaal. *"Quh."*

Nihaal stepped out of the flicker chamber and stopped to stand rigidly beside Khusaaq as Aquila and Izraad approached.

"Doctor Amalfitano, Commander Aquila, Lieutenant Izraad, this is Nihaal T'agoon Tlekuschke, Ha'tat."

Nihaal, at Khusaaq's prodding stare, unenthusiastically unclipped and pulled off his helmet, then clutching it to his chest, dutifully—but *very* briefly—made eye contact with each of the three officers, all of whom, Khusaaq noted, reacting to Nihaal's very sickly appearance with varying degrees of shock.

"Welcome aboard the *Baidarka*, Nihaal Ha'tat," Aquila said.

Nihaal glanced at Khusaaq, then turned back to the Rimmer and replied with obvious uncertainty but in nevertheless perfect trade-use Standard, "It is my... honor, Commander Aquila. Thank you."

Aquila smiled warmly and nodded, then turned his attention back to Khusaaq. "I'm given to understand one of the rescued has gone missing?"

Khusaaq flicked Amalfitano, then Izraad a quick glance before answering with a weary, "Yes—"

"I suggest we adjourn to the conference room," Amalfitano interrupted, critically eyeing the haggard-faced Nihaal and then the equally exhausted appearing Khusaaq.

Aquila nodded his agreement. "Of course. I'm sure you'd both like to sit down, and have something cold to drink—"

Out of the corner of his eye, Khusaaq noticed Nihaal reflexively swallow and lick his lips at the idea of something to drink. For him sitting down, getting his weight off his aching leg had the greater appeal, but he too would happily accept a cold drink.

"—and you can fill us in on all the details and what can we do to help."

Chapter 3

Aboard the freighter, Talakah.

No sooner were Sirin and Qar'qaah released from the flicker effect when his utterly limp body, which she had cradled against her, started to topple sideways. It had been a bumpy trip—hop-skipping via flicker to various chambers around the Gorgon's Lair, all, Sirin assumed, to avoid being followed. She certainly felt like she'd left her stomach behind, somewhere. This was the final stop—she recognized the grimy and paint-peeled interior of the *Talakah*'s flicker chamber. If that hadn't been enough, there was the scrawled rumination on the wall next to the door, written there who knows how long ago, which pretty much summed up her experiences aboard the ship as well: *Fuck this shit.*

She almost breathed a sigh of relief they were back—*and not a moment too soon*—as she tightened her hold to stop Qar'qaah falling face first onto the unforgiving floor, then looked up as Urbat and the Looper hurriedly edged around them, out of the cramped flicker chamber and over to where a heavily armed Syr stood, beside the flicker console.

The Matarran remained behind, and kicked Qar'qaah's boot-sheathed shin. "Get up, Akka'a!"

"He can't!" Sirin snarled. "He's extremely ill, can't you see that? At least give him a chance to recover from being shocked!"

In response, the Matarran shoved the muzzle of Qar'qaah's maser pistol against Qar'qaah's temple and sneered, "He's faking!"

"He's not! *Please—*"

"Then maybe I just put him out of his misery?" He grinned.

"Pava," Urbat replied with a noticeable trace of frustration. "How many times have we been through this? He's worth nothing dead, even less dematerialized."

The Matarran scowled at the man, then took a step back and motioned angrily with the pistol. "I'm sure as *Shôki*'s ghost not carrying him, so get him to his feet—*now!*"

Sirin looked pleadingly at Urbat. "He can't get up—he needs urgent medical attention!"

Urbat stared at her, clearly unsure, and growled, "This better not be some stupid trick—"

"You said he's worth nothing dead, and he will be shortly. *Please*—get Drakin!"

Urbat reluctantly turned and whispered to Syr, and Syr hurried from the flicker chamber.

Sirin turned back to Qar'qaah. Fresh, foamy blood now coated his lips, his breathing came in shallow, rattling gasps and his ashen, exposed skin was ice cold and clammy.

She drew him closer and with her free hand, gathered up one of his limp hands, giving his fingers a gentle squeeze. He responded by taking another, this time even weaker, shuddering breath. *Stay with me—*

"Ssstop poking me wit dat!" came a familiar lisping hiss.

Sirin jerked her head up as Lieutenant Drakin, the *Baidarka*'s Eltannian nurse-surgeon who'd been kidnapped with her, shuffled into the chamber, followed by Syr, who promptly gave the massive reptiloid one last prod with the muzzle of his blaster for good measure. "I sssaid—"

"Drakin!"

The woman jerked her angry scowl off Syr and turned. Her beady eyes widened. "Wat da..." she began as she hurried towards the flicker chamber, to the kneeling Sirin and her hooded, inert companion.

"He's suffering from exposure and exhaustion," Sirin began as Drakin knelt beside her, "and who knows what else."

"Anyting broken?"

"Not that I know of. He was able to walk earlier—until he..." Sirin angrily jerked her chin towards the hovering and visibly agitated Matarran, "shocked him in his sleep."

"How sssporting." Drakin gathered Qar'qaah into her arms. In the process, the hood fell away from his face and she flicked

Sirin a startled look, then she lurched to her feet and turned to Urbat. "Wherez diz ssscow'z sssickbay?"

"Follow me." With that Urbat strode from the chamber, Drakin and Sirin on his heels, with the Matarran right behind them, leaving the Looper and Syr to stare after them, whispering furiously to each other.

Urbat hurried down the brightly lit, narrow corridor and into the bowels of the ancient and dilapidated freighter. Drakin waddled behind him, her tail and Qar'qaah's boot tips keeping cadence with her gait, scraping and tapping along the wall, with Sirin bringing up the rear, deliberately keeping some space between the Matarran and Qar'qaah.

They passed by the cabin Drakin and Sirin had been held in, passed open hatchways that led to the engine room and the galley, passed other closed hatches.

Finally Urbat stopped at a red-framed hatchway. "In here— *lights.*"

Drakin stepped around him as the overheads flickered to life and into the small sickbay and carefully placed her limp burden on the examining table then she began rummaging through the nearby drug cart's drawers.

Sirin positioned herself beside the table, across from Drakin and looked down at Qar'qaah.

He was lying on his back, eyes half-closed, arms and lower legs dangling off the edges of the table, his blistered, blood-coated mouth agape.

She scowled at him. *You have a helluva lot of explaining to do, Buster, so don't you dare die on me!*

Drakin jerked the robe off his shoulder and pressed a loaded ject-it against the exposed, cold-mottled skin, then another and another. That complete, she gave Qar'qaah's chilled, wasted muscle a quick, one-handed massage to hasten the life-saving drugs on their way, then turned back to the cart and withdrew a portable blood warmer.

She placed it between Qar'qaah's splayed legs, flicked Urbat and the Matarran a sidelong glance, then turned to Sirin. "Itz ssshow and tell time."

Sirin arched a brow. "Huh?"

"Witout a rectal probe I can insssert to bypaz hiz ssskinz interference, I'm gonna have to asssez ssstrictly by eye."

"Oh." Sirin couldn't help but wince in sympathy and yes, embarrassment that such was being discussed in front of their kidnappers. It didn't help that the Matarran, noticing her discomfort, smirked.

"Zo, lez ssse wat we got, ssshall we?"

Sirin replied with a less than enthusiastic nod as Drakin carefully sat Qar'qaah up and braced his completely wilted upper body and head against her scaly chest.

Sirin, as she looked at him, had a brief mental image of a rag doll. Granted, a life-sized, tattooed rag doll, but a rag doll none-the-less.

"You gonna help or sssightsssee?" Drakin prompted, to which Sirin replied, "Sorry." Together they undressed him, starting with the cowl and robe then quickly moving on to his filthy under-tunic.

Sirin managed to peel off the under-tunic, in the process reopening a number of scabbed over sores on his bony back.

Drakin wrinkled her snout at the potent, fetid stench as she gently laid him back on the now robe-covered exam table.

To Sirin, Qar'qaah looked even worse off than she had first assumed and she grimaced.

Along with the outward signs of prolonged radiation exposure, the bright lights of the sickbay revealed something far more sinister, something she hadn't noticed before: his mouth, left cheek and chin were discolored by a fresh, reddish-purple bruise and his badly swollen lower lip had been recently split, while his throat, arms and torso were splotched with a multitude of other, yellowing bruises along with a host of scabbed over cuts and scrapes. She could only assume the rest of his emaciated body was similarly marked.

And his trousers... they weren't all over black as she'd first assumed. One thigh and both knees of the morphing fabric were dirty but dun-colored, but his other thigh, crotch and hip of the once form-fitting fabric was stained a dark ruddy brown that smelled like—

"Shit, he stinks!" the Matarran clapped his hand over his nasal slits and mouth as he hurriedly back-stepped into the relatively fresh air of the corridor.

Sirin glanced at Drakin, who replied with a 'Yup, it is what it is' shrug.

Gods.... She swallowed hard then watched in uneasy silence as Drakin slowly and cautiously ran her hands over Qar'qaah's entire body searching for other, less obvious signs of injury.

"Nutting *feelz* broken—aldough dere are sssome resssent healed fracturez." She poked at a scabbed over wound than ran the length of his left forearm, then, plucking at his heavily soiled trousers, shook her head, muttered, "Neverdalez, hez a mez, *inssside* and out."

Sirin briefly wondered if Drakin was going to strip him of the rest of his heavily soiled clothing in front of their hostile audience and was relieved when instead the nurse demonstrated remarkable decorum and went no further.

Instead, Drakin grabbed Qar'qaah's rubbery left arm, draped it across his sunken stomach and quickly attached the blood warmer. She hit the activator, growled, "Blanketz," then turned and squinted at Urbat. "I sssaid *blanketz*! Diz contraption," she tapped the warmer with a talon, "ain't gonna do all da work itzsssef you know—and while you're at it, bring Sssirin ssssometing hot to drink."

Urbat turned to the Matarran. "You heard her."

The alien gave Sirin and Drakin a sidelong glare, then muttering angrily to himself, stalked from the small chamber.

Urbat followed him with his eyes then turned back at to them and smiled sweetly. "Just so we understand each other, if *he* dies, *you* die. *Got it?"*

This time it was Drakin's turn to reply with a withering stare.

"Is that what happened to Tace?" Sirin asked, crossing her arms. "He got in the way, or lost his usefulness, so—"

"Tace broke his damned ankle while we were tracking you—nothing worse, I assure you, and your friend there," he motioned to Drakin, "refused to treat it..."

Sirin looked questioningly at Drakin, who shrugged and smiled.

"...so Syr did, or tried to, and I think caused more damage because according to Tace, he can't even put weight on it, much less walk any distance. Those two, they're more trouble than they're worth if you ask me, but since you're so concerned for your fellow crewman, I'll allay your fears: he's sitting watch on the bridge right now, or he better be or I'll have his hide." With that, he too stepped out of the small sickbay, leaving the women alone with their patient.

Drakin glared after Urbat, then, shaking her head, leaned over Qar'qaah and whispered, *"May I asssk who diz iz?"*

Sirin jerked her chin towards the doorway and lowered her voice to a point it barely reached across the exam table. *"They think he's Khusaaq—and for everyone's sake, I think we best not enlighten them, at least not yet."*

Drakin arched a scaly brow, but taking note, followed Sirin's example. *"But if Taz ssseez him, he'll know—"*

"I know. A lucky break he... well, broke his ankle."

"He didn't—jussst a moderate sssprain. Taz waz alwayz prone to da melodramatic, pluz I overheard him tell Sssyr he waz cold and hungry and "tired of 'hunting yowiez" and wanted an excuz. Dey both tougt it waz funny Urbat "bought it" az Taz sssaid. He waz sssure they could find you in da morning—dat you'd likely come back on your own—"

"Like hell I would've—" She looked at Drakin. *"Sorry, but—"*

"I would've done da sssame, and juz for da record, I would've ssset a broken ankle, even if it waz Taz. But it wasssn't and he waz being sssuch a huge—"

"That might be something we can use against him. I don't think our Mister Urbat would be too pleased to know he's been lied to, especially under those circumstances."

Drakin shrugged, then asked, *"Zo dey tink hez Khoozak. Who do you tink he iz?"*

"I know who he is—he told me. His name is... now, let me get this right... A'uha-larkahn'Qar'qaah Abhijitischinjgra."

Drakin raised both brows. *"And whoz dat when hez at home?"*

"His use name's Qar'qaah."

"Qar'qaah, huh?" She looked down at him and clutching his slack jaw in one taloned hand, gently turned his tattooed face towards her, adding distractedly, *"You sssure have a knack when it comez to Hattoosssinz following you home."*

"He didn't follow me and I wouldn't exactly call this scow home."

"Zo, where'd you find him?"

"We just kinda bumped into each other."

"Uh-huh." Drakin studied his battered face for a moment then unclipped the breather from his nose and tossed it onto the nearby drug cart. *"He certainly doez look like Khoozak—"*

"That he does," Sirin said, and realized it was true, adding, *"and in his case looks are more than just skin deep—"*

"Except hez a lot younger," Drakin interrupted distractedly as she continued to stare at him—all of him, *"da tattooz aren't az elaborate... maybe... at mossst fourteen?"*

Sirin replied with a startled blink and a gasped, *"Fourteen?"*

"Yah."

"How do you figure that?"

"Matooz taut me. Sssee?" Using a talon, she followed the elaborate, interconnected tattoos and deeply incised patterns that flowed across his forehead, down his nose and then spread across his bruised, blistered and blood-smeared cheeks. *"Deez are hiz cassste glyphz—Elkanaghalli. And deez,"* she traced out the mirror-image tattoos that snaked from behind each ear, along his jaw line to meet at his chin, forming a complex double spiral just below his lower lip, *"markz him az Abhijit'tisssinjgra."*

Sirin nodded; the tattoos that covered his face and throat were indeed almost identical to Khusaaq's, albeit noticeably paler under all the grime and sores and dried blood.

"Diz," Drakin pointed to the markedly less complex tattoos that enveloped his entire left arm from shoulder to fingertips, *"iz hiz record of military achievementz—not much zo far."* She

then gestured to his right arm, which bore a markedly different, more graceful, almost sinuous pattern. *"Doz sssignify hiz religiouz accomplisssmentz—again, not much.*

"And deez," she motioned to the intricate design that encompassed his slat-ribbed chest and hollow, abraded belly, *"denote hiz family hissstory, hiz family tree, zo to ssspeak. Each barb, each... curlicue markz an event of deep sssignificanz to him or hiz family. If you learn da patternz, itz easssy to know a lot about da person... like dere age. Going by deez,"* she motioned to his tattoo-decorated arms and face, *"hez jussst a bah-bee."*

Sirin acknowledged the woman's unexpected expertise with a nod—clearly the hours spent tending to Matoosh's injuries while he was aboard the *Baidarka* had not been completely wasted in idle chitchat, or, nearer to the truth, verbal combat. She found herself taken aback by Drakin's estimate of her latest foundling's age.

She gave the Hahtooshan another, much closer look and realized Drakin was very close to the mark. At almost two meters in height and even in his emaciated state fifty three and a half kilos—according to the exam table's readouts—he was not exactly a *baby,* but behind the elaborate tattoos, the peeling, bruised and blistered skin and the hollow, scarified cheeks was indeed the face of a teenager, an eerie glimpse of an adolescent Khusaaq and she found herself transfixed by his hauntingly, achingly familiar—albeit alarmingly skeletally thin and deathly—features.

As she stared at him, wondering if she would ever see Khusaaq again, she reached out and lightly touched Qar'qaah's swollen, blood caked lips with a fingertip.

Drakin coughed softly—breaking the spell—and Sirin jerked her hand away, looked up at the other woman and flushing deeply, stammered, *"I... really don't know much else about him except that he's one of those left behind on Rasal Ghul and later abducted by the* Huui'teh—"

"Ahhhh." Drakin looked down at her patient with renewed hope. *"Dat would explain a lot,"* she replied as she eyed the

raw, clearly infected self-inflicted welts that crisscrossed his tattooed belly. *"And givez me more to work wit."*

Sirin nodded, then, feeling something lightly brush against her thigh, glanced down to find Qar'qaah's fingers touching her.

She wrapped her hand around his—wincing at just how icy-cold his skin felt was despite the blood warmer—and was taken aback when he responded by weakly curling his fingers around hers. She almost smiled. Instead, she motioned for Drakin to lean closer. *"He's also awake."*

Drakin dropped her gaze to find Qar'qaah staring dully up at her. She smiled, whispered, *"Hi dere, Pilgrim."*

His sunken eyes slowly shifted to Sirin but before she could explain, she overheard the sound of approaching footsteps. She put her finger to her lips then whispered in his ear, *"Play dead—uh, wait—make that unconscious,"* and he dutifully closed his eyes while Drakin adjusted the temperature on the blood warmer.

The Matarran appeared in the doorway, several blankets draped over one multi-jointed arm, a steaming mug in the other hand. "Blankets and... soup?"

Sirin accepted the proffered mug while Drakin took the blankets.

"Now *ssshoo.*" Drakin motioned for him to leave.

The Matarran, faced with the nurse's taloned fingers, grudgingly did as he was told.

Sirin tapped the hatch release and it closed. Then she turned back to the examining table to find—to her utter amazement—Qar'qaah weakly struggling to sit up.

"Whoa, dere cowboy," Drakin said, "Not zo fassst." She planted her hand in the middle of his bruised, bony chest and *very* gently pushed him back onto the table. "You need to ssstay put." She draped one heavy blanket over him, then another. "Lez get you defrosssted before you ssstart wiggling around, okay? Udderwissse you're gonna sssnap sssometing off."

Qar'qaah stared up at her for a moment then slowly turned his narrowed and clearly baffled gaze on Sirin. Parting his blood-sticky lips managed a thin, raspy, *"Sseh...?"*

"Drakin here's a trauma nurse, with a lot of experience treating Hahtooshans—*and* a good friend of Khusaaq's—Matoosh's as well," she added for good measure. "You'd be smart to do exactly as she says."

He gave the massive reptiloid another dubious glance, then his nostrils flared and his gaze fell on the mug Sirin held in one hand. He wet his blistered and swollen lips with an equally blistered tongue and lifting his head, whispered, *"Chadran-uha'ne."*

Sirin looked down at the mug, then back at him as he made a desperate grab for it.

"Chadran-uha'ne!" he demanded feebly, almost a sob as his fingers closed around air. *"Tu-kadjiti—"*

"First things first," she replied firmly as she backed up a step. "Let's have Drakin check you out thoroughly, then you can have something to eat, all right?" Out of the corner of her eye, she saw Drakin reply with a quick, sharp shake of her head and a silently worded but emphatic, *'No'.*

Qar'qaah, for his part, let his head fall back onto the table with a soft *thud*, squeezed his eyes shut and began mumbling furiously in Hahtou.

Sirin set the cup on another cart, well out of his reach, out of sight and hopefully out of mind—there was nothing she could do to put it beyond a Hahtooshan's acute sense smell. As Drakin again rummaged around in the drug cart, she tucked the blankets more tightly around Qar'qaah and said, "You really had me worried."

Sirin let her tentative smile of relief fade as she realized his angry mutterings had abruptly turned to soft, wincing grunts.

She watched him in growing concern, suspecting that his hunger pangs had triggered something far more ominous. Then, confirming her suspicions his face contorted. As he began to gag, she hissed, *"Drakin...!"*

Drakin turned, instantly sized up the situation. She grabbed his hip and shoulder and rolled him towards her, almost to the edge of the table and onto his side as he continued to dry heave. "Hold him dere."

As Sirin grasped Qar'qaah's shoulder with one hand and got a firm hold on his trousers' waistband with the other, Drakin looked down at him. "I'm gonna give you sssometing for da pain, nausssea and crampz, okay?" She pressed the ject-it against his upper arm, followed in rapid order by another and then another.

After several tense minutes he stopped retching and began hungrily gulping for air.

Drakin turned back to the cart and began sorting through its stock. "I sssure hope dere's sssometing here for radiation poisssoning…"

He pushed back against Sirin's supporting hands, and taking the hint, she helped him roll onto his back. Then he tried to draw his blanket-covered legs up onto the table as his fingers dug into his sunken belly.

Sirin watched his increasingly desperate struggles to get at the source of the searing pain. Finally, unable stand it any longer, she grabbed his hands and pulled them away. "Stop it—that's not helping!"

Qar'qaah opened his eyes, briefly, then squeezed them shut and clenched his teeth as his body was gripped by another spasm.

Whimpering, he writhed in exhausted agony, his legs feebly flailing, in the process managing to kick the blankets completely off him and she grimaced as his fingers tightened painfully around hers.

"Ah!" Drakin pulled out a purple-capped vial. "Diz ssshould do da trick—at leassst for now." She loaded the ject-it, added, "Diz may sssting quite a bit." Grasping his bony shoulder firmly, she pushed it down on the table and pressed the ject-it against the taut muscle as he continued to squirm, oblivious. "Dere."

She snatched up another, blue-capped vial and loaded it in the ject-it, then set it on top of the cart and turned back to him.

Sirin risked a brief, expectant look at her. "Now what?"

"Now we wait."

"For what?"

"For dat," Drakin replied as he abruptly stopped thrashing around.

Sirin realized his fingers too had abruptly eased off on their death grip and she wasted no time freeing herself from his loosening hold. She gave her hands a vigorous shake to get the blood flowing again. Then, as she watched, Qar'qaah's body appeared to deflate.

Drakin pressed a fingertip to his throat and felt for a pulse for what to Sirin seemed like an inordinately long period of time then the nurse carefully pried up a bruised eyelid. With her other hand, she gave his prominent breastbone a quick knuckle rub.

Getting no response, she straightened and met Sirin's anxious stare.

"Is... is he dead?"

"Nah. Juz out. Like da proverbial light."

Overwhelming exhaustion, in combination with the potent drugs, had finally won out.

Sirin slowly released the breath she didn't realize she'd been holding. She snatched the blankets from the floor. "Now what?"

"Now we let da drugz do dere ting." Drakin turned back to the cart, pulled out an infuser and fluid cylinder, snapped them together, then attached them to his right forearm and pressed the activator. "Dere."

Sirin quickly covered Qar'qaah with the blankets and using the corner of one, carefully wiped some of the caked blood and fresh saliva from his lips.

"I do tink he'd be a tad more comfortable in our quarterz dan on diz cold hard table," Drakin said as she tapped the surface with the tip of a talon, "I know I would."

"Yeah, me too." Sirin gave her own chilled shoulders a brisk rub.

Drakin again gently gathered Qar'qaah's wilted, blanket-wrapped body in her arms. "Bring dat ject-it," she motioned with her scaly chin towards the nearby drug cart, "and grab a coupla extra vialz of painkiller while you're at it—dey've got red capz, and anudder blue one too, daz a sssedative—juz in caz he decidez to get frisssky—and anudder of doz sssilinderz. And sssome burn sssalve—dere's gotta be a tube in dere sssomewhere."

With that, Drakin tapped the hatch release with her elbow and shuffled out of the small sickbay. "We're taking him to our cabin," she announced to the Matarran, who'd been loitering just outside.

Sirin grabbed the ject-it, quickly located the requested vials in the cart's top drawer along with a tube of salve, snatched up a fluid cylinder and her mug of soup then hurried after her.

Drakin headed back down the corridor to the small cabin that had been their makeshift prison for the past several days.

Sirin followed, as did the Matarran, but as soon as she entered the cabin, she thumbed the release and found herself immensely pleased when the door snapped shut in the alien's startled face, so close in fact that if he'd had a protruding nose rather than nasal slits, he'd have lost it.

Drakin stretched Qar'qaah out on one of the cabin's two bunks and said, "Temperature. Up five degreez," which was instantly followed by a steady burst of warm air from the overheads. She held out her hand. "Ject-it."

"Well?" Sirin whispered as she handed it to her.

"Dunno. Right now da biggessst enemiez to hiz immediate sssurvival are extreme exhaussstion, hypotermia and dehydration. Diz," she pressed the ject-it against his arm then handed it back to her, "ssshould guarantee a few hourz of ssshut-eye—for all of uz."

She adjusted the settings on the blood warmer, adding, "Diz, and dat," she pointed to the overhead vent, "ssshould make him all toasssty warm, but not *too* quickly—dat would be very bad—and diz," she tapped the infuser with the tip of a talon, "will pump sssome much-need fluidz and caloriez into him."

Sirin nodded as she stared down at Qar'qaah's gaunt face, again struck by just how much he looked like Khusaaq. Despite his skin losing some of its ashen hue, his tattoos had not regained a Hahtooshan's typical inky-black color. In fact they looked even paler than before, barely darker than his underlying skin.

"What do you make of this?" She lightly touched the elaborate, albeit shadowy pattern that swirled over his left cheek. "Think this is normal for him?"

"He'z likely anemic," Drakin replied as she applied some of the salve to his blistered chest. "Radiation poisssoning does dat."

Sirin shrugged, then as Drakin continued to fuss over her charge, she did a thorough check of their Spartan quarters, assuring herself that the cabin's listening and viewing devices— devices they'd disabled within hours of being kidnapped and confined to the small room—hadn't been replaced or repaired during Drakin's brief absence. Satisfied, she turned back to Drakin. "I think we can speak freely."

Drakin nodded as she pressed her scaly palm to Qar'qaah's forehead and muttered, "Much better," then carefully, almost dotingly combed his tangled hair away from his face and mouth with one talon. She gently turned him onto his side, bending one knee to keep him from rolling onto his stomach. "He needz to ssstay on hiz ssside—in caz he pukez again."

Sirin nodded her understanding.

Drakin straightened and blinked back a yawn. "I don't know about you, but I'm bussshed," she continued as she set the expended ject-it in the bedside table, "haven't ssslept a wink sssince you left."

"Now that you mention it, neither have I—"

"Wake me if he getz ressstlez, okay?" With that, she plopped down on the opposite bunk and sprawled out.

"Uh…" Sirin looked down at Qar'qaah, then back at Drakin and realized that somewhere along the line, she'd ended up with no place to sit, much less sleep… except on the deck. "Yeah… ah, sure."

She looked at the deck, and then at Qar'qaah as he shivered in his sleep. "I assume that's not what you meant?" She favored the other woman with a sidelong glance only to find Drakin already sound asleep—and to add insult to injury, she suddenly began to snore.

Sirin shook her head and with a sigh, sat on the deck, crossed her legs and braced her back against Qar'qaah's bunk—*my appropriated bunk*, she scowled.

With that, she turned back to her mug of soup and took a cautious sip. It had an odd, sour taste, but it was warm, and she realized she was very hungry. She took another sip, and then a deep gulp as she willed her own exhausted body to relax and her mind to come to terms with the fact that she was right back where she'd started, except now there was the added complication of being held with a critically ill, probably dying Hahtooshan who also happened to have a disquieting physical connection to Khusaaq.

She was also struck with an unsettling sense of déjà vu: she had, *yet again*, saved a Hahtooshan for likely a far worse fate than the death he had so closely succumbed to and she squeezed her eyes shut. *Damn, damn, damn and damn...*

Behind her Qar'qaah began to shiver in earnest and then his teeth began to chatter loudly.

She tried to ignore him as she reminded herself that it was actually a hopeful sign that he was shivering again. But when he began to twitch and moan softly, she wearily staggered back to her feet and stared down at him as she gulped down the rest of the soup. *Drakin's right—you're a complete mess.*

As if in reply, he moaned again, his face wincing as another prolonged shiver gripped his body.

She set the now empty mug on the bedside table then tucked the blankets more tightly around his throat and shoulders. His only response was another bunk-shaking shiver.

"Temperature, up five degrees," she sighed and resuming her uncomfortable seat on the deck, back pressed against his bunk, added, "Lights... off."

Chapter 4

Aboard the Baidarka, *in orbit above Poonda Five.*

Amalfitano, seated the conference room table directly across from Nihaal, listened in uneasy silence as Khusaaq retold in detail the events of the past several days. Izraad was seated to his left, and next to her was Aquila. Standing off to one side were Amalfitano's three Hahtooshan bodyguards.

To Amalfitano's trained eye, Khusaaq looked overly fatigued. Clearly the tremendous emotional strain of the so far fruitless search for his missing man and worry over Sirin had taken its toll, but otherwise he appeared none too worse for wear. His companion was another matter.

The young trooper was clearly extremely ill, not to mention very, *very* scared. Except during the brief introductions, Nihaal had not spoken and had pointedly avoided all eye contact. He hadn't even taken a sip from the large glass of water that sat in front of him, whereas Khusaaq had greedily downed his in three loud gulps. A plate of sandwiches had been left untouched by both. Now the soldier's intense gaze was fixed on the shiny tabletop, his armored hands tightly clutching his helmet to his chest as if it offered a sense of security.

"...and so far you've been unable to find any trace of your missing man, Lieutenant Drakin or Ensign Corsali," Aquila concluded, drawing Amalfitano's concerned stare.

Khusaaq slowly shook his head, sighed then added, "Since Kon'ta'aq was, I believe, at far greater and more immediate risk, I made his recovery my priority, using every resource I had at hand while abiding by Narbrooi Hahtra'tzrhi's orders to avoid detection if at all possible. I believed, and still do believe that Sirin and Drakin are in no immediate danger—they were kidnapped to be used as bait to entrap me. As long as their abductors think that's still possible, they won't harm them, might even want to use them as bargaining chips to be given safe passage into neutral space if cornered. But..." he looked away, added, "I am close to accepting the regrettable conclusion that Qar'qaah Kon'ta'aq is deceased."

Amalfitano couldn't help but catch Nihaal's quickly concealed wince.

Aquila, also painfully aware of Nihaal's response, replied, "I'm very sorry we didn't arrive sooner."

Khusaaq flicked his companion a sidelong, worried glance. After a moment of strained silence, he turned his attention back to Aquila. "We now must focus our combined abilities on locating and safely retrieving Sirin and Lieutenant Drakin, sadly not an easy or straightforward task in itself as the Gorgon's Lair has surprisingly effective jamming capabilities, so much so our ship-board sensors were hard-pressed to track us while we were within the city's boundaries.

"We were monitoring Sirin and the lieutenant's kidnappers via their intraship communications, and an unknown number—but clearly not all of those aboard—left the freighter shortly before dawn yesterday not long after the vessel made planetfall. At the time I felt this level of surveillance was adequate—at any sign of trouble and Sirin and the Lieutenant could be flicked out of harm's way. Granted doing so would cost us the element of surprise, but..." Khusaaq shrugged, then continued, "Those who debarked made rendezvous with some yet unknown party shortly after noon, going by a brief message sent to their companions who remained aboard the freighter, and then a few hours after that, one requested to be flicked back to the ship—it appears the individual suffered an injury of some sort..."

"Serves whoever it was right if he was mugged," Amalfitano muttered under his breath, to which Aquila nodded.

"...but since then both ship and those on the planet have gone silent as far as transmissions," Khusaaq continued, seemingly oblivious to the whispered remark. "Nerik'ah Sha'ashahn of *Illuyanka*—one of the koursans tasked with shadowing the freighter from Tuli," he amended at Amalfitano's mildly baffled stare, "has had the vessel under visual surveillance since last night, shortly after we lost the ability to monitor its internal communications."

Now it was Aquila's turn to look baffled.

"Due to the unfortunately timed landing of another craft, a Thalamian trader, in the space next to the freighter, and the trader's jamming on top of the planet's make any intraship eavesdropping impossible."

"You say visual surveillance...?" Izraad asked.

"Eight troopers from the *Illuyanka* are strategically positioned around the freighter. Any attempt by the kidnappers to leave or re-board will be observed. For now the troopers have orders not to interfere, but to follow if the remaining kidnappers do abandon the ship. Unfortunately, due to the jamming, we cannot detect a flicker signature with any accuracy, so it is possible they could flick a few individuals at a time onto or off the freighter without us picking up the signal." He exhaled forcefully, then grabbed the nearby pitcher, sloshed more water into his glass and gulped down its contents, wincing as he did so.

"What about your sensors while on the surface?" Aquila asked after giving Khusaaq a moment.

"Marginally better," he replied, wiping his chin with the back of his hand, "contingent upon where one is relative to areas of the Gorgon's Lair that the Poondians find particularly sensitive. Since it is remotely possible the kidnappers were able to move Sirin and the lieutenant elsewhere before we set up our cordon, I suggest we focus our sensory searches on Eltannians—they're not particularly common in this part of the Rim. Purely by chance we located two while we were searching for Kon'ta'aq, but we didn't have the time to investigate if either was your missing lieutenant. Hopefully, when we find Lieutenant Drakin, she will either be with Sirin, or be able to tell us where Sirin is."

"Done." Aquila toggled the com unit on the table and relayed the orders. He then looked back at Khusaaq. "Anything else?"

"The men retrieved from Rasal Ghul. They too are in urgent need of attention. Our medic had begun treatment, but he's been fully occupied in the ground search..."

Amalfitano looked at Nihaal to find that the soldier was now watching him intently.

"...I would like to entrust the four to the expert care of Doctor Amalfitano, until such time as we return to Tuli and *Faridour,*" Khusaaq added.

"Of course." Amalfitano smiled warmly at Nihaal.

Nihaal stared back, unblinking as he nervously wet his blistered lips; his expression clearly indicated his absolute worst fears realized.

"Which means you'll need replacement resources on the ground," Aquila said. "Replacements that can move about openly, possibly even act as blinds for your troops?"

Khusaaq arched a brow.

"I've already been in contact with the planet's governing body," Aquila continued. "They're under the belief that this is a routine resupply stop. So as not to arouse unwanted suspicion on the part of the Poondians and possibly warn the kidnappers, I suggest I send a detachment of twenty marines to the surface under the guise of shore leave—in fact not to take advantage of a resupply stop by allowing the crew R and R would arouse suspicion."

"Thank you, Commander. Their assistance will be most welcome." With that, Khusaaq rose.

As Nihaal followed suit, Khusaaq turned to him. "Contact the others. Have them regroup at the appointed location, and notify Endooki, Raudah and Laihiri to prepare to be flicked aboard *Baidarka.*"

As Nihaal brought his tac-net to his lips to convey the order, Khusaaq turned to Amalfitano. "I leave them in your able custody."

Amalfitano nodded to his three Hahtooshan bodyguards as he replied, "We'll take good care of them."

Murh'sooli responded with an ever-so-slight nod of his own as Khusaaq briefly met his gaze.

"And now, Commander," Khusaaq continued, "Perhaps I might prevail upon Lieutenant Izraad for one more favor?" He turned to the woman.

"You want me to try to find out exactly who this Cisne, or, should I say Mizahn is, assuming she's one and the same person—"

"She is."

"Of course, Sha'ashahn. Knowing she's indeed human will, I hope, help narrow down the search."

"Thank you, Lieutenant." He then gave Nihaal a sidelong, questioning glance.

"Guk-katl t'buu—"

"In *Standard*, Ha'tat," he prompted gently but firmly. "*Always* in Standard while in the company of our Rimmer allies."

Nihaal replied with a slight nod and, "The teams are on their way to the assigned location, ta'ahn—Matoosh Ruh'ta'aq reports no sign of Qar'qaah Kon'ta'aq, or the two Rimmers. Nerik'ah Sha'ashahn is requesting orders."

"Maintain surveillance—and notify Nerik'ah Sha'ashahn I am returning to the surface and that crew from the *Baidarka* will now be assisting in the ground search—all information regarding the freighter or its crew is to be relayed to Commander Aquila of the *Baidarka* as well in order to best coordinate operations."

"Yes, ta'ahn."

Khusaaq waited until Nihaal had again relayed the orders, then he motioned to Amalfitano. "Go with the doctor, Ha'tat—and do *exactly* as he tells you—regard his orders as if they are my orders."

Nihaal murmured, "Yes, ta'ahn." Then pulling himself up to his full height, he strode around the table and, after one last beseeching look at Khusaaq, which garnered only a frown, he followed Amalfitano, slump-shouldered, out of the conference room as the three Hahtooshan bodyguards fell in behind.

Chapter 5

Aboard the Talakah.

Sirin very reluctantly opened her eyes and was immediately struck with an odd combination of noises: the muffled sound of sobbing and a soft, rhythmic *thunk... thunk... thunk.*

She sat bolt upright and whispered anxiously, *"Lights— quarter power."*

The overheads immediately complied and she spotted the source of the sounds: Qar'qaah was huddled in the far corner of the cabin's small head, wedged into a narrow space next to the sink, knees drawn up against his chest, head buried in his kneecaps, skeletally thin arms wrapped around his legs. He was sobbing.

The intact infuser lay across the threshold to the head and the automatic door kept trying to close, in the process bumping against it, causing the soft *thunk... thunk... thunk.*

What the...?

She rose, slowly, and started towards him. *"Qar'qaah? Qar'qaah, it's Sirin."* She stopped in the doorway, locking the door open then she squatted not far from him—but just out of easy grabbing or kicking range. *"Qar'qaah?"*

He turned away and clutching his head in his hands whimpered, *"Chulh... tohiss-mat... chulh."*

"Drakin...!" she hissed out of the corner of her mouth, then reached back and felt around until her fingers finally latched onto a scaly foot. She gave it a hard tug.

Drakin grunted then replied sleepily, *"Yeeeezzzz?"*

"Something's terribly wrong with Qar'qaah."

Drakin, instantly awake, turned her beady, emerald green eyes on Sirin, then, following her frightened stare, fixed them on Qar'qaah.

She levered herself up onto one elbow as she favored Sirin with a decidedly unhappy look. "How'd he get in dere?"

"I don't know... I fell asleep. Next thing I knew he—"

"Zo much for keeping an eye on him," Drakin grumbled as she lurched to her feet.

"But—"

"Lightz, full power." She placed herself next to Sirin and crossing her arms, watched Qar'qaah for a moment.

Sirin followed her lead, only then realizing he was seated in a pool of blood-tinged watery vomit and she couldn't help but wince. "What's happening?"

"I have no idea. But I tink we need to find out." With that Drakin cautiously stepped into the cramped head, knelt beside him and lightly touched his shoulder. "Qar'qa—"

"Chulh!" He flinched violently and tried to curl into an even tighter ball.

Drakin flicked Sirin a sidelong glance. "Hez having a bad dream."

"More like a nightmare."

Drakin shrugged, "You sssssay tomato, I ssssay tamato," then tightening her hold, gave him a rough shake. "Wake up!"

His eyes snapped open and, seeing her, he screamed and tried to scramble away but his booted feet couldn't get purchase on the vomit-slippery floor, plus there was simply no place to go.

Drakin clamped one hand over his mouth and jaw, instantly muffling his terrified shrieks while the palm of her other hand easily kept him pressed against the wall.

He began frantically kicking her as his hands grabbed hers and tried to break her hold.

"Get hiz legz!" she grunted as his left knee managed to hit her squarely in the stomach.

Sirin grabbed his wildly thrashing, booted feet and pulled with all her strength, then knelt on his shins and pressed down on his knees with her hands, effectively pinning his writhing hips to the deck.

After a few more desperate attempts at freeing himself, he abruptly gave up, too exhausted, too ill to fight any longer.

Sirin looked up to find him staring, wide-eyed at her over Drakin's scaly-fingered gag. "Qar'qaah? Do you recognize me—*us?*"

His frightened eyes, following Sirin's, slid to up to Drakin, then darted back to her. To her relief, he blinked and managed a slight nod. To confirm it, he let go of Drakin's wrists and his arms fell limply to his sides.

"Now," Sirin said, "if you promise you won't fight us, *we'll* let go. Agreed?"

He nodded again.

"You're not just agreeing just so you can try to get away, are you?"

He replied with a slight shake of his head—as much as Drakin's restraining hold on his jaw would allow.

"All right." Sirin immediately released her hold.

Drakin also let go and he slumped back against the wall and gulped hungrily for air.

Sirin gave him a moment. "What the hell was that all about?" she asked as she cautiously seated herself beside him, making sure it was on a dry section of deck.

Drakin grabbed a washcloth, wetted it in the sink and handed it to him.

"Qar'qaah?" Sirin prompted as he blotted his split lower lip, reopened during the struggle.

He closed his eyes and in a husky stammer, replied, "E'kku-tath-whe... ar'quu—"

"In Standard, Qar'qaah. Please, speak in *Standard.*"

He squinted at her, swallowed hard, then managed, "I was..." he closed his eyes, took a deep, shuddering breath then again staring intently at her, continued, "...I was somewhere... *else.*"

"What were you doing up in the first place? If you needed something, you should've—"

"I... I was thirsty."

"Zo you drank sssome water and promptly puked?"

This time he only nodded, rubbing his belly and wincing.

Drakin tapped him on his bony chest with a talon. *"Don't* do dat again—your gut *can't* handle *anyting. Uddersssstood?"*

"I'm... just so... so *thirsty...*" he replied, his weak voice barely above a frantic whisper.

Drakin flicked Sirin a sidelong glance.

"I think you best get back to bed. Can you walk if we help you, or should Drakin carry you?"

He roughly wiped his eyes, then his nose. "I... I can walk..." He held up his hands. "Assist me to... to my feet."

Drakin pulled him to an unsteady stand, but realizing his chest and arms were streaked with vomit and his lip was continuing to bleed, leaving thick, sticky rivulets of bright red blood on his chin and throat, she offered, "How 'bout a quick wasssh up firssst—and while we're at it, maybe we can do sssometing about dat lip?"

He surprised them when he nodded.

Drakin wet another washcloth then as he held onto the sink with both hands to steady himself, she gently scrubbed his face, throat, arms and back, rinsing the cloth frequently while blood dripped from his mouth into the sink, tingeing the increasingly filthy rinse water with a ruddy hue.

She washed his chest, then, as she ran the cloth across his sunken belly, she eyed his heavily stained trousers. "Qar'qaah?"

He lifted his gaze from his intense study of the blood-swirl in the sink and gave her a sidelong look.

"I tink it would be a good idea if I wassshed da ressst of you."

He continued to stare as if not fully grasping what she was suggesting then his suddenly frightened eyes jerked to Sirin as she blotted his lip.

Sirin replied with what she hoped he would interpret as a reassuring smile and a nod. "It really might make you feel a little better," she added for good measure. One thing she had learned early on was that Hahtooshans bordered on the neurotic when it came to personal cleanliness, in large part due to their acute sense of smell.

"Sssirin can leave if you'd prefer—I'm a nurssse. I ssseriousssly doubt you have anyting I haven't ssseen a tousssand timez over zo dere'z no reasssson to be modessst."

He blinked and looked down at himself, at his soiled trousers as his breathing came in short, sharp bursts.

"Qar'qaah?" Sirin gently prompted. Hahtooshans were not, by her admittedly very limited experience, body modest, far from it. Displaying their tattoos—*all* of their tattoos—was part and parcel of their informal social interactions. It was a cultural quirk that had taken her by surprise when Matoosh, within a day of taking up residence on Tuli, took to walking about their small, shared bungalow wearing nothing but his braces—until Khusaaq, noticing her discomfort, mentioned to him that they were not sharing quarters with fellow Hahtooshans. Matoosh being Matoosh suggested that she adopt their customs, rather than the other way around, since it was, as he said, two against one. And when that failed to sway Khusaaq, Matoosh repeatedly "forgot" the rule and clearly delighted in her averted-gaze embarrassment.

Qar'qaah however was clearly extremely apprehensive at the idea of stripping down, even if by doing so he got some relief from the putrid stench. *Personal shyness?* She doubted it—what she saw in his eyes, his face, in the telltale quiver of his blood-streaked chin wasn't embarrassment. It was genuine, raw fear. Perhaps it was the appalling self-realization that he was so weak, so ill they could force the issue if they chose—could, in fact, do what they pleased with him. Their brief struggle had left him barely able to stand—and only by gripping the sink with both hands. What little reserves he had he'd thrown against them to no avail and now even those were gone.

She'd dealt with Khusaaq when he was so critically injured his very life depended upon the actions of people his experiences had told him were the most treacherous of enemies. But that was a sudden incapacitation—and mercifully short-lived.

Qar'qaah had been this ill for *weeks*—a slow, degrading downward slide that no amount of willpower or arrogance could stop. She couldn't even begin to imagine what it was like for a Hahtooshan, someone who was raised to believe he was close to invincible, to be faced, in such a public and humiliating way with his utter defenselessness. Perhaps he was just so ill, so far gone he no longer cared how much he stank, especially if lessening that somewhat also revealed just how vulnerable he truly was.

"It's okay, Qar'qaah—*really*. We're not going to hurt you, I give you my word."

He again met her gaze but this time held it, as if sizing her up, sizing up her intentions.

"If you'd rather not, that's all right—we just thought it might make you feel a little better."

He continued to stare, blood-shot eyes watering.

"How 'bout if I leave?"

As she started to slip around him he touched her arm, mumbled, *"Chulh,"* and with an expression of resignation and without further ado, ran the fingers of one shaky hand down the seal-seam of his trousers.

He took another ragged breath then briefly let go of the sink with his other hand in order to pull the trousers down and almost lost his balance before he grabbed the sink again with both hands.

"Allow me." Drakin carefully tugged his trousers down around his boot cuffs. As she used her foot to gently wedge his legs apart, he squeezed his eyes shut and tightened his hold on the sink.

Sirin at first looked away, fully intent on giving him some semblance of privacy while Drakin and several washcloths got *very* personal. Overhearing his sharp intake of breath, followed by a muffled sob, concern got the better of her.

What she saw left her feeling sick: his emaciated lower body was a patchwork of livid bruises overlaid with oozing, infected sores and peeling, macerated skin.

Gods... She lifted her horrified stare to his taut, tear-streaked face.

Qar'qaah for his part stoically endured the impromptu bath with his eyes tightly closed, wincing occasionally and shivering uncontrollably while he sucked on his still oozing, swollen lower lip.

"Burn sssalve," Drakin whispered out of the corner of her snout.

Sirin tore her eyes off him, nodded, then retrieved the tube from the outer cabin and handed it to Drakin.

"I'm gonna ssssmear cream on you," Drakin said as Sirin squeezed a goodly amount of the bright yellow salve into the nurse's palm. "It ssshould help wit da pain—ssstop your troussserz from ssssticking."

Qar'qaah, his eyes still squeezed shut, nodded.

Drakin quickly used up almost the entire tube on his lower half alone, then finished up by doing what she could for his filthy trousers, which wasn't much while he was still in them. Done, she stood back and eyed her work while discretely shoving the filthy washcloths into the small, over sink disposa-chute. "I tink daz da bessst we can do." She pulled his wet trousers up around his now salve-greasy hips. "Dere, now you finisssh, okay?" She pried one of his hands free of the sink, squeezed what little salve remained into his palm and motioned to his crotch.

He nodded again, applied the salve then after a moment's one-handed fumbling, managed to get everything tucked into place and his trousers resealed.

"Better?" Drakin asked as she wiped his hand free of the remaining salve.

"Jaas-nhe," he replied wearily; he even managed a relieved smile as his glassy eyes slid first to Drakin, and then to Sirin.

"You're welcome." Drakin, realizing he was starting to sway, added, "Okay, *now* bedtime," and pointed to the outer cabin. "Tink you can make it on your own?"

He nodded, then shuffled very slowly back to the bunk unassisted, as Sirin walked along side, her arm at the ready just in case. No sooner had he eased himself down on the bed than he dropped his head into his hands and let out a long, exhausted and shivering sigh.

Drakin followed, snatching up the infuser as she went, then glanced at the empty fluid cylinder and nodded. Nearby lay the discarded blood warmer. She picked that up too then placed both on the other bed.

"Now," Sirin began as she seated herself beside him, "Tell us what this dream was about."

He reluctantly lifted his head from its cradle and squinted at her with still sunken, blood-shot eyes. *"Dream...?"*

"You said you were 'somewhere else'—you were *dreaming."* She mentally rifled through her limited Hahtou then added tentatively, "Uh... *tasse?* Reliving something in your sleep?"

"Tass-eh... dream... *paq,"* he murmured huskily, then wiped his nose with the back of a very shaky hand and fixed his red-tinged gaze on the far wall.

Sirin looked up at Drakin; Drakin shrugged.

"Qar'qaah," she tried again, this time with an audible trace of frustration, "we can't help you if we don't know what's going on."

His only response was to hug himself as he began to shiver again.

Damn. Sirin grabbed the blanket and draped it around his bare shoulders. *"Please* Qar'qaah. We really do want to help you."

He nodded and replied unsteadily, "When... when I sleep, I—" He inhaled sharply and squeezed his eyes shut.

"You have that dream."

He answered with a vigorous nod.

"Of what?" she asked softly.

His mouth twisted, then he forced out, "Of... of being... being put in a stasis pod... awake... and... and..."

"And...?" she prompted with another sidelong look at Drakin.

This time he only shook his head as his bruised, blood-smeared mouth worked in mute horror.

Sirin scooted a little closer. "It's not *just* a bad dream, is it?" She slipped her arm around him, to instinctively offer comfort in the form of physical contact. "Someone actually did that to you—"

"Tu-mazneri...!" His eyes snapped open and he lurched unsteadily to his feet as he felt her encircling arm—startling Drakin into stepping back—and turned his back to them.

Sirin stared—glared—at him and wanted to say, "I just saw you buck naked and you have absolutely *no* secrets from Drakin and now you decide to get all twitchy when I touch you?" But Hahtooshans were like that: while they had little if any body modesty, they took great exception to being touched unless asked, *first*.

The fragile thread of trust between them had been snapped by a simple—culturally thoughtless—act of kindness. And she couldn't even claim ignorance. It was something Khusaaq had alerted her to, early on. *Damn, damn, damn.*

"I'm sorry, Qar'qaah, really I am—I didn't mean to startle you. I promise neither of us will touch you again without your permission, all right?"

He kept his back to them and finally replied with curt nod.

"Now, *who* did that to you?" Sirin persisted, also getting to her feet. Then her eyes widened. "The people who kidnapped you, took you from the *Briseis*—claiming to be Hahtooshans!"

He flicked her an over the shoulder squint and replied hoarsely, "I don't know what you're talking about." He again wiped his nose on the back of his forearm. It wouldn't stop running, forcing him to alternately sniff and wipe, sometimes both at the same time.

"You were rescued from Rasal Ghul by—"

"*Rescued?*" he snarled as he unsteadily turned to face her, his tattooed hands balling into bone-prominent fists as the rest of his body trembled, but she wasn't sure if it was strictly in anger or a combination of rage, fear and overwhelming fatigue. "We were surprised and overrun by Rimmers, taken prisoner—"

"The *Briseis*. She was sent to rescue you. Your safe retrieval—the retrieval of all left behind on Rasal Ghul was part of Khusaaq's demands."

He scowled at her, his expression slowly turning from perplexed to openly suspicious as he braced himself against the wall and gave his nose another, this time very annoyed wipe. "I've heard these lies before—"

"Lies? But how—"

"Sha'ashahn would *never* have handed us over to be tortured, to be—"

"*No*, you don't understand—something went terribly wrong. Those sent to retrieve you didn't follow Khusaaq's very specific instructions. They were supposed to follow them to the letter, and once they had you safely aboard you and those with you were to be brought to Tuli—"

"Tuli...?" His eyes darted briefly to Drakin, then back to Sirin as he began to shiver again. "Wh-wh-who is th-th-this... *Tuli?*" Another wipe, followed by a loud sniff.

"—only a ship claiming to have been sent by the Orthodoxy got to the *Briseis* first and the *Briseis'* captain, not realizing he was being duped, handed you and your companions over."

He abruptly looked away and watching him, Sirin could see him visibly struggle to get his suddenly panicky breathing under control.

Gods... what in hell did they do to you?

She took a step closer and continued in a calm, and what she hoped was a reassuring voice, "Qar'qaah, *we're* not the enemy. Drakin and I were kidnapped too, by people who hoped to use us to get to Khusaaq, and now... they think they have him: meaning *you.*"

He flicked her, and then Drakin, a quick, over the shoulder suspicious glance.

"Itz true," Drakin lisped.

He hugged himself tightly and clenched his teeth to stop them from chattering.

"And while I have no idea what their end game is, why they have gone to such great lengths to try to entrap Khusaaq, they *have* without a doubt gone to great lengths and taken great risks." She gave him a moment to absorb what she'd said, then continued, "I don't know if the people who grabbed you are in any way connected with the people out there," she jerked her chin towards the cabin's locked hatch, "who kidnapped Drakin and me. The timing might have been pure coincidence, or it might have been part of some coordinated and in their eyes presumably fail-proof plan to draw Khusaaq out where they could capture or kill him.

"And now..." she exhaled, "*now* that our kidnappers think they have him, they won't have much use for Drakin and me once we get you stabilized. And they won't have any use for *you* when they discover you *aren't* Khusaaq, so if we don't work together, we're all going to die," Sirin added for good measure. "*Please*, Qar'qaah. We're telling you the truth. We want to help you—and we need you to help us."

He slowly turned around and stared at her for a moment, then Drakin. *No,* she amended, *he's not staring, he's studying us*—with his eyes watching them in a most peculiar way as his nose twitched. Finally, and to her immense relief he stuttered, *"P-p-paq."* His expression, however, was less than enthusiastic.

Keeping one bony shoulder firmly pressed against the wall, he leaned down and cautiously patted the inside of his left boot. A thin smile spread across his bruised and swollen lips and he flicked Drakin a sidelong and decidedly smug glance. "Lizard, c-c-can... you give m-m-me something to... keep me on m-m-my feet and f-f-functional?"

"I'd have to get wat I need from sssickbay, but yez, altough I have to warn you, I couldn't guarantee more dan a couple of hourz and itz not witout a great deal of risssk—"

"That... th-that should be more than enough t-t-time." He staggered back to the bunk and sat down heavily.

Sirin risked a glance at Drakin; the nurse responded with a slight shrug, then they both turned their attention back to him as he slipped his hand deep inside his left boot, only to withdraw a small, innocuous-looking silvery tube. To Sirin, it looked oddly familiar but she couldn't immediately place it.

"And," Qar'qaah said, "I'm m-m-more than willing to accept the risk." That was followed by another wipe of his nose, followed by a sniff—now more a nervous habit than necessity.

Sirin pointed to the object he held and asked, "Uh, what's that?"

"I suppose you could say it's our deliverance," he replied cryptically as he eyed the peculiar object in a way she found particularly unsettling.

Suddenly she remembered why it looked so familiar: Pardix had been wielding something almost identical to it when he and Urbat had kidnapped them, had, in fact threatened to kill the guard with it—

"Someone's heading this way," Qar'qaah hissed an instant before Sirin overheard the muffled echo of approaching

footsteps. Grimacing, he carefully eased himself back onto the bed. "Allow... allow them to think... think I'm extremely ill."

"But you are—"

"And... and therefore... utterly *incapable* of defending myself."

Shouldn't be hard, she thought sourly then arched her brow as he unexpectedly stuffed the tube in his mouth. *What the—*

The door snapped open and she stepped back.

The Matarran warily entered, followed by Urbat. Both had their weapons drawn and Sirin noticed the Matarran was still proudly brandishing Qar'qaah's appropriated pistol.

Urbat glanced down at the seemingly unconscious Qar'qaah then turned to Drakin. "Wake him up."

"But I juz gave him a sssedative." Drakin motioned to the expended ject-it on the nearby table.

"I don't give a shit. We need him awake to answer some questions and we don't have time for him to sleep off whatever the hell you gave him—*now hurry up!"*

"I have to warn you dat in hiz condition dere'z a sssignificant danger dat he—"

"And I'm not going to ask again," Urbat growled as he turned his shocker from Qar'qaah to Drakin.

Sirin immediately stepped between the two. "Why the hurry? Not long ago you were threatening to kill us if he died; now you're more than willing to risk killing him? Plus, who's to say if Drakin does manage to counteract the sedative without doing serious harm that he'll even be able to answer these questions of yours? What could a few hours possibly mean, when letting him sleep might mean he'd be better able to answer you—*assuming he even knows the answers?"*

He chuckled and shook his head. "Good try, Blondie. As for your lover boy there," he jerked his chin towards Qar'qaah, "he knows the answers all right." He lifted his hard gaze to Drakin. "And if you don't do exactly what I say, and do it now, there's really no point in me keeping either one of you alive, is there?"

"But if you kill uz, who'll keep your preciouz prisssoner alive?"

"Well, to be totally blunt about it, it won't be my problem in say…" Urbat flicked his Matarran companion a sidelong look, smiled, then looked back at Drakin and added, "…three hours, give or take? So, do what I tell you, or I'll kill you both, starting with Blondie here. You have ten seconds to decide. Ten. Nine. Eight. Seven. Six—"

"Fine," Drakin snarled. "But I have to take him back to sssickbay, juz in caz he haz a *bad* reaction."

Sirin privately grinned. *Clever girl—*

"Then stop wasting time and do it!" the Matarran barked, motioning impatiently at the door with the maser pistol, while holding his other hand over his nasal slits, a very eloquent response to Qar'qaah's rather potent stink, which had not been helped at all by the impromptu bath or the enclosed cabin's sweltering temperature.

Drakin hesitated, clearly hoping Qar'qaah hadn't in fact slipped back into an exhausted sleep and would react reflexively as he had when Sirin touched him, then with a sidelong, anxious glance at Sirin, she very carefully scooped a believable, and surprisingly limp Qar'qaah into her arms. With an ever so faint sigh of relief only Sirin would appreciate, she shuffled out of the cabin and down the corridor, as the Matarran, Sirin and Urbat followed closely behind her.

A few moments later Drakin stepped into the sickbay, gently placed her burden on the examining table then turned to the drug cart as the Matarran positioned himself across from her and pointed the pistol at Qar'qaah's head.

Sirin, followed by Urbat, entered next. She placed herself not far from the Matarran, to be out of Drakin's way and yet close at hand—for exactly what she wasn't sure—then she crossed her arms and turned her full attention on Urbat only to find him staring back at her. "So why?"

"Why what?"

"Why the big rush?"

"Let's just say I like to know who I'm dealing with."

"I don't follow."

"You will, soon enough." Urbat winked at the Matarran; the alien replied with a slight nod. "For now, I'd rather keep it a… *surprise.*"

"Okay, then answer me this: why the obsessive interest in him?" Sirin jerked her chin towards Qar'qaah.

"It's far too late to play dumb with me, Blondie."

"Humor me," she growled, crossing her arms.

"Okay, for starters, your dear darling here is the Hero of Cotopaxi—"

"Yeah, so?"

"So he's worth a helluva lot of money—your *beloved* Orthodoxy would willingly pay a hefty sum to get him back alive, but then there are the colonial loonies who are willing pay even more—*a lot more*—just to have the pleasure of making a public spectacle of stringing him up for what he and his kind did at Cotopaxi."

"You mean trying to protect the colony?"

He snorted. "Protect? The Hahtooshans massacred the colonists, just like they did at Raumalle then tried to blame it on the Matarrans—"

"That's not true and you know it!" She briefly turned to the Matarran. "And so do you."

Urbat shrugged. "Maybe, but it's what these colonial crazies think—"

"Like Tace."

"Yeah," Urbat replied cheerfully, "except even *more* fanatical."

"Like you?"

He grinned again. "I'm not crazy, or fanatical. I just know a golden opportunity when I see one."

"So, you plan on playing one off against the other? Not very smart if you ask me—Hahtooshans don't react well to double-crossers. And I seriously doubt if these colonists will be any more understanding. And what about Tace? You think he'll willingly go along?"

"Tace does what I tell him. Besides, we don't plan on playing anyone off against another. We plan on using your lover boy here as… well, I guess you could say we plan on using him as the fuse."

"Fuse…?"

"We're gonna hand him over to the colonists, take their money, and then, when the mercs sees what they do to their 'hero', well… something tells me this Coalition-Hahtooshan 'alliance' will go… *boom.*"

"You honestly think the death of one individual can have that effect?"

"In his case, yeah, I do," Urbat sneered. "But I guess we'll find out soon enough if I'm right... and speaking of," he turned his attention onto Drakin to find her still sorting through the drug cart's stock. "What's the hold-up?"

"Just looking for... ah, dere you are." She held up vial in such a way the color-coded cap was hidden. "Diz iz a counteractant, but I again feel compelled to warn you—"

"Quit stalling and give it to him!" the Matarran snarled as he motioned angrily with the pistol.

Don't claim she didn't warn you, Sirin thought.

"Sssure ting. Anyting you sssay." Drakin slipped the vial into a ject-it, pressed the tool against Qar'qaah's shoulder, then quickly and pointedly stepped back as she fixed the agitated Matarran with a frigid, beady-eyed gaze. "He'z prone to projectile puking, zo I'd do da sssame if I waz you if you don't wat to sssmell az bad az him and get your pretty uniform dere all... *messssy.*"

The alien squinted at her, his enormous black eyes crinkling to slits, but he remained where he was, and when nothing untoward happened he responded with a smirk.

It was just the opening Qar'qaah had been waiting for. Taking Drakin's not-so-subtle hint, he moaned, heaved himself onto his side, facing the Matarran and cupping his hand to his mouth, began retching violently.

The startled Matarran jumped back into Sirin, who, unbalanced, in turn stumbled into Urbat.

In that brief moment of chaos, Qar'qaah pointed the tube he now held at the Matarran and the Matarran instantly and mysteriously dropped where he stood, all without making a sound beyond the meaty thud of his body hitting the deck. Qar'qaah then turned the silvery cylinder on Urbat only to find that he'd grabbed Sirin and was now holding her in front him, one arm pinning her arms to her body, the other around her neck.

Qar'qaah, keeping his eyes locked with Urbat and the small tube aimed at the two of them, slowly eased himself off the exam table and to his feet. Once standing, he said, "I suggest that you release her."

"So you can kill me?" Urbat replied, incredulous. Unable to let go of her, even with one hand in order to unholster his own weapon for fear she'd move just enough to give Qar'qaah a clear shot, he had to satisfy himself by tightening his stranglehold on Sirin as she violently squirmed against his grip.

Qar'qaah drew his lips back against his gaunt, blistered and tattooed face in a chilling imitation of a death's head grin. "I think we both know the answer to that."

Urbat risked a glance over his shoulder as he began to back-step towards the open hatch. "But you're not going to risk killing your *beloved* wife..."

Qar'qaah arched a baffled brow at that then as he made the instantaneous translation into Hahtou, he flicked Sirin a startled look and mouthed, *Wife?* To which Sirin replied with a curt, confirming nod.

"...so how 'bout you just drop the *t'jing*—"

"Ah, so you're acquainted with it." Qar'qaah replied sweetly, shoving aside his shock in preference for something far more familiar—and comforting—as he caressed the silvery weapon with his bony, tattooed fingers. "But what am I thinking—of course you'd be, since it's a favorite among the bottom-feeding biota of the galaxy."

"You should know," Urbat fired back, pointedly dropping his gaze to the weapon before again meeting Qar'qaah's feral gaze.

"As for her, well..." Qar'qaah shrugged, "I have some very bad news for you. You see, you've made a *very* serious tactical error, likely one of many as you clearly don't have the smarts for intrigue—"

"Really?" Urbat interrupted, edging closer to the hatch, dragging the struggling Sirin along with him. "And what tactical error is that?"

"I'm *not* Khusaaq, and this..." he looked Sirin up and down as he added with a disgusted sneer, "this *kaa-schat* is certainly not *my* bond-mate."

Urbat replied with a laugh, albeit a clearly forced laugh. "Really."

"Yes. *Really*. I'm Khusaaq's *doh'ha*—his genetic double... right down to the last... what was it now?" He looked thoughtful for a moment then smiled, his sunken and shadowed gray eyes sparkling maliciously. "Oh yes, right down to the last *short tandem repeat.*" At Urbat's startled blink, he tapped his right ear with his forefinger. "They do say the hearing's the last thing to go. In other words, I'm Khusaaq's *clone.* If you'd bothered to learn more about A'tuu'shahn'i and Elkanaghalli'i in particular, you might've realized your mistake earlier. But..." he shrugged and sighed, feigning deep regret, "you didn't. Pity that. As for me... I'm really getting quite fed up with being mistaken for Khusaaq, especially now, when it means I'm slated for a *very* unpleasant end that's actually meant for him."

"It's true," Sirin managed to say, "He's not Khusaaq—"

"SHUT THE FUCK UP!" Urbat snarled, tightening his stranglehold while she tried her best to break his grip.

Qar'qaah watched their struggle, calmly waited until Urbat had regained control then added, "And as for using me as a fuse to ignite a galactic war... *well*, as much as I'd *love* to believe I'm a critical component in the greater scheme of things and that, without me, the universe would come to a crashing halt, the awful truth is that this human female is right: I'm not Khusaaq, which means I'm of absolutely *no* consequence—no one cares whether *I* live or die, *not even Khusaaq,"* he added bitterly as his narrowed gaze briefly met Sirin's wide-eyed stare. "So your grand stratagem to destroy this alliance has some *teensy*, but sadly very critical, flaws. One might even call them fatal flaws, because someone's going to die very shortly, and I have no plans on it being me. This *kaa-schat* means nothing to me, so I could care less if I kill her if it means I kill you—"

"That's classic merc *gratitude* for you, Blondie," Urbat hissed in her ear as he took another back-step towards the hatchway, Sirin still held tightly against him.

"Now that we understand each other," Qar'qaah continued, "I ask again, nicely. Let. Her. *Go.*"

"Why? If you don't care about her, then why not just kill us both?"

"Because my argument is with *you.* Contrary to your truly slanderous Rimmer propaganda, we A'tuu'shahn'i do not kill for the sake of killing—"

Urbat snorted loudly.

"—we kill when we're ordered to do so, paid to do so, or to defend ourselves. Since you've made it abundantly clear that your intent is to hasten my death, and, by your own admission, in an *exceedingly* ugly way, I consider killing you first fully justifiable. *But,*" he raised the *t'jing* so that the business end now pointed directly between Sirin's eyes, "if *you* insist that I kill her in order to kill you I *suppose* I can bend the rules this once..."

Urbat nervously wet his lips.

"No...? Well, if you do as I ask—" he winced, grabbed the edge of the exam table to steady himself and added tightly, "I'll give you a head start—since I'm obviously not in top form, you... stand a decent chance of getting away and... warning your confederates." As if to emphasize the point, he winced again, then released his hold on the table and straightened up. "Four, at the very least, to one? Best odds you're likely to get on a planet like this—"

"How do I know if that thing's still loaded?" Urbat jerked his chin towards the tiny weapon while sidling ever closer to the hatch.

"You... don't," Qar'qaah forced out through clenched teeth.

"How much of a head start?" Urbat stalled as he edged even closer to the open hatchway.

"I suppose it all depends on how fast you can run—"

Urbat shoved Sirin towards Qar'qaah and made a dash for the hatch.

Qar'qaah caught her with his free hand, roughly jerked her to his side and fired the *t'jing*.

The dart hit Urbat in the back of the head, exploding it and splattering the far wall of the small chamber with blood, bone and brain matter as the rest of his corpse hit the deck with a substantial *THWUMP!*

"Obviously not *quite* fast enough," Qar'qaah sighed as he released his hold on Sirin, then, without missing a beat asked, "Exactly how many others are there?" as he strode over to the hatchway. He gave Urbat's body a rough shove with his boot to shift it just enough so the hatch could close, hit the release with his fist then thumbed the lock, sealing them inside.

Sirin blinked, then tore her horrified gaze off what remained of Urbat, looked up at him and, after a moment managed to stammer, *"Wha...what...?"*

"How many others are there?" he repeated impatiently, his pretenses of another fit of abdominal spasms having completely evaporated.

"Uh..." She knit her brows, forcing her stunned mind into concentrating on the task at hand. "Let's see. There's... there's Tace... and another human—"

"Sssyr," Drakin finished for her. "And a Looper—"

"So there *are* only three others?" His feral eyes darted between the two. "Are you *absolutely* certain?"

"Daz all we ever sssaw, right, Sssirin?"

Sirin nodded, murmured, *"Yeah..."* as her gaze, like a moth to flame, shifted back to Urbat's headless, gore-covered corpse. *Gods...*

After a moment of awkward silence, she forced herself to look back at Qar'qaah to find him angrily combing his fingers through his tangled hair. "Did... did you mean what you said?"

He scowled at her as he made quick work of plaiting his now only marginally less disheveled hair. *"Said?"*

"About Khusaaq and you—"

"Being his *doh'ha*?" He tossed the thick braid over his shoulder as he pushed by her, to the drug cart.

"Yes," she replied softly.

He nodded distractedly as he began rummaging around in the cart.

"And about me?"

He looked up, briefly, before resuming his search. "You mean about not caring if I killed you?"

Sirin hesitated as she realized that she wasn't sure if she really wanted to know the answer. His sudden—horrifying—metamorphosis from a very ill, frightened boy cowering in a corner to a calm, cunning killer had left her deeply disconcerted. Could his uncanny physical resemblance to Khusaaq have lulled her into a false sense of thinking that he was, in fact, Khusaaq—or, more accurately, the Khusaaq *she* knew? *But you're not, are you? You're pure, unadulterated yowie.*

As if sensing her thoughts, he gave her another sharp, sidelong glare—then quickly looked away, jaw muscles bunching.

As she stared at him, she suddenly recalled what she had, at time, considered an off the cuff comment he'd made, shortly after they'd met, of proving to everyone that he was nothing more than a poor copy.

At the time it made absolutely no sense to her. Now it made perfect sense, and his current, hateful expression the curdled resentment of a long and tightly-held bitterness—*Oh...boy. Bet even Adler, even in* his *wildest dreams, never considered this kind of inferiority complex—*

"You showed me... *compassion,"* he growled as he angrily dug around in the cart, as if the mere mention of such an attribute left him deeply unsettled. "You could've killed me, or—or just left me at any time and escaped, I couldn't have stopped you, but instead you stayed with me while I was incapacitated—"

"Juz goez to prove da old adage about no good deed goez unpunisssshed," Drakin interjected softly.

Qar'qaah pointedly ignored the remark as he rummaged through the cart's assortment of surgical instruments. "You... you risked your life to protect me when there was no immediate gain to you in doing so. I am therefore indebted to you. And if you are truly Sha'ashahn's bond-mate—"

"I am."

"—then I'm obligated to do everything in my power to protect you from harm until I can return you safely to him."

"If you don't mind me saying so, you don't sound particularly thrilled about it."

"If you don't mind me saying so, I'm *not,*" he replied, mimicking her voice, her inflections, perfectly—and it suddenly occurred to her that he *wasn't* mimicking her, per se. Mocking, clearly, but mimicking... not precisely. He'd in fact done exactly as Khusaaq had done within a brief time of meeting her: he was speaking with a familiar Selkis accent, and had been, she now realized, for some time.

It was just another form of Hahtooshan camouflage, every bit as effective as their chameleon-like armor and tattoos. Only this particular camouflage was being employed to provide a sense of commonality, to put at ease, rather than to conceal, obscure or to strike fear. She wondered if he was even consciously aware of doing it.

He picked up a tool, peered furiously at it then hurled it back in the drawer. "It complicates things tremendously."

Sirin blinked as his sharp rebuke jerked her back to the present reality. "What... oh, well, I'm really sorry."

He flicked her another sullen squint.

"And wat about me?" Drakin asked, clutching her tail in one taloned hand as she gingerly stepped over the dead Matarran, careful not to slip in the surrounding pool of silvery-blue blood as Qar'qaah did not appear to be in a mood for *any* sudden movements—even unintentional ones.

He favored her with a baleful glance. "My obligation extends to you, too, lizard, since you've kept me alive, if only so I can keep you two alive."

Sirin started to open her mouth to protest, then decided against it as he withdrew a very wicked looking instrument she recognized as a heavy-duty laser cutter. He gave it a closer look, nodded and shoved it into the cuff of his knee-high boot. He then selected and snatched up a ject-it and several red-capped vials of painkiller from the drawer, which he slipped into a trouser pocket.

He squatted beside the Matarran and relieved the corpse of its holstered blaster and gave it a quick pat down for other, hidden weapons. Finding nothing, he retrieved his maser pistol from where it had skittered under the examination table.

Still in a crouch, he carefully checked both weapons.

Satisfied, he rose and turned to the two women as he stuffed the blaster and pistol into the waistband of his trousers. "You're absolutely positive there are *only* three others?"

Sirin and Drakin exchanged glances then Sirin replied, "That's all we ever saw."

He stooped to snatch up his filthy under-tunic from where it had been discarded. Instead of slipping it back on, he tore a long strip of fabric from its hem then shoved the remains in another trouser pocket.

Drakin and Sirin again looked at each other, then back to Qar'qaah as he worked the strip of stiff fabric with his fingers. Once it was soft, he reached back, grabbed the long braid and twined the strip of fabric around it. Closing his eyes and mumbling to himself, he twisted the plait even tighter.

Watching him, Sirin realized this was no casual act: she was witnessing a highly formalized ritual. She could only guess that its purpose was, at least in part, to prepare him mentally and physically for what lay ahead.

Finally he stopped whispering to himself and, swaying slightly, reopened his eyes.

For a moment his gaze remained unfocused, then Qar'qaah blinked several times and gave his head a quick shake to clear it.

"You all right?" Sirin asked.

He scowled at her as he gave plait another quick twist, and it neatly folded back on itself.

Answer enough.

"I alwayz meant to asssk Matooz," Drakin said, drawing his suspicious squint, "why da long hair? Doesssn't it... well, get in da way?"

"It marks me as... " he paused, took a breath, then continued, "it marked me as an untouched Elkanaghalli." He took the ends of the fabric strip and tied the braid in place, the plait now a short, extremely thick queue that reached to just below the top of his bony, blistered shoulders. "Defender of the true faith, keeper of the past and as first caste, beloved guardian of the Elkanasu—" He bit his swollen lower lip before adding angrily, "It serves a purpose, or at least it did, in more civilized times when one's standing was determined by hand-to-hand combat."

Drakin raised her brow ridges in begging interest.

"It was… and still is a very effective guard against a blow to the back of the neck, especially when dressed with a *quj'schah*—a thick, metal studded thong. But in the less… *enlightened* times we now live, one must make do with what's available—and this keeps my hair out of my eyes," he added with unexpected pragmatism as he briefly fingered the filthy, fabric-wrapped queue before starting for the hatch. "Relock this after I leave." His emaciated face briefly tightened in a wince that to Sirin appeared to be all too real, then added tightly, "When all those aboard have been dispatched, I'll come back for you."

Sirin easily beat him to the hatch, blocking his path. "Do you have a death wish?"

He met her gaze with a genuinely perplexed one of his own. "Yes, of course I do—"

"Did it ever occur to you that we don't?"

"You mean to tell me you have no wish as to the manner of your death?"

"Well no, not exactly, but I do know I don't want to die on this goddamned ship! The flickerstage is just down the corridor, we have a chance to escape before they realize—"

"You wish to allow these individuals to live so they can continue to pose a threat to Sha'ashahn?"

"No, not when you put it like that, of course not, but—"

"Then I must deal with them, here and now."

"But... but you're extremely ill—"

"I never said I wasn't, but success lies in the element of surprise."

"Okay, I'll grant you that, so you grant me this." She paused then committing not only herself but Drakin, without so much as asking her friend, said, "The chances of success would be greater if you did not go alone."

The remark was followed by several rapid heartbeats of hostile silence then Qar'qaah countered testily, "The chances of *you* surviving are much greater if you remain here."

"Itz uz againssst dem," Drakin replied, briefly drawing his fierce, over the shoulder glare.

"Besides," Sirin refused to budge from her spot in front of the hatch despite Qar'qaah's ferocious expression, "we just might surprise *you."*

"If anyone's to be surprised," he replied testily, "I would much rather it is someone else if it's all the same to you."

She crossed her arms and scowled up at him.

He stared down at her.

Finally, with an exasperated sigh and an impatient shake of his head, he slipped his hand into his trouser pocket and withdrew his wadded up undertunic... and the *t'jing*. He quickly separated the two, furiously returned the undertunic to his pocket and offered her the weapon. "Here."

She carefully plucked it from his blood-sticky, tattooed palm.

"It fires exploding darts—"

"So I noticed," she replied as she stared down at the slim, innocuous looking silver cylinder that was no longer or thicker than her little finger.

"This one is fitted with a silencer so it doesn't make its trademark sound... *tah-JING,* as it discharges. It's designed to carry only armor-piercing explosive darts, both suggesting this once belonged to a professional, not a second-rate criminal like your friend here." He gave Urbat's corpse a kick for emphasis.

"Which begs the question... where did you get it if you don't mind me asking?" She wanted to add, 'This isn't standard Hahtooshan issue' but stopped herself, sensing such a remark, in light of his comments to Urbat about the weapon, would definitely be taken the wrong way. And Qar'qaah did not look like he was in a particularly forgiving mood.

"Let's say a... *benefactor*. Yes, a very generous benefactor, and be happy I did have it and leave it at that." He stepped close, surprisingly so, almost but not quite touching her hip with his and she glanced up at him, suddenly wary. "You fire it by pressing here." He pointed to the recessed trigger and glanced at her face, assuring himself that she understood. "We have a limited number of darts left—six to be precise—so I do ask that you not test it on me."

"Huh?" She briefly met his stern gaze, then looked down at the weapon and realized she was pointing it at his stomach. "Oh... sorry! Didn't mean to do that."

"I'm *sure* you didn't, and I strongly suggest you never do it again... unless, of course, you plan on pushing the trigger."

Don't tempt me. As he turned his back to her to snatch up Urbat's gore-splattered shocker, she stuck out her tongue at him.

Drakin pretended not to notice and fixed her eyes on the ceiling.

Qar'qaah, oblivious to the gesture—or the exchange—gave the Rimmer weapon a cursory wipe off on his even more filthy trousers, then offered it, grip first, to Drakin, who wisely accepted it without comment. "You know how to fire this?"

"Yez."

"Decent aim?"

"Very."

"Good, but I must warn you," he continued disdainfully, "I don't think much of females—*even female A'tuu'shahn'i*—as fighters."

"Indeed? Who'd have guessed," Sirin replied sourly. "But in this case, *buggars* can't be choosers."

He stared at her for a moment, sensing she'd slipped an insult past him, then, with a shake of his head, grumbled, "Ready?"

"About as ready as we'll ever be," Sirin replied with a sidelong look at Drakin.

"Then come," he hit the hatch release. As it slipped open, he sniffed the air then cautiously peered around its red frame, looking first one direction, then the other. Satisfied the corridor was deserted, he crept out, hurriedly motioning for them to follow.

Sirin stepped into the corridor, all of her senses on edge, with Drakin right behind her, both women constantly glancing behind them. Progress was slow as Qar'qaah stopped just before each hatch and emergency stairwell to sniff the air before moving on.

Using his sensitive nose to guide him unerringly to their quarry, he led them up two flights of stairs and finally onto a landing that gave access to the dilapidated freighter's main deck.

He glanced back at them, gestured for them to remain where they were, then he peered around the hatch's frame.

Satisfied, he withdrew into the relative cover of the emergency stairwell. "The bridge is… is down the corridor to the right… about… about twenty meters. Ready?"

Sirin nodded, albeit reluctantly. Qar'qaah was breathing hard, and his pasty skin and pallid tattoos were glossy with oily sweat, sweat that trickled down the grooves etched in his gaunt face, adding an extra component to the decoration: the scarification now glittered like streams viewed from high above.

He lifted his gaze to Drakin. "Lizard?"

"Ready."

He again peered out of the stairwell and, motioning them to follow, slipped out into the dimly lit passageway.

They had traveled no more than a few meters when he stopped. Just… stopped. And for no reason Sirin could immediately grasp.

Then she noticed that he was shaking—no, *twitching,* like a dog in its sleep, little muscle jerks in a body suddenly drawn taut. And his eyes… He was just staring, not *at* anything, just staring, eyes wide and his breath coming short and ragged.

"Qar'qaah?" she whispered, knowing better than to touch him. He was gone, suddenly gone somewhere else, no longer aware of his current surroundings, no longer aware of her or

Drakin or the danger they were in, and wherever he was he was scared, *frozen* scared.

Sirin had seen that look before, on green troops. One of her first assignments after graduating from the Coalition Expeditionary Forces academy on Selkis was to the troop carrier *Hector* where a large part of her duties required her to process the paperwork for soldiers deemed unfit to return to active duty. And part of that process was to be present for and to record their in-depth psychological evaluations.

Qar'qaah's distant expression was an immediate, eerie and unnerving reminder of those troops who'd witnessed something horrific, or done something horrific. Something so horrific the suddenly resurfaced memory would paralyze them. It would force them to stand there, transfixed, as the images replayed themselves over and over inside their heads. It was the stare of someone sparking off something beyond an outsider's understanding.

But this wasn't a base psych unit or even a trauma bed in the *Baidarka*'s sickbay. Here there were no trained personnel with restraint webbing and seds only a yell away. There was no prolonged stay at a base hospital in this soldier's very near future. They were in a passageway aboard a freighter with a crew who weren't looking out for anyone's interests but their own, and wouldn't be particularly happy to find out that two of their own were no longer around.

At any moment one of the crew could come across them, with Qar'qaah unable to move, unable to see, unable to react, just... *gone*.

Sirin had to get him back, no matter the risk. With a quick, over the shoulder nod to Drakin, she braced herself for a possibly violent response and again whispered his name while she very lightly touched his arm.

Qar'qaah flinched and gasped sharply as his free hand balled into a white-knuckled fist while the other clutched his maser pistol as if it was a lifeline.

Sirin whispered, *"Qar'qaah?"* a little louder, *"you okay?"* A stupid question, but... She cautiously tightened her hold, ready to duck. "Qar'qaah. Answer me—*ithsu baktai."* The softly worded command was followed by a not so gentle tug on his noticeably clammy arm.

Then, with a slow blink, he was back. By the expression on his face his recovery was clearly as much as a surprise to him as his unexpected departure to parts unknown had been to her and Drakin.

At least Drakin looked relieved. Qar'qaah still looked scared as he gave Sirin, then Drakin a quick, sidelong glance—like someone who was barely keeping it together and suddenly realized everyone around him knew it. And it wasn't *just* that he was scared. He was a scared *kid*, his Hahtooshan bluster, his swagger all a façade—and a rapidly crumbling façade.

She felt their chances of survival drop several percentage points—not that they were very high to begin with. *If we do survive this, my friend, you're gonna need to spend some quality time in a padded room with lots of happy drugs.*

Qar'qaah nervously wet his lips. He was still shaking; his skin was positively ashen, drawn and sparkling with beads of oily sweat. He looked like a ghost—or like he'd seen one.

"Maybe you should sit down for a bit?"

He shook his head, slowly, not trusting his voice to give any more away.

"Then I suggest we keep moving before someone finds Urbat and wants answers."

He nodded, still refusing to speak, and sniffed the air. Then, with a beckoning gesture—with a still visibly trembling hand—he again started down the passageway.

They'd managed no more than a half dozen meters when Qar'qaah abruptly stopped yet again. Before Sirin could wonder if he'd gone again, she heard what he'd heard: somewhere not far ahead someone was laughing.

But not for long, she thought grimly to herself as she caught the look in his pale eyes.

He put his finger to his lips, then, using the same finger, pointed to a blue-framed airlock further up the passageway.

She nodded.

He sniffed the air then turned to her and continued in a series of rapid, indecipherable hand signals to which Sirin answered with a blank stare.

He stared back—she had to assume he was waiting for her response.

The only one she could think of was a shrug and a shake of her head.

He scowled—clearly he understood what *that* meant—leaned close and whispered: *"A Looper and a human are on the bridge."*

"And the other one?"

He irritably mimicked her shrug. Then wiping the sheen of sweat from his forehead, he muttered, *"Stay here. I'll deal with those on the bridge. While I will endeavor to be as quiet as possible, I cannot guarantee their willing cooperation so the noise might draw our missing accomplice."* He motioned with his chin to a hollow between two major bulkheads, not far from the bridge. *"Position yourselves in there. You'll be relatively safe from any possible crossfire and in an ideal spot to deal with the other human."*

He dropped to a crouch, but as he turned away Sirin whispered, *"Wait."*

He met her worried gaze with an annoyed stare.

"Uh... a little bit ago, you... well, you left us for a moment."

He continued to stare as a jaw muscle visibly twitched.

"What happened?"

He shifted his narrowed gaze back to the nearby airlock as he chewed on his swollen lower lip. *"I saw someone—I mean I thought I saw someone,"* he finally admitted then wiped his lip with the back of his hand as he realized he'd accidentally reopened the split, in the process smearing the blood across his cheek and jaw, giving his ashen skin false color.

"Who?"

"Doesn't matter."

Sirin looked over her shoulder at Drakin. Now it was the nurse's turn to shrug. Sirin looked back at Qar'qaah to find him watching her out of the corner of his eye.

"If you two are finished conferring about my sanity?"

"We're worried about you."

"Worry about yourselves. I can take care of myself." His eyes darted to the *t'jing* she held. *"Now remember, do not fire unless you're absolutely sure who you're aiming at—I'll be exceedingly annoyed if you kill me by mistake."*

Sirin swallowed a startled chuckle and he favored her with another sidelong, and this time exasperated squint as he hissed, *"What now?"*

She replied with a contrite shrug and a whispered, *"If I didn't know better, I'd say you have at least a rudimentary sense of humor."*

"I find nothing amusing about being blown to bits by someone I'm attempting to rescue." With that, he crept silently towards the open airlock.

Well, Sirin thought, as another hand gesture, an ancient human gesture—the perfect, all-encompassing comeback—came to mind, one she wasn't sure he was familiar with but one she promised she'd test out the first chance she got. *You're clearly back to your usual charming self.*

Once he was beyond casual earshot, Drakin leaned close and whispered, *"Hattoosssinz will be Hattoosssinz."*

Sirin sighed, *"He's got panache, I'll give him that."*

"Panaz...?"

"Verve."

Drakin stared back in mordant surprise. *"Of courssse hez got nerve. All Hattoosssinz got nerve, and far too much, if you asssk me."*

Sirin leaned back and cupping her mouth close to Drakin's ear, whispered, *"Not nerve, although I'll grant you that they are all overly endowed in that department. No, what I said was verve. It means zeal, fervor, daring do—"*

"Az I sssaid," Drakin slumped back into the hollow and crossing her scaly arms, huffed softly, *"Hattoosssinz will be Hattoosssinz."*

Chapter 6

Sickbay, aboard the Baidarka.

Nihaal, wearing only a surgical drape across his lap, sat rigidly on the examination table, his frightened eyes following Amalfitano's every move as the doctor calmly and quietly relayed orders to his staff.

Murh'sooli stood off to one side, thick arms crossed, his own piercing gaze fixed on Nihaal, as if that alone would keep the soldier from bolting.

Finally Amalfitano turned back to Nihaal and looked him up and down. Blood metabolites had put his age at thirteen Standard years, give or take a few weeks, slightly younger than Amalfitano had guessed—the combination of tattoos, scarification, muscle wasting and radiation burns had added a few years to his overall appearance—but Amalfitano needed no diagnostic computer or blood test to tell him Nihaal was positively terrified. "You're not Elkanaghalli."

Nihaal hesitated before answering softly, "No, ta'ahn." His pale eyes flicked to Murh'sooli, then back to Amalfitano. "Chah'duu."

"It's one of the older clans."

"Yes, ta'ahn."

"Chah'duu means *guardian,* doesn't it?"

"Yes... ta'ahn."

Amalfitano smiled a private smile at the trooper's look of surprise—not to mention Murh'sooli's—at his unexpected knowledge. Izraad's late-night and often rather fractious tutelage over coffee and anisette cookies was clearly going to pay unexpected dividends. Dumbfounding Murh'sooli, even a little, was, by itself, worth all the effort and trouble. "Open your mouth and stick out your tongue."

Nihaal did as he was asked.

Amalfitano peered inside and inwardly winced. Nihaal's mouth and tongue were covered with blisters and small, bleeding ulcers and he knew the same could be said for his entire gastrointestinal tract—the fetid smell of his breath was evidence enough.

"Okay."

Nihaal snapped his mouth shut.

Amalfitano scooped up a handful of vials and a ject-it from the nearby drug cart then held them out for him to see. "I need to give you a series of injections—for the poisoning. Do I have your permission?"

Nihaal hesitated as he looked at the ject-it, at the vials, and then, after another sidelong glance at the stern-faced Murh'sooli, he finally replied, "Yes, ta'ahn."

By Nihaal's tone, Amalfitano suspected the trooper's unhappy consent was said more out of fear of disobeying Khusaaq—and angering the nearby sergeant—than in hopes of obtaining relief from the agonizing effects of sustained exposure.

"Shouldn't sting too much." With that, Amalfitano lightly grasped his tattooed shoulder, felt Nihaal's entire body stiffen in response, and pressed the ject-it against it before the trooper could react instinctively and pull away. "So, tell me about yourself."

It was a tried and true method, one he'd used on countless soldiers facing the terrors of combat... or suffering from its equally horrific consequences. Get the patient talking, about himself, about home, about anything... get him distracted and eventually he'd calm down—at least that was the plan. But this was no ordinary soldier. This was a Hahtooshan—a merc, and a *very* scared, *very* ill merc at that.

Nihaal replied with a bewildered, *"Myself...?"* as he gave Murh'sooli another glance to which the sergeant grumbled,

"If you don't, he'll just keep asking."

Amalfitano shot the medic a look as he walked around the exam table, to which Murh'sooli replied with a slight twitch of his armored shoulder. "For instance," Amalfitano continued as he reloaded the ject-it, "what's your area of expertise?"

"I'm a technician, ta'ahn," Nihaal replied, watching as Amalfitano pressed the tool against his other shoulder.

"What kind of technician?"

"Weapons, ta'ahn—specifically rail guns."

"Ever hear of Asopus-Sastani syndrome?"

"Yes, ta'ahn."

"So your rail gunners get it too?"

"Of course not, ta'ahn," he replied with a trace of contempt. "It's completely preventable with proper shielding."

Amalfitano raised his brows, made a note to speak to the *Faridour*'s CMO and, if Narbrooi permitted, her chief engineer about it, then happened to notice a freshly healed wound that ran from Nihaal's left elbow to wrist. "What happened here?" he asked as he lightly palpated the ragged scar.

"Tissue samples."

As Amalfitano and Murh'sooli shared puzzled looks, Nihaal slid his arm out from under Amalfitano's curious touch.

Amalfitano looked back at Nihaal. "Tissue samples...? It looks like someone—"

"Cisne's...*doctor,*" Nihaal replied as he covered the injury as best he could with the fingers of his other hand.

"Oh." *And you don't want to talk about it—at least not yet. Fair enough.* He stood back and reloaded the ject-it. *We'll just take it one step at a time.* "Lie down."

Nihaal hesitated only moment before he reluctantly eased himself back onto the table, but his entire body remained tense, like a coiled spring.

"Were you assigned to the *Makhaira* at the same time as Khusaaq Sha'ashahn?" Amalfitano asked as he pressed the ject-it against Nihaal's bare thigh.

"No, ta'ahn. I was already serving aboard her."

"So, how'd you come to end up on Rasal Ghul Seven?"

"It was my part of duty rotation to be a member of the landing party, ta'ahn."

Lucky you, he thought, eyeing Nihaal's badly blistered and peeling face. Then he reminded himself, *But if you hadn't been, you'd be dead, blown to smithereens over Tuli—which begs the question, did we kill a shipload of children?* He jerked his mind back to the present, to Nihaal's tattooed, and, he realized, expectant face. *No, not children, per se...* "I need to palpate your abdomen—do I have your permission?"

"Won't your instruments tell you everything you need to know?" Nihaal's suspicious gaze darted to a nearby darkened monitor.

Amalfitano followed his pointed stare—he'd deliberately not activated the sensors in the examination table. Without some sort of internal probe that could bypass the dermal interference generated by Hahtooshan tattoos, they were little more than flashing lights—and about as useful. And he wanted to build up a little bit of trust with his young patient before he raised the idea of inserting a probe or attaching a signal suppressor.

"Yes... and no," Amalfitano answered. "Yes, they can tell me everything, but I find a hands-on approach has its added benefits." And that was true: all the medical paraphernalia which filled his sickbay certainly could speak volumes on a patient's health and quickly and accurately pinpoint hidden issues, but actually touching the patient, simple skin-to-skin contact, dropping any pretense not to mention barriers, physical and psychological, often left an unspoken bond between patient and physician no diagnostic computer could ever hope to achieve. His skilled hands had never failed or misled him; technology had. "Plus our external sensors can't pierce the 'noise' given off by your tattoos and provide any accurate data."

Nihaal again looked at Murh'sooli, and at his affirming dip of the head, reluctantly nodded his go-ahead then held absolutely still, barely breathing, while Amalfitano pressed his fingertips against Nihaal's taut stomach.

"Painful?"

"No, ta'ahn."

"This missing soldier Khusaaq Sha'ashahn mentioned—"

"Qar'qaah Kon'ta'aq—he is Sha'ashahn's *doh'ha*, ta'ahn."

Amalfitano, aware of Murh'sooli's quickly concealed response, pretended not to notice as he moved his fingers slowly across Nihaal's sunken abdomen while asking with feigned distraction: "His what...?"

"His *doh*—" Nihaal clenched his teeth as Amalfitano pressed down.

Amalfitano made another mental note to ask the medic about what that meant. Right now he had far more urgent concerns: his patient's belly was a cornucopia of bad, albeit not entirely unexpected, news. "Painful?"

"Paq—I mean, *yes*, ta'ahn. Very... very much so."

Amalfitano shifted his hand slightly and pressed down again. "And that?"

Nihaal's grimace was answer enough.

"Your spleen's enlarged—not unexpected." He moved his hand again and again pressed down. This time Nihaal's only response was a sharp intake of breath. "But it's salvageable."

Amalfitano slipped both hands under Nihaal's back and with well-practiced technique felt for other problems while Nihaal fixed his pinched stare on the ceiling.

"Had it not been for Qar'qaah Kon'ta'aq," Nihaal volunteered unexpectedly, "we would've died."

Amalfitano stopped his exam to meet the trooper's intense gray eyes. "He sounds like a remarkable individual, to have kept you all alive—"

"Kon'ta'aq is exceedingly... *resourceful*, ta'ahn..."

Amalfitano nodded his appreciation. For a Hahtooshan, that was high praise indeed. "Resourceful—in what way?"

"He managed to power up the diffusion screen on the island, and somehow kept it running, along with fabricating a protein synthesizer and water purifier out of little more than rusting scrap—in the process spending long hours outside of the bunker, exposing himself to the radiation while ordering the rest of us to remain inside—" Nihaal broke their uneasy staring match and turned his narrowed, watery gaze on the bank of darkened monitors. "The rest of us... we would've given up— he wouldn't let us. Even when a Blatto—one of the crew of the craft Sha'ashahn had taken to reach the mainland—managed to reach the island and told us the boat had foundered in the storm... Kon'ta'aq kept telling us Sha'ashahn would come back for us, Sha'ashahn wouldn't abandon us. Sha'ashahn wouldn't leave us there to..." he squeezed his eyes shut and added softly, "*...to die.*"

Amalfitano looked to Murh'sooli and was surprised to see the normally grim-faced sergeant reply with a commiserating shake of his head.

Amalfitano nodded and lightly touched Nihaal's shoulder, and Nihaal's eyes snapped open. "You just said that he's very resourceful, Ha'tat. It's far too soon to give up hope."

Nihaal replied with a less than confident nod as his eyes again darted to Murh'sooli, and then, as Amalfitano palpated his left kidney, he gasped.

"Okay, that's the worst of it." Amalfitano crossed his arms. "When did you last eat a normal meal—meaning solid food—and keep it down?"

"I… I do not remember, ta'ahn. Before Rasal Ghul…?"

Amalfitano loaded another vial into the ject-it and pressed the tool against Nihaal's other thigh. "Are you able to hold down liquids without getting nauseated?"

"Some of the time, ta'ahn… but that might be due in part to Jaa'qwah Kon'ta'aq's idea of what's actually palatable."

Amalfitano squinted at him as he realized Nihaal had actually tried to make a joke and he chuckled, "That bad, eh? Well, we have *really* good cooks aboard the *Baidarka*—just ask Murh'sooli here…"

Nihaal's eyes obediently darted to the medic, who—for Murh'sooli—nodded enthusiastically.

"…and as soon as you're able, you can eat your fill. In fact as soon as I give you the go-ahead, I want you to eat as much as you want, whenever you want—get some meat back on those growing bones, okay?"

Again, Nihaal only nodded.

Amalfitano gave him another head to toe visual exam as he returned to the business at hand. "Blood in your urine?"

"Yes, ta'ahn."

"All the time?"

He nodded.

"Okay, sit up." He stepped back and as Nihaal quickly pushed himself back into a seated position, he turned to the drug cart. "In treating Sha'ashahn and Matoosh we had to figure out a way to override the interference those tattoos of yours emit."

He turned back to him and held out two small devices. "With Murh'sooli's help, we've come up with these." *And a hell of an improvement over the prototype—for all concerned.* "Nothing more than a fancy signal suppressor and a continuous blood sampler probe. I need to attach them to you. This," he held up the probe, "slips under the top layers of skin—a little pinch going in, that's all. The other just sticks to your skin." He tried not to look as expectant as he felt as he hoped his prep for this was going to be enough to sway the trooper into agreeing voluntarily; he did not want to resort to making it an order.

Nihaal gave the innocuous looking objects a wary glance, then meeting Amalfitano's steady, friendly gaze and after a moment of hesitation, nodded.

Amalfitano breathed a silent sigh of relief then said matter-of-factly, "Give me your arm."

Nihaal did as he was told and Amalfitano inserted the tiny, thread-like probe, affixed it to his wrist, then attached the suppressor to his chest. Then he turned his attention to the bank of nearby monitors as, one by one, they came to life and filled with data.

Reassured by what he saw, all the readouts affirming what he already knew, Amalfitano looked back at Nihaal. "Your medic—you said his name was Jaa'qwah? Well, he did a great job at reversing the effects of your poisoning—plus you have that indomitable Hahtooshan physiology working in your favor." He gave Nihaal a pat on the shoulder. It took him a moment to realize that the soldier had not responded by tensing up. *So it works on Hahtooshan s too.* "Do exactly as my staff and I tell you and you should be over the worst of it in a couple of weeks."

Amalfitano smiled as he saw a glimmer of relief in the young Hahtooshan's haggard eyes. "I want to keep those on you," he pointed to the suppressor and then the probe, "to monitor you. So don't remove or tamper with them, understood?"

"Yes, ta'ahn," he replied as his eyes darted to Murh'sooli.

Murh'sooli replied with a stern nod.

Amalfitano pulled an infuser from the cart. "You're still severely dehydrated and extremely malnourished—I want to attach this to your other arm and pump some high calorie fluids into you over the next seventy-two hours, all right?"

Nihaal startled him by immediately extending his free arm.

As Amalfitano attached it, Nihaal gave Murh'sooli another sidelong glance, then at the sergeant's prodding stare and silently mouthed, *'Jaas-nhe,'* he dutifully repeated in Standard, "Thank you, Doctor."

Amalfitano had noticed the interaction but pretended he hadn't. Expressing appreciation to someone for that person just doing their job was not, he'd come to learn, a Hahtooshan habit and he wondered if perhaps Izraad had been tutoring Murh'sooli in human customs, just as Murh'sooli had been enlightening Izraad to the intricacies of Hahtooshan culture, bribed, according to Izraad, with liberal offerings of all things chocolate. "You're most welcome, Ha'tat." He then stepped back and motioned for him to get to his feet and Nihaal obediently eased himself off the examination table.

Amalfitano loaded the last of the vials. It contained a combination of a potent painkiller and an equally potent sedative. "Now," he said as he pressed the ject-it against Nihaal's shoulder, "how does a few hours of uninterrupted sleep in a nice warm bed sound to you?"

This time Nihaal actually smiled—no prompt from Murh'sooli required.

"Excellent." Amalfitano snatched up a pair of sickbay shorts one of the nurses had placed on a nearby cart, next to Nihaal's discarded armor, and handed them to him. "Here."

Nihaal accepted them and quickly pulled them on.

"Now, come with me." Noticing Nihaal's sidelong glance at his armor, he added, "Don't worry about your armor— Murh'sooli will store it and it'll be under his control at all times, not ours, all right?" In fact Murh'sooli had insisted that only he or one of the other medics be present while Nihaal and the others stripped down, strongly hinting this was being done for everyone else's protection as armor did, on rare occasion, according to Murh'sooli, detonate while being removed.

Amalfitano, while not totally disbelieving the medic—Murh'sooli was, after all, the epitome of no-nonsense—nevertheless suspected there was more to it. That perhaps their armor was booby-trapped as many rumors proposed, and Hahtooshans were as yet unwilling to let their new allies in on the secret of how to safely separate it from the wearer.

Nihaal followed Amalfitano out of the examination room; Rosen was standing just outside, along with three other equally ill and frightened Hahtooshan adolescents, along with Bar'ahani and Amalfitano's other bodyguard, Tayya'shan.

"Ah, perfect timing. Althea," Amalfitano said to the nurse as he lightly grasped Nihaal's bare shoulder, "how 'bout you take our young friend here to ward one and find him an empty bunk." *And quickly.* He gave Rosen a pointed look, to which she replied with an understanding nod. He then turned to the three soldiers and smiled. "So, who's next?"

When no one volunteered, Tayya'shan pointed to Laihiri and barked, "You! *Go.*"

Chapter 7

Aboard the Talakah.

Sirin stared at the open hatchway as she mentally counted off the seconds.

Qar'qaah had slipped unnoticed onto the bridge some moments before. Despite his promise, she found herself increasingly uneasy as time ticked by without her overhearing a startled cry or muffled thump, or the sharp report and accompanying flash of something—or someone—being blown to bits.

She struggled with images of him frozen in place, unable to tell what was real and what was a figment of his exhausted mind—or worse yet, doubling over at a crucial moment and now that Urbat was dead, completely at the mercy of Tace.

Finally she could stand it no longer; she started to rise from their hiding spot within the curve of a bulkhead, whispering, *"Maybe he's in trouble—"*

"Maybe we ssshould do exactly wat he told uz to do," Drakin replied in kind, tugging her back down.

"But—" she was cut off by a muffled *'boom'* that reverberated down the passageway. An instant later, the corridor was plunged into utter darkness… and total, deafening silence as even the ever-present background hum of the overhead air vents abruptly ceased.

"Oh, diz can't be good," Drakin whispered.

"We better go find Qar—"

"Quiet!"

Sirin flinched at the unexpected male voice behind her, then reached back and quickly located what she immediately realized was the toe of a boot, and not just any boot. It was unmistakably a Hahtooshan campaign boot, with all its attendant and rather revolting wriggling. She quickly let go and reflexively wiped her hand on her thigh. *"Qar'qaah…?"*

"You were hoping it was someone else?"

Yes— "No, of course not, but—what the hell happened?"

"I did just as I said I would. I dealt with the human and the Looper..."

She felt him crouch beside her.

"...then I cut the power."

"Oh," she replied, perplexed. *"Uh... why?"*

"Because we A'tuu'shahn'i have very acute vision—even in the dark. And what we cannot see we can smell or sense. It offers me a very distinct advantage."

"Zo, now wat?" Drakin hissed, her bifurcated tongue tickling Sirin's cheek; she absently swatted it away.

"Now we... we wait for the... remaining human to... to come to uuuus..."

Overhearing his hushed voice taper off into a stifled groan, Sirin whispered, *"Are you okay?"*

He didn't answer immediately, and when he did it was a strained, *"No."*

"Have you been injured?"

He startled her by clutching her shoulder to steady himself. *"No—"* He gasped sharply as his fingers tightened their hold, then he buried his forehead in the center of her back and muffled: *"I'm... I'm just feeling really sick to my stomach."*

Oh, please don't puke on me... She wanted to scoot a little further away but Drakin's bulk blocked her path. She gave the nurse a futile shove, but there was simply no space for Drakin to shift, even a little bit.

Qar'qaah took several deep, gulping breathings before finally lifting his head and adding, *"It... it will pass—"*

"Syr?" an all too familiar voice to Sirin echoed up the passageway, accompanied by a moving beam of light and shuffling footfalls.

Qar'qaah instantly released his hold on Sirin and maintaining his crouch, twisted towards the voice.

"It's Tace," she whispered just loud enough for Qar'qaah to hear, not that it mattered to him who it was, Sirin realized a second afterwards. All that mattered was the last kidnapper had delivered himself to them, rather than them having to go looking.

"Mathoc?" Pardix called out again. "What the hell's going on?"

Sirin pushed herself back against the unforgiving wall as the narrow shaft of light swept uncomfortably close to their hiding spot.

The oddly cadenced footfalls stopped—*no,* Sirin realized, *not oddly cadenced, he's limping*—and the light beam suddenly streamed past them, down the length of the corridor. "This no time to play games—you heard Jonathan—Cisne'll be here at any time!"

Sirin felt Qar'qaah's entire body twitch against her and she gave him a wary, sidelong look. *Oh, please, this isn't the time to go spacey on us—*

"I can't leave you two imbeciles alone on the bridge for five goddamned minutes while I take a piss without you screwing things up!" The light swept back and forth. "Mathoc? Where the hell are you, you maggot-brained moron!"

Sirin flicked Qar'qaah another quick glance as the beam swept past them again and saw him roughly wipe his eyes with the back of his free hand, then blink several times as if he *was* having problems seeing, despite his earlier boast.

But at least he was with them, instead of gone somewhere. That in itself was a small relief.

"Syr...?" Pardix continued, his voice now tainted with fear as he pulled his blaster from its shoulder holster. *"Dammit, answer me!"*

A bleat of an alarm startled Pardix into wheeling towards the bridge's open airlock. He pointed the hand light at it and leading with the blaster, took a cautious step, and then another, his body silhouetted by the wavering halo of light. "Syr...? Is that you?"

Sirin, while on route to Poonda Five, had spent countless hours fantasizing about Pardix meeting an untimely and *extremely* unpleasant end. But now, as Qar'qaah took careful aim and fantasy was about to become reality...

She squeezed her eyes shut.

Nothing happened.

She slowly opened one eye a crack, and then the other.

Pardix was still alive and very much in one piece and peering into the bridge as he swept the light back and forth. "Syr…? Mathoc…?"

Qar'qaah whispered in her ear, *"Remain here."*

"But not just shoot—"

"He's standing in front of a major power bus. If I fire, I risk hitting it as well, and if we want to get you and your scaly friend safely off Poonda Five and back to Sha'ashahn, then we need a functioning ship." With that he slipped silently around the bulkhead.

Oblivious, Pardix warily stepped through the airlock, onto the bridge, taking the only source of light with him. Qar'qaah's stooped silhouette was immediately swallowed up by the surrounding, now stifling darkness.

Gods… Sirin swallowed hard as she leaned back into Drakin's familiar, comforting bulk. She expected another quiet kill, perhaps at most a startled grunt, followed by a dull *thud* as something heavy hit the deck.

Instead the emergency lights flickered to life, bathing the corridor, as well as the interior of the bridge in a deep ruby light.

"Uh-oh," Drakin whispered an instant before the bridge exploded with weapons fire.

Chapter 8

Aboard the Talakah.

Sirin covered her nose and mouth as best she could as smoke billowed from the bridge airlock and into the corridor. Beside her, Drakin hunkered down and covered her snout with both hands as the acrid cloud began to swirl around them.

The choking fumes stung their eyes and burned their throats and lungs and for several minutes Sirin had to fight a growing sense of panic. Just as she felt as if she was about to suffocate, the smoke began to dissipate as the ship's emergency air scrubbers abruptly kicked in and a vent directly above them blasted them with fresh oxygen.

She hungrily sucked in the air as she wiped her streaming eyes with her sleeve, then she cautiously peered around the bulkhead. The oval airlock was barely visible in the ruddy haze, illuminated from within by the intermittent flash of exploding circuits.

She leaned back and whispered to Drakin, *"I'm going after Qar'qaah—"*

"He waz pretty emphatic about uz ssstaying here."

"Then you stay here, I'm going to find him!"

"And how, may I asssk, are you going to do dat? In diz sssmoke, hez almossst az invisssible az da proverbial needle in a hayssstack... and a hundred timez az prickly—"

"And he might be seriously injured." Or, more likely, dead, she admitted to herself.

Drakin replied with a heavy sigh, *"Den I better come wit you."* She rose stiffly and helped Sirin to her feet then they peeked around the bulkhead.

The smoke had cleared enough that they could now see the bridge airlock… and the shadowy form of a body sprawled face down not far from its raised threshold.

Sirin glanced up at Drakin.

Drakin stared back at her. *"Only one way to find out."*

Together they crept cautiously towards the lock and the unmoving body.

Sirin stopped. Unprepared, Drakin bumped into her.

"Wat?"

"Tace," Sirin whispered. *"It's Tace."*

Drakin shuffled closer, then squatted beside him, grabbed a limp wrist and felt for a pulse. Finally she looked up at Sirin and shook her head.

Sirin turned to the open airlock as more acrid smoke belched forth: somewhere within that hellish maelstrom was Qar'qaah.

She stuffed the *t'jing* in her jumpsuit's pocket and pulled its collar up around her mouth and nose, then motioned for Drakin to stay where she was and cautiously stepped over the threshold and onto the bridge.

She swept the chamber with her burning eyes, using the smoke-diffused ruby glow of the emergency lights and the occasional waterfall of sparks from consoles. The bridge was in ruins; everywhere she looked, she saw wrecked and smoldering equipment.

"Qar'qaah!" she called out as she carefully eased herself under a dangling loop of wiring. "Where are you—uh… *Guuch-sseh?"* Taking another wary step, she peered into the murk. *"Guuch-sseh!"*

Her own lungs were now burning, her eyes were streaming and she knew if she didn't find him soon, she'd have to retreat or risk succumbing herself. *"Ithsu baktai! Answer me, damn you!"* She took another shuffling step and felt her foot bump into something soft—something that *didn't* feel like composite.

She dropped her watery gaze. "Qar'qaah…?"

Realizing her foot was planted next to a soot-covered human hand, she knelt and felt for a pulse. *Please be alive… please…*

After what seemed like an eternity, and not feeling anything, she bit her lip as tears began to well up in her burning eyes, then she suddenly realized the hand was attached to an arm that was encased in a sleeve—

And Qar'qaah's stripped to the waist… which means—Syr!
She jerked her hand away, scrambled back to her feet and

wiping her fingers on her own sooty clothing, hastily backed away from the body.

Damn it, where are you? She looked around once more and spotted the rotund, smoldering mound of the Looper, slumped over a nearby console.

"Qar'qaah!" she called again, her smoke-hoarse voice now barely above a raspy whisper. "Qar'*qa*—*!"* she squeaked as a hand landed on her shoulder and she started violently then turned to come face to bare chest with him. She looked up. Only his eyes were visible by their reflective glitter. His nose and lower half of his face was masked behind the remains of his undertunic, skin and fabric coated in a very effective camouflage of soot. "Stop sneaking up on me!" she snarled as she punched him in the arm. "I thought you were—*what the hell are we standing here for?* Come on!" She slipped around him and marched off the bridge.

As she emerged from the thinning smoke, Drakin rose from where she'd been squatting beside Pardix and started towards her. "You okay?"

"I'm fine," Sirin snapped.

"I meant *him,"* Drakin replied, looking past her.

"Oh." She also turned her stare on Qar'qaah. To her relief, aside from being covered in soot, he appeared unhurt from his most recent ordeal. "What happened back there? We saw the emergency lights go on then all hell broke loose—"

"The Rimmer activated the emergency overrides," he replied hoarsely, "panicked when he saw me and started firing wildly. I was forced to take cover under a console, next to an air vent—"

"Why didn't you answer me? You scared me half to death!"

He tore off the mask, coughed explosively then replied, "I was… otherwise occupied."

"Occupied?"

He angrily wiped his mouth with the undertunic then grumbled, "Being sick, if you really must know." He coughed again and clutching his stomach in one hand, audibly gulped down the urge to heave. Once the spasm passed, he shoved his free hand into a trouser pocket, withdrew the vials and ject-it he'd taken from the sickbay and managed to rasp, "Lizard?" As he held out the ject-it and vials Sirin couldn't help but notice that his hand was trembling. "I... I may have need... of these shortly."

Drakin nodded her understanding and accepted them, but not having any pockets herself, she in turn gave them to Sirin as Qar'qaah stumbled over to Pardix and gave him a cautious prod with his toe.

Drakin followed. "Hez dead. Have to asssume due to sssmoke inhalation, sssince I couldn't find any udder obviouz cauz."

Sirin looked at Pardix, then up at Qar'qaah and felt a fresh wave of irrational anger wash over her. "You mean all that shooting and you... *you missed?*"

He scowled at her and replied in a deeply aggrieved, albeit hoarse and cough-disrupted voice: "For your... your infor... formation, I didn't do *any* of... of the shooting. Your... friend here," he gave Pardix's body another angry poke, "was the... the one with... the overly excitable trigger finger—"

"But...*but the bridge is in ruins!*"

"And why is this suddenly my fault?" he snarled before he succumbed to another violent—albeit mercifully brief—fit of coughing.

"I didn't say it was your fault! It's just—*oh, never mind!*"

He took an unsteady step back, yanked his pistol out of his waistband, pointed it at Pardix and pulled the trigger. The resulting blast vaporized the body and left a large, gaping hole in the deck. He then shoved the weapon back into his waistband and turned to her. *"There!* Now I shot him *and* further damaged the ship! *Satisfied?"*

Sirin opened her mouth to reply. Then, realizing she had no suitable retort she cared to use with a Hahtooshan who was this angry, she wisely snapped it shut.

"We must leave—*now!*" He staggered down the corridor, back to the emergency stairwell. There he stopped and waited for them, coughing sporadically as his soot-blackened fingers tapped out an angry, impatient cadence on the doorframe.

A loud popping sound coming from within the bridge, accompanied almost immediately by another puff of acrid smoke which rolled out of the airlock prompted Drakin and Sirin into hurrying after him.

"So," Sirin asked as she came abreast of him, "what's the plan? Clearly we can't use this ship to get off planet—and I suspect the com station is beyond quick repair."

He squinted at her. "Thanks to your... friend, everything on the bridge is beyond repair, period. Assuming this vessel's flicker chamber is still functional and *Huui'teh* hasn't been moved, we can use her."

"*Huui'teh?*" Drakin asked, beady emerald eyes darting between the two.

"The appropriated Hahtooshan koursan that brought me here," Qar'qaah answered curtly. "Fully powering up even her most basic systems would alert those on *Jirah* and prompt Khusaaq Sha'ashahn to investigate—as good if not better than contacting him via com-net as it would not draw the attention of our Poondian hosts... or *others*," he added as he gave the smoky stairwell a dubious glance. *"Go."*

"You're not coming with us?" Sirin asked as she stepped aside to allow Drakin to pass.

"I'll take up the rear... just in case—" He turned away, coughed several times into the wadded up undertunic as the cloud of smoke overtook them, then irritably jerked his chin towards the stairwell and managed to add in a raspy, almost pleading whisper, *"For once—just once—do as I tell you."*

She sighed, and shaking her head, followed Drakin into the dimly lit, smoke-filled maw. She heard him right behind her, his breathing coming in short, wheezing gulps punctuated by everyone's muffled, hacking coughs.

Halfway down, almost to the next landing, a loud *'boom'* sounded from somewhere above them.

Startled, Qar'qaah stumbled and barely caught himself before he collided with Sirin.

She glanced back up at him to find him nursing his elbow. "Are you all right?"

"Thank you for asking," he replied tartly, "but I've never been better."

"Then watch your step, okay?" she fired back in kind. *"Sheesh!"* She again started down the stairs, muttering, "I try to be nice, try to show concern and what do I get? I get atti—"

His hand landed on her shoulder, startling her into silence.

He leaned close and as his bony fingers tightened their grip, he hissed in her ear, *"I can fall faster than you can run, so I strongly suggest you keep your comments to yourself or you might find yourself acting as a cushion for my hard landing."*

Point made, he released his hold.

The rest of the descent was made in awkward silence and a short time later the three found themselves back on the same deck as the sickbay.

"Da flicker chamber iz dat way," Drakin pointed. With a nod from Qar'qaah, they hurried down the corridor and finally into the small room.

Qar'qaah headed for the flicker console and checked to see if the mechanism had enough power to safely transport them.

"Will it work?" Sirin prompted as they overheard another explosion, this one much closer than the last.

"I think so..." he replied distractedly as he scowled at the console's fluctuating energy levels. With a muttered curse, he kicked the console, winced and again peered at its power display.

Sirin flicked an equally nervous Drakin a sidelong glance as Qar'qaah squatted beside the console, jerked open an access panel and reached inside.

They watched in edgy silence as he tinkered. Seeing his expression darken even further, Sirin sidled close to Drakin. *"Maybe we should walk?"*

"Tah!" He lifted his gaze and grinned. "I've diverted all available power to the mechanism." He scrambled back to his feet, began hurriedly tapping in commands—then suddenly stopped, his bony and soot-blackened fingers hovering above the console, his smug grin dissolving. He knit his brows as he stared down at his hands.

"Uh, something... wrong?"

He slowly lifted his head and stared at Sirin—more precisely *through* Sirin. It did little to quell her growing anxiety.

Oh, please. Not again. "Qar'qaah...?"

He blinked and shifted his point of focus back to her. "I'm... I'm not sure exactly where *Huui'teh* is."

Sirin exhaled, relieved; beside her Drakin shifted uneasily.

"Den maybe you ssshould give yousssef plenty of wiggle room?"

He fixed Drakin with an exasperated squint as he mopped his sweaty forehead with the tattered undertunic. *"Wiggle... room...?"*

"You know," Drakin wiggled her scaly hips, "wiggle room."

He shifted his narrowed gaze to Sirin for translation.

"She means you don't have to plant us right beside the *Huui'teh*' main access hatch—a few dozen meters away would be just dandy."

"A few hundred would be even dandier," Drakin muttered under her breath.

He blotted his soot-streaming eyes. "I think it best that I flick us to the periphery of the southern landing field then find *Huui'teh* by sight. She might be several tens of meters away. Here." He pulled three breathers from a nearby wall-mount and tossed two towards them.

Sirin caught them and handed one to Drakin.

"So," he continued, clipping the third to his own nose, "once we're released from the effect, you mustn't dawdle..."

Sirin and Drakin exchanged indignant looks as Sirin mouthed, *Dawdle?* It was not exactly a word one expected to find in a merc's top-shelf vocabulary.

Qar'qaah, obviously aware of the silent interaction, added irritably, "I'll point out *Huui'teh* to you then you must run as fast as you can to her while I cover you. I have no idea the situation we might be facing, or *whom* we might come across," he added pointedly, "and I think it prudent to assume the worst. *Understood?"*

"Uddersssstood," Drakin replied, nodding vigorously.

He shoved the undertunic back into his pocket and his pistol into his waistband. "Then move—I'll set the delay then join you."

Sirin and Drakin hurried into the chamber. They had no sooner braced themselves for what promised to be a rather bumpy trip when he dashed in and positioned himself between them.

Breathless, he turned his full attention back to the mechanism.

Nothing happened.

He glanced down at Sirin; she stared up at him.

"Perhaps I was mistaken about the power," he admitted an instant before the door jerkily slid closed followed by their cramped surroundings quivering ever-so-slightly—prelude to the actual flicker effect taking hold.

Sirin wrapped her arms around him, not thinking—at that instant not giving a damn—how he might react, and held on for dear life as the dim interior of the flicker chamber suddenly receded, leaving a series of quickly fading after-images across her visual field.

Chapter 9

Surface of Poonda Five.

Sirin reluctantly released her hold on Qar'qaah's skeletal waist and, shading her eyes with her hand, peered into the mid-afternoon dazzle.

The searing light and heat ripples made identifying anything at any distance almost impossible. To make matters worse, the landing field was unusually crowded with vessels of all descriptions and she realized that they had been exceedingly lucky. Had Qar'qaah set the coordinates just slightly differently, they might have ended up inside an impeller, or as a permanent—but not factory-issue—part of a particle cannon.

She shook her head, then, overhearing a litany of what she immediately recognized as whispered Hahtooshan curses, she looked up to find Qar'qaah angrily wiping the stinging, sooty sweat out of his streaming eyes with the equally sooty undertunic.

"Well?"

Still grumbling, he blinked several times then scanned their surroundings only to fix his squinting, blood-shot eyed attention on something off in the hazy distance.

"What is it?"

He looked down at her and grinned a decidedly triumphant grin, his teeth luminous against his soot-blackened skin. *"Huui'teh."* He pointed to a large, battered but otherwise nondescript dun-colored ship crouched like some ancient tortoise on the hard-pack between two very sleek, gleaming white atmospheric craft some one hundred and fifty meters to their left.

"That's 'space worthy'?" Sirin asked, dubious and his pleased grin abruptly vanished.

"As with all things A'tuu'shahn'i, it's a mistake to be so easily deceived by outward appearances," he replied hoarsely as he angrily jerked his maser pistol from his waistband. *"Go."* He gave her a not-so-gentle nudge with his free hand as he warily scanned their surroundings.

Sirin and Drakin hurried across the flat expanse and finally ducked under the ship's low-slung belly.

Once hidden within the ship's shadow, Sirin turned back to find Qar'qaah loping awkwardly towards them, across the hard-pack, maser pistol held at the ready in his right hand while the other was tightly clutching his left thigh.

As he joined them, she whispered, *"Why are you limping?"* She looked down to find a large rip in his left trouser leg, visible only when he crouched beside her, exposing his paler, less sooty, tattooed skin and a deep, gaping wound that ran from mid-thigh to knee.

"What the hell?" Before he could back out of reach, she grabbed his boot cuff and holding it firmly, peered at the injury while allowing Drakin to do the same.

Drakin scowled at him. "Why da hell didn't you tell uz you were hurt? We could've ssstopped by sssickbay and—"

"It didn't strike me as important at the time. Getting you two away from the freighter as soon as possible was."

"You really are a pain in the ass." Sirin sighed. "You *do* realize that, don't you?"

He grinned, then, gesturing for them to stay where they were, crept on, further along the *Huui'teh*'s battered and blast-scarred undercarriage and over to an emergency escape hatch. He pressed the palm of his left hand to the hatch and it instantly and silently swung open.

He sniffed the oppressively hot, dusty air then gave the deserted landing field one last scan with narrowed eyes as he searched for any movement. Satisfied, he looked back at Sirin and Drakin and motioned impatiently to them.

Once they'd joined him, he shoved the pistol back in his waistband, grabbed the rungs on the hatch and with a labored grunt, pulled himself up and into the bowels of the ancient koursan.

He glanced around, again sniffed the air, then knelt by the opening and reaching down, offered Sirin his hand.

She grabbed it and he lifted her off the ground and into the ship.

Drakin was another matter. She handed him the shocker, which he placed on the deck behind him, but instead of trying to lift her, he instead took her clawed hands and placed each on a rung. He then scrambled back as the huge reptiloid heaved herself up into the ship with surprising grace and with a few millimeters to spare.

He stumbled back several more steps then abruptly sat down on the deck. Drawing his knees up against his chest, he took several deep, wheezing breaths, followed by a bout of violent coughing.

Sirin eased herself down beside him, waited for the coughing spasm to pass, then said, "Now, let's have a look at that leg," as she pulled the ject-it and a vial of painkiller from her pocket.

He nodded, and as Drakin squatted beside Sirin, he sprawled back and straightened out his injured leg for them to examine.

Sirin looked down at it and was startled to realize that the dutifully morphing trouser fabric had not only started to reseal itself, but had also adhered to the wound bed, creating a temporary, but very effective dressing. Despite that, the deep wound continued to ooze, leaving large, brilliant red droplets on the deck, and his trouser leg, already saturated with blood, left a wide, soot-sticky smear.

Drakin carefully probed what she could see of the ragged gash. "How'd diz happen?"

"I—" He grit his teeth as her talon touched an especially tender spot, then added tightly, "I tripped and fell against something... on the bridge, and—"

"Well, you're really lucky—you didn't sssever anyting critical, but you've ssstill lossst a fair amount of blood dat you couldn't afford to looz, and I bet it sssmartz like hell."

Perplexed, he shifted his gaze to Sirin.

"She means she bets it hurts a lot."

"Paq..." He closed his eyes, took several ragged breaths, then using one elbow, tried to lever himself into a seated position.

"And where are you going?" Drakin asked, rocking back on her haunches.

"I need... I need to get... get to the bridge, power up—"

"Get up now and I promiz you, you'll paz out."

The best he could muster was a less than menacing glare.

"Tink itz likely da people who kidnapped you might return and take off?"

He gave his head a slight shake as he continued to struggle, trying to get purchase on the polished surface made slippery by the blood, which made him struggle all the more. "Sha'ashahn... had all systems on *Huui'teh* disabled... she can't take off... not without knowing how to override the overrides and in the correct sequence—"

"But they might not know that." Sirin glanced around her. What at first had seemed a welcome refuge suddenly looked like a trap.

He shook his head. "No, once we were rescued, they likely abandoned *Huui'teh*, suspecting a trap. There are plenty of other ships to commandeer." He gestured around him, to the unseen and thickly populated landing field that surrounded them.

His logic wasn't perfect, but clearly the best he could manage.

"Den da bridge can wait an hour or zo." Drakin pushed him back down and held him there.

He stopped resisting, too weak and too ill to be in a panic for long and stared up at her with glassy, sunken eyes.

"Agreed?"

"Paq...."

Clearly surprised by his unexpected acquiescence, she released her hold. "Derz not much I can do right now witout sssuppliez, zo I'm going to give you a painkiller, den I want you to lie perfectly ssstill and let doz magic pantz of yourz do what dey can do to ssstop da bleeding and ssstabiliz your blood presssure, okay?"

He nodded and as Drakin pushed the ject-it against his bare shoulder, he shifted his dull, now sleepy-eyed stare to Sirin.

She smiled, wiped a lock of tangled and soot-greasy hair off his forehead, and leaning down, lightly kissed him on his equally soot-greasy cheek.

Clearly puzzled, he touched the spot with his fingers and rasped drowsily, "What... what was that for?"

She smiled again. "For rescuing us."

"Perhaps... perhaps you should wait until you are actually safely aboard *Jirah,"* he managed before he succumbed to a fit of body-jolting coughs.

Sirin looked up at Drakin; Drakin shrugged as she handed her the expended ject-it.

Sirin stuffed it in her pocket then scrambled back to her feet. "Let's get that hatch sealed."

With Drakin's help she managed to close and lock it. Then she looked back at Qar'qaah to find him still sprawled, spread-eagle, on the deck, eyes closed, one hand clutching his stomach, the other his thigh and still coughing feebly. He looked utterly spent.

"I tink we could all uz a breather."

"Yeah." Sirin eased herself down next to Qar'qaah and after a moment's hesitation, gently lifted his head and placed it in her lap. She hid her reaction but was pleased when he didn't resist. He didn't even open his eyes—he was in fact fast asleep, nudged into a comfortable darkness by the painkiller.

She lifted her own gaze and looked around at the otherwise empty staging bay and was suddenly struck by how... *organic* it appeared. Just as with the exterior, there were no straight lines, no sharp edges, only gentle curves and rounded surfaces. She realized that every surface—including the deck—was decorated in a faintly glowing sinuous pattern reminiscent of Hahtooshan tattoos.

She looked up only to find the domed ceiling similarly adorned. As her eyes followed one of the coiling designs that snaked overhead, she realized that it was pulsing, albeit ever so slowly. The effect was extremely unsettling, as if the ship itself was alive—and perhaps just like Qar'qaah, deeply asleep.

She dropped her gaze only to find that the pattern on the deck was also throbbing. At first she thought it was just the reflection of the ceiling, but on closer examination it became obvious that the design on the deck was not a mirror image. She also wasn't sure if it was just a trick of the eye—maybe a trick of her own exhausted mind, but it appeared to be more complex and slight brighter immediately around Qar'qaah.

Then, as she watched, it also appeared to *move,* to slowly eel around and then under him... *and her*—she almost expected to *feel* it slither beneath her and instinctively tensed, then shivered at the creepy-crawly sensation.

Drakin checked Qar'qaah's leg again, then, with a shrug and a muttered, "It'll have to do," settled on the deck and curled around them, in the process carefully draping her tail over Qar'qaah's hips, heedless to the shifting pattern beneath her, or his morphing trousers.

Trying to take her cue from the nurse, Sirin cast another quick glance around as she leaned back into Drakin. *Just your imagination, that's all.*

Nestled in the Eltannian's solid embrace and with Qar'qaah's head and shoulders pillowed in her lap, she suddenly found herself intensely sleepy. She let out a weary sigh and, lightly resting one hand on his bare shoulder, the other on Drakin's tail, closed her eyes.

Chapter 10

Control room of the Baidarka.

Izraad, overhearing the nearby airlock open, lifted her preoccupied gaze from her console.

"Anything?" Aquila asked as he strode towards her, across the *Baidarka*'s control room.

"No sir," she replied. "I've searched all databases containing the names of known provocateurs and colonial fanatics—no Cisne or Mizahn. I've even contacted colleagues back at Intel Command but no one has ever heard of either one. Clearly they're aliases, which is what we all suspected from the start, but people usually pick an alias that has some significance to them, some connection—so, after coming up dry elsewhere, I approached it from a linguistic standpoint—"

"And?"

"Cisne means 'swan' in an old Earth language—Spanish. It was their name for the constellation Cygnus."

His mouth formed a silent *'O'*, then, "So?"

She shrugged then shook her head. "So... nothing. Ditto with Mizahn. Turns out it's not even A'tuu, it's ancient Gorm, meaning deity."

He raised his brows. "So we're dealing with someone with delusions of ornithological grandeur?"

Izraad couldn't help but chuckle wearily, "Perhaps," then continued, "I tried every conceivable phonetic spelling and had the computer jumble the letters of both Cisne and Mizahn in every possible combination, but still nothing. I also interviewed the four soldiers from Rasal Ghul we have onboard, but as it turns out, only Endooki Ha'tat—along with Sha'ashahn's missing man—had any interaction with her. The others were forced to witness this soldier being beaten, repeatedly, but only by Cisne's crew. She was never present during these... *educational sessions,* as her crew referred to them.

"Endooki saw her only twice, each time briefly when she and her accomplices came to collect the missing soldier for, as she called it, "some friendly conversation." He describes her as at least superficially human, middle-aged with reddish brown hair, pale skin, tall for a human, and—interestingly—she spoke fluent A'tuu. He said she also spoke Standard with an inflection he could not place."

"Significant?"

"All Hahtooshans, even ones as young as Endooki, are extraordinarily well versed in languages, as well as regional variations and dialects, so for him not to recognize an accent is, well… unusual—he suggested she was perhaps trying to mask her true accent. He also told me that the missing soldier was repeatedly put *awake* into a stasis pod and left there for extended periods of time, then brought back to Endooki and this Cisne's doctor to tend to."

"Gods." Aquila couldn't help but visibly wince before he replied, "Clearly not someone who subscribes to any existing treaties on the treatment of prisoners—"

"Or maybe has a particular antipathy towards Hahtooshans."

"—and possibly as a way of goading the Orthodoxy—and perhaps specifically, Khusaaq—into reacting rashly?"

"Precisely. You see this missing soldier is Sha'ashahn's *doh'ha*—his genetic double."

Aquila stared at her, head cocked to one side. "You mean… *a clone?"*

She nodded. "Nihaal let this rather critical detail slip while William was examining him and from what Murh'sooli told me, this is a very ancient custom, practiced these days only among the most ultra-orthodox Elkanaghalli, of creating a backup copy of someone who shows great promise—"

"So if that person's killed, this copy can step into their boots—"

"Not… *exactly. Doh'ha* were once created to be a living organ bank."

"What?"

"Elkanaghalli—as we found out the hard way—have very strict religious beliefs on remaining pure and to that end do not permit non-autologous tissue donation, or, say, even the *temporary* replacement of damaged bone with synthetic.

William mentioned this with Khusaaq. When he offered to replace his badly fractured femur with synth—"

"So you're saying this missing soldier is Khusaaq's *organ bank?*"

Izraad shook her head. "No. *Doh'ha* are still created, but it's now more of a way of recognizing someone whose genetic makeup is deemed to be in some way outstanding—to protect a promising lineage, a living genetic reservoir so to speak. They're still the clone of the individual but they're not expected to sacrifice themselves to their *ta'katleh*—their genetic progenitor. Donate stems, tissue, what have you, certainly, but not die in order to save the other. Elkanaghallis, who are the smallest caste as well as the oldest, are simply hedging their bets—which, considering their line of work is, well, actually quite sensible."

"I don't get it." Aquila braced his hip against Izraad's console and crossed his arms. "If this clone was created, as you say, as a way of recognizing Khusaaq as an exceptional individual, then how could he be an adult? Khusaaq, by his own admission, only came into his own at Cotopaxi—and that was a little over eleven years ago. Now, I realize Hahtooshans go into the 'family' business at a *very* young age, and mature faster than we do, but—"

"Khusaaq is, or should I say, *was* a *doh'ha*, too."

"Oh. No... wait. That still doesn't explain things."

"It does if you'll bear with me."

Aquila eyed her and wisely pursed his lips.

She smiled, continued, "According to Murh'sooli this whole *doh'ha* business is a dying custom, performed, as I said, only by the oldest, *most* orthodox Elkanaghalli families."

"But... I still don't—"

"Khusaaq's *ta'katleh,* his progenitor, was killed at Tindari, and upon *his* death, a new *doh'ha* was cloned, but—"

"So, this missing soldier, who would then be, what, about...?"

"Fourteen."

"What about Matoosh? And I remember William mentioning that another soldier we rescued from Rasal Ghul who was a close genetic match for Khusaaq—"

"Gienah."

"Yeah. So, you're telling me they're clones too?"

"No," Izraad shook her head. "Antigen tests were conclusive: Matoosh and Gienah are what are called *a'itat'ahtaqh*, meaning siblings through strict genetic selection within the family, so they are extremely close, genetically speaking to Sha'ashahn, but they're *not* clones. They were also created the 'old fashion' way—"

"You mean—"

"Yes. It's a way for Hahtooshans to maintain some variation within the *dor'balth*, the immediate family, not to mention providing those carefully selected to reproduce with a strong incentive to keep making babies, since to most Hahtooshans— not just Elkanaghallis—sex is deemed to be a deeply religious act, performed strictly for procreation, *not* for pleasure..."

"Well," he muttered, "that would certainly explain why they're all so damned short-tempered—"

"...at least that's the 'company line', even among Elkanaghallis, according to Murh'sooli..."

Aquila raised his brows in begging interest.

"...who, as it turns out, is not only a veritable gold mine of information on the intricacies and idiosyncrasies of Hahtooshan society, but has a truly wicked sense of humor, especially when it comes to his fellow Hahtooshans and their many foibles."

Aquila favored his intelligence officer with a very dubious expression. "My admittedly limited interactions with Murh'sooli left me with the distinct impression that he has, like every other Hahtooshan I've so far met, absolutely *no* sense of humor about anything, least of all themselves."

"As with any highly complex culture," she countered, "especially with one such as theirs that has developed in relative isolation, the collective Hahtooshan view of themselves doesn't exactly match with the views and mores individual Hahtooshans have about themselves or their views of other Hahtooshans. To the collective, they are a noble race who, through no fault of their own, have fallen on hard times but who have excelled in adversity, where personal honor, duty and sacrifice to the Orthodoxy reign supreme. Individuals, though, see their fellow Hahtooshans as petty, foul-tempered, self-serving and greedy—but not themselves of course, oh no. So you could say they're more like us... than us."

Aquila frowned at that. "But... why post both Khusaaq and his clone on the same ship? That would sort of defeat the whole, 'let's have a back-up copy if the original gets blown to bits' concept, wouldn't it?"

"I asked Murh'sooli that very thing. He said it's customary for close family members to serve aboard the same ship—in fact many serve together for their entire military careers—the same was true of humans until only a few centuries ago. Hahtooshans clearly consider familial or caste loyalty as a far stronger bond than being Hahtooshan and probably always have—each recognized caste was clearly created from a separate and distinct group of Neanderthals and as hunter gatherers, they would've strongly perceived anyone not from their natal group as an outsider and therefore suspect. And clearly, based on my own observations of individuals from different castes interacting, that remains the case."

"So they don't even trust or like each other." Aquila nodded. "I noticed a definite tension between Khusaaq and Murh'sooli after Khusaaq and the trooper flicked up, but at the time I just chalked it up to Murh'sooli being hand-picked by Narbrooi—and Khusaaq just being, well... Khusaaq."

"Upon *first* meeting," Izraad amended. "Once the immediate sense of threat is eliminated, they work extremely well together—far more cohesively than we non-Hahtooshan humans do, due in large part to their genetically enhanced synesthesia.

"But back to families serving together. Again according to Murh'sooli, Hahtooshans keep a genetic bank somewhere—he wouldn't say where, not that I can blame him, and likely in more than one place, so even if everyone in an immediate family were to be wiped out, it would be technically possible to entirely reconstruct the lineage given time—note I said *technically.*"

"Meaning he wasn't so sure?"

"He didn't say so in so many words, but he definitely thinks that's the case. Anyway, he said is not an entirely unheard of occurrence of losing entire families—no surprise there—in fact he hinted that something truly catastrophic occurred not all that long ago, something that took place likely in or near the Nyaat cluster—"

"Nyaat Cluster? Never heard of it."

"Neither had I, until I started digging. It's on the far side of the Vela Molecular Ridge, and, as it turns out, Intelligence had picked up chatter about Nyaat, about something 'big' as they put it, taking place—lots of activity, mostly inside the cluster itself. The Ti'finagh collective were involved—"

"Damned bugs," Aquila muttered under his breath.

Izraad smiled briefly; Aquila's aversion for 'bright bugs' as he called insectoids, was well known. It was a common human phobia after all. "But whether the Hahtooshans were fighting for or against the collective is open for debate, although what we know of the Ti'finagh is that they are highly xenophobic, so unlikely they would have hired alien mercenaries."

"Unless things were going really badly," Aquila offered.

"And that appears to have been the case. All Intelligence could gather was that there were major losses on all sides, and, if this is indeed the same event Murh'sooli hinted at, an astonishingly large number of families were wiped out.

"That all said, it's not all that surprising they choose to serve together, knowing if the worst case scenario does happen, their exact bloodlines will likely continue. However, this isn't an absolute guarantee of genetic immortality."

"So we're back to the *technically* caveat."

"Yes. Natural selection trumps genetic manipulation in the long run when it comes to the overall vigor of a species, and as we both know, the Hahtooshans were heavily, one might even say, recklessly manipulated on a genetic level by their creators to serve a particular niche. It's possible the Elkanasu never intended for their creations to outlive or outlast them, that the

Hahtooshans were, one could say, *purpose-built*, and so the Elkanasu didn't factor in such things as the diminution of alleles at the locus over tens of thousands of years."

Aquila nodded. "I remember Will mentioning something about that—that they were in fact quite fragile, on a chromosomal level. Maybe the Elkanasu intentionally built-in a genetic kill switch so to speak, which the Hahtooshans, over the centuries, intentionally or strictly through fortunate happenstance managed to circumvent, at least up to a point?"

"Possibly," Izraad replied. "Murh'sooli did say that after this catastrophic event took place, it was discovered that some of the banked genetic material had become corrupted over the centuries, simply due to age, external contamination, what have you, so it's definitely no guarantee of genetic immortality and it will take decades, generations in fact to reconstitute lineages, to weed out the weakened chromosomes and refabricate more stable ones, time the Hahtooshans don't have. Especially now that everyone knows who and what they are—"

"And their Achilles heel."

Izraad nodded. "Precisely."

"This could, in part, explain why the Orthodoxy was willing to enter into an alliance with the Coalition. Having no resistance to common human diseases was the straw that broke the proverbial camel's back."

"My thoughts too. But back to the matter of Khusaaq and this missing soldier. When Elkanaghalli create a *doh'ha,* they always opt for genetic material harvested from a living donor rather than from banked material if at all possible. And wisely so—fresh is always better than frozen, right?"

Aquila squinted at her, unamused.

She shrugged, continued, "Hence this soldier was cloned directly from Khusaaq, rather than from material they already had on hand from Khusaaq's immediate progenitor, or that progenitor's progenitor ten times removed."

Aquila gave his head a shake as if to clear it.

Izraad said, "Trust me, I just gave you the highly abridged version. In truth it's far, far more complicated and—"

Aquila held up his hand. "Abridged is just dandy, thank you."

Izraad chuckled. "It's also possible Khusaaq felt his *doh'ha* needed to be protected, which is why he kept him so close."

Aquila arched a brow. "From his fellow Hahtooshans?"

She nodded. "While Khusaaq is considered a cultural icon, a hero by most Hahtooshans, he's attracted his fair share of enemies, due in large part to his adamant refusal to *play* hero. If Narbrooi's any guide, Khusaaq clearly didn't win over many of his detractors by allying himself with us, even if by doing so, he single-handedly saved his people from at best a crippling pandemic they'd be hard pressed to recover from, at worst complete annihilation. Again, per Murh'sooli, Khusaaq's actions only seemed to further entrench the views of those on either side of the fence—each claiming his latest actions proves their side of the argument—but, as I was going to say, according to Endooki, this *doh'ha* of Khusaaq's appears to have an uncanny knack for regularly getting himself into serious trouble—"

"And needs big brother to constantly pull his ass out of the proverbial fire?"

"In a word, yes." Izraad settled back in her chair and crossed her arms. And there's something else..."

"Of course there is," Aquila muttered, massaging his forehead. "There always is."

Izraad favored him with a commiserating smile. "There's another very immediate need to find this missing soldier beyond the obvious. There's this weird... physiological phenomena, for lack of a better word, that happens to Hahtooshans who find themselves separated from their kind. Murh'sooli called it *turee*—the diminishing.

"If they are alone for an extended period of time, their tattoos, their... *kaa-shaai* begin to fade. Reach a certain point and the *kaa-shaai* will not return to their original intensity even if the individual is safely reunited with his or her fellows—and those who are so afflicted are shunned, forming something close to an untouchable caste within Hahtooshan society—and if the *kaa-shaai* disappear completely... well, they believe that person dies."

"Likely?"

"Murh'sooli doesn't question this, but did say he'd never seen a case himself—where the *kaa-shaai* disappear completely. I'd say there's at least some kernel of fact within the belief, but how and why this occurs, I have no idea. William couldn't explain it either from a medical standpoint. It might simply be yet another example of a cultural mythos, a way of keeping Hahtooshans close to home, so to speak, and not be tempted to go walk about. They're all terrified of being abandoned, so being abandoned in a cultural sense, being an untouchable... well, I would think it likely most who find themselves so afflicted would kill themselves rather than exist as a pariah. So yes, they would die, just not from a physiological cause.

"But this cultural phobia, for lack of a better term, serves a very rational purpose: they do all they can do not leave their people behind, dead or alive in order to maintain the mystery as to whom they really are. Up until very recently, it's served them very well, although per Murh'sooli, Hahtooshans have gone missing, lots of 'em, some have just vanished, others... well, he said it's never mentioned, but it's suspected they deserted—as you can imagine, that's a concept the Orthodoxy keeps a lid on. But none have ever vanished in Coalition-claimed space, until now with this *doh'ha*. At least none he's ever heard about and in his position as a senior medic aboard this sector's flagship, he's bound to hear most of the scuttle-butt."

"So it would seem," Aquila replied dubiously. "But then that survey ship vanished, albeit not in Coalition-claimed space, and now it's turned up, a year later, here on Poonda Five and in Cisne's hands, rebranded with the deliberately provocative name of *Huui'teh,* but with no sign of its former crew."

Izraad only nodded.

"And how long can a Hahtooshan remain isolated before this happens?"

"Murh'sooli said it depends on the situation, the physical and emotional stress the individual is under, or if there's an underlying medical crisis—"

"Such as advanced radiation poisoning."

Izraad nodded. "Yes, and as I started to say earlier, this *doh'ha* matter adds yet another facet to the issue of the kidnapping and the subsequent singling out of this particular soldier."

"You think this Cisne mistook him for Khusaaq?"

"I'm more inclined to believe Endooki's take on it: the *doh'ha* deliberately drew her attention, to spare the others—he is Khusaaq's clone after all, and therefore probably shares Khusaaq's strong altruistic streak. It's also possible this Cisne knew precisely who and what he is even before she abducted them. If so, Cisne would know the other Hahtooshans— specifically Khusaaq, would make every reasonable attempt to retrieve him. She does speak fluent A'tuu after all, so one could assume she is equally well-versed in their cultural practices, even the archaic ones."

"Which means she might be connected with the likes of Behardien and Mladić," Aquila offered.

"Possibly."

"Or maybe Hahtooshans weren't as enigmatic as we—and they—thought."

"It's a hell of a big galaxy," Izraad replied. "While Hahtooshans have made a supreme effort to limit their interactions with humans by strictly controlling what contact there was—up until now only by com-net or, like the Cotopaxi awards ceremony, through very effective sensory camouflage, or plying the majority of their trade in parts of the rim not frequented by humans or, for that matter, other Coalition races—the Coalition did at one time employ them, far preferring Hahtooshans over other mercenary groups, and, I must say, to great effect and the enrichment of both parties, so it's not unreasonable to assume that there have been times when humans and Hahtooshans have found themselves in more than brief, face-to-face contact, such as what happened on Rasal Ghul. Perhaps this Cisne is, like you, Ensign Corsali and

Corporal Gianakis, one of those rare survivors of such an encounter."

"But in her case came away from it with a seriously pathological grudge?"

"As we've both come to learn, not all Hahtooshans are as affable and forward thinking as Khusaaq."

"Uh-huh," Aquila replied. "So, if she knew so much about them, why keep that a secret? A lot of money could be made selling that kind of information—lots and *lots* of money."

"Perhaps her hatred for them is so deeply personal, she didn't want to share or sell it, at least not until doing so would create the maximum amount of damage. As you said, her behavior does appear to border on the pathological."

Aquila straightened up, inhaled slowly through his nose, exhaled forcefully the same way as he looked around him, then his gaze again settled on Izraad. "Have you informed Khusaaq of what you've found, or, should I say, not found?"

"Yes. He was, understandably, disappointed, but not particularly surprised as Narbrooi's Intelligence people had already done their own very thorough research and had come to the same dead end." Izraad looked down at her console, sighed and shook her head. "And still no sign of Sirin or Drakin. Ensign Cyllo and the sensor officers aboard Khusaaq's ship and the two koursans working together have detected a total of six Eltannians on the planet, and possibly a seventh, using both surface and ground penetrating scans. The coordinates have been transmitted to Sha'ashahn and his men, as well as Delatorre and his teams, but it'll take time for them to check out each one as they're widely dispersed both within the city itself, the outlying settlements, mining camps and landing fields. Time we really don't have."

Aquila gave her shoulder a squeeze. "As we've all learned in the past few weeks, Lieutenant, never, *ever* underestimate Hahtooshans, highly motivated Hahtooshans doubly so. If anyone can find them, it'll be Khusaaq."

Chapter 11

Aboard the Huui'teh.

"Hey, sssleeping beauty…"

"Huh…?" Sirin slowly opened her eyes and turned them towards the familiar lisping voice.

"Your Prinz Charming haz vamoosssed."

"What!" Sirin sat bolt upright as she looked down.

Only a smudge of greasy soot and a smear of dried blood marked where she'd last seen Qar'qaah, seemingly fast asleep, his head and shoulders cradled in her lap.

She scrambled to her feet and glanced around the roughly circular staging bay: the nearby escape hatch's lock light still glowed bright red, and Drakin's shocker, which Qar'qaah had placed next to it, was exactly where he'd left it.

Sirin then looked at each of the four oval airlocks that broke the bay's otherwise smooth, curved walls. All were closed, each of their lock lights' also a telltale red. *"Shit, shit, shit…"* She stomped her foot on the deck for emphasis. *"SHIT!"*

As Drakin rose, Sirin turned to her. "He couldn't have just vanished into thin air."

"Wouldn't put it passst him."

"If he was wearing his armor," Sirin said as she snatched up the shocker and handed it to Drakin, "I'd agree, but he isn't."

"Den don't asssk me. But da next time we dessside to take a nap, I ssstrongly sssuggessst we tie him up firssst. I don't like diz nasssty habit of hiz of not ssstaying where we put him."

"Yeah," Sirin nodded distractedly as she looked around her once more. Something about their surroundings niggled at her, something that wasn't quite… right. She shrugged it off; there were more pressing concerns at hand. "But he wouldn't have just left us here."

"Why not? He made it abundantly clear dat he didn't exactly enjoy our company… wit da exception of your lap, dat iz—he ssseemed to like dat a *lot.*"

Sirin squinted at Drakin. "I agree he's a huge pain in the ass, but he's also risked his life, not once, but repeatedly, to get us this far. Which means he wouldn't just leave, now that we're this close to getting off this pisshole of a planet."

"Den where iz he?"

"Well, assuming he's still onboard, he couldn't have gone too far, which means it shouldn't be all that hard to find him, besides—"

"I dunno. Diz iz quite a big ssship and he ssstrikez me az sssomeone who would be really, really good at hide and ssseek—wit armor or even witout and diz iz an Hahtoosssin ssship after all."

"Agreed, but I'd wager he's gone in search of the bridge, or maybe sickbay first and then the bridge?"

"But which airlock? Dey all look da sssame."

Sirin looked around once more and it suddenly struck her what was different: the deck, ceiling and walls were now completely unadorned. *What the...?* Before she could ponder the matter further, she noticed a small bright red spot on the deck not far away and, a little further on, another one. She looked back at Drakin and smiled. "Well, it seems he was kind enough to leave us a trail of breadcrumbs... or, in this case, blood drops." She pointed and started following them. Directly ahead stood one of the airlocks.

Sirin thumbed the release and it hissed open. A smear of soot-streaked blood, approximately Qar'qaah thigh-high on its inner seal and a drip of blood on its threshold were the corroborating clues she'd been hoping for. She knelt and touched the drip with a finger. It was still tacky.

She rose and murmured, "This way," as she pulled the *t'jing* from her pocket. Clutching it tightly in one hand, she hit the inner lock release then cautiously stepped into the adjoining corridor.

Drakin followed, shocker held at the ready.

Ahead, on the deck, Sirin spotted another glistening blood drop, and then another and further on, yet another, which happened fall just short of the open hatch to an emergency stairwell. But there the trail of blood spots stopped.

She peered into the stairwell, then up the stairs and as far as she could see the grated steps were free of any further spoor. *Damn!*

"Zo, which way'd he go?"

"I dunno." Sirin smiled feebly. "But look on the bright side, at least he's stopped bleeding."

Drakin only stared at her.

"How 'bout you take the high road and I take the low road and I bet I'll find Qar'qaah before you."

Drakin's stare crumbled into a glower. *"Cute."* She stepped into the stairwell and began trudging up the steps, her tail whacking out an angry cadence on the shaft's walls as Sirin, wasting no time, started down the curved, hatch-lined corridor.

Sirin stopped at every doorway, looked inside and cautiously called his name. Hearing no reply she moved on, well aware she might come across his kidnappers instead of Qar'qaah—his logic had been shaky at best after all.

With that thought foremost, she tightened her hold on the *t'jing*, her thumb resting lightly on the trigger.

Just as she was beginning to question whether he really was still onboard, or worse—she came to the end of the corridor. Ahead stood another open airlock.

She sidled up to its double ruby rings, peered around the airlock's seal into the chamber beyond, and realized that she had found the ship's bridge. The gloomy chamber was ominously silent, its numerous consoles dark. The only illumination came from the now familiar, but nevertheless eerie, faintly pulsing designs that coiled and slithered overhead, along the walls and across what was visible of the deck, instantly suggesting to her overly active imagination some sort of high-tech cave art. *Apropos,* she thought with a private smile.

She warily stepped across the threshold and out of the relative glare of the corridor lights, paused then asked softly, "Qar'qaah? Qar'qaah, it's me, *Sirin.* Are you in here?"

She looked around and warned by a muffled cough, finally spotted him, seated at a console at the far end of the bridge, his skeletally thin back to her.

She walked over to him and, stopping behind him, crossed her arms and asked with a tone of irritation she couldn't quite suppress, "Why didn't you answer me?"

"I'm busy." He rose from his chair, pulled the blaster from the waistband of his trousers, placed it on the top of the console next to his pistol and the laser cutter, then got down on hands and knees and yanked open an access panel beneath the communications station.

Sirin's eyes were now fully adjusted to the dim lighting and everywhere she looked she saw evidence of his hurried handiwork: other access doors left ajar, and in one case forcibly pried open, another crudely accessed by way of the laser cutter, a scattering of tools… faintly glowing power cables draped over chairs and snaking around stations—as if the iridescent patterns that flowed across the floor, ceiling and walls had somehow managed to escape their two dimensional limitations.

Setting that disturbing idea aside, she found herself amazed at what he'd accomplished—or the damage he'd done, depending on one's perspective—in such a short period of time. "We've been searching all over for you—"

"And now you've found me. So, do you get the prize, or do I for managing to cunningly elude you for so long despite the fact that I'm exactly where I told you I'd be?"

She ignored the snide remark. "Why did you leave without waking us? You scared us half to death."

Instead of answering, he eased his head and shoulders through the access hole and inside the bowels of the console.

"Well?"

He rolled over, onto his back and cautiously slid himself a little further inside. "If I'm ever to get you off this accursed planet," came his muffled reply, "I must contact *Jirah*. To do that, I must get the com-net powered up as quickly as possible."

"So, you just left us there."

"Obviously."

"But—"

"Are you an engineer?"

"No, but—"

"Is the lizard?"

"You *damn* well know she's a nurse—who saved your life in case you forgot—and you also know *damned* well her name is Drakin, so how—"

"Then what would have been the point of waking the two of you? Besides, you both looked quite comfortable and clearly in need of some… *beauty sleep?"*

She glared at his skeletal lower torso and legs and found herself sorely tempted to kick him in the bony shin. *Obviously the nap did nothing to improve your lovely disposition.* Aloud she said, "Very funny. But now that I'm here, what can I do to help?"

"Nothing."

Sirin sat in his chair then studied what she could see of him as he coughed and cursed and tinkered with the console's inner workings. "Sure?" She leaned forward and her elbow accidentally bumped the precariously placed blaster, which promptly skittered down the sharply sloping console and onto Qar'qaah's unguarded groin.

Startled, he flinched violently and she winced as she overheard a loud *thump* from inside the console.

It was followed by a *very* awkward, prolonged and unhappy silence.

"You *can* help," he finally replied tightly just as she started to retrieve the blaster, "by *not* touching anything else."

She immediately withdrew her fingers. "Sorry."

He grunted.

A moment later he withdrew, snatched the blaster from where it had fallen between his legs, then, rubbing his freshly abraded forehead, lurched unsteadily to his feet. *"Up!"* He irritably motioned for her to relinquish the chair, using the heavy weapon to emphasize the order.

She barely had a chance to get out of the way before he threw himself onto it, slammed the blaster down on the console then began tapping in commands. She eased herself onto the chair at the console next to his, turned to face him and crossed her arms.

"Has anyone ever told you that it's very impolite to stare?" He favored her with a sidelong glower.

"Can't help it."

"Yes, you can. You have conscious control over your eye muscles. So, you can look at your own lap, your own hands... even that console." He jerked his chin towards another nearby station. *"Anything.* Just stop staring at *me."* With that he turned his own narrowed gaze back to the communications console.

"But... *damn it,* you look just like Khusaaq—okay, well a lot younger, and a hell of a lot thinner Khusaaq—you sound just like him..." she said as she suddenly realized how true it was, "...you walk just like him... you have the same mannerisms— do you have any idea just how unsettling it is for me to see his very sickly double?"

He chuckled softly and keeping his own sunken eyes fixed on the console, replied in a quiet, but nevertheless very bitter voice, "Do you have any idea what it's like to be judged—your entire life—not on who you are, but *what* you are? Nothing I've ever accomplished means anything!" He held out his bare arms for her to see his tattoos then just as quickly dropped them back to his sides with a look in his eye as if he'd seen a ghost.

"The only thing that matters to *anyone* is that I'm his *doh'ha*!" He smacked himself in the bony chest with his balled fist. "Those who hate him and hate what he represents, hate *me!* Those who idolize him—when they realize I am not him—get very ugly, as if I was trying to fool them. Or conversely they flatter me, hoping that they can get to him through me." He snorted. *"Yeah!"*

Sirin studied him, studied his very angry, down-turned face for a moment then asked quietly, "What about you?"

"What about me?" he replied warily.

"What matters to you?"

"Nothing."

"I don't believe you."

He resumed his reprogramming of the console. "And I honestly don't care what you believe."

She slumped back in her chair and then began to count, aloud and very slowly, starting at one.

She had gotten as far as seven when he asked, "What is the significance of this ritual of yours?"

"Ritual?"

"Counting out loud. You do it all the time."

"I don't do it all the time. I just do it when I'm around you."

He hesitated, jaw muscles twitching, then, "So?"

"So I do it to stop myself from saying or doing something we both might regret."

He stared at her for a moment then fixed his gaze on the console and replied, "Then you do not do it often enough."

"I was wrong. You aren't a huge pain in the ass, you're a stupendously *colossal* pain in the ass."

He favored her with another sidelong glance. "Clearly you don't apply this technique of yours with any logical consistency."

She took a deep, steadying breath, then said, "Qar'qaah, I want to help—can't you see that?"

"And I just told you I don't need—or more importantly, *want* your help."

"I'm not talking about this," she motioned expansively, if incautiously, towards the communications console, narrowly avoiding knocking the blaster off its perch and back into his lap. "I'm talking about you. I want to help *you*—"

"Why?" He abruptly turned to face her and sneered, "Because I look just like your *beloved* Khusaaq? *Didn't you hear what I just said?"* He abruptly rose and struck his clenched fists against the console with enough force to send the blaster and laser cutter sliding off the console, each falling harmlessly to the deck with a loud clatter, and snarled, *"I'm not him!"*

"No, you're not."

He stared at her for a moment, clearly taken aback, and just as clearly swaying slightly then grabbing the lip of the console, he eased himself back into his chair. "Yet another missed opportunity—"

"What I mean, Qar'qaah, is that despite you being his *doh'ha* and all, you are *you*—a very different, very distinct individual—"

"Are you so sure?"

"—and don't ask me why," she continued, pointedly ignoring the muttered comment, trying and failing to ignore the underlying unease it conjured up, "because you certainly don't make it easy, but I really do like you for who *you* are—is that so hard to believe? *Is it?*"

He dropped his stare to the console, gave his head a shake to clear it, then resumed his work, his sooty fingers tapping out a very angry cadence.

"Is it? Granted, you've raised the celebrated Abhijit'tischinjgra family trait of mulishness to a whole new, dare I say stratospheric level, but then again, if you weren't so doggedly single-minded, we'd all be dead. Anyone else—even Khusaaq—would have dropped in his tracks long ago, but not you."

She sat back and waited, but when he refused to even look at her, she added, "You're utterly exhausted and very, *very* ill. Once we're aboard Khusaaq's ship and you've had a chance to rest and recuperate, things won't appear so bleak   "

"I'm not going back."

"What...?"

"I said I'm *not* going back. You are. I'm not."

"Of course you are!"

He leaned back in his chair, crossed his arms and met her gaze. "Do you also disagree with everything Sha'ashahn says, too, or am I the only one who is the incredibly privileged recipient of this special treatment?"

"But—"

He held up a soot-blackened finger, silencing her. "I talk, you listen; you listen, I talk—*got it?*"

She clamped her lips shut.

"Excellent, now permit me to repeat myself. I'm *not* going back. Period. End of discussion."

"Why not?"

He sighed heavily and rolled his eyes. "I should've known..."

Sirin fixed her eyes on the far wall. He resumed his work, angrily tapping code into the computer interface.

After several minutes, he surprised her by muttering, "I've yet to accomplish what I came here to do."

She held up her index finger.

He peered at it, then upwards. Seeing nothing unexpected, he squinted irritably at her. "What?"

"Permission to speak?"

He reluctantly began, "I suppose—"

"A minute ago you said nothing mattered to you." Suddenly, all the words she'd been bottling up for the past several minutes began pouring out in an angry rush: "So now what's so goddamned important you're willing to die for it, because you will die, Qar'qaah, and very, very soon if you don't get expert medical care. You may be a pig-headed Hahtooshan, but you're not fucking indestructible—quite the contrary—even you have to have realized that." She waited, tapping her foot on the deck then prompted irritably, *"Well?"*

He bit his sooty, split lip, grimaced, tried to wipe the grime onto his equally grimy fingers, grimaced again then replied quietly, "Find Cisne."

"Cisne?" She knit her brows. The name sounded vaguely familiar, but she couldn't immediately place it. "Who or what the hell's—"

"Take back from her what..." he winced then began to massage his temples with his fingers, adding softly, "...what she took from me."

She watched him, not sure what to say, not sure what to think. But as his fingertips started to dig into the blistered, soot-streaked and peeling skin behind his eyes, as if trying to reach some deeply buried pain, her own eyes widened in sudden comprehension. *Gods!*

Without considering how he'd react, she lightly grasped his blood-sticky knee, mindful of the injury.

He jerked his hands away from his temples, glanced down at her hand then scowled at her.

"Do you honestly believe that finding this Cisne will end the nightmares, stop the paralyzing space-outs?" She tightened her hold. *"Do you?"*

He swallowed hard before answering softly, "I won't know until I find her—"

"You're in no shape to find anyone, *dammit!*"

He chuckled harshly, "That's just what Sha'ashahn said. He ordered me to stay aboard *Jirah*, told me I was not... *fit* to accompany him—"

"That's not what he meant and you fucking well know it!"

"—that he would find her and the others and deal with them, but—"

"But you disobeyed his direct orders—what am I thinking," she smacked herself in the forehead for emphasis, "of course you would!"

He gave her another quick, sidelong glare. "I didn't disobey, per se. I just chose to interpret my orders differently."

"You went fucking AWOL!"

He arched a brow.

"It means you deserted—"

"If that's how you care to characterize my actions, then fine."

"But Hahtooshans don't desert."

"Who told you that? Sha'ashahn?"

"Matoosh."

He snorted. "He knows better—presumably he told you that to shut you up. I'd wager it didn't work."

Sirin pursed her lips, decided to let that swipe slide and said, "Okay, so after you... *reinterpreted* your orders, which now included you flicking down to the planet in order to conduct your own search for this Cisne, which explains why you were all alone when I ran into—*when we happened across each other,*" she amended quickly as she saw his jaw muscles bunch.

He shrugged tetchily but this time did not look at her.

"But... why? Why disob—I mean why reinterpret your orders, why flick down alone—even you had to have known you were extremely ill. *Qar'qaah?*" She tightened her hold on his knee. "Please, tell me. *Why?*"

He lifted his head, fixed his gaze on the console and replied harshly, "I can never be what he expects, what he demands—he won't even allow me to seek my own way, my own ship postings. He keeps me near, just so he can humiliate me at every opportunity, so he can constantly remind me what a failure I am—"

"He, meaning Khusaaq—"

"—I've tried, repeatedly, to meet his expectations, but... but I'm just not... not capable."

"What do you mean, not capable? You're more than half dead, barely able to keep on your feet, yet you managed to take out five heavily armed and very determined kidnapp—"

"Four."

She blinked. "Four...?"

He looked at her out of the corner of his eye. "The fifth died of smoke inhalation, if you recall. Vaporizing a corpse doesn't count."

She almost laughed. *A fine time to stand on particulars*—but such was Hahtooshan vanity. They were inordinately proud of whatever they did, even if that was to leave a trail of utter destruction in their wake, but they drew a very strong and indignant line at taking credit—or blame—for anything they didn't, in fact, do. Instead, she replied with audible exasperation, "Okay, *four*, but you still managed to rescue me and Drakin without either one of us even getting a scratch! That in itself is an incredible feat—*why the hell can't you admit that?"*

He shook his head and replied quietly, "You don't understand—you... you *can't."*

Rapidly losing patience with him, she angrily released her hold on his knee, roughly shoving his injured leg aside in the process and drawing his sidelong, wincing stare. "Oh, I think I do!" she replied harshly, "I think you flicked down not in hopes that you'd find this Cisne, but that she'd find you and *finish* what she started—"

His eyes widened.

"—your way of punishing yourself once and for all for failing to measure up to some impossibly high standard—not a standard Khusaaq set for you, oh, no, but one you set for yourself!"

He continued to stare at her as his mouth twisted and his bruise-shadowed eyes watered. After a moment he whispered, almost plaintively, *"Go away."*

"No."

He resumed tapping in commands.

"Qar'qaah, *dammit*, talk to me! Tell me what's going on inside that amazingly thick, *incredibly* screwed up head of yours!"

"Leave me alone—"

"Why? So you can wallow in self-pity?"

"No, because I cannot concentrate with you jabbering at me."

She crossed her arms and squinted at him. "I'm not going anywhere."

He scowled at her, then with a shake of his head, broke their glaring match and turned back to the console.

She remained silent as he worked on the com-net, but kept her eyes on him. As she studied his down-turned face, she found herself yet again taken back by just how incredibly young he was, and yes, just how much he looked and sounded like Khusaaq. *Would I feel the same about you if you didn't?*

Suddenly very uncomfortable with that train of thought, she found herself confronted by another that was even more unsettling, one that had been worming its way around her subconscious ever since she'd learned of his true relationship to Khusaaq, and jolted to the surface by his muttered aside: *maybe you're right, maybe you are more like him than I want to consider—maybe I* am *seeing the real Khusaaq, not the enlightened veneer gained through experience.*

Suddenly furious, but unwilling to consider the anger might be at Khusaaq for possibly lying to her, keeping hidden his true self, she fixed her preoccupied stare on the open hatchway and shifted her rage onto an far less complicated, more straightforward target. *Gods help you, Cisne, if I ever get my hands on—*

A bleat startled her. She blinked and, looking down, realized the console was now alight with flashing telltales. She lifted her gaze to find Qar'qaah staring at her, eyes glittering.

"Count to one hundred this time... *slowly*, then press this button." He pointed.

"What? I... I don't understand."

"Powering up to com-net should have been enough to alert those manning the sensors aboard *Jirah*, and prompt them to investigate, but just to be on the safe side, when you press this button it will send a distress call—"

"And you want the time to get as far away as possible."

"Yes." He rose slowly and very unsteadily and watching him, Sirin wondered if he'd even make to the nearby airlock.

"But you have no idea where she is—she could be anywhere, she could have even left the planet—"

"I know where she is, or, should I say, where she will be, at least briefly." He looked at Sirin, too miserable, too ill to be crazy. Clearly he'd thought this one out, knew full well the chances, the consequences. Knew the outcome. Didn't care.

"What? But... but how—"

"Your *friend,* back on the freighter. When he was looking for the others, he said that they were expecting Cisne?"

She stared up at him for a moment, baffled, then her eyes widened.

"He thought it was Cisne who'd double crossed them and cut the power. He was most surprised when he realized it was *just* me." The corners of his blistered mouth twitched at a clearly very satisfying memory before he added, "And the other human—remember he mentioned a colonial fanatic, one who'd pay more than A'tuu'shahn'i to get her hands on Sha'ashahn in order to... *string him up?"*

"Cisne."

"One and the same."

"But... when she realizes—"

He chuckled harshly as he angrily wiped the beads of sooty sweat from his forehead and scarified cheeks with the back of his soot-grimy hand. "By then, you'll be back in the hands of Sha'ashahn, aboard *Jirah*, and both of you will be safely out of her reach."

"Which is why you wanted to get us away from that freighter as quickly as possible. You knew if she arrived while we were still aboard—"

"She would use you to entrap Sha'ashahn."

Sirin watched as he awkwardly stooped to retrieve the blaster and laser cutter from the deck and replied angrily, "All very heroic."

"No," he said as he straightened up. "Just practical. Everyone gets what they want."

"Including you?"

He stuffed the blaster into his waistband and tossed the laser cutter onto his now empty chair. "According to you, yes."

"I'm so sorry, Qar'qaah, that was a terrible thing for me to say."

His replied with a slight shrug as he fixed his narrowed gaze on the nearby airlock as if measuring the distance and said, "It was. But perhaps you're also right."

She got to her feet, placed herself between him and the airlock. Having run out of all other options, she played her last card. "As your… your *ta'ashan* I order you to remain here!" She placed her hands on her hips for extra emphasis.

He managed a soft chuckle which was cut short by a belly-rubbing wince. "So, you've taught yourself some of our more arcane, and, I might add, *asinine* customs. Well, since I only have your word that you are who you claim you are, and since Rimmers are notorious liars," he motioned to her, as if seeing something she couldn't, "I simply do not recognize your authority to command me to do anything. Besides, as a deserter—your label, not mine—I'm under no obligation to follow anyone's orders."

"But—"

"And when you next see Sha'ashahn, you really should ask him to fully explain the potentially very unpleasant consequences of a *ta'ashan* invoking his or her claim of command through marriage."

"Like what?"

"All obligations will be shifted from your bond-mate's kin to you and yours. All debts, all dishonors become yours whereas your bond-mate's record of any wrong-doing is expunged."

"That doesn't sound very fair."

"And wielding authority one has not legitimately earned is?"

She stared up at him, realized he was now swaying slightly and said, "This is suicide, or worse—much worse, you know that! Besides, by the time you get back to the freighter, she'll probably have already come and gone—"

"Then I'll track her—that is the one thing I am very good at—reading the book, as they say. Even Sha'ashahn says so."

"Qar'qaah—look at yourself! You're barely able keep on your feet as it is—you're running on nothing more than painkillers and adrenaline—what happens when you run out of both? Because you will, sooner rather than later."

"Then I'll die," he replied flatly, "just as you say." He held out his hand. "May... may I have the *t'jing*?"

"Qar'qaah...*please.*" She made a grab for his outstretched hand but he managed to step back, just out of reach without unbalancing himself and falling. "You don't have to do this!"

"No, I don't have to. I want to." He again held out his hand, adding softly, almost urgently, *"Tohiss-mat."*

She shook her head and slipped her hand into her pocket, then withdrew the small weapon and blinking back tears, placed it on his grubby, tattooed palm.

"Jaas-nhe," he murmured as his sooty fingers curled around it. He pushed it down into the cuff of his boot then picked up his pistol and stuffed it in his waistband next to the blaster.

"I can't talk you out of this."

He shook his head, as if no longer trusting his own voice, and again started for the airlock.

Then you leave me no choice. "Wait."

He stopped but refused to look at her.

She angrily wiped her eyes, then dug into her other pocket and pulled out the ject-it and the remaining vials. She palmed the blue-capped sedative as she said, "At least let me give you something to keep you on your feet... for a little while longer,

maybe even long enough to have a fighting chance against her."
She stepped closer and he glanced down at the two red-capped
painkiller vials she held out for him to see.

"I'll take them with me." He reached for them.

"The last couple of times when you desperately needed
something to keep you going," she countered harshly, "you
couldn't give it to yourself, *remember?*"

He immediately jerked his hand away as if burned, then
turned his bare, emaciated shoulder towards her and fixed his
narrowed eyes on the far wall.

She quickly loaded the ject-it with the blue-capped vial,
shoved it against his upper arm, then hit the activator and
pumped its entire contents into the wasted muscle.

He grimaced, and as she stepped back, he again held out his
hand, still refusing to make eye-contact.

She popped out the empty vial, hoping he wouldn't look to
see that she'd in fact given him a sedative, then slapped the ject-
it and one of the red-capped vials into his awaiting palm. "So,
now I'm to count to one hundred—you're absolutely *sure* that's
enough time?"

He nodded as he slipped the ject-it and vial into his trouser
pocket, then he staggered off the bridge.

She waited until he was well beyond the airlock, hit the
button on the console then followed only to find him just a few
meters down the corridor, leaning heavily against the curved
wall, in the hollow of a bulkhead.

She approached, murmured, *"Qar'qaah?"* and lightly
touched his shoulder.

He promptly slid down the wall and onto his knees.

She knelt beside him. One look at his slack face and half
closed eyes confirmed that the potent drug had taken hold.

She pulled the blaster and pistol from his waistband, placed
them on the deck behind her, then, grasping his shoulders,
carefully eased him down onto the deck, onto his side. She
slipped her hand into his boot, carefully withdrew the *t'jing* and
placed it beside the other weapons.

She leaned down, wiped a lock of sooty hair from his forehead then kissed him on his equally sooty cheek. "I'm so terribly sorry, Qar'qaah. Really I am... but I couldn't let you—"

An odd heaviness washed over her; an instant later she felt a very unsettling sensation, as if she was being nudged by scores of unseen hands against the unforgiving bulkhead.

Startled, she lifted her gaze and looked around only to find that the entire length of the corridor had begun to quiver faintly as if seen through heat ripples.

Then the peculiar phenomenon vanished as quickly as it had come and the corridor returned to its dim stillness.

She had no sooner begun to question whether what she'd just experienced had been real or just a figment of her own exhausted and overwrought mind when six Hahtooshans in full battledress solidified in the corridor, between her and the bridge, with eight more between her and the bay airlock. All had their weapons drawn and although none were pointing them directly at her she instinctively tightened her protective hold on Qar'qaah, using her own body as a shield. *"Don't shoot! We're unarmed!"*

The nearest soldier immediately shoved his maser pistol back into its holster, then unclipped and pulled off his helmet.

Sirin, seeing who it was, gasped, *"Khusaaq...!"*

He winked at her then said to his companions. "Secure the ship—"

"Drakin's aboard, too," Sirin interrupted hastily before the others could obey.

"Anyone else?" Khusaaq asked, the soldiers hesitating.

"Not that we know of—Drakin's somewhere on the deck above."

"Lieutenant Drakin is Eltannian," he explained to the others then added, "go."

All but one of the soldiers disbursed. The remaining trooper slowly approached, his full attention on Qar'qaah as Khusaaq smiled at Sirin, opened his arms and murmured, *"Toq-bhir."*

She leapt to her feet, ran to him and as he tightly wrapped his arms around her, she buried her face in his armored chest.

"Are you injured?" he asked quietly but with an audible tone of worry, immediately loosening his hold. "Jaa'qwah Kon'ta'aq here is a medic," he motioned to the soldier, who had removed his own helmet and was now kneeling beside Qar'qaah.

"I'm fine."

"And Qar'qaah, Kon'ta'aq?" Khusaaq asked, looking past her.

Jaa'qwah looked up, nodded, "We got to him in time, ta'ahn—barely. It will take me a few minutes to stabilize him for transport."

Khusaaq nodded then fixed his eyes on Sirin as she said, "I thought I'd never see you again."

He wiped her soot-streaked cheeks with a gauntleted finger. "I must say I did not have the foresight to arrange our reunion on such an incredibly romantic locale as Poonda Five, but..." He stooped down and kissed her lightly on the lips, then, drawing her more tightly against himself, mindful that he was wearing armor and she was not, kissed her again, this time passionately.

She responded in kind and for a moment they were oblivious to everything but each other.

Finally, breathless, he broke the embrace.

Smiling, she reached up and wiped the smear of soot from around his mouth. "Bet that didn't taste very good."

"But you do," he replied, bringing her sooty fingertips back to his lips and giving them another kiss, then he looked down and sighed, "I see you've become acquainted with Qar'qaah Kon'ta'aq."

"Yeah." She followed his gaze, noticed Jaa'qwah had spread out an impressive array of ject-its on the deck next to Qar'qaah and was still pulling supplies from his equipment belt. "Small universe."

"We've spent the better half of the last two days turning this planet inside out, using every resource at our disposal, searching for him... and *you* found him."

"Actually," Sirin replied, "we kinda found each other."

Khusaaq replied with a quizzical arch of a brow but before she could explain they both overheard a familiar, echoing hiss from the nearby emergency stairwell: "All I can sssay iz itz about damned time da cavalry ssshowed up!"

Sirin looked around Khusaaq to see Drakin emerge from the hatchway, followed by three Hahtooshans. All had removed their helmets. The first two were strangers and one, Sirin immediately realized to her surprise was not only female, but also going by her facial tattoos, *Elkanaghalli*. Unlike Mir-Suhjai, this woman, like Amalfitano and Tasende's female bodyguards, was every bit as tall and muscular as her male counterparts.

Sirin quickly shifted her startled gaze from the woman to the last of three and found to her immense relief that it was none other than Matoosh.

He acknowledged her pleased grin with a tight smile of his own, but as his gaze fell on Qar'qaah, his smile faded. He quickly slipped past Drakin and the other two Hahtooshans, hurried over to Qar'qaah and knelt beside the medic.

Drakin too, realizing who was lying on the deck, waddled towards them. "Waz he being da hero again?"

Khusaaq jerked his head up and squinted at Drakin as Sirin replied,

"Yes… and no."

Drakin stopped to stand behind the kneeling Matoosh and placed her hands on her hips. "Yez *and* no?"

"Okay, yes, although he'd vehemently disagree—"

"If he weren't presssently unconsssciouz."

"There is that," Sirin conceded.

"Zo…?"

"So I… uh… knocked him out."

"You… knocked him out?" Matoosh repeated, incredulous, as the other two soldiers warily joined them, the female placing herself beside him, her intensely curious gray eyes darting between Khusaaq and Sirin while the other trooper hung back, keeping his eyes and his weapon, trained on the corridor.

"Told him I was giving him a painkiller," Sirin continued, suddenly fearful she might have overdosed him. "Instead I injected him with an entire vial of sedative."

The medic jerked his head up and stared at her, then shaking his head and muttering angrily to himself in A'tuu, turned back to Qar'qaah.

"I had no choice," she continued hastily, defensively, "he was going back to the freighter, to confront someone named Cisne—"

"Cisne?" Khusaaq repeated as he and Matoosh exchanged startled glances.

"You know about her?" she asked, her eyes darting between the two.

"Indeed we do," Matoosh growled as he angrily gathered up the weapons Sirin had placed on the deck. He handed the blaster and pistol to the female trooper, then arching a disdainful brow, offered the *t'jing* to Khusaaq with a cryptic: "Traceable evidence, ta'ahn, to the killings of the Tulian security guards?"

Khusaaq accepted it, muttered, *"If* it's the same t'jing." He gave the small dart gun a quick, curled-lip glance, adding, "Definitely professional grade," and checked how many darts it still held before slipping it into a concealed slot on his armored hip. He then turned back to Sirin. "Are you absolutely certain it was Cisne?"

"No, but he was." She looked down at Qar'qaah. "He was planning on acting as a diversion, bait as it were, until Drakin and I were safely back aboard your ship. I... I couldn't let him do that."

Khusaaq and Matoosh again looked at each other; Khusaaq shook his head and said, "So much for this whole experience breaking him, once and for all, of his—"

"Pigheaded selflessness?" Sirin interrupted.

Khusaaq shrugged.

"It's a family curse," she added, just loud enough for him to overhear—or so she thought. Then she happened to catch the quickly concealed smile on the female soldier's full lips and Matoosh's uneasy, sidelong glance at the male trooper, who, for his part, pointedly refused to look at anyone.

Khusaaq cleared his throat then asked, "This freighter... is it the same one that brought you here?"

Sirin nodded.

He turned to Matoosh and started to open his mouth, but was cut off by a new voice, a deep, decidedly irritated voice: "Sha'ashahn, the ship's not as we left it…"

Khusaaq, Sirin and the others turned to find two soldiers striding abreast down the corridor towards them, helmets tucked under arms, as the taller and heavier of the two continued, "…thanks to Kon'ta'aq's 'unique' approach at overriding my sequential overrides and getting the com-net powered up."

Khusaaq looked at Sirin and said, "This is Tejat Ruh'ta'aq—Second Engineer of *Faridour*. And beside him is Rukoobi Kon'ta'aq, weapons officer. Ruh'ta'aq, Kon'ta'aq, this is my bond-mate, Sirin, and this," he motioned with his chin, "is Lieutenant Drakin, medical officer of the Coalition Patrol Ship, *Baidarka*."

Tejat acknowledged the two with a cold glance and an equally cold nod while Rukoobi responded with a decidedly disarming smile and a murmured, "A pleasure to meet you both, at last." He even extended his gauntleted hand in a very un-Hahtooshan gesture.

Sirin replied with a friendly smile of her own along with a firm handshake, then she happened to catch Drakin's decidedly predatory grin. *Uh-oh.*

"My oh my. Da pleasssure iz all mine," Drakin lisped softly as she gave the well-built Rukoobi a *very* thorough once-over with her eyes while also shaking his hand. "Yez, definitely all mine—"

"How long will it take you to get the ship space-worthy?" Khusaaq fixed his hard stare on the engineer while Rukoobi discreetly tried to free himself of Drakin's grip.

The massive trooper irritably combed his armored fingers through his shoulder-length blue-black hair. "It's not just a simple matter of reactivating all bridge systems, ta'ahn. Each must be powered up slowly, and one at a time—plus we first must undo *everything* Kon'ta'aq did and reinitialize in the *proper* sequence or risk a catastrophic power cascade." His narrowed eyes darted briefly to the unmoving object of his obvious exasperation, as if to affix blame as well.

"We don't have the luxury of a lot of time, Ruh'ta'aq."

"I know, ta'ahn, and I will do what I can to hurry things up, but—"

"Pity Kon'ta'aq cannot offer his assistance," Matoosh offered helpfully, patting the inert Qar'qaah on his hip. "As I'm sure you noticed, he is an extremely able, not to mention very ingenious engineer."

Tejat responded to that remark with a noticeable tightening of the corners of his already thin-lipped mouth and a low rumble that seemed to emanate from deep within his barrel chest.

"Since he is presently... *incapacitated*," Khusaaq added, pulling his tac-net from his weapons belt, "I'll contact *Baidarka...*"

Drakin and Sirin stared at each other, stunned as Sirin asked, *"Baidarka?* But—"

"She's in orbit." He flashed Sirin a smile and a wink, then turned back to Tejat. "I have no doubt her engineering staff, once apprised of the situation, will be more than willing to offer their assistance, Ruh'ta'aq."

Tejat's pale eyes widened and he replied a little too hastily, "That will not be necessary, ta'ahn! Shu'hah and the others are already hard at work undoing Kon'ta'aq's... *ingenious* efforts. If you'll permit them to continue to assist me, I have no doubt we can complete repairs and power up all essential systems within an hour—perhaps less."

"Are you sure?"

Tejat nodded vigorously.

"Then you'd best get to it, hadn't you?"

Tejat replied with another nod, then turned on his heel and hurried back down the corridor, leaving Rukoobi behind.

Rukoobi, who'd managed to free himself from Drakin some moments before, stared after the retreating Tejat, then looked at Khusaaq and hid a soft, barking chuckle behind the same armored hand.

Khusaaq grinned in reply then looked down at Jaa'qwah. "Is he ready to be flicked out of here?"

"Yes, ta'ahn."

Khusaaq brought the tac-net to his lips. *"Baidarka...?"*

"This is Baidarka, *Sha'ashahn,"* came Aquila's familiar voice and Drakin and Sirin smiled at each other.

"We've succeeded in locating *all* of our missing, Commander—*alive."*

"That's wonderful news!"

"Indeed. Ensign Sirin and Lieutenant Drakin are unharmed," Khusaaq added as he eyed Sirin's soot-grubby face and tattered clothing. "Qar'qaah Kon'ta'aq, however, is in desperate need of medical attention."

"We have a team standing by, Sha'ashahn."

"I'll be back in contact with your momentarily, Commander." With that he cut the link then turned as the remaining soldiers reappeared from searching the rest of the ship.

"All secure, Sha'ashahn," one reported.

"Excellent. Notify those on the bridge that the rest of us will be leaving shortly; they now have possession of the ship."

The soldier nodded and darted past, towards the bridge.

Drakin knelt, carefully eeled her arms under Qar'qaah and gently tugged him against her and after a brief struggle with his limp body and rubbery limbs, lurched back to her feet.

Khusaaq wrapped his arm around Sirin's waist, in the process drawing her worried gaze from Qar'qaah. "I want you to return to *Baidarka* with the lieutenant—"

"And you?"

His eyes narrowed to angry slits as he took in Qar'qaah's soot-smeared, slack face. "I think it's high time I meet this Cisne. We have much to... *discuss.*"

"But—"

He put a gauntleted finger to her lips. "This is an A'tuu'shahn matter." He lifted his gaze, acknowledged that the soldier who'd gone to alert those on the bridge had returned then said, "Everyone, with me."

The soldiers immediately donned their helmets and formed up.

"Jaa'qwah..."

The medic, who'd been in the process of hurriedly gathering his equipment from the deck, looked up. "Yes, ta'ahn?"

"You're to accompany Kon'ta'aq. Doctor Amalfitano is well trained in treating A'tuu'shahn'i, as is Lieutenant Drakin," he nodded to her, "but not in dealing with one quite as headstrong as Qar'qaah—"

Drakin muffled a pointed cough.

Khusaaq glanced at her, adding, "I'm sure they'll find your particular medical expertise most welcome."

Jaa'qwah dutifully nodded, snatched up his helmet and leapt to his feet, then very reluctantly looked at the massive reptiloid.

"You're a medic?" Drakin asked, Rukoobi instantly forgotten as she gave the stocky Dakkeesh an appraising once over, her bifurcated tongue fluttering millimeters from his overly prominent nose.

Jaa'qwah risked a quick, sidelong glance at Khusaaq.

"The best in the fleet," Khusaaq answered for him. "So please... *don't* eat him."

Drakin wiggled her brow ridges and grinned suggestively at Jaa'qwah, displaying a mouthful of razor sharp teeth.

He visibly paled, swallowed convulsively and instinctively backed up a step.

Khusaaq chuckled, then met Sirin's worried gaze and tightened his hold on her waist.

"Be careful," she murmured.

"Always."

She touched his lips and he kissed her fingertips, then he murmured, *"Go now."* She reluctantly released her embrace and joined Drakin and Jaa'qwah.

As Khusaaq and the others backed away, he brought his tac-net back to his lips. *"Baidarka...*the lieutenant, Ensign Corsali, my medic and Kon'ta'aq are ready to be flicked aboard."

There was a brief pause before Aquila replied, *"We have their coordinates. Flicking aboard... now."*

Chapter 12

Sickbay, aboard the Baidarka, *1558.*

Sirin stopped just short of the open doorway of Amalfitano's office. She looked down at herself and realized that no amount of smoothing or tugging would make the tattered, grubby and oversized jumpsuit look like anything other than a tattered, grubby and oversized jumpsuit.

She lifted her head and tucked a lock soot-greasy blond hair behind her ear. *Ready?*

The answer came quickly as she exhaled. *Not really—but I can't put this off any longer.*

Over six hours had passed since she and the others had flicked aboard the *Baidarka*—hours spent enduring the lengthy ordeal of a complete physical by Doctor Fleming, followed by an equally exhaustive debriefing by Izraad. But her thoughts had never strayed far from Khusaaq... and yes, Qar'qaah.

She'd reminded herself that Khusaaq could take care of himself and Qar'qaah was in the best hands possible, but neither assurance, no matter how many times she repeated them, was enough to keep her nagging fears for their welfare, their safety at bay.

There was nothing she could do to speed up Khusaaq's return. That left one thing she could do.

So here she was, standing just outside Amalfitano's office and seated inside was the one person who could confirm her worst fears about Qar'qaah—or put them to rest.

She squared her shoulders and stepped across the threshold.

Amalfitano sat at his desk, unaware of her arrival, his attention fixed on a flimsy he held in both hands.

"Doctor?"

He jerked his head up, and, seeing who it was, placed the report on the desk. "Ensign." He started to smile then his eyes narrowed. "Lieutenant Izraad said she'd told you to go have a shower, get something to eat and then have a nap. Now, I can't speak for the meal, but clearly you haven't showered or had a nap, unless of course you favor the exhausted escapee from the clutches of hell look."

She replied with a contrite shrug.

He shook his head and motioned for her to approach. "I was just reviewing the results of your physical. Aside from some smoke inhalation, mild dehydration and a few bumps and bruises, you're in remarkably good shape, but I want you to take it easy for the next few days and once Khusaaq's back ab—"

"What about Qar'qaah?"

He fingered the flimsy, long enough for her to feel as if the bottom had dropped out of her stomach. *He's dead.* She sank down into one of the chairs in front of his desk. *That's what you're going to tell me. Qar'qaah's dead—*

"I won't mince words with you, Sirin. He's in really bad shape—"

She jerked her head up.

"—much, *much* worse than the four who were kidnapped along with him."

"But he's alive?"

He nodded. "Which is a miracle in itself—maybe there is something to that Hahtooshan stock phrase that they were engineered to survive. Hell, Neanderthals were, and did for hundreds of thousands of years... until we came along and pushed them over the edge by sheer numerical superiority. He's certainly beat the odds..."

She sagged back into the chair, but her embryonic smile of relief was instantly wiped aside by Amalfitano's next comment.

"...but it's no exaggeration to say that he wouldn't have survived another day—in fact he wouldn't have survived another few hours without intensive medical intervention. Both kidneys had shut down, he was well on his way to liver failure and his entire gut—"

"May I see him?"

Amalfitano eyed her. "I think it would be for the best if you did as Zarijan suggested." He began to shuffle the flimsies. "Maybe later, okay?"

"Going by what you just said, there may not be a 'later'."

He visibly winced, then met her gaze and said, albeit very reluctantly, "All right." He wearily pushed himself out of his chair. "But understand, he won't be able to speak with you. In fact he won't even be aware of you."

She raised both brows.

"He's in a drug-induced coma—"

"Because of the sedative I gave him?" she gasped, horrified. "I didn't mean to overdose him, I just—"

"Whoa! I induced the coma, not you. The Hahtooshan medics and I agree it's for the best while we try to treat his complex medical problems. Only after we've stabilized him medically, will we start to wean him off the sedatives and allow him to wake up... slowly, and at his own pace. You didn't harm him by doing what you did. According to Jaa'qwah, you stopped him from further harming himself, so calm down." He paused, shook his head, then added, "You've earned yourself quite a reputation among the Hahtooshan medics, Sirin—even Murh'sooli and he's not easily impressed, believe me. And yes, I suppose you can even sit with him for a little while—but I better warn you, you're gonna have company."

"Company?"

"You'll see." He guided her out of his office, and into the main infirmary then through a doorway and into the same small, cubicle-lined intensive care unit which had housed Khusaaq and Matoosh not all that long before.

As they came to the unit's airlock, Amalfitano reached out to press the activator.

"Is he going to pull through?"

Amalfitano dropped his hand back to his side as he met her gaze. "Murh'sooli and Jaa'qwah assure me they've successfully treated much worse cases of poisoning. And clearly Hahtooshan tolerance for sustained exposure is far greater than ours due to their ability to lessen the impact of ionizing radiation on their DNA—something to do with what Murh'sooli called nanophase biomineralization—he said it's another property of their tattoos—but it's not just a matter of the poisoning. Zarijan and I have had a chance to speak to the others rescued from Rasal

Ghul and simply put, Qar'qaah suffered tremendous physical and psychological abuse at the hands of his kidnappers—"

"I know."

"You mean he told you? Anything you can tell me about what was done to him could be of great help in determining the best approach—"

"He didn't exactly tell me. It was obvious to me, almost from the start, that along with being physically ill, he was also suffering from severe psychological trauma. Later, Drakin and I were witness to a nightmare—he said something about being put in a stasis pod awake—but there was clearly more to it than just that, as horrific as that is all by itself."

Amalfitano arched a brow, but said nothing.

"He also kept, well, *spacing out*—just *gone*, gods know where, and he admitted to seeing things that weren't there—"

"Matoosh told me when he tried to convince him to return after he'd deserted he refused," Amalfitano interrupted, "in large part because he was convinced Matoosh was a hallucination. Not an unexpected symptom in someone with advanced radiation poisoning and extreme physical exhaustion."

She gave him an oblique stare. "You do realize he's Khusaaq's clone."

"Yeah," he exhaled, "I know. Leave it to our Hahtooshans to keep life interesting."

"He made it very clear that he felt that being, as he put it, 'a poor copy' of Khusaaq was wholly untenable. To that end, he deliberately disobeyed Khusaaq and flicked down to Poonda Five alone, utterly ill-equipped to survive on the surface, but intent on finding this Cisne at all costs when deep down he knew the likelihood of finding her was next to nil."

"So, we're dealing with someone who was already suffering from some pretty complex and long standing psychological issues well before this... this *creature*, Cisne, got her hands on him."

"In a word, yes."

"Great," he grumbled, rubbing the back of his neck. "Just... great. I think I'd best contact the *Faridour's* CMO—ask if she's ever had to deal with anything like this before..."

"Couldn't hurt." She nodded.

"...maybe Narbrooi too, since he's Elkanaghalli and therefore has to be extremely familiar with this whole bizarre *doh'ha* business."

"Matoosh, I'm sure, will do anything you ask. I came away with the strong feeling that he and Qar'qaah are—or at least were at one time—very close."

"And Khusaaq?"

She dropped her gaze to the deck. "I honestly don't know. The Khusaaq Qar'qaah spoke of and clearly hates with every fiber of his being isn't the man I know and love. But then again, there's a lot about Khusaaq I don't know—for one thing, I didn't know he had a clone... until I literally came face to face with Qar'qaah down on the planet. It was, to say the least, a bit of a shock."

She took a deep, steadying breath, then continued. "I often overheard Khusaaq and Matoosh speaking in A'tuu of those left behind on Rasal Ghul when they didn't think I was listening, or, I suspect, even if I was, that I wouldn't understand them. Both were deeply distressed, and Matoosh once mentioned to me that three of the five were related to them. For the most part both were tight-lipped about them—but still, how can you fail to mention to your wife that you have a clone?"

He gave her arm a commiserating squeeze. "When it came to discussing family, Khusaaq was the same way with me—he became quite agitated when I asked him about his parents, his childhood. I came away thinking it was a Hahtooshan cultural norm not to discuss one's immediate family, one's background with outsiders."

"Yeah," she replied softly. *"Outsiders."*

Amalfitano lightly grasped her shoulder, drawing her gaze. "Sirin, this isn't a case of him not wanting to open up fully to you. You're dealing with a lifetime of intense social and religious indoctrination—he can't be expected to shed that training in a short few weeks, no matter how much he loves you. Give him time, he'll come 'round."

This time she only nodded. *I sure hope so.*

"Ready?"

Not really, but... She nodded again and he pushed the release, the airlock snapped open and they stepped inside then waited in silence as the small unit cycled. The inner door opened and he stepped out and motioned to the nearest cubicle. "In here."

Sirin entered the dimly lit unit only to find three Hahtooshans standing off to one side, and a forth seated on the fold-down seat next to the room's single bunk. All were clad in loose fitting sickbay jumpsuits. The seated soldier immediately rose and stepped back as the others came to rigid attention.

"It's okay, boys," Amalfitano murmured. "This is Ensign Sirin Corsali, Khusaaq Sha'ashahn's bond-mate. Sirin, this is Endooki Ha'tat," he motioned to the trooper who'd been seated, "and that's Nihaal Ha'tat on the left, Laihiri Ha'tat, and Raudah Ha'tat on the right."

Sirin acknowledged each with a nod and a smile then she turned her full attention to the person on the narrow trauma bed.

At first she didn't recognize Qar'qaah. He was no longer covered in soot and grime; now his skin was smeared with a creamy white salve which gave him a death-like pallor and concealed his tattoos and bruises, even the scarification, as well as the overt signs of his poisoning.

His blue-black hair had been washed and re-plaited and now lay in a neat, glossy coil just above his right shoulder. Infusers were strapped to his forearms, a signal suppressor was attached to his left shoulder, and two ventilator pods cradled his bare chest. A sealer dressing encased his sunken abdomen and a myriad of tubes, lines and cables snaked out from under the thin drape that covered his lower body, only to disappear into the base of the trauma bed.

"We had to remove his spleen and most of his liver, and one kidney was unsalvageable." Amalfitano motioned to the dressing. "So we replaced them, along with his largely necrotic stomach and intestines with analogous donor tissue we had left over from Khusaaq."

Sirin gave him an arched look.

"The medics had anticipated recovering him and the others alive and suspecting what we'd need, started the replication process within hours of us leaving Tuli." He glanced over his shoulder just as the sphinxlike Murh'sooli entered the small cubicle.

"Given a choice," Amalfitano continued as the medic busied himself with one of the ventilator pods, "I'd have preferred to hold off, get him stabilized before putting him through major, multi-organ transplant surgery, but... we, or, should I say, *he* couldn't wait. Luckily, having Murh'sooli and three other Hahtooshan medics assisting, everything went without a hitch and in record time." He paused, then added, "Ironic, yes? I guess one could say that this whole *doh'ha* business *cuts* both ways."

"As it was intended," Murh'sooli interjected softly, drawing both Amalfitano's and Sirin's surprised stares. He replied with a cryptic smile, then pivoted smartly on his heel and walked out of the cubicle.

"Damn I wish he wouldn't do that," Amalfitano muttered, scowling after the man.

Sirin shook her head and looked back at Qar'qaah. The combination of the cool lightening and the salve gave his skin an eerie translucence, like polished alabaster, and without the distracting camouflage of tattoos and scarification he looked even younger and more... *human.*

She stepped close to the bed and reluctantly touched Qar'qaah's upper arm, half expecting it to be as cold and hard as stone. To her relief, it was warm and yielding.

She bit her lip and looked at Amalfitano. "As sick as he was, he repeatedly risked his life to save ours."

"I know."

She dropped her gaze back to Qar'qaah. "I never got the chance to thank you properly for that so don't you dare die on me."

Overhearing a nervous shuffle of feet, she looked to the soldier standing across from her to find him staring covertly at her.

She gave her eyes a rough wipe, asked, "Endooki Ha'tat, correct?"

He replied with an uncertain nod and a murmured, "Yes, ta'ashan."

She stared at Endooki for a moment and then looked at the other three. They looked to be even younger than Qar'qaah and almost as ill. "Go get some rest. I'll stay with him."

Endooki looked at Raudah, who in turn looked at the other two. Laihiri finally nodded and started for the doorway, Nihaal and Raudah very reluctantly on his heels.

Sirin pulled down the other seat, sat down and wrapped her fingers around Qar'qaah's salve-smeared wrist. She smiled to herself as she felt his surprisingly strong pulse, then looked up to find Endooki still standing across from her. "I'll come get you if there's any change, now... *go on.*"

"Yes, ta'ashan, we'll be in Ward One." With one last worried glance at Qar'qaah and a nod to Amalfitano, he followed the others out of the small cubicle.

Amalfitano waited until Endooki had entered the airlock and the lock had closed then said, "From the moment he came out of surgery they've refused to leave his side—during the four and a half hours of surgery they all stood outside Op Room Two, refusing even to take advantage of the chairs the staff brought for them. I've been trying to get them to get some rest themselves, or barring that, opt for some sort of rotating shift—nope. Clearly you have the touch when it comes to dealing with pig-headed Hahtooshans."

"I wish I could take credit."

He cocked his head to one side. "I don't follow."

"As their commanding officer's bond-mate—his *ta'ashan*—my wish is his order, or so goes Hahtooshan custom."

"I'll bear that in mind—could come in real handy."

"It does have its limits, like I couldn't tell them to go sack a planet."

"Oh." He snapped his fingers. "Well... damn. That was at the top of my to-do list."

She managed a soft chuckle. "Plus, according to my friend here," she jerked her chin towards Qar'qaah, "invoking this old custom does have some rather unpleasant consequences."

"Unpleasant...?"

"Very. Something about taking on your spouse's debts and obligations."

"Sounds like any marriage to me."

"Yeah," she replied, "except it only goes one way."

"As I said, sounds like any marriage."

Sirin eyed him. "And how would you know?"

"Observation, Ensign. Utterly *unbiased* observation."

She couldn't help but chuckle at that.

"You need your rest, too, you know."

"I know, but—"

"Thirty minutes, Ensign."

"But I just promised—"

"If there's any change in his condition, I'll tell you first, so you can tell them, deal?"

She sighed and nodded. "Deal."

Amalfitano gave her shoulder a squeeze, then turned and walked out of the cubicle.

Once alone with Qar'qaah, she tightened her hold on his wrist and with her other hand, lightly stroked his salve-greasy cheek. *"I mean it—don't you dare die on me."*

After some slight wriggling, she managed to find a relatively comfortable position on the hard-backed chair while maintaining her hold on his wrist. Then she settled in to watch the slow rise and fall of his chest, listen to faint rhythmic hiss and click of the ventilator pods, feel the reassuring thudding beat of his heart.

Slowly, lulled by the soft, comforting sounds and sensations of life, and extremely tired herself, she found herself nodding off.

Then she became aware of a new noise—that of someone softly but insistently clearing their throat.

She blinked herself back to full wakefulness, glanced at Qar'qaah. Realizing he was not the source of the muffled cough, she looked at the doorway, expecting to find Fleming or Amalfitano or even one of the Hahtooshan medics standing there.

Instead she saw Izraad and her throat muscles instinctively tightened—this unassuming woman knew things about Khusaaq she could never know, never comprehend—Izraad had felt *his* blood coursing through *her* veins, had drawn *his* breath into *her* lungs, had seen *his* world—as well as her own—through *his* eyes, *his* perceptions. Fears, friendships, battles, pain and pleasure, subconscious pettiness, unspoken hopes, utter despair—she had been completely immersed in who and what he was, had embraced the core of his being in a way no other person ever could.

For a few precious minutes during the mind-strip, Izraad had *been* him.

It was an intimacy beyond sex, beyond love, beyond complete acceptance... beyond pure hatred. It was far beyond anything Sirin and Khusaaq were capable of attaining and Sirin still wasn't sure if she was jealous of Izraad for that, or relieved—sometimes it was better not to know everything about someone one loved as deeply as she loved him. She couldn't even explain why she felt the way she did about him—she and Khusaaq were factually worlds apart in life experience, opposite sides of the same coin.

This truly unique familiarity was also an issue both women had avoided; in fact they'd avoided each other if at all possible since Khusaaq's mind-stripping.

And now here Izraad was, standing in the doorway, alone.

"May I come in?"

"Oh... yes, of course, Lieutenant." Using her free hand, Sirin motioned to the other fold down chair, across the bed from her as she straightened up.

Izraad slipped onto it, then, as she studied Qar'qaah's relaxed face, she murmured, almost distractedly, "It's truly astonishing how much he looks like Sha'ashahn—downright eerie in fact."

"Yes," Sirin replied, the not completely unexpected observation making her even more ill at ease.

Izraad gave her a sidelong look. "You're worried you don't really know him, aren't you? It terrifies you to think I do."

The woman's comment cut right to the bone and Sirin had to stop herself from visibly flinching. Then she answered softly, "Yes."

"If it helps, I don't, truly. I know only a single facet of him, a kernel of his experiences."

"But—"

"I know what you've gone through, what you've seen and who you've met over the past days," she dropped her gaze briefly to Qar'qaah before again looking at Sirin, "have made you question everything. And reasonably so. All I can tell you is to trust your heart, your gut—love isn't logical, Ensign. It isn't rational, it simply is or it just as simply *isn't*. The man you fell in love with remains the man you fell in love with. Don't overcomplicate it."

Sirin took a breath, slowly exhaled. *Easier said than done.*

Izraad smiled tightly then added, "Speaking of Sha'ashahn, that's why I'm here."

Sirin sat bolt upright, bracing herself for the worst.

"We just heard from him—he and his crew are all safely aboard the *Huui'teh*—they expect to make orbit shortly and rendezvous with *Jirah* within the hour."

Sirin relaxed, just a little, then asked, "And Cisne?"

"He said they'd searched the freighter, and found evidence that she'd been there but had left shortly before they arrived."

"Evidence?"

"He didn't elaborate—as you might imagine, he wasn't in the best of humors so Commander Aquila and I didn't press him for details. But clearly whatever he found was enough to convince him that she would not be returning. I gathered from what little he told me that they'd tracked her for some distance, but eventually lost the trail."

Sirin looked down at Qar'qaah and gave his wrist a squeeze. *Pity they couldn't have taken you with them—you'd have found her, I know you would've.* Then, looking back at Izraad and realizing the woman had overheard the thought, she managed a tight smile, incredibly thankful that Khusaaq, Matoosh and the others were all safe, but at the same time, intensely frustrated that the person who had caused so much damage—so much pain—had escaped yet again. "Now what?"

"Despite Sha'ashahn's well-intentioned efforts, we really don't know who we attempting to find. While Endooki Ha'tat saw her, each time it was very brief, and under carefully controlled conditions. He readily admits he might be mistaken about some of the details. Kon'ta'aq, however, told Endooki he'd made sure he got a really good look at her, he even memorized her scent along with the minute fluctuations in her aura—something Endooki tells me is as unique as an individual's fingerprints, so he's the *only* one who can positively identify her—"

"But it might take days, maybe longer before he'll be stable enough to be interviewed—and that's assuming he survives the next twenty four hours—"

"And the longer we wait, the greater the chance Cisne will make good her escape."

Sirin, instantly suspecting what Izraad was proposing, tightened her hold on Qar'qaah's wrist. *"No!* He's been traumatized enough—to mind-strip him aga—"

"I'm not suggesting he be mind-stripped, Ensign," Izraad replied calmly but firmly. "What I am suggesting—and only if Sha'ashahn agrees and Doctor Amalfitano deems it medically safe—is to slowly taper off the sedatives, allow him to slip into a normal sleep state... then passively eavesdrop on his dreams—no forcible mind-strip, I promise you."

Sirin thought about it for a moment then replied warily, "I'm not sure Khusaaq will agree."

"Neither am I. And you know how insanely protective William is about his patients. But if we're ever to have any chance of apprehending Cisne—and making any charges stick—we must find out who she really is and unfortunately," she dropped her gaze to Qar'qaah, "he's the only one who can tell us."

And if he dies....

"Ensign?"

She turned to find Fleming standing in the doorway.

"We need to make some adjustments on the infusers... and Doctor Amalfitano said to tell you your thirty minutes are up."

Sirin started to protest then realized a Hahtooshan was standing behind the nurse. In the dim light of the corridor, it was impossible to tell who it was, until Fleming entered the cubicle and Jaa'qwah stepped forward, into the doorway.

"I'll remain with him, ta'ashan," the medic said. "You need your rest as well, if you are to help Kon'ta'aq in his recuperation."

Sirin almost smiled. "Then you know what a—"

"Challenge he can be?" he replied, offering her a cloth to wipe the salve from her hands, "Indeed so, ta'ashan."

"But what about the others? I told them—"

"They're all sound asleep, Ensign," Fleming answered. "Exhausted, just like you."

She very reluctantly released her hold on Qar'qaah's wrist, accepted the cloth and rose from the fold down seat as Jaa'qwah and Fleming went about their jobs.

"Ensign?" Izraad prompted from the doorway. "He's in expert hands—now come along."

Chapter 13

Aboard the Baidarka, *1723.*

Sirin stepped across the threshold then took a moment to look around. Her small, neatly organized cabin was just as she'd left it—*how many weeks before?*

Rafe Pierson stood just behind her, in the corridor. The medtech had just happened to slip onto the seat next to hers in ship's largely deserted galley as she picked at a plate of food, a little of this, a little of that that she'd placed on her tray, mostly at the encouragement of one of the cooks who'd spotted her just staring at the array of offerings as if it all just too much to take in, stayed to eat with her and make small talk. After that, he'd made feeble excuses to accompany her to her cabin.

She turned to face him. "Thanks, Rafe. You can tell Doctor Amalfitano that I'll be fine now."

He blinked, feigning innocence. "I don't know what—"

"I know he put you up to it."

Realizing the futility of continuing the pretense, he shrugged. "Was it really that obvious?"

"Let's just say I wouldn't give up your day job, if I were you."

He crossed his arms and huffed, "I volunteered you know—I wasn't conscripted."

That made her laugh. She looked down at herself, at her filthy clothing, then back at the medtech. "You're a very brave man, Rafe."

He chuckled then started to walk away.

"Uh… Rafe?"

He turned back to her, and seeing the look on her face, replied, "I'll call you as soon as we have any news—*promise*. Now get some rest—and, uh," he wrinkled his nose, "if you don't mind me saying so, ma'am, a shower?"

She chuckled, replied, "Definitely a shower," then thumbed the door release and it slipped closed.

For a moment she stared at the door, then turned and looked around once more.

Suddenly her eyes welled up with tears as she remembered that the last time she was here, she was eagerly anticipating her new life with Khusaaq on Tuli. Her future seemed so full of promise, of happiness she never thought she'd find.

Now here she was, literally, back where she'd started.

She angrily wiped the tears away, muttered, "I'm just tired," and strode into the small head.

It didn't help that her shipboard surroundings told her it was mid-morning while her body was under the distinct impression that it was late-evening. On top of that she hadn't slept more than an hour or two at any given time in... she knit her brows and shook her head. *Hell if I remember.*

She slowly, wearily peeled off the torn, soot-stained jumpsuit and reached for the door to the disposa-chute, but just before discarding it, she stopped, fingered the collar and quickly found the tiny, hidden tracking device.

Her face darkened and she whispered, *"Burn in hell for eternity, Tace,"* as she shoved the jumpsuit into the disposa-chute then realized it was evidence—possibly critical evidence in any future board of inquiry, although as far as she could tell, Pardix's complicity was beyond doubt and he'd certainly paid for his crimes. But, she reminded herself, he came from a wealthy family; a family that might go to great lengths to try to clear his name.

She retrieved the jumpsuit, wadded it into a ball and tossed it into the corner, out of the way, then scowled at it. *You're not getting out of a posthumous guilty verdict for murder and kidnapping that easily, you bastard.*

She exhaled, shook her head then stepped into the shower stall.

Fifteen minutes later, and feeling cleaner than she had in well over a week, she stepped out of the stall, grabbed a towel and dried herself off. Then, using it to give her wet hair a quick rub, she walked back into the main cabin... and stopped in her tracks.

Khusaaq sat on the edge of her bunk.

"What..." she gasped, dropping the towel, "what are you doing here? You—"

"Aren't you pleased to see me?" He got back to his feet, the expression on his haggard face deadly serious and worried.

"Of course!"

The expression didn't change as she walked up to him and wrapped her arms around his waist. "What's wrong?"

"You tell me."

She stared into his gray eyes, searching. "Someone's said something, haven't they?"

"Doctor Amalfitano—"

"He had no right to say anything!"

"He felt he did, and we need to talk."

She let go, slumped down on the bed then shivered as a rivulet ran from her still wet hair down her spine.

He snatched up the towel, draped it around her shoulders then eased himself down beside her. "I planned on telling you about Qar'qaah, about who and what he is, truly I did. But the time never seemed right, and I was afraid—"

"Don't you dare say I wouldn't understand," she said with more heat than she intended.

He jerked his gaze off her, fixed it on his knees. After a moment of strained silence, he said, "Quite the contrary. I was afraid you *would* understand."

She eyed him. "I don't... well, I don't understand."

"Understanding and acceptance are not the same thing—"

"And you thought if you told me you had a clone, it would change how I felt about you?"

He turned to face her. "It did, didn't it?"

"Momentarily, well... okay, yes."

"And now?"

"All right, I'm still processing it. And yes, I'm worried about what other bombshells you're withholding, when they might go off. I'd be lying if I said I wasn't. Everyone tells me to give you time, to adjust, that you'll eventually fully open up to me, just as I have with you—"

"But what you don't know about me scares you. *I* scare you." He lurched to his feet.

"That's not what I said! I'm being completely honest with you—"

"You saw part of me in Qar'qaah, and what you saw scared you—*appalled* you, am I correct? You saw an A'tuu'shahn who looks like me, sounds like me, behaving in a way you wanted to believe I was incapable of behaving. Isn't that true?"

She bit her lip, wondering how he had hit so close to the truth. *"Yes."*

He looked away, exhaled forcefully. "I am what I am. I've never hidden *that* from you, I couldn't have, even if I'd wanted to." He shook his head, turned back to her. "You want the truth from me? I kill. I've killed a lot. It's what I do! It's what all A'tuu'shahn'i do! Do I like it? No. I *hate* it. Most of us do. You want to know something else? Qar'qaah is more like me than even I want to admit—he represents everything I hate about myself. And something else. I'm a clone too. And my 'father', Ja'andai? So was he. What else do you want to know—ask me *anything*. Maybe you're wondering how many sentient beings I've killed with my bare hands?" He yanked off his gauntlets, held up his hands for emphasis and she couldn't help but notice they were shaking—from rage, from exhaustion, she couldn't tell. "Or maybe you want to know how many soldiers I've knowingly sent to their deaths, how many innocent civilians—"

"Stop it!" She stood up, walked right up to him and grabbed one hand.

"You wanted to know the truth about me, I'm telling you! Ask me anything—"

"Stop it," she repeatedly, softly, and placed a finger to his lips. *"Stop."*

He squeezed his eyes shut, turned his head away, said in a husky whisper, "I was afraid to tell you—I was afraid if I did, I'd lose everything—*again."*

She tightened her hold on his hand; he responded by running the fingers of his free hand through her clean, damp curls, then enveloped her shoulders with his arm and rested his cheek against the top of her head. She felt his pulse pounding in his wrist, heard his rattling breath, but all too quickly the anger bled out of him and she realized he was leaning more heavily against her.

"I'm sorry—truly," he whispered.

"Me too."

"I love you, toq-bhir."

"I love you too, and you damned well better never ever doubt that or there will be hell to pay, Mister."

He replied with a soft snort.

"Come on." She carefully slipped from his embrace and as he straightened up, she said, "You're about to drop in your tracks, let's get you out of your armor, and then you need to lie down, have a good, solid night's sleep—we both need that. Clearer heads in the clear light of morning, as they say."

He nodded, "But first a shower—I positively reek."

"I wasn't going to mention it, but... well, yeah, ya do."

He managed a tired smile then began shedding his ghillie armor, accompanied by frustrated mutterings on his part as his fingers cramped and his stiffening joints protested. Finally, after several minutes of struggle, the last piece fell away and she stepped close and meeting his exhausted but expectant gaze, lightly caressed him.

He responded with a sharp, and to her deeply satisfying, intake of breath.

Encouraged, she got a firm, one handed grip on him then drew him into the cramped shower stall and under the showerhead. She grasped his buttocks and jerked him against her, then slid her hands up, over the dense knot of tattoos that covered his lower back.

He gasped again and managed, after a moment's distracted fumbling, to press the activator behind him then arched his head back and let the hot water stream over his face and down their naked bodies as he let out a long, contented sigh.

She stepped back, just enough, and took him in, savoring the moment, the nearness of him then grabbed a tube of soap. "Turn around."

He did as he was told and plunged his face into the pulsing stream as she washed his long hair, her hands occasionally straying to his buttocks, his spirit lock and in between his soapy legs. He responded with soft, satisfied sighs.

She thoroughly rinsed the soap from his hair, back and legs, made quick work of plaiting his hair then murmured, "Now turn back to me."

He turned around and watched intently as she washed his arms, his chest, his stomach, his eyes following her every move as her hands ran over his soap-slick skin, her fingertips tracing out his tattoos.

She smiled as she felt his entire body respond to her touch, her lingering caresses.

Finally she washed him off, then stood back and admired her handiwork. Exhausted he might be, but he wasn't *that* exhausted—and suddenly neither was she. She met his now eager gaze, grinned, and licking her lips in anticipation, crooked a finger at him to follow.

Chapter 14

Ensign Corsali's quarters aboard the Baidarka, *0815.*

"Ensign...?"
Sirin groggily opened her eyes and looked around.
"Ensign Corsali, please respond."
For an instant she thought she was dreaming. *Am I really in my cabin?* She recognized the ceiling and felt Khusaaq's familiar warm bulk beside her. *Are you really here?*
Almost afraid to look at him for fear it would break the spell, she carefully wrapped her hand around his wrist. He felt very real—and he sounded very real as he mumbled in his sleep, sighed heavily and smacked his lips.
"Ensign Corsali?" the voice came again, this time more insistent.
Instantly wide awake, realizing it was no dream, realizing it might be sickbay, she carefully levered herself up onto one elbow, so as not to awaken her bedmate, cautiously reached across his bare chest and softly clearing her throat, tapped the activator. *"Yes...?"* she whispered, hoping the person on the other end would respond in kind.
"Ensign, is Sha'ashahn with you?" the day shift comp op's voice boomed from the speaker and she winced.
She leaned over Khusaaq and whispered, "Yes... in fact he's *sound asleep* beside me so will you *please* keep your voice down?"
There was a pause then the comp op replied awkwardly but to her immense relief, softly: *"Oh. Uh... well, um, ma'am, the Commander asks that you and Sha'ashahn please come to Doctor Amalfitano's office as soon as it's... uh, convenient..."*
Amalfitano's office? She felt her pulse leap and she squinted at the speaker, trying not to let her fears get the better of her.
"...but he did say to tell you that this isn't an emergency."
Gee, thanks for not saying that at the start, you—
"Should I tell him this... ah... isn't a good time?"

Her squint crumbled into a glower. *What the hell do you think?* Aloud she whispered, "Tell him we will be there as soon Sha'ashahn wakes up." With that she hit the activator, cutting the connection. *Dammit—*

"Which I suppose means now?" came Khusaaq's sleepy voice.

Sirin looked down at him.

"What's up?" he mumbled as he rubbed one eye.

She carefully eased herself off him and down onto the bunk beside him. "Commander Aquila wants to see us." She lay her head on his shoulder, then slowly ran her hand over his bare chest and down onto his stomach.

"About what?"

Sirin lightly probed his navel. "Didn't say—"

"Shouldn't we get dressed?"

"I… suppose… *so,*" she replied slowly as her fingers began to trace out the tattoo that coiled around Khusaaq's right hip, the same tattoo that completely encircled his upper thigh.

Khusaaq lightly grasped her hand before it could follow the tattoo any further, although it was clearly too late and murmured, "Perhaps you shouldn't start something we don't have time to finish right now."

Sirin lifted her head, scowled at him and grumbled, "Spoilsport."

He sighed and shaking his head, sat up and looked back at her. "Coming?"

"That *had* been my plan if you'd just played along."

He eyed her. "I mean are you going to get up?"

Sirin stuck her tongue out at him.

"That had been my plan, too," Khusaaq grumbled as he knuckle-rubbed one eye.

Sirin snorted in laughter.

Khusaaq rose and offered her his hand. She grasped it and he pulled her to her feet, but instead of letting go, he jerked her against him and nuzzled her neck.

Sirin responded with a throaty moan, then, as he gently fondled one breast while nibbling her earlobe, she managed to stammer, "Didn't... didn't you just... say something about... not... not starting anything?"

He let go and stepped back, well out of reach and grinned wickedly. "Let's just say I owed you."

Doctor Amalfitano's sickbay office, 0907.

"Absolutely not!" Khusaaq shook his head vehemently and, using both hands, angrily pushed himself out of the chair and to his feet. Having no other options, he'd worn his ghillie armor to the meeting, which only added to his intimidating stance.

Izraad, Aquila, Sirin and Amalfitano remained seated, Amalfitano behind his desk, the others in three of the four the chairs that formed a half circle in front of it.

"Sha'ashahn," Izraad continued, *"please,* just hear me—"

"You're asking *me* to give *you* permission to enter his mind! Passive or not, to do such is a direct violation of our most deeply held beliefs and therefore a violation of who and what he is!"

"I'm not asking your permission *to enter his mind,* Sha'ashahn—I thought I made *that* perfectly clear," Izraad replied with audible exasperation. "I'm asking your permission, as his commanding officer, to allow me to *eavesdrop* on his dreams, to see what he's seeing and more importantly, see *whom* he's seeing."

"Sha'ashahn," Aquila said, drawing his fierce gaze. "We all want to catch Cisne. But to do so, we *must* know who she is— and only Qar'qaah had direct and repeated contact with her. Perhaps she even let it slip what her real objective is, which, I suspect, is far more sinister than just the appalling abuse of a Hahtooshan prisoner. We wouldn't ask, wouldn't even consider this if it wasn't our only option."

"Khusaaq," Amalfitano added, "we all know he was horribly brutalized by this person—"

"Indeed," he replied coldly, shifting his hard stare to the doctor.

"So there's something else to consider."

Khusaaq's menacing expression remained unchanged as he asked warily, "Such as?"

"There's an old truism in combat medicine," Amalfitano said, "physical pain is a constant reminder that you survived—psychological pain makes you question if it was worth it." He paused, looked Khusaaq in the eye and added, "If we knew exactly what was done to him, then we'd have a much better idea of how to treat him, and without immediate, effective treatment, this sort of psychological trauma will, no doubt, have long-term, profound effects on his ability to function..."

Khusaaq fixed his slitted stare on the nearby certificate and award decorated wall, his jaw muscles visibly bunched in silent, impotent rage.

"...assuming he doesn't succeed in killing himself at the first opportunity." Amalfitano waited, but when Khusaaq failed to acknowledge the remark, the warning, he looked at Sirin to find her watching Khusaaq, oblivious to all but his intense anger, his profound anguish.

Amalfitano shifted his questioning gaze to Izraad and Aquila.

Izraad shook her head; Aquila only shrugged.

Amalfitano rose, slowly circled his desk and walked over to him, lightly placed his hand on Khusaaq's ghillie-armored shoulder and said quietly, "Please, son, allow us help him."

Khusaaq squeezed his eyes shut and grit his teeth.

"If you wish, you and any of the others can be present. Zarijan *won't* hurt him, we promise you—he won't even be aware of her presence."

"He's Elkanaghalli," Khusaaq whispered, just loud enough for Amalfitano to hear. *"And my doh'ha."*

"I know." Amalfitano tightened his hold on his shoulder, despite his hand's reflexive urge to let go from the armor's rapidly morphing surface. "I also know that I'm painfully ignorant of the complexities of your relationship with him and the full ramifications of what was done to him and why. But I do know this—what Zarijan is offering to do very well might be his *only* hope." He paused then added softly, "You've entrusted me with his body, son. Now you must entrust us with his soul. If we do not do this, we risk losing both."

Finally, and to Amalfitano's immense relief, he felt Khusaaq's rigid shoulders slump.

Khusaaq blew out his cheeks, slowly lifted his head and opened his eyes, then looked back at Izraad. "You have my permission, Lieutenant."

"Thank you, Sha'ashahn." She turned her stare on Amalfitano.

"I'll start weaning him off the sedatives… it'll take several hours. I'll notify you all when it's time." He flicked Izraad a sidelong glance and walked out of his office.

Chapter 15

Isolation unit 2, sickbay, aboard Baidarka, *1406.*

Khusaaq followed Amalfitano into the small isolation cubicle. Izraad was already there, along with Matoosh and Murh'sooli.

The veteran medic had been an obvious choice; Matoosh had requested to be present, as had Sirin.

Khusaaq at first had adamantly refused both, fearful of the effect it might have on Matoosh, and unwilling to expose Qar'qaah and his intensely personal horrors to Sirin, both for his sake and hers.

Sirin had reluctantly agreed to his reasons, but Matoosh had been persistent, his arguments impassioned, persuasive.

Khusaaq, in turn had finally, very grudgingly, agreed.

He acknowledged the three with a glance and a nod, and then crossing his arms, studied Qar'qaah's gaunt face for a moment. Finally he lifted his narrowed stare to the cluster of monitors above the head of the trauma bed.

Amalfitano had timed it perfectly. Critical neurotransmitter levels had dropped dramatically; Qar'qaah's heart rate was increasing in response and his breathing was no longer deep and regular, but shallow, rapid and erratic. Most telling of all: his eyes had begun to dart back and forth beneath closed lids.

His body was now free of the sedatives, his mind loosened from its chemical moorings and drifting slowly upwards, into dream state.

Amalfitano motioned to one of the fold-down chairs and Khusaaq slipped onto it, then he looked across the narrow trauma bed at Izraad as she eased herself down onto the other chair.

Amalfitano then joined Matoosh and Murh'sooli near the doorway.

All had been briefed: no one was to speak; no one was to touch Qar'qaah aside from Izraad.

Khusaaq clasped his hands in his lap, not quite sure what to expect—despite Izraad's assurances that all she was going to do was "eavesdrop" on Qar'qaah's dreams—and at first nothing out of the ordinary happened. Qar'qaah was clearly dreaming. But going by his slight body twitches and slurred mumblings, he was not experiencing anything particularly fearful.

Just as Khusaaq began to question if he'd made the right decision, Qar'qaah groaned and began to breathe heavily.

Khusaaq met Izraad's even gaze.

She nodded, slightly, and turned her full attention on Qar'qaah.

Khusaaq steeled himself, watching her as she lightly stroked Qar'qaah's upper arm, which had been thoroughly cleansed of the salve and firmly secured in a restraint for this very reason.

The faint, sweet scent of a pheromone unleashed a host of all too fresh memories of his own *forcible* mind-strip, in a room only a few meters from this one, by the very woman he was now entrusting with the life—the very soul of his *doh'ha.*

He knew her chempathic touch was needed—the compounds released from her palm and readily absorbed into the pores of Qar'qaah's skin were the final nudge his mind needed to step into his nightmare and, more importantly, remain trapped there, unable to escape into startled wakefulness until Izraad was able to see Cisne through his eyes—Khusaaq had reluctantly agreed to that, too.

It has to be done! he angrily reminded himself. *We have to know. I'm sorry... I'm so terribly sorry—*

"Chulh..." Qar'qaah twitched and mumbled softly, "...chulh, chulh... tu-mazneri..." Then, abruptly, he started to struggle for air as the terrors took hold. *"Tohiss-mat...chulh, chulh...!"*

The over-bed monitors confirmed it: heart rate, breathing, brain activity had increased significantly.

Amalfitano turned to the nearby drug cart and quietly withdrew a preloaded ject-it.

Izraad flicked him, then Khusaaq a warning look as she tightened her hold on Qar'qaah's restrained arm.

"Tu-mazneri...!" Qar'qaah sobbed and tried to pull away from her as he tossed his head back and forth. Then he began to whimper in mounting fear.

Khusaaq found himself fighting the almost overwhelming urge to shake him awake.

"Chulh... tohiss-mat," Qar'qaah groaned. *"Chulh... chulh..."* He began to pant, then suddenly his back arched and he groaned again, this time in sheer agony. He no sooner fell back onto the bed then his body convulsed again, and then again and again.

Khusaaq, unable to witness his helpless terror, the excruciating pain any longer, fixed his wide-eyed stare on Izraad to find that she'd lost her expression of intense, but detached interest. Her face was now a mirror of Qar'qaah's, twisting and grimacing as his mind relived the horrors that had tormented both his sleep and his waking hours from the moment he had fallen into Cisne's clutches.

Izraad was now in the midst of the nightmare, living the recalled experiences just as Qar'qaah had experienced them first-hand and was experiencing again—feeling, seeing, hearing exactly what he felt, saw and heard. Until that moment, Khusaaq hadn't comprehended the full scope of what she had volunteered to do. And going strictly by her rapidly changing expressions, what she was experiencing was truly horrific—

Qar'qaah screamed, startling everyone, as he feebly struggled against unseen attackers then he began gulping noiselessly, his chest muscles straining as if he was suffocating.

Izraad yanked her hand away. Clutching her own throat, she lurched to her feet and stumbled back into a very shaken Matoosh.

He instinctively grabbed her, steadying her as she continued to gasp for air while staring wide-eyed down at Qar'qaah.

Amalfitano gave her shoulders a firm shake and whispered, *"Zarijan—break the connection!"* as Khusaaq leapt to his feet, not sure what to do, what to say.

When Izraad failed to respond, but continued to strain for each breath, her wild, unblinking eyes fixed on Qar'qaah, Amalfitano turned to Matoosh and hissed: *"Get her out of here—now!"*

Matoosh wordlessly scooped her up into his arms and hurried from the cubicle.

Amalfitano shoved the jet-it he'd been holding against Qar'qaah's knotted thigh as Qar'qaah continued to struggle for breath.

"What's happening?" Khusaaq demanded in a harsh whisper.

"Hell if I know!" Amalfitano dropped all pretense at speaking quietly. "But we're heavily sedating him again—and until we know exactly what we're dealing with, he's gonna stay that way." He smacked the intercom with the flat of his hand as Murh'sooli began pulling more vials from the drug cart. "Meerut... *get the hell in here!"* Then he turned to Khusaaq. "You—*out!"*

"But—"

"Now!"

Khusaaq started to back-step towards the door as Meerut slipped around him and over to the bed. He hesitated as he gave Qar'qaah one last look—Qar'qaah no longer struggled for air; he was now breathing peacefully, his body and tear-streaked face completely relaxed, as if nothing was amiss.

"Out," Amalfitano said again, but this time a little more gently. "Go on, son."

Khusaaq wet his lips, then reluctantly turned and strode into the airlock.

As he stepped out and into the main infirmary, he saw Fleming, Rosen, Pierson and Bar'ahani clustered around Izraad. The woman was sprawled on the floor next to the nurses' station. Matoosh stood nearby, powerless to do anything but watch.

Khusaaq strode over to Fleming just as she pressed a ject-it against Izraad's shoulder and asked huskily, "Is she going to be all right?"

"I think so." She handed Rosen the ject-it, then looked up at Pierson. "Rafe, get a stasis board."

"No." Khusaaq knelt, carefully slipped his arms under Izraad's back and knees then drew the now unconscious woman against him and rose. "Where?"

Fleming jerked her chin towards one of the triage bays. "In there."

He nodded and followed the doctor into the bay, but he'd no sooner placed Izraad on the triage bed than he was squeezed out of the cramped bay by the crush of staff. He exhaled and as he walked back over to Matoosh, he realized that the soldier looked to be as deeply shaken by the entire experience as he was, if not more so.

Matoosh cautiously met his gaze, but there was nothing to say, no words to share. So they stood together in uneasy silence, unsure whether to remain or leave while sickbay staff hurried by, oblivious to them and their pleading, helpless stares.

Chapter 16

Isolation unit 2, sickbay, aboard Baidarka, *1443.*

"That went well, don't ya think?" Amalfitano growled.

Meerut exchanged sidelong glances with Murh'sooli then the nurse and medic both looked at the doctor as Meerut replied, "We'll stay here with him, sir." She jerked her chin towards the door. "I think Khusaaq and Matoosh are in dire need of some fatherly reassurance."

"What about me?" Amalfitano snapped.

Meerut replied with a forced chuckle. "Sorry, Chief. You're on your own."

He squinted at her, shook his head, then handed Murh'sooli the expended ject-it. As he turned to the doorway, Murh'sooli suddenly reached out and grabbed him by the shoulder.

Amalfitano glanced at him, startled.

Murh'sooli gave his shoulder a commiserating squeeze, then let go.

Taken aback by the medic's unexpected and totally out of character gesture, Amalfitano momentarily forgot what he'd been doing. Then he remembered: 'fatherly reassurance.' He hurried out of the cubicle and into the airlock.

A moment later he stepped out to find the two Hahtooshans in question standing not far from the door to his office. Both looked utterly despondent.

"You two." He motioned to them. "With me." He started towards the doorway to his office.

Realizing they hadn't moved, he looked back at them. "Come on, both of you. *Now.*"

This time Khusaaq followed. Matoosh, with a quick glance back at the isolation unit, silently took up the rear.

Amalfitano headed for his desk, motioned to the group of chairs still clustered in front of it, and muttered, "Sit." Then he eased himself down into his own chair and looked first at Khusaaq and then Matoosh. "Qar'qaah's all right—*okay?* No harm done. So relax."

"And the Lieutenant?" Khusaaq asked quietly.

"Zarijan's a helluva lot tougher than she looks," Amalfitano said. Only then did he realize he wasn't sure if he'd said that for Khusaaq's sake or for his own.

Khusaaq shook his head and fixed his slitted eyes on his knees. Suddenly his face contorted in impotent rage and he smacked the arms of his chair with his fists with enough force to dent the composite and bring tears to his eyes. *"I never should've agreed to this!"*

Amalfitano shifted his startled, unblinking stare from Khusaaq to Matoosh.

Matoosh was watching Khusaaq, a stricken look on his face.

Cazzo. Amalfitano yanked open the bottom drawer of his desk and withdrew the hidden decanter of his best whisky—not the cheap, rotgut stuff he'd bought on Tuli for unwelcome guests—and three mismatched glasses. "I think we could all use a stiff drink."

At the clink of glassware, Matoosh slowly pulled his uneasy gaze off Khusaaq and fixed it on Amalfitano.

Amalfitano filled each of the glasses almost to the rim then pushed one across his desk to Matoosh, and the other towards Khusaaq. He then picked up the third. "Go on."

Matoosh followed suit, but Khusaaq continued to stare dejectedly at his knees, lost in his own thoughts, his own horrors.

Amalfitano sighed, then brought his glass to his lips and was privately relieved when Matoosh did the same, albeit with little enthusiasm.

Finally Khusaaq looked up and saw the glass. Without saying a word, he grabbed it, downed its potent contents in several loud, grimacing gulps, slammed the glass down on the desk, lurched to his feet and stormed from the office.

Matoosh put his now half empty glass on the desk and began to push himself out of his chair, to follow.

"No."

Matoosh stopped in mid-push.

"Sit back down, son. I think he wants to be alone. You, on the other hand, look like you are in dire need of some company."

Matoosh glanced back at the now empty doorway as he slowly sank back down onto the chair.

"Your brother just needs to work off some steam."

"Steam...?"

"Anger—guilt, or more accurately, a combination of both."

Matoosh nodded, picked up his glass and after a moment, took a deep gulp. He swallowed, frowned at the liquor's unfamiliar taste. Then staring at the glass clutched in his hand, he asked, "Now what?"

"Hope to hell whatever Zarijan saw is enough to finger this goddamned monster." Amalfitano took an angry sip, and then another.

"And if the Lieutenant *didn't* see enough?" Matoosh's normally gravelly voice was a harsh, hoarse whisper. His question had occurred to Amalfitano as well, one he had been unwilling to voice aloud.

"I don't know, son." He took another, deeper gulp, then grabbed the bottle and quickly refilled their glasses. "I just don't know."

Chapter 17

Sirin's quarters aboard the Baidarka, *1710.*

"They're waiting for us," Sirin murmured as she stared down at Khusaaq.

He'd appeared, extremely distraught, at her door over two hours before. She didn't have to ask why; she'd been waiting anxiously for word of what Izraad had gleaned from Qar'qaah's dreams. As if she couldn't have guessed, Pierson had given her a heads up.

The pungent smell of alcohol on Khusaaq's breath had confirmed her worst fears.

She'd just been thankful he'd come to her, instead of retreating into the bastion of the *Jirah*, which was now berthed in the *Baidarka*'s cargo bay, sealing himself physically and emotionally inside while shutting everyone else out.

He'd wordlessly paced her small cabin like a caged tiger for several minutes then had abruptly sprawled out on her bunk only to stare up at the ceiling. She'd seated herself next to his hip, then tentatively interlaced her fingers with his and was relieved when he didn't pull away, in fact he'd tightened his hold and with a weary sigh, closed his eyes.

Then came the unexpected page from Amalfitano, requesting that they return to sickbay.

At first, when Khusaaq failed to react, Sirin thought he'd managed to fall into an exhausted asleep, or, more likely, was so caught up in his own chaotic thoughts that he hadn't heard the page. Then she looked down to find him staring up at her.

She smiled, released her hold and rose.

He slowly pushed himself to a seated position, dropped his booted feet to the deck, raked his hair off his forehead with both hands then stood.

She held out her hand.

He took her hand in his, and together they walked out of her cabin.

A few minutes later they found themselves seated beside each other in Amalfitano's office, staring at Amalfitano's untidy desk and empty chair. To Khusaaq's left sat Aquila. To Sirin's right sat a very drawn, and, to her critical eye, mildly intoxicated Matoosh.

Realizing he was watching her out of the corner of a rather blood-shot eye, she gave his knee a gentle, commiserating squeeze. Matoosh surprised her when he didn't immediately pull away. Instead he responded with a quick and decidedly half-hearted smile.

"William said he'd be with us shortly," Aquila said as Khusaaq's apprehensive gaze flicked back to the doorway, the second time in less than a minute.

"Yes," Khusaaq replied and shifted uneasily in his chair. He jerked his eyes back to the doorway as they heard approaching footsteps. Then he hurriedly rose and turned; Matoosh, Aquila and Sirin followed suit.

Amalfitano was the first to enter, followed by Izraad, assisted by Bar'ahani, and behind them the faint, ghostly distortion of another of Amalfitano's bodyguards, and lastly, to Sirin's surprise, Endooki.

"Please." Amalfitano motioned for them to resume their seats as Bar'ahani helped Izraad to another chair, the woman still shaken by her ordeal.

Once Izraad was seated, the imposing and normally standoffish Bar'ahani positioned herself behind Izraad, one tattooed hand lightly resting protectively on Izraad's shoulder. Sirin almost smiled.

Bit by bit, shared experience by shared experience, the gulf between Hahtooshan and human, which at first had appeared unbridgeable, was shrinking—the shock of the other had finally begun to wear off, at least among those aboard the *Baidarka*. Each no longer looked upon the other as implacable adversaries with inexplicable motives, enigmatic enemies to be feared, distrusted and hated. They were now individuals who stood together on common ground and with common humanity. It gave her a glimmer of hope for the alliance as a whole.

Amalfitano slipped onto his own chair, looked around at the expectant faces and cleared his throat. "Let me first say that due to the expert care of Murh'sooli and Jaa'qwah, and of course Tayya'shan and Bar'ahani here," he looked first at the grim-faced medic who stood behind Izraad, then acknowledged her invisible companion by nodding to where he assumed the medic might be standing, not far from the doorway, "Qar'qaah's poisoning is responding much quicker than expected to treatment. Same's true for the other four rescued from Rasal Ghul." He paused and smiled warmly at Endooki. Then, with a sidelong look at Khusaaq, he added, "If Qar'qaah continues the same rate of improvement, my plan is to wake him up perhaps as early as tomorrow morning and start him on some limited physical therapy within a few days."

Khusaaq replied with an apprehensive nod.

That was the good news, Sirin thought as she too braced herself for the other shoe—or in this case campaign boot—to drop.

Amalfitano leaned back in his chair, crossed his arms and looked at Izraad. "Zarijan?"

The diminutive woman made eye contact with each, then locked gazes with Khusaaq and began without preamble, "I *saw* Cisne, Sha'ashahn. I now know who, or should I say more importantly, *what* she is."

Matoosh breathed an audible sigh of relief; he almost smiled as he again shared a sidelong glance with Sirin.

"And what is that?" Khusaaq leaned forward in his chair.

"Hahtooshan."

"What?" Sirin gasped. "No! She's a colonial fanatic—"

"That's what she wanted everyone to think," Izraad replied, again fixing her eyes on Khusaaq. "She is, without a doubt, Hahtooshan, Sha'ashahn, and not just any Hahtooshan, but *Elkanaghalli*—she said as much to her most trusted confederate, this oft-mentioned Matarran doctor—"

"Some doctor," Amalfitano grumbled, *"more like butcher."*

"—while Qar'qaah was unconscious and his subconscious mind heard, and *remembered.*"

Khusaaq digested that, then turned to a still stunned Sirin and said, "It's never been a secret that many A'tuu'shahn'i, even some Elkanaghalli'i wanted me dead, especially now, but—"

"Why would she do what she did to Qar'qaah?" Sirin asked as she lightly rested one hand on Khusaaq's taut forearm and the other on Matoosh's knee. "Of all people she would have known to mind-strip him—"

"Qar'qaah wasn't mind-stripped," Izraad interrupted.

Sirin blinked, suddenly wondering why she'd assumed he had, as if mind-stripping was the worst possibility and explained all. "But—"

"We know he was placed in a stasis pod," Izraad continued, "not just once, but repeatedly and always without any proper prep. He was also severely and repeatedly beaten."

Khusaaq nodded curtly, clearly anticipating more and much worse.

Izraad paused then added, "It truly pains me to tell you this, Sha'ashahn, but he was also sexually assaulted by Cisne... and by each of her crew."

Khusaaq stared at her. Then clenching his teeth, he squeezed his eyes shut.

Matoosh muttered an obscenity as his hands balled into white-knuckled fists.

Endooki and Bar'ahani reacted with wide-eyed horror.

Gods, Sirin thought as she suddenly recalled his reaction to the impromptu bath. *That's what you were trying to tell me—that's why you were so scared—*

"I'd surmised as much," Amalfitano murmured, "due to the nature of some of his physical injuries."

That news left everyone looking like they were about to be physically ill.

Izraad gave all of them a few minutes then rose unsteadily. Waving off Bar'ahani's proffered hand, she walked up to Amalfitano's desk. She cleared her throat, drawing their uneasy stares. "With Endooki's help, I've created an image of what she looks like." She reached over, tapped a series of commands into the desktop computer interface and then turned the small desk mounted screen outwards.

Khusaaq and Matoosh leaned forward and stared at the image, each with a look of absolute murder in his eyes.

The middle-aged woman's face that stared back was—at least to Sirin—disappointingly ordinary. Then she reminded herself that monsters rarely looked like monsters—true evil more often than not came guised in commonplace blandness, all the better to insinuate itself—her brief experience with the late Captain Mladić was proof enough of that.

Beside her, Khusaaq shifted uneasily in his chair, his expression one of growing apprehension... coupled with hesitant, almost reluctant recognition. Suddenly his eyes widened and he gasped, *"Ekkorh-tath...!"*

"You know her," Izraad replied as a statement of fact.

Khusaaq swallowed convulsively then managed to stammer as he pointed a shaky finger at the image, "That's... that's Pashna'gaalan ket Tashar'anhi—*I'm sure of it.*"

"Pash...ah who?" Aquila asked.

Khusaaq eyes darted to Aquila then back to Izraad. "Pashna'gaalan ket Tashar'anhi. Gaalan... she was Nahru'tzrhi of *Huui'teh*—the original *Huui'teh.* But she was killed when *Huui'teh* was destroyed defending Cotopaxi—"

"That's what you," Izraad interrupted, "what all Hahtooshans were supposed to think. And it worked. She was, in a word, *smug,* about just how easy it was to fool the entire Orthodoxy when she discussed the matter in front of Qar'qaah to her Matarran confidant."

"But... but *why?"* Khusaaq asked, his voice cracking.

"Why fake her death? Why want you dead? Why do what she did to Qar'qaah?"

He dropped his stunned gaze back to the image and slowly shook his head. "Nahru'tzrhi was one of the most highly decorated officers in the fleet—she inspired such loyalty in her crews..." He took a deep, steadying breath then continued huskily, "I would have willingly died for her—all of us would have."

"And all but five of you did on Cotopaxi," Izraad replied.

He bit his lip, added huskily, "And now I'm the last. The sole survivor of Cotopaxi."

"Precisely."

Khusaaq stared at her for a moment. Then his gaze returned to the image as if it held the answers he so desperately sought.

"But what about her tattoos," Sirin asked, "the scarification—"

"When an A'tuu'shahn is completely isolated from other A'tuu'shahn'i for even a short period of time," Khusaaq said, "their tattoos, their unique *kaa-shaai*—"

"Grow fainter?" Sirin interrupted.

Khusaaq nodded, as did Bar'ahani and Endooki, but it was Matoosh who answered: "It's called *turee*—the diminishing, the physical manifestation of being left behind, utterly alone, abandoned *even* by the Elkanasu."

"Why didn't yours fade?" Sirin turned back to Khusaaq.

"You mean why didn't mine fade while I was here, in sickbay? Because Matoosh was near me and I was near him and there were other A'tuu'shahn'i aboard as well. Proximity, that's enough. But we're speaking of cases of total separation, complete isolation." He paused, then added, "Those who prefer a more secular explanation," his eyes flicked to Bar'ahani, "claim it's nothing more a physiological response to extreme stress. Regardless of the cause, it's a well-documented phenomenon. Eventually, as the theory goes, the *kaa-shaai* will disappear completely, along with the individual's unique interference pattern and aura. Elkanaghalli'i, Kri'taaka'i and Chah'duu'i believe when that happens, the individual dies. Clearly this is not the case."

"Which is why Qar'qaah did not recognize her as Hahtooshan," Izraad said, "despite doing all he could to memorize her scent, her appearance." She nodded to Endooki. "Even her aura had transformed to the point she no longer read as what she really was, but rather as simply human."

"Indeed," Endooki replied. "I never had any suspicion, any doubt she was anything but human."

"And as for the scarification," Amalfitano said, "it would be a simple cosmetic procedure for even the most mediocre surgeon—say, like this *doctor* of hers?"

"I'd heard rumors," Khusaaq continued, "we all have." He looked at each of the other Hahtooshans present, "Of renegade A'tuu'shahn'i, those who chose..." his voice trailed off as his gaze turned inward.

Everyone turned to him, wondering, suddenly worried, waiting for him to continue and when he didn't Sirin prompted gently, *"Khusaaq...?"*

He blinked then turned to her and in a voice barely above a whisper said: "I've lived my entire life for this moment, anticipated the ultimate freedom, to experience... *everything.*"

Sirin raised her brows. "What? I don't understand—"

"Those... those are almost the last words Gaalan said to me." His gaze shifted to Izraad. "For A'tuu'shahn'i, to speak of the ultimate freedom... I took it she was fully embracing her imminent death by remaining aboard *Huui'teh,* to keep the Matarii occupied while the surviving crew, myself included, flicked down to the planet. But... that's not what she meant at all." He squeezed his eyes shut, shook his head and exhaled slowly.

Sirin risked a sidelong glance at Amalfitano to find his anguished expression mirrored Khusaaq's.

"Gaalan was hailed as an Elkanaghalli martyr." Khusaaq opened his eyes to again stare, unblinking, at the image with a look of utter bewilderment. "An intoxicating symbol of the ultimate sacrifice for those of us who longed for our ancient, honorable way of life. To that end I've always maintained that she, and all who died aboard *Huui'teh* and on the surface defending the colony, protecting the colonists, were the true heroes of Cotopaxi..."

Sirin couldn't help but wince at the profound betrayal in his voice.

"...but what happened afterwards, in combination with other *concurrent* events," he added cryptically as he again made brief eye contact with his fellow Hahtooshans, each of whom nodded knowingly in response, "left such a terrible, open wound on our collective psyche that the Q'shaathrah decided a *living* symbol was needed—not a martyr, we had far too many of those. Proof to all that despite the terrible costs, despite unspeakable duplicities, we had ultimately prevailed."

He shook his head. "For the longest time I shunned the 'honor' until I was convinced by others that by doing so, I drew even more unwanted attention on myself, as well as betraying the memory of those who died, Gaalan most of all."

"When in truth she was the one who betrayed her ship," Izraad said gently, "her crew, her people, to the enemy—"

Khusaaq looked sharply at her. "Many say I have done the same."

Izraad acknowledged that simple, painful truth, not to mention the menacing look in his eyes with a slight dip of her head. "Indeed."

Khusaaq chuckled bitterly, said, "Her very last words to me were, 'Do me proud, Ruh'ta'aq,' so perhaps she knew me better than I thought."

An awkward silence followed, then:

"But… why kidnap Qar'qaah and the others in the first place?" Sirin asked, wanting to shift the subject away from Khusaaq and back to Cisne.

Izraad turned to Khusaaq. "I'd say her rationale was pretty straightforward: she hoped it would provoke you into reacting recklessly, without thought for your own safety, drawing in the Orthodoxy with you and plunging the entire Rim into all-out war, a war she and her confederates would profit nicely from."

At Khusaaq's arched stare, she added, "It was evident from the snatches of conversations Qar'qaah's subconscious overheard that she and her companions are arms merchants, and very successful ones too—but there's more to it, a lot more." She paused again, clearly wanting to give everyone a chance to digest what she'd said.

Khusaaq exhaled forcefully. Matoosh shifted in his chair as he slowly shook his head.

Sirin murmured, *"So, you were wrong,"* in the process drawing everyone's sidelong, puzzled stares.

"Wrong...?" Izraad repeated.

Sirin jerked her head up to meet the woman's questioning stare. "Not you, Lieutenant, no. Qar'qaah. Something he said to Urbat, while we were still aboard the freighter. Urbat told us that he was planning on using Khusaaq as the fuse to ignite a galactic war," she nodded to Izraad, "by handing him over to the colonial fanatics—*to Cisne*—and then, according to Urbat, when the Orthodoxy saw what the colonists did to their… *hero*," she tightened her hold on Khusaaq's wrist and met his gaze, "the Hahtooshan-Coalition alliance would go *boom*. Only problem was—unbeknownst to Urbat—he didn't have you in his grasp, he had Qar'qaah. Qar'qaah, as you can imagine," she favored Matoosh with a glance, "was quite happy to enlighten him as to this critical blunder in mistaken identity."

Matoosh managed to chuckle softly, acknowledging her astute grasp of Qar'qaah's own penchant for reckless impertinence.

"He said…" Sirin knit her brows, "now let me get this right… ah, yes… he said, 'As for using me as a fuse to ignite a galactic war, as much as I'd love to believe I'm a critical component in the greater scheme of things and without me the universe would come to a screeching halt, the truth is I'm of absolutely no consequence—no one cares whether I live or die…'" she looked at Khusaaq, "'…not even Sha'ashahn.'"

Khusaaq winced, then blew out his cheeks and shook his head.

"As I said," she gave his hand another squeeze, "he was *wrong*… about a lot of things."

Izraad gave Khusaaq a moment before she continued. "I have no explanation, no rationale for why she took matters one step further and abused Qar'qaah in such a truly horrific manner aside from the obvious, which is that he was a stand-in for you—which begs the question, *why* you. But I can tell you this with absolute certainty: she may claim to be sympathetic to the colonial fanatics, in fact vehemently maintained such to her hired crew, along with selling colony worlds contraband arms and the like at highly inflated prices, but as I started to say before, there's more to it. You see, her true loyalties, without question, lie with the Matarrans and have, for a very, *very* long time."

"Before Cotopaxi?" Khusaaq asked, almost reluctantly.

She nodded. "Her betrayal of the original *Huui'teh* and its crew, not to mention the colony, was not some last minute decision to save herself. She had everything planned well in advance. She said as much to her doctor, her close confidant and likely Matarran handler, and again, within earshot of Qar'qaah, believing him to be unconscious or she simply didn't care if he overheard as I doubt she planned on letting him live once she had entrapped you."

"But... that doesn't make sense," Khusaaq countered, "we were at Cotopaxi to defend the colony against the Matarii!"

"And so you did, heroically, I might add—and I mean that *truly*, Sha'ashahn," she added quickly as he opened his mouth to deflect the comment, "but if someone wanted to fake his or her death, what better way than to go out in a blaze of glory? With no evidence remaining to the contrary, no one would have suspected a thing—and by your own admission, no one ever did."

He gave his head a shake as if to clear it, followed by an almost dismissive look in his eye that said, 'I'll deal with this later—too much now'.

Izraad continued, "Along with your name, Sha'ashahn, she mentioned another to her confederate—"

"Ja'andai," he interrupted with absolute certainty.

Sirin looked at Izraad, then back at Khusaaq as she gave his balled fist a gentle, prodding squeeze. The name was familiar—but before she could recall why, Aquila asked,

"Who's this... Ja'andai?"

Izraad answered, "Ja'andai'yalhah Abhijit'tischinjgra was Sha'ashahn's *ta'katleh*—"

"My... genetic progenitor," Khusaaq interrupted, "One could say he was my father." He briefly met Amalfitano's worried stare.

"You spoke of him to me," Amalfitano replied. "You said he'd been killed when you were very young—"

"At Tindari, yes," Khusaaq finished for him. "Gaalan was there too and served with him. She was awarded our highest commendation for her actions, as was Ja'andai—posthumously. But what should have been a shining moment in our two families' shared history was tainted by rumors that Ja'andai and Gaalan had had a physical relationship—an absolute taboo on so many levels and an accusation that was immediately dismissed by Tashar'anhi'i and Abhijit'tischinjgra'i. Elkanaghalli'i as a whole blamed it on the Khighalli'i—yet another blatant attempt on their part to discredit our caste's accomplishments, especially in light of their less than spectacular feats during the campaigns at Grus's Ghost and Peshitta.

"Had Ja'andai survived, he would have been able to successfully rebuff the obviously trumped up allegations, but Gaalan, while extremely charismatic, was not as politically adroit. Her rapid rise through the ranks had upset a lot of people, even some of the more orthodox Elkanaghalli'i, who while defending her publicly, privately felt her ruthless, even what they deemed as shameless methods for advancement were unbecoming of someone of her lineage and more befitting that of a Khighalli or Barkaat.

"After Tindari she was offered, one might say forced into what was a step-back in such an illustrious career: to train officer-candidates. While it was promoted as a tremendous honor, a way of recognizing her unique military skills, sharing them with a new generation, it was in fact nothing more than a way to side-line her, to diminish her power..."

"A good enough reason to want to seek revenge," Aquila interjected softly with a sidelong look at Izraad.

Izraad for her part stared back, tight-lipped. Sirin caught her expression, realized there was more, but the woman was holding back, clearly waiting to see what Khusaaq already knew.

"...or so her detractors thought," Khusaaq added, oblivious. "She used that position to raise a generation of A'tuu'shahn'i from all castes who were fanatically devoted to her. Not only that, as their direct mentor, she could rightfully claim—and did—a sizeable percentage of any profits these officers made from the very lucrative contracts she, using her connections, funneled to them. Which made these now high ranking and very successful officers even more faithful to her. So the plan to defang her... backfired and backfired spectacularly. And many have remained fiercely loyal to her memory, even after all these years, after *everything...*"

Sirin studied Khusaaq's distant expression as he continued to speak. She was amazed, stunned in fact, that he was suddenly so candid, and not just with her, but with others. It was as if the shock of seeing Gaalan, realizing she wasn't dead and worse, was a turncoat, made everything he'd believed in a lie, a lie he now desperately wanted to fully expose as if by doing so, it would somehow all make sense.

She risked a sidelong, anxious glance at Amalfitano; he held up a finger, signal not to say or do anything to interfere, to let Khusaaq speak while he was in an uncharacteristically talkative frame of mind.

"By the time I was old enough to begin my official training," Khusaaq obliged, lost in his own memories, "she was a very wealthy, very powerful woman. She demanded that I serve under her, saying she'd been following my progress, had promised Ja'andai she'd watch over me, to train me up to be every bit as good as he was, if not better—"more than a suitable replacement", as she said to the Q'shaathrah when she requested me.

"Ja'andai had remained very popular, a now greatly idealized defender and symbol of the old ways, which made this a controversial move on her part as it instantly rekindled the rumors about her alleged relationship with him—Khighalli'i again began to whisper things, ugly things, eager as always to exploit any scrap of damaging hearsay about an Elkanaghalli, no matter how farfetched; many Elkanaghalli'i and Kri'taaka'i urged her to pick another Abhijit'tischinjgra, there were certainly plenty of suitable candidates—more promising in fact, but she thought she was untouchable and I suppose she was. To placate them, she also demanded Sahr'qharubi ket Rasharawan'tischinjgra—Qharubi, a close kinsman—we ended up serving together until... until *Makhaira* was destroyed over Tuli.

"At the time, Qharubi and I were too young to understand the power struggles going on behind the scenes. We were both deeply honored—I was shocked, to be truthful, when I was told she'd personally requisitioned me for her next training tour. I'd been a rather... well, mediocre student you see, easily distracted—and worse, I questioned everything, even our core beliefs, naïvely believing nothing should be off-limits..."

Sirin couldn't help but notice Matoosh's sad smile and nod.

"...and despite being Ja'andai's *doh'ha*, I never felt as if I was truly his clone. He never wasted an opportunity to let me know just how supremely disappointed he was in me. By the time Gaalan asked for me, my family had accepted that my prospects were, to be kind, not good, not like Ja'andai. They were as stunned as I was; to them the old allegations were of no matter. Gaalan would, they were convinced, finally mold me into a faithful copy of Ja'andai, maybe even something better.

"Every officer-trainee wanted to serve under Gaalan as it almost guaranteed you your choice of assignments, your choice of ships and crews when the time came. For her to pick me... well, I didn't believe it until I received my official transfer papers. Of course there were those who whispered that I was being singled out for special treatment because of her supposed relationship with Ja'andai, but on that first tour and the second—which ended at Cotopaxi—she never once behaved towards me in anything less than a purely professional manner, at least not that I, an admittedly very naïve young Elkanaghalli, was aware of.

"I had no unexplained privileges, no special treatment—and she was a very hard, very demanding taskmaster, especially on that second tour. I felt as if I was never good enough, that I'd never live up to Ja'andai's reputation or Gaalan's expectations—but she always said she had full faith in me, that she could see things in me that Ja'andai hadn't seen, that I couldn't see, wouldn't see until I was older. But that was her way, with *every* member of her hand-picked crews—she demanded more than you ever thought you were capable of, could cut you to the bone with just a look or a single word, but she also encouraged in a way that made you want to try even harder."

He shook his head and looking down at his knees, added softly, "Gaalan was also the major force behind creating Qar'qaah, and while the immediate family was still in the official mourning. Her actions were considered most... *inappropriate*, especially in light of the fact that there was already a *doh'ha—me*, and what's more, she was Tashar'anhi, not Abhijit'tischinjgra, the two families separated by a number of blood lines.

"Two *doh'ha* from the same *ta'katleh*—the same progenitor—alive at the same time... it was simply unheard of, at least in recent times, and few believed Ja'andai, despite his truly impressive achievements, warranted such an unprecedented honor. And of course her pushing so quickly for another *doh'ha* stirred the rumor pot. But she had the political clout to make it happen, playing on her status as Hero of Tindari, and before that Ladjah-Höyük and Pu'taak's Rift, playing on Ja'andai's immense popularity especially among Elkanaghalli'i and Kri'taaka'i, which had only increased a thousand fold since his death. The Q'shaathrah was loath to refuse her and her supporters, or, perhaps in truth they were afraid to refuse her, fearing she could in fact force the issue.

"But then more rumors, even uglier rumors, began... that Qar'qaah was not in fact a *doh'ha*, but instead the product of Gaalan and Ja'andai's illicit union—that she wanted a cover story to hide her pregnancy, thus saving her hard-won reputation, along with Ja'andai's. Many believed the Q'shaathrah would have gone along with such a cover-up to avoid such a major scandal that would have destroyed her career and Ja'andai's legacy and likely torn the Q'shaathrah apart along religious and secular caste lines, risking civil war. Of course I knew nothing about this, not until much later, once Qar'qaah was well into childhood and after Gaalan's death—I mean, when she was no longer there to shield either of us."

Sirin couldn't help it—she gave Matoosh an oblique look.

He stared back, his heavily scarred and tattooed face now expressionless.

"If you don't mind me asking," Aquila said, "why did she insist on another *doh'ha*—she had to have known beforehand the consequences of doing so?"

Khusaaq shook his head. "I never thought to ask her, believe it or not... well, that's not entirely true. Truth was, I was afraid to ask, and Qar'qaah and I have dealt with the fallout ever since. Perhaps she was testing just how far she could push things, demonstrating to those who'd tried to sideline her just how powerful she truly was. Gaalan did love to see people she felt had wronged her squirm." He shrugged, added, "Perhaps it was nothing more than that."

For several minutes no one spoke, no one moved as they waited for Khusaaq to elaborate. Instead he abruptly pushed himself out of his chair and to his feet.

Matoosh followed as Endooki and Bar'ahani, who'd been standing at parade rest, snapped to rigid attention.

"Commander," Khusaaq said as he turned to Aquila, "I must contact Narbrooi Hahtra'tzrhi and notify him of developments."

"Of course."

Khusaaq looked at Sirin, at Amalfitano and Izraad, and finally, Aquila. "Those officers I mentioned, the ones who have remained ferociously loyal to Gaalan all these years?"

Aquila nodded.

"Many are also ferociously opposed to the alliance between your peoples and mine—using Cotopaxi and what happened afterwards as their own rallying cry...."

"Remember Raumalle," Amalfitano murmured, then met Khusaaq's gaze. "The ultimate opportunists, like the Raumalle Revengers—none of whom were actually *there*, as the loudest of loudmouths rarely are, politicizing a tragedy to advance their own extremist agendas."

Khusaaq nodded, then continued, "Gaalan's sudden reappearance, regardless of the cause, will likely cause a great deal of turmoil, possibly even a public split among the two factions. She was a master of manipulation after all—I doubt she's lost any of that skill, living as she has with the Matarii for all of these years."

"You're suggesting a Hahtooshan civil war," Aquila replied, "with a Matarran collaborator lighting the fuse—"

"Instead of me igniting one between the Orthodoxy and the Coalition, *yes.* Now, Commander, I ask that you immediately recall your people from the surface, break orbit as soon as they are aboard—and return to Tuli as fast as you can."

Aquila arched a brow. "I don't—"

"You do not want to be here when *Faridour* and her outriders arrive."

"Arrive? But—"

"Gaalan *was*—correction—*is* Narbrooi Hahtra'tzrhi's *li-a'itat*... his older sister."

Sirin eyes widened as it suddenly dawned on her that *this* was the mysterious reason the officer had been so vindictively unhelpful in setting up Tuli's com-net. In Narbrooi's eyes, Khusaaq had supplanted his own sister as the Hero of Cotopaxi, which perhaps to the sanctimonious admiral was an even greater sin than his oft-voiced contempt at Khusaaq for willingly turning his back on the Elkanasu—

"And you think he will come to her support?" Aquila asked, clearly horrified at the idea. Others too shifted uneasily in their chairs as the implications of such came into sharp focus.

Khusaaq shook his head. "Quite the contrary, Commander. Trust me when I say I have absolutely no doubt Hahtra'tzrhi will be most... *displeased* to learn that Gaalan is not only inconveniently still very much alive but a Matarii collaborator and he'll most certainly want to eliminate this stain on his family's otherwise spotless military and religious record before she can foment trouble—and by the most expeditious means without undo concern for... *collateral* damage."

Chapter 18

Isolation unit 2, sickbay of the Baidarka, *1836.*

Sirin stepped into the dimly lit isolation cubicle, acknowledged the seated Matoosh with a slight smile and motioned for him to remain where he was as he started to rise. Then she turned her attention to Qar'qaah.

Outwardly he looked the same, perhaps even a little better, but now she couldn't help but see him through the prism of his horrific experiences at the hands of Cisne—*No, not Cisne. Gaalan.*

She bit her lip, then looked back at Matoosh and was somewhat taken aback at just how haggard the young Hahtooshan appeared. Clearly the revelations had had a profound effect on him as well. "I'll stay with him—why don't you go get something to eat and then get a few hours of sleep? We can order you up a tray and you can use my cabin if you'd like—"

"I'm not hungry," he replied as his own preoccupied gaze drifted back to Qar'qaah.

"You, *not* hungry?"

"Or sleepy," he added in a tone that left absolutely no room for argument.

She shook her head and started for the other fold down seat on the opposite side of the narrow bed—then thought better of it. Instead she walked over to stand beside him, and after a moment, asked, "May I?" and held out her arm.

He nodded.

She wrapped her arm around his shoulder and was incredibly pleased when he actually leaned into her.

She lightly kissed the top of his head.

"Khusaaq Sha'ashahn is aboard *Jirah,*" he murmured. "In discussions with Hahtra'tzrhi and the Q'shaathrah."

"I know. I wasn't looking for him. I was looking for you."

He glanced up at her, surprised.

"I'm worried about you, Matoosh, every bit as I am about Qar'qaah and Khusaaq."

He shifted his blood-shot gaze back to Qar'qaah. "Doctor Amalfitano has warned me the odds are against him surviving— that the psychological damage..." He squeezed his eyes shut.

She tightened her hold on him. "He told me the same thing. And I told him never underestimate a Hahtooshan's will to survive."

Matoosh again looked up at her, but this time his pale eyes glistened, catching the flickering, multihued telltales of the nearby monitors. "You do realize that even A'tuu'shahn'i don't believe that. We just know our will to survive only has to be just a teensy bit stronger than that of our opponents'."

"Perhaps so, but he's certainly beat the odds so far. And this *is* Qar'qaah we're talking about. I don't think he's quite finished raising hell in this existence, do you?"

Matoosh managed a half-hearted chuckle at that. "I'd very much like to think not—besides, he's my vicarious outlet."

"Then don't give up on him, okay? I haven't, and neither have Doctor Amalfitano and his staff."

He nodded then stared at Qar'qaah's relaxed face for several minutes before he spoke again. When he finally did, his normally gruff voice was barely above a strained whisper: "When we were children... he was always getting into trouble. Of course so was I, but *I* rarely got caught."

She couldn't help but smile.

"He, on the other hand, was *always* getting caught. I sometimes wondered if that's what he wanted all along—to *get* caught—because of how angry it made Khusaaq." He snorted softly. "Qharubi told me once that Khusaaq did much the same with Ja'andai and went out of his way to enrage Ja'andai by questioning everything, but I'd never heard him admit it until today. Qar'qaah *is* Khusaaq—or, should I say the Khusaaq before Cotopaxi—not that either would ever admit it, not even to themselves..."

Sirin couldn't help but shift uneasily at the worrisome comparison.

"...Khusaaq hated being a *doh'ha* too, you see, hated growing up in the shadow of someone bigger than life, with all the attendant obligations, restrictions and unrealistic expectations heaped upon him. Khusaaq at least had the benefit of a proper introduction to the role and was accepted without question. Qar'qaah did not and was not."

Sirin slipped her arm from Matoosh's shoulder and carefully eased herself down on the edge of the bunk, next to Qar'qaah's hip. Taking Qar'qaah's warmly pliant and salve-covered hand in hers, she met Matoosh's gaze squarely. "And you?"

"I understand Qar'qaah better than he understands himself. I desperately wanted to be him you see—I would've given anything to trade positions with him, and he with me." He roughly wiped his gaunt cheeks with the back of his tattooed hand. "But..." he shrugged, "...we were born who we are, and no amount of wishing can change that. He is Khusaaq's *doh'ha*, I am not—and yes, he really is his *doh'ha* in case you had any lingering doubts." He fixed her with his gaze.

"I know he is, but Khusaaq didn't exactly put that topic to rest, in fact he just left the whole issue hanging, which—"

"He's had to deal with those rumors most of Qar'qaah's life—despite all the genetic testing that always confirmed Qar'qaah's true legacy, testing that the skeptics always found reason to question. Perhaps he no longer feels the need to justify who and what Qar'qaah is... or, in this case, who and what he is *not*."

Least of all to Rimmers, Sirin added privately as she gave Qar'qaah's wrist a gentle squeeze. "Perhaps so."

"You must understand that he had to shield Qar'qaah not just from those who wished him—*meaning Khusaaq*—harm for his role in Cotopaxi and the ensuing fallout, but from extremist Elkanaghalli'i who wholeheartedly believed the rumors about Gaalan and Ja'andai and wanted to eliminate their physical manifestation by the most efficient means."

She couldn't help but shake her head while wondering if she'd ever fully understand the complex and convoluted Hahtooshan psyche. "Like Narbrooi?"

Matoosh eyed her. "Hahtra'tzrhi is not an extremist. He's just... extraordinarily uncompromising in his views."

Sirin couldn't help but arch a brow at that; Matoosh did have a wicked sense of humor, along with an exceedingly good grasp of irony, but something told her he wasn't being ironic or trying to make light of the situation. To him there was a clear difference, which begged the question: what constituted a Hahtooshan extremist in Hahtooshan eyes? *I hope I never find out...*

"So, answer me this..." she began, drawing his wary eye, "Khusaaq said he was afraid to ask Gaalan about Qar'qaah. What was he afraid of, if he knew Qar'qaah was in fact his clone?"

He smiled, briefly. "Ah, yes, I can see where that left you wondering. *No,*" he shook his head. "He was afraid Gaalan was going to tell him that Ja'andai and his family had been right about him all along, that even she couldn't make him into anything close to suitable replacement for Ja'andai and so wanted to start fresh, with a new *doh'ha.*"

"Well, he certainly proved her and them wrong."

"Actually, he didn't."

She arched a brow at that.

"Ja'andai would have died, would have rather had all A'tuu'shahn'i die than ally us with the Coalition. He *was* an extremist. Utterly uncompromising."

"Well..." she blew out her cheeks, "then we're all exceedingly fortunate that Khusaaq turned out the way he did."

Matoosh didn't answer immediately, and when he did it was with a less than unequivocal, "Yes, I suppose so." He paused for a moment then continued as his gaze shifted back to Qar'qaah. "I've come to terms with way the things are and my hope—assuming he survives—is that he and Khusaaq can somehow find common ground, that each can accept the other as they are, acknowledge their similarities, their differences, and not try to make the other into something he cannot be. That Khusaaq will finally, publicly recognize just how capable Qar'qaah really is."

She glanced over her shoulder at Qar'qaah and smiled before again meeting Matoosh's steady, albeit watery gaze. "He's certainly an amazing engineer."

Matoosh smiled again, but this time it was a genuine, very proud smile. "He's always been able to fix things, even from the youngest age. No matter how badly broken, no matter if critical pieces were missing, no matter that he had no idea if he even had all the pieces, damaged or not. He'd make it work, somehow, and more likely than not, better than it had before.

"You know how children like to take things apart?" he asked.

She nodded, eager and encouraging—surprised and pleased he too had suddenly opened up in a way she'd never imagined possible.

"I was great at it—anything and everything I could get my hands on, from Khusaaq's prized maser pistol that had been Ja'andai's and the even more celebrated Shus'hnu's before him, to the engines of Qharubi's personal and much loved speeder, I took apart, and with, I might add, immense skill." He flashed her a decidedly smug grin and she couldn't help but chuckle.

"Qar'qaah put them back together. *Always*. He'd watch me, watch how things came apart, how they fit, how each part interacted with another. Then he'd put it back together, faster than I'd taken it apart. I never understood how he did it—I still don't. Taking things apart is easy. Putting them back together is hard. Putting them back together so they *work* as they are supposed to is even harder. He made it look simple... like child's play."

He paused, took another deep and weary breath, then continued. "Sometimes, when I was left to watch him, I'd deliberately smash something just to give him something to do, knowing I could go off with my friends and he'd be just where I'd left him when I returned."

As he spoke, the veneer of the battle-scared veteran, the brusque, raspy-voiced mercenary, the fearsome yowie suddenly disappeared, revealing to Sirin a boy no different than any boy, with friends and the almost universal desire of boys—if left to their own devices—to get out of responsibilities and into serious mischief.

Matoosh, lost in his own memories, was oblivious to her distraction. "Of course there were times when I wrongly judged just how long it would take him to effect repairs and he'd come find us and want to tag along." He shook his head with feigned disgust. "I always told him that he was more innately talented than any Quu'dahn engineer ever born."

She leaned close and whispered, "I wouldn't let Khusaaq's engineer hear you say that."

"Tejat? Oh, no. Definitely not!" He smiled briefly and added quietly, "Pity he cannot fix himself."

Sirin asked, "And what about you?"

He eyed her with a suddenly suspicious stare. "What about me?"

"You've always been there for Qar'qaah. You're Khusaaq's right hand. So who do you turn to when you need advice, need guidance?"

He shrugged, little more than an offhand twitch of the shoulder as if it was of no importance but she could tell she'd hit a nerve.

"I used to seek out Qharubi," he finally answered. "He always had the answers, or at least seemed to."

"Wasn't he was aboard—"

"Makhaira." Matoosh nodded. *"Yes..."*

"I'm so sorry." And she was; she'd been keenly aware that Khusaaq had mourned, and was still mourning the deaths of many aboard *Makhaira*, but up until that moment it hadn't occurred to her that Matoosh, and by extension, the other survivors of Rasal Ghul, had been experiencing the same anguish over lost friends and family—

"In our line of work," Matoosh interrupted her mentally kicking herself, "you accept that nothing is permanent and no one is immune from loss."

Sirin sighed then added, "Well, you can't continue be everyone else's stalwart support without needing some of your own."

"Are you volunteering?"

"Yes."

"You have no idea what you are getting yourself into."

She couldn't help but laugh at that. "Oh, of that I have no doubt, but... there it is. Anytime, anywhere you need to talk, I'll be there. And you really need someone to talk to, Matoosh. You can't keep everything bottled up—"

"Or I'll end up like Khusaaq?" he said, voicing her thoughts.

She exhaled. *"Yes."*

"Then I accept your generous, if, I must warn you, extremely ill-advised offer. In case you haven't realized it yet, we A'tuu'shahn'i are a seriously dysfunctional lot."

She grinned, started to reply then overhearing the faint hiss of the airlock, looked expectantly, almost apprehensively, at the doorway.

A moment later, Fleming stepped into the cubicle, followed by Tayya'shan, who was carrying several infuser cylinders.

Sirin rose from the bed and turned.

"Ruh'ta'aq," Fleming murmured with an acknowledging nod to Matoosh, "Ensign," she added as she flicked Sirin a quick, pointed stare.

Sirin knew that look and she turned to Matoosh. "How about we give Doctor Fleming some room to work?" When he hesitated, she added, "Let's go get some dinner—I hear the cooks made chocolate cream pie…"

If the temptation didn't immediately grab Matoosh's attention, it certainly grabbed Tayya'shan's, who suddenly looked like a man who desperately wanted to be elsewhere.

"…my treat?" she added, trying not to laugh at the medic's poorly concealed lip licking and she made a mental note to have the cooks send up a large piece, in fact a whole pie, just for him. She held out her hand. "Please?"

Matoosh rose stiffly and surprised all of them when he took her outstretched hand in his.

"Come on then," Sirin said. And Matoosh, with one last look at Qar'qaah, followed her out of the cubicle.

Chapter 19

Commander Aquila's quarters aboard the Baidarka, *2018.*

Aquila stared at the desk-com as he ran his fingers through his close-cropped, brown hair that had begun showing streaks of gray of late. Then with a slow shake of his head, he looked across his desk to his seated exec, Lieutenant Teague and Izraad. "You heard the Admiral." He rose wearily from his chair.

Izraad followed his lead but Teague remained seated, arms crossed.

"But if what Sha'ashahn says is true," Teague said, his narrowed eyes fixed on the com unit's speaker grille, "we can't just leave Poonda Five to the *mercies* of Narbrooi." He looked sharply at Aquila.

"Yes, we *can*, Edwin." Aquila jerked his chin towards the desk-com. "Admiral Keon didn't ask us if we'd like to leave, he *ordered* us to leave as soon as all security teams are back aboard—this is now strictly a Hahtooshan matter. Besides, Poonda Five claims to be non-aligned but we all damn well know the planet's governing body's been in bed with the Matarrans for a *very* long time. The fact that the Coalition's secret negotiations with the Poondians over a status of forces agreement collapsed after the Matarrans found out and objected—"

"So, if Narbrooi attacks the planet," Teague interrupted, "a largely defenseless planet with a population of over a million humans and nonhumans—you're telling me the Coalition is just going to stand by and let them?"

"I'm not telling you anything Edwin. The Central Council made the decision—a *unanimous* decision I might add—and Admiral Keon just gave us a direct order to break orbit. With luck the Poondians will find Cisne and hand her over—"

"And if the Matarrans attempt to interfere?"

"They won't. Collaborator or not, she's now on her own—the Matarrans aren't going to risk going to war for one person, least of all a Hahtooshan defector and arms peddler."

"But they might go to war over Poonda Five."

"I doubt it. Again, in the greater scheme of things, Poonda Five just isn't worth it to them. From what I've heard, they were more than just a little peeved that the Poondians were in clandestine discussions with the Coalition. Hell, knowing the Matarrans, they might find it works in their favor to let the Hahtooshans 'clean house'—let the Orthodoxy do all the dirty work and get all the blame, so to speak."

"So Poonda Five, like Cisne, is on its own, facing a Hahtooshan planet-killer."

"That about sums it up, yes. And the sooner the Poondians realize that, the sooner they'll capitulate. One might even argue that if we stay, our mere presence might embolden the Poondians into defying the Hahtooshans' demands."

Teague angrily pushed himself out of his chair. "I never thought the Coalition would knowingly stand by while Hahtooshans massacred the population of an entire planet! Is this what a Coalition-Hahtooshan alliance means? Because if it is, I want no part of it!"

"I suggest you reread your history, Edwin," Aquila snapped back, furious that the officer was forcing him to defend an order he too found morally repugnant—to say the least. "For well over a hundred years the Coalition and its allies were the Orthodoxy's happy customers in doing just that. The very tactics you find so repellent resulted in the founding of a number of new colony worlds for the Coalition, including, I might add, the planet you were born on!"

Teague's indignant scowl crumbled into a frigid glare. "I don't see what that—"

"It wasn't until Raumalle and Isandhlwana," Aquila interrupted, "when the very same tactics were used against *our* colonies, that the Coalition publicly and with great fanfare banned the use of Hahtooshan mercenaries. As if by doing so, we somehow cleansed ourselves of any association with such... *despicable* conduct, a loosely applied ban that was in effect until we suddenly found we again had need for their particular, 'ask no questions, feel no buyer's remorse' skills... defending what was, unbeknownst to the Hahtooshans, a blatantly illegal colony—you might remember it. It was called Cotopaxi. And we all know that the Coalition only placed a permanent, binding prohibition on their use *after* Cotopaxi not because the colony was lost, or because of rumors about what happened at Chhotri and Tharus—the *official* reason for the ban—but because the Hahtooshans demanded so damned much to keep their mouths shut about what they'd really found at Cotopaxi!"

He paused, then in a more appeasing voice added, "Look, Edwin, I don't like this any more than you do, but we have our orders. Besides, Narbrooi is *not* Tarqk. He no doubt fully appreciates the complexities of the situation and will not just start shooting the minute he arrives. He *will* show restraint—"

"Hahtooshans?" Teague snorted. "Restraint? I'm not sure they know the meaning of the word! After seeing that interrogation vid of the Thalamian—"

"—and the Poondians have survived a very long time living on the edge; one might even say they've thrived in the high-risk environment they've created for themselves over the last century and a half. And it's certainly not the first time someone's come gunning for them."

Teague replied icily: "This is a Hahtooshan planet-killer we're talking about, Commander, not some Gorm privateer or Thalamian border—"

"I'm painfully aware of what the *Faridour* is, Lieutenant."

Teague shook his head, then stalked over to the door of Aquila's office and smacked the release. The door snapped open and he stormed out.

Aquila watched him leave and muttered, "Dismissed." As the door closed, he turned to Izraad and shook his head.

She started for the door, then looked back and said, "I certainly hope you're right about Narbrooi, Commander."

He wearily resumed his seat. Massaging his temple, he replied quietly, "So do I, Lieutenant. *So do I.*"

Chapter 20

Isolation unit 2, sickbay, aboard the Baidarka, *2125.*

Amalfitano stood in the doorway of the small, dimly lit isolation cubicle, his arrival having gone unnoticed, or, he suspected, deliberately ignored by Khusaaq.

Khusaaq stood with his back to the door, at the foot of Qar'qaah's bed; the only sounds were the soft, rhythmic click and hiss of the ventilators and the faint, regular bleat of the over-bed cardiac monitor.

Amalfitano hesitated, not sure whether to leave Khusaaq to his thoughts, or intrude and offer some words of solace, of reassurance.

He no sooner realized he had none to offer when Khusaaq whispered, *"I never meant for this to happen."*

Amalfitano stared at Khusaaq's armored back, unsure if the remark was meant for him or for the heavily sedated Qar'qaah. Then Khusaaq slowly turned to face him, eyes glittering. "I never intended to abandon him, *husahn*, either on Rasal Ghul or Poonda Five."

"I know." Amalfitano placed a comforting hand on Khusaaq's shoulder. "The first thing you asked me about, after we rescued you from Rasal Ghul and once you were able, was about those left behind. Your first condition to Admiral Keon was their safe recovery. The minute you learned of their abduction from the *Briseis,* you mounted a rescue—a successful rescue I might add, against overwhelming odds—"

"Yet I could not save him." Khusaaq flicked Qar'qaah another sidelong look, then startled Amalfitano by turning for the door.

"Where are you going?"

"Jirah." He stepped across the threshold and into the narrow corridor.

"Mind if I tag along?" Amalfitano asked as he followed Khusaaq into the airlock, along with his ever-present but to human eyes invisible bodyguard—Bar'ahani this time, and

Bar'ahani only, after Amalfitano had finally convinced Murh'sooli that one bodyguard, fully camouflaged, was sufficient, and a better use of the other on duty was in the virology lab.

The inner lock slipped shut behind the three, instantly sandwiching Amalfitano between the visible Khusaaq and the invisible Bar'ahani, tight quarters with the two Hahtooshans wearing full armor. He tried not to grimace at their ghillie armors' odd, morphing feel, palpable through the fabric of his medreds.

Oblivious, Khusaaq clasped his hands behind his back and fixed his unblinking stare on the outer lock, and as the small chamber cycled, Amalfitano gave his brooding companion a sidelong look, painfully aware that Khusaaq had not actually agreed to his company.

But you also didn't say I couldn't come—

The outer door snapped open and they stepped out, then walked out of the quiet sickbay, Amalfitano's long legs easily able to match Khusaaq's purposeful stride, with Bar'ahani's slight distortion just visible out of the tail of Amalfitano's eye.

It was past twenty-one thirty and the evening-lit corridors and stairwells leading to the cargo bay were largely deserted. Those crewmembers they happened across, now somewhat habituated to seeing Hahtooshans in full armor aboard the *Baidarka*, murmured their polite, "Good evening, sirs," to Khusaaq and Amalfitano, and stepped aside so as not to accidentally bump into what they couldn't see.

The cavernous bay itself was quiet and unmanned except for one marine guard, posted just outside the main airlock to keep the overly curious away. As the trooper saw who approached, she came instantly to attention then wordlessly tapped the release and the lock hissed open.

Khusaaq strode through without making eye contact with the woman.

Amalfitano acknowledged her with a slight nod; the marine, in turn, replied with a poorly concealed look of envy as Amalfitano followed Khusaaq into the brightly lit bay itself.

Beyond, *Jirah* floated silently a meter or so above the polished deck. As Amalfitano walked towards it he was suddenly struck by the craft's uncanny likeness to a dozing Earth squid suspended in the water column. Even its opalescent skin and the faint scintillations that rippled across its surface perfectly mimicked natural caustics and lent itself to the appearance of the underwater predator caught in a shifting sunbeam.

Jirah, like her aquatic doppelgänger, was beautiful, sleek and once awakened from her slumber, lightning fast and deadly.

"Mah'cheh."

At Khusaaq's softly worded command, a hidden airlock silently dilated open amidships, revealing a tantalizing glimpse of the interior; an instant later, a ramp unfurled, only to stop within a few centimeters off the deck, as if it was reluctant to make contact with the *Baidarka*.

Khusaaq, not looking to see if Amalfitano followed, strode up the ramp and into the awaiting craft.

Amalfitano took a more measured pace, his eyes taking in every square centimeter of the alien ship, savoring the irony that, of all people, he was being permitted aboard.

The *Baidarka*'s chief engineer, Lieutenant Perou—in fact the entire engineering department, not to mention the marines tasked with guarding it—had talked of nothing else from the moment *Jirah* at silently settled into the bay. Without Khusaaq's express permission—which had not been forthcoming—they knew better than to enter the craft, assuming they could even figure out how that was possible. That hadn't stopped them from gawking at it, walking around it, whispering to each other in awe as they tried to make sense of each sinuous curve, each vaguely ominous bulge... briefly touching it and marveling at the skin's peculiar organic feel—like living tissue—and its eerie, undulating color pattern.

None had ever seen a Hahtooshan ship 'in the flesh'; their only contact had been in the form of vid images. The *Faridour* while in orbit around Tuli had been studied as extensively as passive scans allowed—active scans had been strictly forbidden. And admittedly the *Faridour* was so massive, so down right unnerving—if one believed its rumored planet-killing abilities—it was almost too much to take in.

But the foldboat was potentially understandable… and therefore the object of intense, bordering on obsessive curiosity on the part of the *Baidarka*'s engineers, not to mention her weapons techs, marines, navigators and helmsmen. All wanted the opportunity to experience what the craft—rumored to be capable of a sustained and mind-boggling fold twelve—could do, first hand.

Even Aquila, first and foremost an engineer, had privately admitted to Amalfitano a certain amount of frustration over not being invited to take a tour of the incredibly alien vessel now berthed within his own ship.

And now, like a modern day Lord Carnarvon, Amalfitano was about to enter the engineering equivalent of Tutankhamun's tomb, in the company of the Hahtooshan version of Howard Carter. He almost laughed out loud at the perversity of the situation, but *Jirah*, and its ominously silent, almost *watchful* presence created a decidedly chilling effect.

Amalfitano picked up his pace, hurrying up the ramp and to the open lock before the ship could, literally, withdraw its open invitation.

He stopped just long enough to glance back at the gaping marine and gave her a quick, finger-wiggling wave, and to acknowledge Bar'ahani, now visible and who'd taken up a parade rest stance at the base of the ramp, then he stepped inside… and immediately stopped again as he realized he was now in a staging bay, its rounded walls completely covered in a frightening display of exotic weaponry. It didn't help that the instant he was aboard, the ramp was indeed withdrawn and the airlock noiselessly closed—as if the ship *had* been waiting on him.

Amalfitano suppressed a shiver as he walked on, through the inner airlock and into the adjoining corridor. There he stopped yet again and looked first to his left, then to his right, not sure which way Khusaaq had gone. *Minchione…*

"Khusaaq…?" Getting no immediate reply, he tried again, this time a little louder, more insistent, bordering on annoyed. *"Khusaaq?"*

Where the hell'd you go? Amalfitano looked around again and was struck by the simple, but rather disconcerting fact that there was not a straight line to be seen. The passageway snaked away and oval hatchways appeared at odd intervals, like so many blood vessels branching off from a main artery. And the walls—the walls pulsed faintly. He looked up only to find the arched ceiling covered with an intricate, glowing latticework of patterns evocative of Hahtooshan tattoos. The whole effect made his skin crawl and he nervously wet his lips.

"Khusaaq!" he called out. *"Damn it, where the hell are you?"*

Then he slowly became aware of something else, something even more unnerving. He was being watched, and every fiber of his being told him it he was not being watched by Khusaaq.

He very reluctantly turned around.

Standing not far away was a very grim-faced Hahtooshan. The huge soldier was wearing only his trousers and one campaign boot, clutching the other in his hand. By the disheveled look of him, Amalfitano had the sneaking suspicion that the merc had been rousted out of a sound sleep by his angry bellow and was none too pleased about it. *Uh-oh.*

"How'd you get in here?" the Hahtooshan growled as he tugged on his boot.

"Uh… I… uh, I came with Sha'ashahn."

The Hahtooshan dropped his now booted foot to the deck, drew himself up to his *very* impressive height, crossed his equally impressive muscular arms and, looking past Amalfitano, replied in perfect, albeit sneering Standard, *"Indeed? I* don't see him." He again fixed the doctor with his fierce, gray-eyed glare.

"I know," Amalfitano glanced around again before returning his gaze to the soldier, "but he was here just a minute ago. Honest—"

The Hahtooshan replied with an exceedingly dubious squint.

"—but I don't know where he is now." Amalfitano favored him with a feeble smile.

The Hahtooshan started towards him. "Permit me show you the quickest way out."

"Uh, that really won't be necessary." Amalfitano began to back-step towards the staging bay. "I can find my own way, really... so sorry for waking you—"

A gauntleted hand landed on Amalfitano's shoulder and he almost jumped out of his own skin. *Cacchio!*

"He's my guest, Tejat," came Khusaaq's familiar voice.

Amalfitano breathed a silent sigh of relief as Khusaaq released his shoulder and stepped forward, to come abreast of him. "Doctor Amalfitano, this is Tejat Ruh'ta'aq, Second Engineer of *Faridour*. Ruh'ta'aq, this is *Baidarka*'s Chief Medical Officer."

Tejat responded with a very slight, clearly unenthusiastic tip of his head and a frosty, "Doctor."

"Ruh'ta'aq," Amalfitano replied in kind, emboldened by Khusaaq's presence.

With that, Tejat spun on his heel and, muttering angrily in Hahtou, quickly disappeared through another hatchway.

Amalfitano stared after him then, giving his jumpsuit's collar a nervous tug, said, "I sense he's not a real people person?"

"Tejat is Quu'dahn—*all* Quu'dahn'i are like that."

"Quu'dahn, huh?"

"Yes."

"Always that... uh, *big?"*

"Yes."

Amalfitano's eyes flicked back to the hatchway as he gave himself a shake, thoroughly unnerved by the chance meeting. "Any more like him aboard? Just kinda like to know, so I don't upset anyone else and get myself blown to pieces in the process."

"No. *Just* him." With that, Khusaaq gestured to the bow of the foldboat. "Come with me." He started down the corridor, towards the bow.

"Oh, trust me when I say I'm not going to let you out of my sight again," Amalfitano said as he hurried to catch up. "Must say, he makes a very good guard dog," he added as he cast a quick, over the shoulder glance back to where he'd last seen the engineer.

"Yes, he does," Khusaaq replied. Reaching another airlock, he stopped, murmured, "the bridge," and motioned for Amalfitano to step through.

Amalfitano did as he was directed, only to find himself inside a relatively small but incredibly well organized oval chamber. Ergonomically designed stations were evenly positioned around its perimeter while its curved walls bristled with monitors and interfaces of all descriptions. Here, both deck and domed ceiling were covered with the same sinuous, glowing ornamentation.

Noticing the doctor's uneasy preoccupation, Khusaaq smiled. "It disturbs you, yes?"

"It looks alive."

"That's because *she* is," Khusaaq replied. Leaving Amalfitano staring, wide-eyed at him, he walked over to a nearby console.

"What the hell do you mean, *'That's because* she *is'?"*

Khusaaq slipped onto the seat. *"Jirah*'s alive—sentient, as are all of our vessels—"

"Sentience does not necessarily mean *alive,"* Amalfitano said as he gingerly walked over to him, nervously eyeing his strangely curious surroundings. But his comment did stir a recollection. Aquila had mentioned Narbrooi saying something to the same effect about their ships, not to mention their—

"Not to you, perhaps." Khusaaq tapped in a series of commands. Then, leaning back in his chair and crossing his arms, he stared at the computer's response as he continued, "But then again, we A'tuu'shahn'i were genetically engineered by sentient machines, and so perhaps that gives us a slightly *broader* definition of what it means to be alive."

"So," Amalfitano looked around him again, "she's sentient, like your daggers?"

Khusaaq fixed him with his own startled stare. "How do you know about our daggers?"

"Narbrooi told us, well, to be totally correct, he told Robert and Zarijan."

"Ah."

"Must say, the one time I handled that damned knife of yours—"

"Siah'ushu," Khusaaq interjected softly as his right hand, out of habit, lightly touched his bandoleer, now missing not only the dagger but its sheath. He quickly dropped his hand back to the console but not before Amalfitano saw him do it.

"—it gave me the cold creeps—I thought I saw the design move, slither as it were, across the surface and assumed it was just my imagination getting the better of me, but—"

"It was not."

"Oh, gee, *thanks,"* Amalfitano replied sourly as he involuntarily wiped his hands on his thighs.

Khusaaq's mouth quirked into a slight smile and motioned for Amalfitano to take the seat at the console next to his.

"Siah'ushu was reacting to your unfamiliar touch—I suspect they were as disconcerted by the experience as you."

"They...?" Amalfitano asked with audible unease as he sat down.

"Siah'ushu, like all Elkanaghalli daggers, is a conduit through which we communicate with the one true source."

Amalfitano raised his brows.

"What you experienced was the Elkanasu, doctor. I hope you fully appreciate what an honor that is."

"I suppose—*wait a minute.* I thought your machine masters died out thousands of years ago."

"More accurately, they ceased to exist in *this* dimension thousands of years ago."

"But... but... *wait."* Amalfitano held up his hand. *"Never mind.* I'd rather not know."

"Yes," Khusaaq said as he shifted his gaze back to the console. "Perhaps that *is* for the best."

For several minutes neither spoke as Khusaaq stared intently at the data that flowed across the console's interface.

As Amalfitano watched him, watched the multicolored reflection of the data in his intense eyes, watched the information stream across his face, blend with his tattoos, bleed into the scars, he was suddenly struck by the realization that this—not the cold-blooded 'merc', not the critically injured patient or desperate fugitive—was the real Khusaaq. A professional soldier calmly, quietly, methodically preparing himself. *But for what, exactly? Only one way to find out.* "So, now what?"

"You mean, what happens when *Faridour* arrives?"

"Yeah."

"Hahtra'tzrhi will deliver an ultimatum: turn over Gaalan or he will destroy the planet."

"No, seriously."

"Seriously. *Faridour* is a *kotla'gau*—a true planet-killer. Alone, she has enough firepower to wipe the face of a planet twice the size of Poonda Five clean of all life within a matter of a few hours. Even microbes hidden deep within its cave systems could not survive. Or," he added with a casual shrug, "Hahtra'tzrhi could just blow it up."

"Blow... it... *up?* A whole damned planet?"

"As you Rimmers like to say, 'to smithereens.' Yes."

Amalfitano couldn't help but swallow convulsively.

"We prefer not to do that as it wreaks absolute havoc with foldspace navigation, and habitable planets, while not rare, are not so common as to be reduced to so much interstellar rubble simply for the sake of proving that A'tuu'shahn'i do not make idle threats. We are *not* Matarii," he added with a note of bitterness. "Far from it."

"I seriously doubt anyone thinks Hahtooshans make idle threats—"

"And *Faridour* will not be coming alone. Which is why it's vitally important *Baidarka* be on its way back to Tuli when *Faridour* and her outriders arrive. Some of the gunners will, undoubtedly, have very twitchy trigger fingers. I would not wish *Baidarka* to become nothing more than target practice before the real shooting starts."

"But..." Amalfitano spluttered, *"we're allies!"*

Khusaaq favored him with a sidelong look. "That didn't stop your Captain Mladić, under cover of authority, from plotting my murder, now did it? Or stop your Ensign Pardix from kidnapping Sirin and Lieutenant Drakin in order to entrap me—"

"They were extremists—and they certainly weren't functioning under any orders from the Coalition!"

Khusaaq only eyed him.

"Okay, no official orders. Narbrooi on the other hand—"

"Is also acting alone—officially."

"You mean—"

"I mean as Hahtra'tzrhi, Narbrooi does not require the prior approval of the Q'shaathrah in what is, in essence, a matter of personal and family honor."

"He can't just kill an entire planet over a matter of honor!"

"Oh, yes Hahtra'tzrhi can, and very well may, if the Poondians do not hand over Gaalan."

"But what if she's already left? What if they can't find her? Poonda Five's a very big planet—"

"Have no fear, Hahtra'tzrhi will be *most* reasonable. He will give them time to search for her, or, at the very least the time to demonstrate to him their sincerity in the effort."

"And if they refuse, or are unable to 'demonstrate their sincerity', he'll turn the *Faridour*'s guns on the planet and start blasting away?"

"No. Hahtra'tzrhi will most likely first choose to employ a single, massive electromagnetic pulse—"

"*An EMP?* But... but that's ancient technology, even I know—"

"It may be *ancient* technology, *husahn*, but it's still very effective. It leaves the planet and its inhabitants relatively unscathed while rendering its defense systems, not to mention its com-net, power and water purification systems beyond quick repair. And these days few planets bother to protect themselves against such, assuming any attacker will use much more advanced weaponry." He paused and flicked Amalfitano a decidedly wicked grin. "Our basic philosophy is that the most effective weapon is always the one the enemy least expects, even if that weapon is nothing more than a rock—or your bare hands."

Amalfitano shifted uneasily, forcing himself *not* to reflexively glance down at Khusaaq's hands.

Point made, Khusaaq again fixed his stare on his console. He continued in a matter-of-fact tone, "Then we'll make planetfall, *en masse*, and look for her ourselves. Only *if* we find that the Poondians were knowingly abetting Gaalan's efforts to escape, or to simply escape detection, will Hahtra'tzrhi order the planet be—" he inhaled sharply, squeezed his eyes shut and whispered, "...*wiped clean*."

"It's a populated planet!"

"I know—Narbrooi knows." He paused, collected himself then added in a louder, steadier voice, "As your human philosopher, Sun Tzu, so succinctly said, 'All warfare is based on deception'."

Amalfitano knit his brows. "I... I don't follow."

"What I mean is I seriously doubt it will come to that. Most species, when confronted by an A'tuu'shahn assault force, are smart enough to immediately capitulate to our demands without a shot being fired, by either side. It's a deception we've employed many times and with great success."

Amalfitano slumped back in his chair and muttered, "There've been notable exceptions... like Raumalle."

This time Khusaaq only nodded as he returned to his intense study of the data flowing across the interface.

Amalfitano, left to his own devices, tried not to think about exploding planets. He willed himself not to visualize tens of thousands of Hahtooshan shock troops precipitating out of the thin, chill and dusty Poondian air only to turn the planet inside out. Tried to distract himself by again looking around at his surroundings.

It was not exactly a calming alternative. It only made it worse when Amalfitano realized that Tejat had silently joined them and now sat directly across the bridge—

"Why did you want to 'tag along'?"

"Huh?" Amalfitano flinched, jerked his uneasy stare off the engineer's broad, now ghillie-uniformed back and looked at Khusaaq. "What?"

"You asked to 'tag along' when I told you I was coming here. Why? I cannot imagine it was to satisfy your curiosity about *Jirah*. You are the only person aboard *Baidarka*—aside from Sirin—who has not expressed a strong interest in a... tour."

Amalfitano didn't answer immediately. When he did, it was a softly worded, "I was worried about you. I was afraid you might—"

"Do something foolish?" He leaned back in his chair and crossing his arms, looked squarely at him.

"All right, as a matter of fact, yeah."

"No. I have everything to live for." Then Khusaaq chuckled softly, startling Amalfitano.

"Mind if I ask what's so damned funny?"

"I just realized that I really do have everything to live for. That's something I never thought I'd say, much less truly believe. I have my crew, who are depending upon me." He flicked the silent Tejat a quick, over the shoulder glance. "I have Sirin—"

"And Qar'qaah?"

"Yes, *Qar'qaah*." Khusaaq paused, his smile fading. "I must find a way to make amends for what was done to him... *what I've done to him*," he added. "Had it not been for me, this never would've happened to him."

"Tell me, how could you have prevented it? Did you know ahead of time about Gaalan's plans to intercept the *Briseis*? Hell no—"

"I knew when we made planetfall on Rasal Ghul that we were going to be marooned." He turned back to the console.

"So, why'd you take him with you? Why'd you take Matoosh or the others for that matter?"

Khusaaq looked at him out of the corner of his eye.

"I'll tell you why: because you knew damned well if you left them behind, Tarqk would find some horrible end for each and everyone one of them. You told me once that he hated you, hated all Elkanaghallis—that he methodically singled out your caste, but as long as you were aboard, you could protect them, at least to a degree. But leave them, and in particular your *doh'ha*, to the mercy of Tarqk when you knew you and they might have a fighting chance on the planet? Of course you opted to take them with you!"

"I didn't take everyone."

"I know, and I know that haunts you, but there was no way you could've known that your ship would be destroyed and all aboard her killed. You took those you could—in other words you did the best you could under the circumstances. *Why can't you admit that?* Why the hell can't you give yourself credit for trying to do the right thing?"

Khusaaq fixed his narrowed stare on the computer. "I did… once."

"It must've been a hell of a long time ago," Amalfitano snarled. Out of the corner of his eye, he saw Tejat twist around in his chair to face him but he was on a roll and he wasn't going to let the massive soldier or his icy, albeit astounded stare slow him down. "Because I've never *once* heard you give yourself credit for one damned thing and that's not a habit one learns overnight—"

"Cotopaxi," Khusaaq whispered, flicking Amalfitano a sidelong, accusatory glance. "I learned it from my experiences at Cotopaxi."

"But—"

"As you know, I was the highest ranking officer to make it off *Huui'teh* before she was destroyed by the Matarii—" He stopped, took a breath, then continued, "I'd had plenty of combat experience, even had some limited command experience, but I'd never had to deal directly with non-A'tuu'shahn'i, much less non-A'tuu'shahn'i civilians. And we were facing overwhelming odds.

"The colonists were terrified—over half of them were women and children. The colonists looked to me, to my soldiers to protect them. There were only forty three of us—*to defend an entire planet."* He grimaced at a memory, then continued huskily, "My troops trusted me, the colonists trusted me and… *and I gave the orders that killed them all."* He squeezed his eyes shut and clenched his jaw muscles.

Cazzo. Amalfitano looked away so as not to intrude on Khusaaq's intensely personal agony. *No wonder you—*

"When I was awarded the Coalition Battle Commendation," he continued, his voice a little stronger, drawing Amalfitano's oblique stare, "I thought it was validation that I'd done the right thing, that I'd made the best choices with what I had to work with, despite the appalling costs—I thought it meant that the Coalition was finally acknowledging that we too bleed." He met the doctor's gaze. *"I was wrong."*

Chapter 21

Commander Aquila's quarters aboard the Baidarka, *2312.*

Aquila scowled at the speaker grille. "What do you mean, Beta Team hasn't checked in? I gave the order for all teams to flick back aboard..." he squinted at his desk chronometer, "...well over *three* hours ago. And you're just now notifying me they haven't returned?"

"Yessir," came Delatorre's anxious, disembodied voice. *"When Corporal Pappas didn't check in as scheduled seventy minutes ago, I assumed it was because she and her team were still too deep in that abandoned mining complex they'd been searching on a tip—there are unmapped pockets of pretty intense radioactivity at those lower levels, which wreaks havoc on communications. I was sure she'd make the next hourly check in and felt there was no reason to wake you—"*

"But she hasn't." Aquila exhaled and angrily massaged his forehead. "Report to my cabin—on the double!"

"Yessir." Delatorre quickly cut the connection.

"Shit!" Aquila smacked the desk with the flat of his hand. He added, "In fact, double shit!" then punched the desk-com's activator with more force than was needed.

The voice of the night shift's comp-op answered, *"C and C—"*

"Masursky, where's Khusaaq Sha'ashahn?"

There was a pause, and then the comp-op replied, *"Still aboard the Jirah, sir."*

"Notify him we have a serious problem and ask him to report to my quarters immediately."

"Yessir—"

"And keep trying to contact Beta Team!" He cut the connection, slumped back in his chair and added, "And hope to hell the Hahtooshans don't arrive ahead of schedule."

Commander Aquila's quarters, 2329.

"I'll have a team ready to go planetside in ten minutes, Commander," Delatorre gave a sidelong, upwards glance at Khusaaq and a curt nod to Aquila, pivoted on his heel and started for the door of Aquila's cabin.

Khusaaq followed him with tired eyes. "I believe it would be best if my crew and I were the ones to go after them, Sergeant."

Delatorre stopped just short of the door, slowly turned around and fixed his surly stare on Khusaaq. Delatorre had never concealed his deeply held hatred of Hahtooshans and the assigning Hahtooshans as bodyguards for Amalfitano and Crewman Xosé Tasende had only added insult to injury.

Aquila shook his head. *And now this.*

Delatorre stared up at the taller man. "Meaning no disrespect... *sir,"* he said frigidly, "but my men are perfectly capable of finding our own. We don't need—"

"Merc help?" Khusaaq replied calmly, his hands loosely clasped behind his armored back.

"As a matter of fact, yeah... *sir."*

Khusaaq favored Aquila with an arched look. "I see no need for further secrecy, Commander, so perhaps you should enlighten the sergeant?"

Delatorre looked first at Aquila, then at Khusaaq, and then back at Aquila. "Sir?"

Aquila crossed his arms and leaned back in his chair as he fixed his gaze on the marine. *"Faridour* is on her way to Poonda Five, Sergeant, along with a Hahtooshan assault force."

Delatorre's expression turned from openly hostile to frankly appalled as his wide eyes slid back up to Khusaaq as Aquila continued:

"Baidarka was ordered to break orbit before they arrive, to avoid any... miscalculations."

Delatorre's eyes darted to Aquila, then back to Khusaaq.

"This Cisne we've all been searching for?" Khusaaq said and Delatorre nodded, albeit reluctantly. "Her real name is

Pashna'gaalan ket Tashar'anhi… she's Narbrooi Hahtra'tzrhi's elder sister—*and* a Matarii collaborator."

Delatorre blinked then turned back to Aquila, bewildered. "But… but I don't—"

"Hahtra'tzrhi will not differentiate between Poondians and missing members of your crew if the planet refuses his demands to hand her over," Khusaaq continued before Aquila could explain, again drawing the sergeant's uneasy gaze. "However, if my men and I go, Hahtra'tzrhi will give us a chance to locate and retrieve your search party before he... demonstrates his displeasure." He paused and smiled coldly at Delatorre. "We A'tuu'shahn'i have only *one* steadfast rule when it comes to warfare, Sergeant. We don't *knowingly* kill our own."

Chapter 22

Isolation unit 2, sickbay, aboard the Baidarka, *0843.*

Amalfitano stopped beside Meerut, crossed his arms and stared down at their star patient.

The machines told him Qar'qaah was indeed waking up, but the young Hahtooshan taking his sweet time. *Of course if I'd been through what you've been through, I'm not sure I'd want to wake up, either.*

Using a carefully concocted cocktail of serotonergic and noradrenergic neurotransmitters, which had successfully inhibited the cholinergic neurotransmitters responsible for REM sleep, he'd kept Qar'qaah asleep, but in a blissfully dreamless state, ever since Izraad's 'eavesdropping'.

On top of that, he'd made judicious use of painkillers. Now those had been withdrawn, and Qar'qaah, in response, was living up to his reputation of being exceedingly mule-headed by refusing to wake up on schedule.

Amalfitano turned to Meerut. "I'll be in my office." He walked out of the cubicle and into the narrow passageway then into the airlock.

Once inside, with both inner and outer locks sealed, he leaned against the wall and rubbed his neck. He found himself staring down the nagging doubts that had plagued him since he had learned the full extent of Qar'qaah's mistreatment at the hands of Gaalan—*or whatever the hell that monster calls herself,* he scowled.

He knew how to treat Qar'qaah's poisoning, his physical injuries—but undo the psychological damage done, on top of the already preexisting psychological issues? The *Faridour*'s CMO, Hai'chellah, had tried to be helpful, but she readily admitted that she'd yet to confront such a complex situation.

Narbrooi too had, with surprising candor, willingly offered suggestions. But in the end both had left it up to Amalfitano's judgment, each adding that they had complete faith in his abilities.

Well, that's all well and good for you. I hold this boy's life in my hands, and for the first time in my career, I have absolutely no idea how to treat him. He looked down at his hands, realized they were trembling. *I don't even know where to start!*

He had toyed with keeping Qar'qaah in a drug-induced stupor until such time as he could be delivered into the hands of the *Faridour*'s medicos, but those plans had been quickly dashed. If things went badly on Poonda Five—especially if the Matarrans did decide to get involved—Hai'chellah and her staff would have their hands full treating casualties on top of caring for those battling the virus, and there were still plenty of them, many critically ill with a few not responding to the protocols, an ominous development in itself.

Besides, he'd given Khusaaq his word that he'd take Qar'qaah and the others back to Tuli and out of harms' way.

Amalfitano exhaled forcefully and straightened up as the outer lock door snapped open. *You're on your own, ol' chum, so best get to it.* He stepped out, walked past the nurses' console, acknowledged Fleming's concerned and following stare with what he hoped was a casual shrug and a muttered, "Still sleeping like a baby," and entered his office.

He slowly walked around his desk, eyeing the untidy stack of flimsies that sat to one side and found himself tempted to lose himself in the reports rather than confront the real issue: how to deal with Qar'qaah's crippling psychological injuries. He slumped down into his chair and fingered the top report.

"What's up?"

He lifted his gaze to find Fleming standing in front of his desk, arms akimbo. *I shoulda known...* "Qar'qaah's refusing to wake up."

She snorted with laughter then said, "No, really."

"I'm kinda hoping he stays asleep."

"Ah. Now we're getting somewhere."

He shuffled the reports.

"Why don't you play it by ear?"

He looked sharply at her. "Play what by ear?"

"How you approach him."

"Thanks, I'll do just that." He resumed his shuffling.

She seated herself, uninvited as she was wont to do, in one of the chairs facing his desk and crossed her arms.

He stopped his shuffling long enough to squint at her. "What?"

"You tell me."

He knew that look. She wasn't going anywhere. When Doctor Jenna Fleming wore that look, she was like a dog with a bone—she'd worry it until she shook the truth loose. "Okay. I have absolutely no idea how to approach him."

"Yes, you do."

"No. I. *Don't.*"

She opened her mouth to reply, but he held up his hand, silencing her and began counting off, using his fingers, "I have an adolescent, an age group well known for their extreme angst not to mention raging hormones, who also happens to be a genetically engineered Neanderthal, which means his brain chemistry is different than ours—but not obviously so, oh, no, in fact very discreetly so, just to make it that much trickier—and who is also a Hahtooshan, who, as we all know, have their own *extremely* peculiar take on things, who also happens to be the clone of not one, but *two*, possibly *three* Hahtooshan cultural icons and because of that was already suffering from a *massive* inferiority complex, who was then sexually debased by someone who goddamned well knew he was a celibate..."

Running out of the fingers on one hand, Amalfitano switched to the other. "And oh, yeah, who many Hahtooshans persist in believing is his mother despite iron-clad evidence to the contrary, and who did what she did just to get at the one person he hates more than he hates himself."

"Yup." Fleming nodded sagely. "That pretty much sums it up."

He glowered at her.

Unfazed, she leaned back in her chair, studied him for a moment, then said, "Look, William, you're going into this far better prepared than you were when you had to treat Khusaaq and Matoosh—"

"Their injuries were strictly physical—"

"Were they?" she interrupted pointedly. "Matoosh maybe—for a Hahtooshan I suppose you could say he's 'well adjusted'—but Khusaaq has, as we both know now, his own long-standing issues, and on top of that he was mind-stripped. With them, you were utterly blind; with Qar'qaah you have four highly experienced Hahtooshan medics at your beck and call, you have Sirin and Drakin who had extensive interaction with him, you have the *Faridour*'s CMO not to mention her Elkanaghalli captain, both of whom are only a call away. You have Zarijan. You have little ol' me to bounce ideas off of. And lastly, and perhaps most importantly, you'll have Matoosh and Khusaaq—"

"But ultimately it's up to me—"

"True, but—"

"No buts! There are no buts allowed here!"

"But you just—"

"I said no buts, dammit!" He smacked the desktop for emphasis.

She sat bolt upright and glanced over her shoulder. "Uh-oh…"

"Uh-oh *what?*"

She turned back to him and smiled feebly. "I just realized I haven't heard hide nor hair from our other Hahtooshan patients in over an hour." She lurched to her feet and started for the door. "Best go see what they've gotten themselves into—can't be good."

"And what about Qar'qaah?"

She stopped at the door and looked back at him. "What about him?"

He threw up his hands in exasperation. "What the hell were we just talking about? I have absolutely no idea how to treat him!"

"Yes you do, you just haven't realized it yet."

"But—"

"No buts, remember? *Your* rules, not mine." With that she strode away.

He stared—glared—after her, then fixed his frustrated gaze on the stack of flimsies. He angrily sorted through them, picked up the most important and with an annoyed huff, settled back into his chair and pretended to read it.

"Doctor Amalfitano…"

He lifted his distracted gaze at Meerut's urgent page.

"…please come to ISO two immediately."

"Well of course *now* you decide to wake up!" He threw the flimsy back onto the pile, rose and hurried from his office.

Chapter 23

Isolation unit 2, sickbay, aboard the Baidarka, *0911.*

Qar'qaah's eyes were open, occasionally following the bustle of
activity around him as if he was a disinterested onlooker, rather
than the center of attention.

He was now propped up in bed, his head and back supported
on several pillows, but he had not spoken, had not reacted in the
slightest to being handled, to the transient discomfort of having
invasive medical paraphernalia removed or replaced or to his
unfamiliar surroundings—*to the utterly alien scents and sounds
and auras*—had not made any attempt to interact with anyone
since awakening from his drug-induced coma ten minutes
before.

Amalfitano, painfully aware of his young patient's detached
stare, looked at the over-bed monitors. What he saw was not
promising. While Qar'qaah's poisoning was responding well to
treatment and his new kidney and gut were functioning far
better than Amalfitano could have anticipated at this stage, he
was clearly having immense difficulty processing the heady
fusion of what he was seeing, hearing, and, peculiar to
Hahtooshans, *smelling*. The Faridour's CMO had confirmed
Amalfitano's suspicions that all Hahtooshans were true
synesthestes—an enhanced legacy of their Neanderthal
ancestors, she'd said. But in Qar'qaah's case it only made the
situation worse: the ultimate in sensory overload when he was
least able to cope with it.

Amalfitano shook his head then flicked Meerut a worried,
sidelong glance.

She replied with an equally worried shrug.

Amalfitano turned back to his patient and finished
unclipping the infuser from Qar'qaah's right arm as he
whispered, *"Go get Jaa'qwah—"*

"Tayya'shan's just outside—"

*"I know, but Qar'qaah doesn't know him—he knows
Jaa'qwah, and get Zarijan and Sirin here too—on the double."*

The nurse nodded and hurried from the cubicle.

Amalfitano resumed his distracted study of the over-bed monitors, but soon found his gaze drifting back to Qar'qaah.

Qar'qaah, for his part, was staring at nothing in particular, just… *staring*.

Amalfitano glanced over his shoulder, mentally prompted Jaa'qwah and the others to hurry the hell up, then looked back at Qar'qaah and found his impatience, not to mention his growing concerns, getting the better of him.

"Kon'ta'aq?" He lightly touched Qar'qaah's forearm and repeated, *"Kon'ta'aq?"* This time he succeeded in drawing Qar'qaah's dull, slow-blinking gaze. "Are you in any pain?"

In response Qar'qaah wet his bruised, gummy lips with the tip of his blistered tongue.

"Thirsty?" Amalfitano picked up the bedside water pitcher and cup and, holding them in the path of Qar'qaah's unfocused stare, sloshed some water into the cup as he repeated in uncertain Hahtou: *"Lotzeh-ne'i?"*

Qar'qaah continued to stare at him. Amalfitano wasn't sure if it was because he couldn't comprehend his terrible Hahtou, or something far more worrisome.

"Lotzeh-ne'i?" he repeated, bringing the cup closer and Qar'qaah finally, to Amalfitano's immense relief, fixed his sunken eyes on it.

His nose twitched; he licked his lips again.

Amalfitano brought the cup still closer, allowing Qar'qaah to get a good sniff of the fluid. "Small sips, okay?" He pressed the cup to his patient's lips.

As if understanding him this time, Qar'qaah took a sip, briefly letting some of the cool water pool in his mouth. Then, as he swallowed, his head fell back against the pillow and he closed his eyes, as if utterly exhausted by the effort.

Amalfitano again studied the monitors and was intensely relieved to see signs that Qar'qaah's higher thought processes *were* finally starting to reintegrate, coalescing around the primal scent and taste of water.

Hearing a soft, smacking sound and realizing Qar'qaah's eyes were again fixed on the cup he held, Amalfitano brought it back to the young mercenary's sticky lips.

Qar'qaah startled him by grabbing the cup. Before Amalfitano could jerk it free, he greedily gulped down its entire contents.

Amalfitano hurriedly stepped back, anticipating the inevitable.

He didn't have long to wait.

Qar'qaah's sunken eyes bulged and he began to gag, his entire body convulsing in response.

Amalfitano slipped his arm under Qar'qaah's bony shoulders and helped him to lean forward.

He vomited explosively, vomited again then sagged back into Amalfitano's supporting embrace and clutching his bandaged stomach, continued to dry-heave.

Amalfitano sighed and eased him back onto the bed. Then he carefully slipped his arm out from behind Qar'qaah. Using the thin drape that had covered his lower body, he wiped his mouth, throat and chest as Qar'qaah's entire body continued to spasm. *Cacchio.*

Catching movement out of the corner of his eye, Amalfitano turned to the doorway and was relieved to see Jaa'qwah. He acknowledged the medic with a quick nod then turned back to Qar'qaah. In a mildly chiding tone, he said, "Next time, *listen* to your doctor, all right?"

Qar'qaah, eyes tightly closed, lips drawn back against clenched teeth, surprised him again by nodding.

"Give your insides a chance to recover from everything they've been through—you might even be able to progress to solid food sooner than I'd thought, but *not* if you keep bolting water like that."

He flicked Jaa'qwah another glance; the medic wordlessly offered him a loaded ject-it, which he took and pressed against Qar'qaah's bare thigh. "I'm giving you something for the cramps and nausea, all right?"

Qar'qaah opened his eyes and stared up at him for a moment then his bruised mouth began to work, struggling to form words.

"Easy... *easy*," Amalfitano murmured. "You're doing fine, Kon'ta'aq—just take it slow—"

"Ah... aduut-sseh...?"

Intensely relieved, Amalfitano almost smiled. "I'm Doctor Amalfitano—"

"Kaa'path-sseh?" he asked in a hoarse whisper.

"I'm supposed to be here. I'm the CMO of the *Baidarka*—"

"Bai... Baidarka?" Qar'qaah squinted at him intensely as if suddenly realizing he was staring at a human, not a Hahtooshan.

"You're aboard the Coalition Expeditionary Forces patrol ship, *Baidarka*, in our sickbay."

Qar'qaah closed his eyes, shook his head slowly and mumbled, *"Tuh maztsaeh...."*

"That's perfectly reasonable. You just have to understand one thing, and that's that no one here is going to harm you."

After a moment, Qar'qaah reopened his eyes and let them wander around the small cubicle. His gaze swept past Jaa'qwah, then stopped and slid back to him. Their gazes locked.

"Jaa'qwah, Kon'ta'aq," the medic offered.

Qar'qaah studied him intently then managed, *"Jirah...?"*

"Yes, Kon'ta'aq. We met aboard *Jirah.*"

Qar'qaah shifted his unblinking stare back to Amalfitano. *"Baidarka?"*

"Yes!" Amalfitano grinned. "You're aboard the *Baidarka*. I'm William Amalfitano, her chief medical officer."

Qar'qaah shook his head and replied in uncertain Standard, "No... no, you're... you're not."

Amalfitano's relieved grin faded. "But—"

"You're... you're a hallucination," Qar'qaah added, his hoarse, weak voice now a little stronger, his speech a little more confident. His eyes flicked to Jaa'qwah. "So are you."

Jaa'qwah clearly took the observation as an insult. "Am not."

"I know a hallucination when I see it—I've been seeing a lot of them lately... and I've gotten quite good... good at knowing what's real and what's not and neither of you is real."

Jaa'qwah crossed his arms. "If I'm a hallucination, why are you talking to me? I distinctly remember telling you not to acknowledge your hallucinations by speaking to them—"

"Yes you did—or," Qar'qaah added, giving the medic a suspicious sidelong glance, "should I say the *real* Jaa'qwah did."

"Then why—"

"Because hallucinations—as you should know *if* you were real—are creations of my own mind and therefore anything I know, a hallucination would know. Which means you should know better than to talk to me."

Jaa'qwah looked at Amalfitano and conceded, "He got me there."

Amalfitano gave his head a quick shake to clear it—just a moment ago the young Hahtooshan couldn't even think coherently, and now he was running logic circles around a medic and a doctor? *This does not bode well...* "Do you always speak to your hallucinations in Standard?" he asked, taking another approach, "rather than Hahtou?"

Qar'qaah pulled his accusatory gaze off Jaa'qwah and fixed it on Amalfitano. Clearly that question left him briefly baffled. "Am I speaking Standard?" He thought about it, and then replied, "No matter. I guess if it's my hallucination, I can speak any language I want. Now, both of you—go away." He motioned dismissively with one bony, blistered hand. "Go on. I have work to do."

"Like what?" Amalfitano asked, refusing to budge.

"Like inspecting the diffusion screen," Qar'qaah replied, mimicking Amalfitano's voice, his faint, northern Italian accent, his intonations, perfectly.

Amalfitano and Jaa'qwah exchanged puzzled looks as Qar'qaah started to ease himself off the narrow trauma bed.

"The power unit hasn't been checked in days, probably needs some adjusting—"

"I wouldn't try standing I were you," Amalfitano offered.

"Then it's fortunate for you that you aren't me." Qar'qaah angrily tossed the vomit soaked drape aside and with a sidelong, challenging stare, dropped his bare feet to the deck.

Amalfitano again looked to Jaa'qwah but the medic replied with a slow shake of his head. They both then turned back to Qar'qaah just as he cautiously stood.

The instant he put his full weight on his legs his knees buckled.

Qar'qaah made a desperate grab for the bedside table, got a handful of the drape instead and pulling it with him, he sat down, in the process bumping the bedside table and knocking over the water pitcher. It promptly dumped its contents on him, leaving him soaked and spluttering in surprise.

Amalfitano crossed his arms, shook his head and leaning close to Jaa'qwah, asked, "Is he always this... um, stubborn?"

The medic replied with a weary sigh, and, "In my limited experience with him, yes, ta'ahn."

Amalfitano turned to find Qar'qaah looking around, clearly unsure as to how he'd ended up sitting on the deck, naked and wet, clutching the vomit-splattered drape in his hands.

He looked up at them with a decidedly accusatory, albeit watery eyed squint. *"Who pushed me?"*

"No one pushed you," Jaa'qwah replied.

"Then how'd I end up here?" Qar'qaah asked, motioning to the deck.

"You fell," the medic answered irritably.

"No, I didn't. I was *pushed."*

"You weren't—"

"Kon'ta'aq," Amalfitano interrupted, "you're very ill— we're just trying to help—"

"By *pushing* me?"

"I already told you," Jaa'qwah growled, "no one *pushed* you."

Qar'qaah looked down at himself, then back up at the medic as he angrily wiped a wet lock of hair from his equally wet face. "And I suppose you didn't dump water on me, either?"

Jaa'qwah started to open his mouth, but Amalfitano quickly placed himself between the two and cautiously held out his hand, palm-side up. "Allow me to help you back to bed."

"I don't want to go back to bed!" Qar'qaah slapped the proffered hand away, adding almost frantically, *"I have to check the diffusion screen—it hasn't been adjusted in days!"*

"You're not on Rasal Ghul Seven, Kon'ta'aq," Amalfitano replied calmly but firmly as he squatted in front of him, "you're aboard the Coalition patrol ship *Baidarka*. You've been aboard, in our sickbay, since—"

"I don't believe you—you're just trying to trick me!"

"Why would I want to do that?"

Qar'qaah's glare crumbled into a baleful, albeit watery squint. "Maybe pushing me wasn't entertainment enough?"

"Then explain your surroundings," Amalfitano reasoned, motioning around him with one hand. "Does this look like Rasal Ghul? And what about me? How do you explain *me?"*

Qar'qaah rubbed his wet, peeling and salve-greasy forehead with both hands and grumbled, "I told you, you're a hallucination, a very *annoying* hallucination, I must say. Now go away, I have work to do."

Amalfitano, hearing the nearby airlock hiss open, rose and turned expectantly. A moment later Izraad and Sirin appeared in the doorway of the small cubicle.

In response to their expectant looks, he stepped aside to reveal Qar'qaah seated naked in a puddle on the deck, wet hair plastered to his skull and now closely examining the base of the trauma bed.

"What the...?" Sirin looked back at Amalfitano.

"He tried to get up—told him not to, but... he thinks we're hallucinations. Thinks he's back on Rasal Ghul."

"Oh."

"I can hear you, you know," Qar'qaah grumbled, not looking up from his intense study of the trauma bed's various foot controls.

Izraad and Amalfitano exchanged glances as Amalfitano motioned for the two women to enter. "Sirin, maybe if you try..."

Sirin nodded, and as Izraad joined Amalfitano and Jaa'qwah near the doorway, she cautiously approached.

"Qar'qaah...?" she said quietly as she slowly, carefully extended one hand. "It's me, Sirin—"

"I know it's you," he answered irritably as he tried to open a small access door on the bed's pedestal. "But you're not real, just like the rest of 'em. Now be quiet! I've got to reconfigure the power supply to the diffusion screen before—"

"You're not hallucinating, you're not on Rasal Ghul and that's not the power supply to the diffusion screen. That's the repair door for the trauma bed and you're in the *Baidarka*'s sickbay."

He stopped trying to pry open the door with his bony fingers and glared up at her as he wiped a trickle of water from his forehead. "I told you to be quiet!"

She knelt in front of him. "Qar'qaah, listen to me—"

"Why?" he replied peevishly as he angrily wiped another rivulet from his cheek then flicked it in her direction. *"You never listen to me!"*

"Okay, talk to me. I'll listen, promise."

"What's the point? You're not real, none of this is real," he gestured wildly around him, "and I have work to do!"

She glanced back at Amalfitano; he replied with a slow shake of his head. She turned back to Qar'qaah to find him now staring intently at her. "It's really me. *Smell*, use your nose... go on."

At her urging, he cautiously sniffed the air. She edged a little closer, still holding her hand out, palm side up.

"You're on the *Baidarka*," she continued, her eyes never wavering from his. "The man standing behind me, wearing the red jumpsuit? That's Doctor Amalfitano. He's the *Baidarka*'s chief medical officer. He and his staff have been taking care of you, treating your poisoning and your other injuries since we flicked aboard several days ago."

Qar'qaah risked a quick glance up at Amalfitano then jerked his wary eyes back to her as she inched a little nearer.

"What's the last thing you remember before waking up here?"

He continued to stare at her, clearly unsure.

"Try to remember, Qar'qaah. *Please.* Try."

He dropped his gaze to his tattooed fingers, and after a moment said, "I was trying to fix something... the... the diffusion screen—"

"Not the diffusion screen. You were powering up the *Huui'teh*'s com-net—"

"No!"

"Yes. You got it powered up, then told me to count to one hundred so you had time to get away before Khusaaq arrived..."

He swallowed hard as he slowly lifted his head to squint at her.

"...you were going to confront Cisne."

"Careful, Sirin," Amalfitano warned as he realized Qar'qaah had begun to tremble.

"I offered to give you a painkiller to keep you on your feet, give you a fighting chance and you agreed—*remember?* We were on the bridge of the *Huui'teh.*"

Qar'qaah slowly shook his head as his breathing quickened. "That's not true—"

"Only I gave you a sedative instead. I couldn't let you go after her, it was suicide—"

"You're lying!"

"No, I'm not. Please, Qar'qaah, *try* to remember."

His frightened eyes welled up with tears as he rubbed his temple with a very shaky hand. "I... I ca... can't..."

"It's okay," she soothed. "It'll all come back. You just have to give yourself some time to recover from everything you've been through. All you have to know right now is that you're *safe*." She risked a quick, over the shoulder glance at the medic, then turned back to him and smiling, said, "Jaa'qwah's here too." She moved a little closer. "You remember Jaa'qwah."

He kept his eyes fixed on her as his entire face began to contort.

"It's really me, Qar'qaah—"

"I want to believe you," he whispered as tears streaked down his hollow, greasy cheeks.

"I know you do, and I know you're really, really scared."

He briefly searched the worried faces of those standing behind her as he roughly wiped his face with his fingers. "You've fooled me before—"

"Me?" Sirin asked, drawing his suddenly fearful gaze.

"I thought it was real, but... but it wasn't. It was just... just another of your mind games—"

"It's *Sirin*, Qar'qaah, not—"

"I don't want to play any more... I want it to stop." He dug his fingers into his temples. *"Please*—I won't fight... just... *just make it stop."*

"I want to—we all do, but we need your help."

He bit his lip as more tears rolled down his gaunt, blister-pocked face; this time he made no effort to wipe them away. *"Please—I'll be good this time..."*

"If you don't trust your eyes, trust your sense of smell," she again held out her hand. "It's really me—"

He lunged forward, grabbed her arm then jerked her onto him as she let out a startled squeak.

Amalfitano and Jaa'qwah started after her, then stopped when they realized that she wasn't hurt, just surprised.

Qar'qaah wrapped his arms tightly around her, pressed his wet face into her chest and sobbed, *"I'll be... be good, I won't fight. I'll do what you want—please, just... just make it stop...."*

She glanced back at Amalfitano and Jaa'qwah and soothed, *"It's okay,"* as much for their benefit as Qar'qaah's as she stroked his head and heaving shoulders. *"You're safe now... shhhh. No one here is going to hurt you. I won't let them."*

Qar'qaah continued to sob uncontrollably, his breathing coming in increasingly sharp, convulsive jerks.

Jaa'qwah slipped a ject-it and vial of mild tranquilizer from the nearby drug cart, met Amalfitano's approving gaze, then loading the tool, carefully eased himself around the trauma bed and squatted not far from Qar'qaah and Sirin.

"Kon'ta'aq?"

Qar'qaah slowly, reluctantly, lifted his head to peer at him, then, happening to see the ject-it in Jaa'qwah's hand, tensed and hissed, *"Chulh!"*

"It's okay," Sirin murmured, tightening her hold, but to no avail with his skin wet and greasy with burn salve. "Jaa'qwah isn't—"

"*CHULH!*" Qar'qaah shoved her aside and, grabbing the lip of the trauma bed, managed to scramble to his feet. Then he promptly slipped and fell, face first onto the deck with a resounding *thud,* followed by an agonized groan.

Jaa'qwah started for him but Amalfitano, afraid any attempt at restraining him would cause more harm, grabbed his arm. *"No."*

Clutching his belly, gripped by pain and panic, Qar'qaah tried again to get to his feet, but his bare feet were unable to get purchase on the deck made slippery by water and—Amalfitano suddenly realized—*blood.*

Jaa'qwah saw it too, gave Amalfitano a sidelong glance and at the doctor's nod, he quickly and expertly pinned Qar'qaah, face down on the floor.

Qar'qaah reacted by shrieking in terror.

Sirin grasped the now wildly flailing arm nearest her before it struck the base of the trauma bed as Amalfitano got a firm hold on a thrashing leg.

Izraad hit the alarm then joined in the fray, grabbing the other leg.

Jaa'qwah managed to seize Qar'qaah's free arm and roughly pried his fingers free of the near-strangling grip they had on the collar of his duty uniform, then he forced it, outstretched, to the deck and held it there.

It was over in less than a minute, but by the look Izraad gave Amalfitano and by mindless terror in Qar'qaah's increasingly feeble, breathless screams, he knew something horrific had just happened. Before he could put words to his fears, he heard the airlock snap open, heard staff running, drawn by the blatting alarm.

He risked a quick, over the shoulder glance just as Meerut and Tayya'shan appeared in the doorway and through clenched teeth managed, "Uh… need a little help here."

Meerut snatched up the ject-it that had gone flying as Tayya'shan carefully edged around Amalfitano, then, with a nod to Izraad, relieved her of her hold on Qar'qaah's left ankle.

Face down and spread-eagle, Qar'qaah continued to struggle against their combined hold, but it didn't take long before he utterly exhausted himself.

The instant Qar'qaah stopped fighting, Meerut slipped between Amalfitano and Sirin and at Amalfitano's urgent nod, pressed the ject-it against his shoulder.

They all waited a moment longer, then at Amalfitano's signal, he, Sirin and Tayya'shan cautiously released their hold.

Jaa'qwah, satisfied Qar'qaah no longer had the strength, much less the will to fight, carefully eased himself off him and staggered to his feet, then helped Sirin to hers.

Qar'qaah, his nose and cut upper lip now bleeding profusely, continued to sob softly, his entire body twitching in response as his fingers slowly curled into his palms. Soon, even the sobbing stopped as the tranquilizer took hold.

Amalfitano cautiously knelt beside him. "Qar'qaah?"

When he didn't respond, Amalfitano wrapped his fingers around his wrist. *"Qar'qaah?"*

He opened his now glassy eyes and slowly turned them towards Amalfitano.

"We need to get you back into bed—make sure you haven't seriously hurt yourself, okay?"

Qar'qaah continued to stare at Amalfitano. There was no fight left in his eyes, not even fear—and it went far beyond the tranquilizer's effects to something much deeper—as if something deep inside of him had finally just... *snapped*.

"Kon'ta'aq?" Jaa'qwah knelt beside Amalfitano. "Allow us to help you."

Qar'qaah's only response was to slowly close his eyes— complete and utter capitulation: *Do what you want. I no longer care.*

"Aganreka'a," Jaa'qwah replied softly as his worried eyes darted to Amalfitano.

Amalfitano reluctantly got to his feet and stepped back as Tayya'shan knelt next to Qar'qaah's other shoulder.

"Hai ti-mat-qu'a." With that Jaa'qwah and Tayya'shan each got a firm hold on an arm, then rose as one, taking the unresisting Qar'qaah with them.

Tayya'shan, in one deft movement, slipped an arm around Qar'qaah's back and scooped up his legs with the other, then pivoted and carefully deposited him back on the bed.

Shivering, Qar'qaah stared dully at the nearby wall as everyone clustered around the trauma bed.

Amalfitano gave him a cursory head to toe visual exam and quickly, to his immense relief, discovered that the source of the bleeding was nothing more serious than a lacerated elbow, along with the bloody nose and cut lip.

Meerut grabbed a warmed blanket from the over-bed bin and quickly covered Qar'qaah as Tayya'shan pressed a sealer to his oozing elbow.

Sirin accepted a washcloth from Izraad, then began to gently dab Qar'qaah's bleeding nose and lip.

Izraad stepped close, then said in a strained, hoarse voice: "They used hallucinogenics on him—to *heighten* the experience—so when he saw the ject-it..." She didn't need to finish.

Amalfitano stood back, gave the over-bed monitors a quick study and with a shake of his head, sighed, "Looks like we have our work cut out for us."

Chapter 24

Khusaaq motioned for the others to stop.

He dropped to one knee and, using the flickering glow of a nearby overhead, peered at the faint footprint left in the dust that lightly coated the passageway's smooth floor.

The joint twelve-man team had been searching the long-deserted mine for hours and this print was the only hint that anyone had come this way in a very long time. They had chosen this particular maze of passageways because it, unlike the others on this level, was illuminated, albeit with an irregular and not particularly reliable pattern of overhead light strips. Clearly someone had recently powered up its grid and Delatorre had insisted this was evidence of his missing team.

Khusaaq, having little else to go on and knowing the labyrinthine underground complex covered several tens of square kilometers and had multiple levels, agreed.

Delatorre squatted beside him as the rest of the search team, A'tuu'shahn and marine, gathered around the two, everyone wearing full battle armor minus helmets. That had been another concession and done by mutual but silent consent. The Rimmers had found their own helmets limiting and Delatorre himself had been the first to remove his, his marines quickly, eagerly following his lead. Khusaaq and his soldiers quickly realized A'tuu'shahn helmet visors didn't offer enough added input to warrant their use, either. Ultra-sensitive noses, eyes and ears worked almost as well, perhaps even better and without the visage their human allies found so unnerving.

Khusaaq sniffed the stale air, hoping it would give him some clue. Like the footprint, the scents his ultra-sensitive nose picked up were months, possibly years old. He flicked the sergeant a glance and shook his head.

Delatorre wearily lurched back to his feet. Not thirty meters ahead, the meager lighting ended and the passageway led into the pitch-dark. He flicked on his hand-held torch and pointed its beam of down its length. "Where the hell'd they go?"

Shu'hah, who stood beside Khusaaq, shifted uneasily, his hand lightly resting on the grip of his maser pistol as his wary eyes probed their dimly lit surroundings.

Khusaaq rose and flicked Shu'hah a sidelong, acknowledging glance. Something wasn't right, in fact something was *very* wrong. He'd expected to find some obvious evidence of the earlier search party—something a little more substantial than a hastily rewired light grid; if nothing else, he expected to still be able to pick up the missing marines' combined scent, suspended in the stagnant air. But the complex, from the top floor down, had been devoid of anything fresh.

His last hope had been this level, this corridor.

"I think we should split up," Delatorre said.

It had not been Khusaaq's idea to include the sergeant, or any of his men for that matter. But Aquila had insisted—they were, after all, searching for *his* missing crewmen, not A'tuu'shahn'i. Khusaaq had agreed only after winning a critical concession from Aquila *and* Delatorre: he was in command of the entire search team, not just his own soldiers. Delatorre had balked, but had ultimately, very grudgingly conceded. It was, however, a very uneasy partnership, a microcosm of the equally fragile A'tuu'shahn-Coalition alliance, a hastily slapped together relationship based on mutual and immediate necessity rather than mutual and established trust.

"No."

Delatorre squinted up at him. "But—"

"They're not here, Sergeant, they *never* were here—in fact no one has been here in a very long time."

"What are you talking about? Their last communication was from *this* level—"

"That's what we were supposed to think," Matoosh growled with a sidelong look at Murh'sooli.

Khusaaq nodded to the five A'tuu'shahn'i and they immediately unholstered their pistols.

Startled, and clearly thinking the worst, Delatorre reached for his own weapon and the five marines did likewise. *"What the hell—"*

"We need to leave, *now,"* Khusaaq interrupted. "Toubeh, take point." He jerked his chin back the way they'd just come then his eyes darted to Delatorre. "We'll cover you."

"But—"

"That's an order, Sergeant—*go!"*

Delatorre hesitated only a moment then angrily motioned for his men to follow Toubeh as she took the lead. Muttering to himself, Delatorre began his own reluctant retreat as the other A'tuu'shahn'i covered their withdrawal with broad sweeps of their hand-held torches, their pistols at the ready. Khusaaq and Rukoobi took up the rear.

Suddenly Toubeh stopped, held up her hand and, glancing around her, whispered, *"Listen...!"*

Everyone froze as their eyes searched the surrounding darkness for whatever had alerted her. Then they all felt it through their feet: an ever so faint rumble but rapidly getting louder.

Then a very fine dust began filtering down from the ceiling.

Delatorre glanced back at Khusaaq and bellowed, *"RUN!"*

Isolation unit 2, sickbay, aboard the Baidarka, *1636.*

Sirin, hearing the faint, telltale hiss of the isolation unit's inner airlock opening, lifted her gaze from the data reader she held and looked expectantly at the doorway. Realizing it was Amalfitano, finally making rounds, she placed her reader on the bedside table.

While Amalfitano had spent most of the day in a closed-door conference with Izraad and the Hahtooshan medics—along with the *Faridour*'s CMO by fold net—as to the best way to proceed with Qar'qaah, she'd implemented her own approach. For the past several hours she had been anticipating the doctor's arrival with a nervous tickle in her stomach. She'd far overstepped herself but...

She flicked Qar'qaah a sidelong glance. He was again propped up on pillows, but this time his eyes were fixed on another data reader he clutched in one hand, a stylus with the other. He appeared oblivious to all else.

Nearby, Nihaal and Raudah sat cross-legged on the deck, backs braced against the wall, also holding data readers.

As Amalfitano stepped into the cubicle, Nihaal looked up. Realizing who it was, he nudged Raudah with his elbow.

They started to get up, but Amalfitano smiled and motioned for them to stay where they were and they happily returned to their single-minded study of the data readers.

Amalfitano gave the over-bed monitors a quick scan, briefly dropped his gaze to the equally preoccupied Qar'qaah then favored Sirin with a very startled, questioning stare.

She rose from the bedside fold-down chair, stepped close, then motioned to the two seated on the deck and whispered, "Ensign Zayyad lent them some of his war game simulators—thought it might keep 'em busy and out of trouble."

Amalfitano replied with a genuinely appalled stare. "Is that such a good idea?"

"You honestly think we've come up with some way to wreak havoc that they haven't already thought of and perfected a hundred times over?"

"Yeah... I, *um,* suppose so."

"And going by their grins and whispered remarks, I think they find our idea of war games rather amusing and.... pathetically unsophisticated."

"Oh—maybe that's something we should keep to ourselves. I can't imagine Ensign Lesedi would appreciate it since she's always bragging that she's the fleet's highest scorer on most of 'em."

"No, likely not."

He leaned close. "Speaking of, where are the other two?"

"Down in the galley, keeping the cooks very busy."

"I guess they took me seriously when I told them they had the go-ahead to eat their fill."

"Drakin's with them, keeping an eye on them—if I didn't know better, I'd say she's actually enjoying her role of mother hen."

Amalfitano couldn't help but smile, but the smile faded as he turned his full attention on Qar'qaah. He stared at his utterly engrossed patient for a moment, then arching a brow, gave the monitors another, more detailed study.

To Sirin's less than expert eye they certainly looked far more promising than they had seven hours before, and Fleming, each time she made rounds confirmed this, had even discontinued the mild tranquilizer earlier in the day. Despite being provided a steady stream of updates on his patient, Amalfitano was clearly rather taken aback to find Qar'qaah not only awake but so thoroughly engrossed in the output of a data reader that he appeared oblivious to all else, including his doctor's belated arrival.

Finally Amalfitano motioned with his chin to the data reader and the iron grip it had on Qar'qaah's attention. "More war games?"

"Specs for the *Baidarka*'s foldspace field generators."

He raised both eyebrows in begging, mildly disconcerted interest. "The foldspace field generators...? But—"

"Matoosh told me Qar'qaah had an uncanny knack for fixing things. According to Laihiri and the others, he amply proved that back on Rasal Ghul with the water purifiers and diffusion screen—and he certainly managed to get the *Huui'teh*'s com-net up and running in record time. Then last night Matoosh said something that stuck with me."

"And what's that?" Amalfitano asked, keeping his voice to a whisper as his gaze slid back to Qar'qaah.

"'Pity he can't fix himself'."

He looked back at her. "And...?"

She took a deep breath. *Here goes.* "I thought maybe if we gave him something to fix, it might provide him with something familiar to occupy his mind, something attainable to attempt, maybe even provide some sense of normalcy."

Amalfitano nodded in growing approval.

"I raised the idea with Commander Aquila and Doctor Fleming—I wanted to clear it with you and Lieutenant Izraad, but—"

"We weren't available—struggling to come up with an idea as solid as yours." He shook his head, said, *"Go on."*

"Well, they both agreed and Commander Aquila spoke to engineering. One of the field generators has been off line since our run-in with the first Hahtooshan warship, and Lieutenant Perou said it needed a complete overhaul at the Mirfak docks—until Narbrooi offered the services of his crews and mobile space dock. While they'd begun repairs on the actual generator, they hadn't started replacing the damaged command circuitry before we left orbit. So, I suggested we let Qar'qaah have a crack at it.

"The lieutenant was more than agreeable—as was the commander—since this type of technology isn't exactly proprietary, so Lieutenant Perou brought us all the specs. And it does seem to be working. He's already come up with one idea to reroute pathways around the worst of the damage, and Engineering's testing it as we speak. Plus he hasn't made a snide remark all day, which must be a personal best for him." In fact she'd been secretly hoping he *would* make a snide remark or two, proof that he was making an effort to regain control, reassert who and what he was.

But he hadn't. Qar'qaah had been painfully quiet, speaking *only* when spoken to and doing exactly as she, Fleming and the nurses told him without comment—*without a fight*. He'd submitted to having his entire body cleansed of the heavy burn salve, followed by extensive debridement, then the application of a lighter cream—a lengthy, extremely painful and humiliating procedure under the best of conditions—with barely a muscle twitch or grimace.

This was *not* the Qar'qaah she knew, nor the one Khusaaq and Matoosh had described and it deeply troubled her, troubled his companions, and by Amalfitano's clearly forced chuckle, it troubled him, too.

Qar'qaah, suddenly suspecting he was the object of their hushed conversation, reluctantly lifted his intense gaze from the reader's small screen and fixed it on Amalfitano.

The doctor met his gaze squarely and Sirin, watching the silent exchange, realized Amalfitano too was momentarily taken aback—now that the distracting camouflage of the thick burn salve was gone—by Qar'qaah's uncanny resemblance to Khusaaq. Not the obvious similarity of a child to its parent, not the echoing resemblance of younger brother to older, but an almost perfect mirror image. *Damned unnerving, isn't it?*

Amalfitano asked, "How're you feeling, Kon'ta'aq?"

Qar'qaah thought about it before answering softly, "Better than I felt earlier, ta'ahn."

Amalfitano had expected defiance; instead he got deference and it clearly left him unsettled. "I'm very relieved to hear that. Now, I need to examine your surgical wounds. Do I have your permission to touch you?"

Qar'qaah flicked Sirin a sidelong, worried look.

She replied with a reassuring smile and a nod.

He looked back at Amalfitano and nodded—no smile. Just the same worried look.

"This shouldn't hurt." Amalfitano pulled the drape aside then carefully peeled away the bandage that encased Qar'qaah's abdomen. Pleased by what he saw, he added, "I think we can leave this off." He pushed the dressing into the wall-mounted disposal unit, then he began to carefully palpate Qar'qaah's stomach, flanks, and finally, his injured leg. "You're doing fine—almost done. There," he murmured, replacing the drape. "Excellent—better than I could have expected. You're healing remarkably quickly—any discomfort?"

"No, ta'ahn."

Amalfitano replied with a mildly skeptical, "Sure?"

"Yes, ta'ahn."

He looked up at a monitor then asked, "Am I real?" as he again met Qar'qaah's stare.

Qar'qaah hesitated, startled by the directness of the unexpected question, then answered, "I… I think so." The wary tone in his voice left little doubt that he'd learned in the very hardest way possible that there was a basic unreliability in faces. They shift, change, deceive right before your eyes and he was not about to commit himself to what was real and what was not—at least not yet.

"But you're not entirely sure."

This time Qar'qaah shook his head while his eyes held an expression that said he fully expected Amalfitano to vanish into thin air—turn into Cisne, one of her henchmen... or *her* doctor.

"That's okay. It's to be expected. You're suffering from extreme exhaustion along with advanced radiation poisoning. Either one can cause hallucinations and leave you unsure about what to believe in."

"Yes, ta'ahn."

"I can't prove to you that I'm real—that I'm really who I say I am—I wish I could. All I can say is that things *will* get better and that no one here is going to harm you."

The look in Qar'qaah's intense gray eyes said it all: *hallucinations can promise anything—promise what you want more than anything else—they've done it before. And their promises are always lies.*

"You're doing fine, all right? Doing just fine. Hungry?" Amalfitano's abrupt change of subject was to Sirin a signal that he too had decided best way to convince Qar'qaah everything he was now experiencing was real, to act as if *that* was a given. That normalcy *was* in itself the best approach.

Qar'qaah answered cautiously, "I am thirsty, ta'ahn," clearly deciding to play along as there was no obvious cost in doing so.

"Again, that's to be expected. Now, you'll need to start out slow—no bolting it this time, agreed?"

"Agreed, ta'ahn."

"We'll begin with some clear liquids, but do exactly as I tell you and you should be able to start on solids sooner than I'd originally anticipated."

"Yes, ta'ahn." Obedient. Respectful. And—because Qar'qaah was starting to wonder if perhaps everything he was seeing and hearing might be *real*—absolutely terrified.

"Good. I'll have the galley send up some fortified broth every couple of hours. If you can keep it down, we'll advance your diet to something a little more substantial tomorrow."

"Like chocolate milk!"

Amalfitano and Sirin glanced back at the two seated on the deck. Raudah, the one who'd made the menu suggestion, grinned, as did Nihaal, but the grins were forced.

Amalfitano replied with a nod, and, "Yeah, like chocolate milk."

"What... what is this?" Qar'qaah looked first at Amalfitano, then Sirin, and finally his fellow Hahtooshans.

"It's a drink," Nihaal offered, delighted by Qar'qaah's wary curiosity. "Much better than barra, better than anything we have, and it comes in a solid, too, which is just as good. It's like kij'a but without the nasty side effects." He made a face for emphasis.

"And they let you have as much as you want," Raudah added enthusiastically. "No rationing!"

Qar'qaah thought about that for a moment, then looked up at Amalfitano, the faintest of hopeful glimmers in his still very sunken, shadowed eyes.

"Clear broth to start, okay? Keep it down and tomorrow you can try some chocolate milk, I promise."

Qar'qaah glanced at his companions, couldn't help but smile at their eager nods then shifted his gaze back to Amalfitano. "Agreed, ta'ahn."

"I'll order up a tray—*remember*, take it slow."

"Yes, ta'ahn."

Amalfitano then turned to Sirin. "Sirin, may I speak with you for a minute?"

Sirin nodded, and was painfully aware of Qar'qaah watching them as they left the room. He was scared—scared she wouldn't come back—or worse, would come back as someone else.

When Amalfitano didn't stop in the corridor, but instead continued on, into the complete privacy of the airlock, she realized whatever he had to tell her was something he did not want Qar'qaah and the others to overhear, and therefore not good news despite his earlier assurances.

Suddenly she was scared too—scared Amalfitano was going to confirm what she had begun to suspect, what the daylong meeting among medical and psychological experts had concluded: that Qar'qaah was incurably insane, trapped in an in-between world, where delusion and reality were seamlessly interchangeable.

She took a deep, steadying breath, stepped in behind him and hit the release.

The instant the inner lock slipped shut, Amalfitano asked, "How'd you explain Khusaaq and Matoosh's absence to him and the others?"

She shrugged. "I told them they were planetside, searching for Cisne. Why?"

"There's been an accident."

She jerked her thoughts off Qar'qaah and onto Khusaaq. *"What?"*

"There was a cave-in—"

"Is everyone all right?"

He hesitated just long enough for her pulse to leap. "We don't know. Two of Delatorre's men and one Hahtooshan made it out." He motioned towards the outer sickbay, "Just flicked aboard and are in triage. But the rest, including Khusaaq, Matoosh and Delatorre are trapped and we can't raise them by com-net."

She slumped against the interior wall of the airlock as she tried to slow her panicky breathing. "Gods, what am I going to tell Qar'qaah—"

"You're not going to tell him *anything*—you're going to act like nothing's amiss, *hear me?"* He gave her shoulders a shake to drive home the point. "I'll be brutally honest with you—this could finally push him over the edge, where there's absolutely *no* hope of coming back." Then a little more gently: "Look, how 'bout I assign one of the nurses, or maybe have Zarijan sit with him until we have a better idea of what's going on?"

"No—he needs me." What she left unsaid, but what she suspected was patently obvious was that she needed him, too, just as much.

"Are you absolutely sure?"

She nodded, took a deep, shuddering breath and squeezed her eyes shut.

"It's too soon to think the worst, Sirin. Way too—" Before he could finish, the emergency klaxons began to howl. *"Cazzo, now what?"*

He punched the release for the exterior door. The instant it opened he stepped out, then stopped and looked back at her. "When I have any news, I'll tell you. Until then, none of them are to know, not even suspect anything has happened. Understood?"

She replied with a less than enthusiastic, "Understood," cleared her throat then tapped the release. The lock closed, instantly plunging the small compartment into complete silence. She stood there for a moment, debating whether to surrender to the good, exhausted cry that had been welling up inside her or collect herself—*Falling apart isn't in anyone's interest*, she told herself, *and besides, it's not like you.*

Damn straight it's not! She angrily wiped her eyes and tapped the inner release. As the door opened and she stepped out, she took a deep, steadying breath, calmed her heart, her thoughts, then walked back into the cubicle only to find Qar'qaah watching her intently.

She felt her pulse leap, worried he'd sense something terribly amiss, possibly even smell her underlying fear, her closeted anxiety. But then he smiled—a faint, but decidedly relieved smile. He too had worried... worried *she* wasn't coming back and that trumped all else.

She smiled in reply. "Broth will be up soon," then motioned to the data reader he held and chided good-humoredly, "now get back to work, you don't want to keep Lieutenant Perou waiting, do you?"

Chapter 25

Control Room, Baidarka, *1653.*

Aquila stared in open-mouthed horror at the tactical screen as Hahtooshan outriders, like a Biblical swarm of locusts, began dropping out of foldspace all around the *Baidarka*. Realizing he was gawping like some raw recruit watching a training sim, he snapped his mouth shut then looked around to find every member of the bridge crew wearing the same horrified expression and frozen in place, hands hovering over consoles, wide eyes fixed on the tactical, mouths agape. Even the usually unflappable Izraad appeared decidedly disconcerted. Teague had lost all the color in his face, not, Aquila reminded himself, that he had much to be begin with.

Then a new alarm began to wail over the din of the klaxons, making everyone jump, warning of a massive spatial displacement. "Something really big's dropping…" Ensign Zayyad, the tactical officer, managed to say an instant before the *Faridour* sparkled into mind-boggling solidity a scant two hundred kilometers off the *Baidarka*'s starboard bow, in the process entirely eclipsing the planet. *"Gods…"* he breathed, to which the helm officer, Ensign Eisele, nodded her hearty agreement.

The *Baidarka* was now totally surrounded by a Hahtooshan armada the likes of which none had ever seen, or even imagined—*feared*—possible. "Where'd they all come from?" Ensign Lesedi flicked the sensor officer a quick glance. But Cyllo, by her own slack-jawed expression, clearly had no ready answer.

"My guess?" Zayyad replied with a sidelong look at Eisele. "Outta the embers of hell."

Aquila slowly twisted around to face the com station and its equally unnerved operator. He cleared his throat, tugged at his uniform collar then said, "Shut that damned racket off!" and motioned around him. The moment the alarms were silenced, he added, "Open a hailing frequency."

Stoker replied with a wordless nod and turned to his station. "F-f-frequency open, sir."

Aquila straightened up in his chair, flicked Teague a quick, sidelong glance, fixed his unblinking gaze on the tactical grid and began, *"Faridour...* this is Commander Aquila of the Coalition Expeditionary Forces Patrol Ship, *Baidarka—"*

"Huuuullo... Commander," came an all too familiar, rich baritone, followed, much to Aquila's chagrin, by an equally deep, barking laugh.

Aquila's apprehensive stare darkened into a deeply indignant scowl.

As if sensing his less than positive reaction, Narbrooi immediately swallowed his laughter, adding, *"I must apologize, Commander for our rather, um, theatrical arrival? You see we so rarely have the opportunity to... make such a grand entrance I simply couldn't deny my crews the experience. Rest assured, it was not for your benefit, but rather the planet... and it appears to have had the desired effect—they're hailing us on every frequency imaginable."*

Aquila shifted uneasily in his chair, far from mollified by the Hahtooshan's voiced regrets, sensing the admiral was still grinning, and grinning broadly. In fact he strongly suspected every single Hahtooshan on every single ship that now surrounded the *Baidarka,* not to mention the planet, possibly even the system, was grinning if not laughing out loud and uncontrollably. *You goddamned fuckin' merc bastards, but,* he quickly reminded himself, *on second thought, a far better outcome than shooting us on sight.* "Yes... well, be that as it may, Hahtra'tzrhi," he replied irritably, "we have a new, and very urgent problem to deal with."

"Indeed?" Narbrooi replied, his voice now all business.

"As you are aware, Khusaaq Sha'ashahn and five of his men, as well as six of my people were searching the lower levels of an abandoned underground complex for another four-member security team, which, on a tip, had gone there in search of Gaalan and had then failed to report in as scheduled."

"Sha'ashahn informed me of this matter and that it might delay your departure. What's happened?"

"A short time ago we picked up an emergency retrieval beacon and flicked aboard one of your soldiers and two of my crew. They reported that the passageway they had been in unexpectedly collapsed, cutting them off from the others. We've been unable to reach any of those trapped via com-net, including Khusaaq Sha'ashahn."

"A most unfortunate series of... coincidences, Commander."

"Yeah."

"Well, all of our resources are, of course, at your disposal."

"Thank you, Hahtra'tzrhi, and since we have no idea what the conditions are like—"

"We will commence searching immediately. Our ground penetrating scanners are far more powerful than yours, and of course we are searching not just for Rimmers, but A'tuu'shahn'i, and some distance from the Gorgon's Lair and its jamming, which should make the task much simpler."

"I'll have my sensor officer transmit their last known coordinates immediately, Hahtra'tzrhi." He flicked Cyllo a sidelong glance.

She replied with a confirming nod and turned to her console.

"Coordinates received," Narbrooi replied a moment later. *"I'll contact you as soon as I have any word.* Faridour... *out."*

Aquila exhaled as his gaze fell on the suspended tactical. Everywhere he looked there was a flashing marker—many of them overlapping—denoting the position of a Hahtooshan vessel. Each had firepower at least equal to the *Baidarka*'s, and that wasn't even taking into account the *Faridour*, which had more sheer destructive capacity than *all* of the other ships combined.

"Never thought I'd say this," Lesedi murmured to herself, "but I'm real happy we're allies."

Realizing Aquila had overheard the remark and was now staring sidelong at her, she pointed to the now frozen grin on her tawny face. *"See?* Happy, sir, very, very happy—one might even say ecstatic."

Aquila chuckled, replied, "Me too." He rose from his chair, gave his jumpsuit collar another angry tug then started for the airlock. As he reached it, he tossed over his shoulder to Lesedi, "I'll be in sickbay, checking on our injured—you have the conn, Ensign."

Chapter 26

Level 5, abandoned mining complex, Poonda Five.

Matoosh staggered to his feet as he peered into the impenetrable murk. Even his incredibly acute vision was of no help, not in darkness this absolute. He could, however, sense others, from their body heat, their smell and most obviously, their harsh coughing.

The stale air was now full of thick, powder-fine dust from the ceiling collapse. It coated the inside of his mouth, his throat and his lungs, leaving him straining for each breath. "Sha'ashahn?" he rasped as he hit the emergency beacon on his armor. "Murh'sooli?" He coughed several times then added, "Toubeh? Rukoo—"

"Matoosh...?" came a weak voice from somewhere behind him.

He turned towards it. *"Shu'hah?"*

"Yes... are... are you hurt?"

"Not seriously. You?"

"Legs... pinned, can't... can't move—"

"Let me find the others and we'll pull you free." Matoosh knelt and began feeling around, hoping to find one of the torches. Instead his fingers brushed across a leg that was encased in distinctly Rimmer body armor.

He quickly patted down the unconscious marine, hoping to find the torch clipped to the man's belt and almost smiled as he happened across its familiar shape. He snatched it up, hit the power button and his surroundings were immediately bathed in diffuse light.

What he saw made his breath catch in his already tight throat.

Most of the ceiling had collapsed, trapping them in a stretch of passageway barely more than four meters long. Murh'sooli was crumpled against the nearby wall, his face badly bloodied but by his weak coughing clearly alive.

Nearby, lay Delatorre and two more marines, all covered with dust and chunks of the ceiling and moving feebly, as well as Shu'hah, his lower body and legs hidden under the toppled remains of what had been, moments before, a wall joist. But there was no sign of Khusaaq or, for that matter, Rukoobi, Toubeh and two marines.

Matoosh hurried to Murh'sooli, knelt beside the medic and gave him a quick once over with his eyes as he hurriedly pulled pieces of debris off of him. The man had sustained a direct blow to the head by a chunk of the ceiling and had suffered a large, bleeding and bone-exposing gash from forehead to just behind his left ear. His right arm was clearly broken, as was his right lower leg and his armor had already reacted by stiffening around the fractures.

Matoosh activated Murh'sooli's retrieval beacon, then quickly separated the medic from his triage kit, in the process prodding the man towards consciousness.

Murh'sooli managed to open one eye and peered up at him, then mumbled through bloodied lips, "What... happened?"

"The ceiling collapsed, you took a blow to the head—"

"Any... anyone else hurt?" Murh'sooli slurred, wincing as he tried to rise.

"Just you," Matoosh lied, gently pushing him back down.

Murh'sooli managed a half-hearted chuckle. "Isn't that always the way?"

"Where's your helmet?" Matoosh glanced around, couldn't immediately spot it.

"Little... little late don't you think?" Murh'sooli replied.

"There's always a chance more ceiling will fall—ah, there it is." He managed to pull it out from under Murh'sooli without causing the man any more pain, then carefully placed on his head and clipped it in place, but not before saying, "Don't try to move, all right? Let your armor do its thing. Help's on the way."

Murh'sooli nodded, and, clutching his helmeted head in his left hand, sagged back against the wall.

Matoosh hurried next to Shu'hah. The soldier was awake but, by his glazed expression, rapidly succumbing to shock despite his armor, like Murh'sooli's, responding to the crushing blow by stiffening and in so doing, taking some of the weight off his body, forcing blood into his core and pumping needed drugs into his system. Matoosh tried to lift the crumpled beam off of him, but alone it was a futile effort.

He located Shu'hah's helmet, carefully slipped it on his head, made sure it was secure, hit his beacon then turned back to Delatorre and the three marines.

He gave the sergeant a quick once over, saw no obvious serious injuries, then, kneeling beside him, gently shook his shoulder. "Sergeant?"

Delatorre groaned and tried to curl into a ball.

"Sergeant, I need your help—*please.*"

"Maybe... maybe I can help," came another voice. He turned to find one of the marines—he placed the human's name as Private Lhota?—staggering to his feet.

He hurried over to him and steadied him, then said, "Shu'hah—he's trapped."

Lhota nodded, stumbled after Matoosh, over to Shu'hah. "First things first, helmets," Matoosh said. Together they donned them, then they tried to lift the joist. Even with two, assisted by their armor, it was just too heavy.

Matoosh knelt down beside Shu'hah, tapped his chin com and said, "Stay with me, Kon'ta'aq."

Shu'hah mumbled something unintelligible.

Matoosh looked around to find Lhota sliding Delatorre's helmet over the man's head, nodded, then he opened the triage kit and sorted through its stock in hopes of finding something to assist Shu'hah's armor's in-built pharmacy.

"What the hell happened?" came a raspy voice.

Matoosh turned to find Delatorre now on his feet, fumbling with his helmet's fasteners.

"The ceiling collapsed—" Matoosh began, but was cut off by a faint, and all too familiar whine. He turned to the two Rimmers. *"They've found us!"*

"Who found us?" Delatorre asked warily.

Before Matoosh could answer, the flicker effect took hold, grabbing all of them and whisking them away.

Main staging bay, Faridour, *end of High Watch.*

Matoosh, still clutching Shu'hah's wrist, released the breath he'd been holding as he immediately recognized the interior of the massive bay; he almost grinned as he looked up at his companions. "We're aboard *Faridour!*"

His comment did not have the immediately reassuring effect he'd expected.

"Faridour...?" Delatorre repeated unsteadily as Lhota's helmeted head snapped this way and that, the marine scanning the brightly lit chamber in uneasy silence. Nearby lay another marine, face down and unmoving on the oddly iridescent floor. Next to him another, and a little further away sat Murh'sooli, his helmeted head cradled in his armored hands. With the supporting rock wall now gone, he abruptly toppled onto his right side.

Adding to Delatorre and Lhota's growing panic—audible to Matoosh by their rapid breathing alone, no need to check his visor's readouts—pulsing lines slithered from the surrounding walls and darted across the surface of the deck only to coalesce around each of the fallen—worse, around their own feet. Both Rimmers turned to Matoosh as Delatorre whispered, *"What the fucking hell...?"*

Before Matoosh could explain, could reassure his nervous companions, airlocks at opposite ends of the bay snapped open in unison and soldiers in full battle panoply, weapons held at the ready, poured into the bay and fanned out to quickly surround them.

For the two Rimmers, the floor and its strange, slithering pattern was instantly forgotten in preference for a far more obvious and immediate danger. Delatorre's helmeted head swung around to face Matoosh as Lhota's softly uttered and deeply sincere protective oath crackled in Matoosh's earpiece.

"It's all right—just standard procedure. No one's going to shoot you," Matoosh offered, but his reassurances had little effect on the two.

A moment later the ring of soldiers parted as unarmored medical personnel and equipment arrived. They converged on

Matoosh and his small, unmoving group, several clustering around Murh'sooli, others around the fallen marines and Shu'hah.

"You can let go now, Ruh'ta'aq."

Matoosh blinked and looked up to find *Faridour*'s Chief Medical Officer, Hai'chellah, standing next to him, along with the *Baidarka*'s pathologist Xosé Tasende.

Delatorre pulled off his helmet, gasped, "Xosé, gods am I relieved to see you!" and clapped Tasende on the back.

The burly Lhota too edged a little closer to the stocky pathologist. Tasende, for his part, looked at little taken aback at his sudden popularity with fellow crewmen who normally barely gave him the time of day.

"We'll take it from here," Hai'chellah added as she knelt beside Matoosh and gently pried his gauntleted fingers from Shu'hah's wrist. "And you have your own injuries that need tending, Ruh'ta'aq."

Matoosh nodded, then, with Tasende and Delatorre's help, lurched unsteadily to his feet. "What about the others?"

Hai'chellah looked up from examining Shu'hah. "They're still searching for Sha'ashahn and Rukoobi Kon'ta'aq, Ruh'ta'aq." She shifted her gaze to Delatorre and added, "The other two members of your team are safely aboard *Baidarka*, Sergeant, as is Toubeh Ruh'ta'aq." She flicked Tasende a pointed glance. "Xosé, if you will?"

"Come with me," Tasende said. "Let's get you three to sickbay." Motioning for Matoosh, Delatorre and Lhota to follow, he started towards the open airlock.

Chapter 27

Level 5, abandoned mining complex, Poonda Five.

Khusaaq opened his eyes only to find himself face down in rubble and something—*someone*, he quickly amended—sprawled across his back. By scent he knew it was Rukoobi; he could also smell fresh blood and lots of it.

His last coherent memory was of Rukoobi yelling a warning then being tackled and knocked to the ground.

"Kon'ta'aq?"

Getting no response, he carefully felt around and finally located one of Rukoobi's armored hands. His wrist was stiff—in fact his entire left arm was rigid, only the shoulder joint was movable—his armor had reacted to his injuries, forcing blood back into his vital organs, to his brain, while stabilizing fractures, evidence enough Rukoobi was seriously, if not fatally injured, hemorrhaging inside his armor. He could also hear the man's breathing. It was shallow and accompanied by an ominous gurgling.

Fearful to move, to further injure the severely injured man, Khusaaq tried to figure out their exact situation. Nearby lay one of their torches, its beam the only source of light. He saw no one else, and, even more importantly smelled and heard no one else. He reached out, carefully. His fingertips lightly brushed the butt of the torch but it was just a little too far away to actually grab. *Chiku!*

His slight movement, however, did elicit a soft groan from Rukoobi.

"Don't try to move, Kon'ta'aq."

Rukoobi, heedless, groaned again then tried to rise, struggling clumsily against his own armor, in the process somehow managing to dislodge the slab of rock that had fallen on his back.

Realizing this might be his only chance, Khusaaq carefully wriggled out from under him and Rukoobi promptly collapsed beside him.

Khusaaq awkwardly lurched to his knees and shoved the slab the rest of the way off Rukoobi, then gave the soldier a quick, head to toe visual exam as Rukoobi weakly coughed up foamy blood.

What he saw confirmed his worst fears. The soldier was surrounded in a faint, cloyingly sweet nimbus of purple, the most obvious sign of pain so severe and on so many levels it had overwhelmed his armor's ability to control it.

Khusaaq gave his own armor's wrist readouts a quick glance to find that he'd been far more fortunate due to Rukoobi's selfless actions and only suffered a dislocated right shoulder and broken left ankle—*and five cracked ribs*, the readouts warned as he started to take a deep, mind-clearing breath.

He activated his emergency retrieval beacon and Rukoobi's, then he staggered to his feet and snatched up the torch.

Sweeping their surroundings with the light only corroborated what he already knew: they were alone. A mass of fallen rock blocked the passageway where he'd last seen Matoosh, Delatorre and the others. It also cut them off from their only route of escape.

He limped over to the rockfall and placed his palm and outstretched fingers against it. A glance at his wrist sensors registered no signs of life within ten meters.

Khusaaq unclipped his tac-pac and brought it to his lips. *"Matoosh? Can you receive?"*

Answered only by the low, warbling whine and crackle of electronic hash, he adjusted the frequency then tried, "*Baidarka? Baidarka*, this is Khusaaq Sha'ashahn. Medical emergency—lock onto my signal... *Baidarka? Baidarka*, are you receiving?"

Again answered by hash, he reclipped the tac-pac to his weapons belt then took stock. His sensors had earlier warned him, warned them all that the surrounding rock at this depth was heavily laced with pockets of highly radioactive ore—the reason for the mine in the first place—making Coalition communications and sensor readings at this depth at worst nonexistent, at best unreliable and the initially accepted explanation for the missing landing party's silence.

A'tuu'shahn sensors and tac-pacs should have had no issue, even at this level, and hadn't up until the collapse, which suggested another, far more ominous explanation: they were being jammed. And if that was the case, signals from their emergency retrieval beacons wouldn't be picked up, either, even if an A'tuu'shahn vessel with its far more powerful receivers was within range—and at last check, *Faridour* and her outriders were not scheduled to arrive in the system for another hour.

Rukoobi didn't have that much time.

Khusaaq had only one option and that was to retreat further into the cave system, away from the unstable section, away from the source of the jamming, in the hopes that his tac-net could get through to the *Baidarka,* or, barring that he could find a com station or flicker chamber. He knew there were many within the sprawling mine—Poonda Five did have regulations when it came to mining operations—with the compulsory two com stations and emergency flicker chamber on every level. He just didn't know exactly where they were located or if any were still functional, and that was assuming they'd been functional in the first place. Mine operators everywhere were notorious for skirting safety regulations they considered superfluous and too expensive after all and placing just the framework of a com station or flicker chamber did address the letter, if not the spirit of the law.

Leaving also meant moving away from the rockfall and, therefore, away from anyone trapped on the other side... or underneath. *Right now my priority is the one person I know is still alive: Rukoobi.*

With that, he knelt beside the man and reassessed the damage. The drugs had clearly cut Rukoobi's agony, the nimbus had faded, and what remained had coalesced around his lower back, but there was only so much the armor could do. At best it could provide a little more time.

He very slowly and carefully rolled Rukoobi onto his back; as he did so, Rukoobi coughed several times then opened his eyes and stared glassily up at Khusaaq.

"What... happened?" Rukoobi whispered as fresh blood foamed from the corner of his mouth and from his nose.

"The roof caved in, I can't find the others and you've been badly injured."

Rukoobi managed a half-hearted, wincing chuckle and a mumbled, "Ah. So... so this isn't... isn't just a... a really, *really* bad dream."

"I'm afraid not, Kon'ta'aq."

He nodded then succumbed to another fit of coughing.

Khusaaq waited until Rukoobi had had a moment to recover then said, "I'll carry you." Aside from the obvious, there was another less altruistic reason not to leave him behind: without immediate care, Rukoobi would indeed die and when that happened, his armor, sensing no living A'tuu'shahn was close at hand, would respond. The resulting explosion would collapse the rest of the passageway, possibly even pancaking the floors above down onto them and anyone else still alive—which begged the question, if others were in as bad a shape, or worse on the other side of the collapsed passageway or under it, then an explosion might be imminent, regardless.

"We have to get as far away from the rockfall as possible," he continued, leaving the rest unsaid. By the look Rukoobi gave him and then the rockfall, it was clear the soldier had come to the same conclusion. "Here. You guide us, all right?" He handed him the torch, which Rukoobi clutched to his stomach, then said, "Ready?"

"Would... would it make... a difference if... if I said no, ta'ahn?"

Khusaaq shook his head.

"Thought not." With that, Rukoobi clenched his teeth and nodded.

Khusaaq, using his good arm, awkwardly scooped up the man's now semi-rigid body.

Rukoobi's face twisted in agony—despite the infusion of painkillers, despite the now cast-like armor—but he didn't make a sound.

Khusaaq quickly cradled his upper body against his dislocated shoulder, wrapped his right arm around Rukoobi then lurched to his feet.

The torch, braced on Rukoobi's stomach, remained clutched in his armored fingers and its beam provided just enough light for Khusaaq to see where he was going and avoid tripping over the rubble. Such a stumble, he knew, would cost Rukoobi his tenuous grip on life.

He adjusted his hold on the man, then, with one last glance at the rockfall, started down the passageway, all the while trying to keep his bearings so he could, if needed, retrace his steps.

Each time he came across a side corridor, he'd stop, and Rukoobi would dutifully point the torch's beam into its maw. No com station or flickerstage presented itself; the featureless, unfinished corridors only led off into the darkness, however, Khusaaq had, momentarily, felt the weakest of tingles race up his left arm from wrist-mounted sensor cluster to his shoulder: his retrieval beacon had picked up a responding signal, too faint to fully activate but just strong enough to cause the beacon to go into reacquisition mode. *Faridour,* or at least some of her outriders, had arrived ahead of schedule.

Or perhaps nothing more than a case of wishful thinking... The tingle had been so brief after all, so faint, the more he thought about it, the less he was sure he'd felt it at all.

Doesn't matter, he told himself. *Just keep moving.*

After leaving a directional mark on the dust-covered floor with his heel, he staggered on, painfully aware that Rukoobi's breathing was becoming more labored and wet by the minute and that the torch's light was dimming. *Just a little farther...*

He figured they'd covered a couple hundred meters when the main corridor suddenly split in two. He stopped and as he caught his breath, he stared first at the left, rough-hewn and darkened passageway then the right, knowing if he made the wrong choice Rukoobi would die—painfully aware there might not *be* a right choice.

"Hero to the last."

He flinched, startled by the unexpected yet oh-so familiar voice, a voice that had haunted him for most of his life, then slowly turned, the torch's beam following.

Its faint glow washed across five individuals as they emerged from the deeper recesses of the left-hand corridor, hidden until that moment from his sensors by just a matter of a few dozen meters: a Looper, two Matarii, a Thalamian and...

"Gaalan."

As she strode purposely towards him, she tipped her head, slightly. "Khusaaq."

Unlike her companions, she appeared unarmed. The other four had their weapons pointed at him and once in the main corridor, they fanned out to surround him.

"I understand you've been looking for me," Khusaaq replied.

"Yes. And you, me." Gaalan motioned irritably to two of her companions. "Disarm them."

One of the Matarii and the Thalamian warily approached, then with obvious distaste at touching armored mercs, nevertheless made quick and unnecessarily rough work of removing Khusaaq and Rukoobi's weapons before hastily backing away again, clutching their rewards for doing the disagreeable work.

Gaalan gestured to the ground at Khusaaq's feet. "I'm sure you're extremely tired—and he's *dead* weight, a virtual stiff," she chuckled, "so why don't you put him down?"

Khusaaq felt the tingle in his arm return, stronger this time—and this time he was sure about it. *Stall...* "It's me you want, not him, so how about we make a deal?"

"You're in no position to make any kind of deal my friend. Now, put him down voluntarily, or I'll ask my friends to do it for you and I suspect they won't be as careful. A'tuu'shahn armor weighs a lot."

Out of the corner of his eye he saw the other Matarii this time and the Looper take a step closer. "I'll go with you— willingly..."

That stopped them and the two looked questioningly at Gaalan; she motioned them to remain where they were.

"...no tricks, I give you my word, if you'll provide him with the medical care he needs and safe passage back to the Orthodoxy."

She briefly studied Rukoobi's bloodied face, then met Khusaaq's pinched stare. "He's Khighalli."

"And you're Elkanaghalli."

"Was Elkanaghalli. But that was a very long time ago. People change."

"And some do not."

"Like you." She sauntered up to him, and, stopping in front of him, met his gaze. For a moment they stared at each other. Her expression softened and she said, "You look so much like him."

His expression remained steely. "Ja'andai."

"Yes. Especially now—you're about the same age he was when he *died.*" She looked him up and down, adding, "Thinner, *yes,* definitely thinner. What's the matter? Doesn't being a Coalition puppet agree with you?"

He gave her a quick up and down glance and replied disdainfully: "Being Matarii puppet does seem to agree with you—perhaps far too well."

Gaalan grinned at that then lightly ran her fingertip along his jaw, following one particular tattoo as it coiled and curled from ear to chin. "He was so beautiful—*just like you...*" Feeling his jaw muscles twitch against her unwanted touch, her smile twisted into a malicious grin. "And your *doh'ha* of course. He's almost too pretty—just like you were as a boy. The curse of the Abhijit'tischinjgra line and the torment of being an Elkanaghalli. *Such a pity.*"

She chuckled and stepped back, arms akimbo. "And now, here you are all grown up, the vaunted *Hero of Cotopaxi*—among other equal and vastly overblown accolades."

"That was a role, a title I never wanted, never sought—"

"So I heard, but that only endeared you to the ignorant masses, didn't it?"

"Not everyone, certainly not your brother." He tried not to twitch as the persistent tingle suddenly turned to a distinct albeit uneven pulsation.

Oblivious, Gaalan shook her head as she dropped her gaze to Rukoobi. "Yes... *Narbrooi.*"

Khusaaq too looked down at him and realized that he'd lapsed into unconsciousness. He could literally feel Rukoobi's life slipping through his fingers and he tightened his hold. *Stall... just a few more minutes until the beacon gets a definite lock—* Using Rukoobi, he realized, as bait, his impending death as an inducement to keep Gaalan here, to keep them all here.

"Narbrooi's a narrow-minded, sanctimonious fanatic." Gaalan's cold stare never wavered from Rukoobi's slack, blood-smeared face. She reached out, gently wrapped her fingers around the man's gauntleted right wrist then lifted his dangling arm and with surprising care, laid it across his chest.

"Just like Ja'andai."

She only shrugged, gave Rukoobi a pat on the arm, murmured sweetly: "Better? Yes, I thought so."

"He's now Hahtra'tzrhi, with *Faridour* as his flagship."

She lifted her gaze and snickered, "Oh yes, I know—I do keep up with things, how else would I have known where to look for you?" She paused, shook her head and said as if to herself, "To think that whiny little brat whose ass I wiped more times than I can remember now commands a planet-killer, not to mention an entire fleet. *Truly* boggles the mind." She looked sharply at Khusaaq. "I do hope he's grown out of his temper tantrums? Could be problematic with his finger so close to a trigger that could wipe out half this sector."

"Let's just say he's learned to control them."

She laughed. "I bet—"

Rukoobi coughed feebly, in the process splattering them both with droplets of foamy blood.

She stepped back, glanced down at herself and made a cursory attempt at wiping the spatter from her expensive clothing and face then she fixed Khusaaq with a smug stare. "Now, about your... *deal.*" She cocked her head to one side, and, looking thoughtful, tapped her fingertip on her chin. *"Humm..."*

He winced as he tried to adjust his slipping hold on Rukoobi. Catching the look in her eye, he realized she too was deliberately stalling, in her case forcing him to stand there, holding Rukoobi until he lost his grip. The armor could augment his strength only so much.

"What, say at most another five minutes?" she asked.

His heart skipped a beat—*maybe she knows, maybe she can sense the beacon, somehow.* His armor should have blocked any signal leak, but... "I don't understand—"

"Until he dies and his armor reacts by detonating."

He tried not to look as relieved as he felt, while out of the corner of his eye, Khusaaq saw her confederates take a collective step back, as if that small distance would make a whit of difference.

Gaalan noticed too and snorted in contempt before again fixing her eyes on him, eyes, a part of his mind realized, were bright blue, not telling A'tuu'shahn gray. He hadn't noticed before—

"Did you really think after all these years I'd forgotten about that lovely failsafe?" she asked. "The ultimate terror weapon for both enemy and wearer alike. Did you know that command can detonate a soldier's armor remotely, regardless of the individual's condition?"

"Yes," Khusaaq hissed through clenched teeth.

"I always thought that was such a wonderfully callous option—one's own officers posing as great a danger to life and limb as any enemy. But then A'tuu'shahn'i as a whole are a very callous lot, don't you agree?"

"But it won't detonate if he dies, not here, not with living A'tuu'shahn'i so close."

"You didn't notice but I just cancelled that failsafe." She motioned to Rukoobi's right arm and the controller on his wrist.

He refused to play into her game by looking down, to confirm she'd in fact managed to hit the recessed button when she'd placed Rukoobi's arm on his chest. An unexpected act of compassion that was anything but.

"Nahru'tzrhi rank and above can also *override* the detonation sequence," Khusaaq countered.

"Oh yes—yet *another* failsafe, but the obverse is that any attempt by someone hoping to somehow guess the correct sequence will only trigger the explosion immediately— absolutely no do-overs, no time to try to get away." She chuckled again, lifted a hand, fingers stopping just short of touching the control panel on Rukoobi's wrist.

She caught a telltale, reflexive twitch of Khusaaq's armored fingers, so close to the panel as well and grinned at him. He was in fact reacting to beacon's pulse pattern—much stronger now, and regular, a throb every eight seconds—but by Gaalan's smirking expression it was clear to him that she'd read the move as something else.

Just a few moments until they can lock on—stall. He winced as he readjusted his hold on Rukoobi, cementing her suspicions—no need to fake that.

"But you being only a *lowly* Sha'ashahn... you weren't given the code, were you?" Gaalan continued. "See? You should have accepted one of those countless offers of a generous bump up in rank. Had you done so, you'd have the knowledge to stop it. But, since I'm the only one here of high enough rank... now, shall we see if I can recall which code is which—"

"Assuming they haven't been changed in the interim," Khusaaq countered.

"Only one way to find out, yes?"

"Yes, I suppose so."

That prompted the others to reflexively shuffle back another few steps, everyone now realizing Gaalan was going to take it right up to the edge—maybe she was willing to die, to kill everyone present to make her point. Then again, Khusaaq reminded himself, she'd always been a master of brinksmanship, and knowingly, voluntarily, standing less than a meter away from a bomb about to go off was as ballsy as one could get.

And he'd been her ever-watchful protégé. *Two can play at this game.*

"Go ahead," he challenged with a smile of his own, fully expecting her confederates to take off running, not that that would've saved them if indeed Rukoobi's armor detonated, not in such a confined space. To his surprise they only edged a little further away and it dawned on him that they were far more afraid of Gaalan, of what she might do to them—if all survived the next few minutes.

The pulse was now coming every five seconds and more intense with each rolling beat.

She laughed, stepped back. "There's no need for *everyone* to die, is there? You've made your point, you've proven to us all that you are the *hero* to the last, yes?" She glanced over her shoulder at the others, all of whom nodded vigorously in response, then turned back to him and continued, "So now, put him down, and we'll flick out of here before he breathes his last and brings this entire complex down on us."

He took a breath, then another. *Stall...* "Please, Gaalan. I beg you."

"You? Begging for the life of a worthless Khighalli?"

"Then kill us both and be done with it." He tried not to twitch as the acquisition pulse again increased in intensity and tempo, now coming every three seconds and prompting the exhausted muscles in his effected arm to quiver in response. He mentally urged Rukoobi: *Hang on, just a little longer...*

"As personally appealing as your offer is, to do such would be such a waste—all that time and effort put into capturing you, and for what? A minute or two of intense, long-denied and well-deserved gratification? Tempting... very tempting, but you see, you're worth a fortune alive, didn't you know? That's something that should appeal to your poorly-hid vanity guised as self-effacement. My companions and I will be able to live very comfortably on what we'll get for you for a very long time, won't we?" She looked over her shoulder, briefly, to again acknowledge the anxious nods of the others. "And your very public death will be worth even more, although not in an immediate financial way, oh no. More like... an *endowment*, a gift that keeps on giving."

"What... *what happened to you?"*

She looked down at herself, then again meeting his gaze, cocked her head to one side. "Are you talking in generalities or something specific?"

"You know what I mean—why... *this?*" He curled his lip and jerked his chin dismissively towards the ragtag group of aliens who formed a loose and very nervous semi-circle around them. "From A'tuu'shahn hero to... to Matarii collaborator?"

"You flatter me," she grinned, eyes sparkling. "And we'll have plenty of time to talk, later, and preferably in far more... agreeable surroundings?" Her expression suddenly hardened, as did her tone. "Put him down. Now."

Khusaaq met her sneering gaze. A moment passed, another. Rukoobi continued to breathe, albeit feebly. He couldn't hold onto him much longer; he wouldn't drop him—he couldn't— but his strength was nearly gone and the pulse was no stronger, the interval between was still three seconds; clearly the *Faridour* was having some difficulty zeroing in on his and Rukoobi's retrieval beacons—

"Contrary Khighalli to the last," Gaalan murmured as she gazed down at him. "But I'm tired of waiting," she sighed, "and I do *so* hate seeing anyone, even a Khighalli, suffer." She motioned irritably to her companions.

As Khusaaq watched them reluctantly approach, he suddenly remembered something—something critical yet overlooked, even by him until that instant.

Time to take matters into my own hands—you're not going to escape, Gaalan, not this time.

He lifted his gaze back to her and reluctantly nodded then slowly, and *very* carefully dropped to his knees. He carefully eased his arm from under Rukoobi's armored legs, and using them as a blind, slipped his hand into the hidden slot on his left hip.

He whipped out the *t'jing* and fired four darts in rapid succession, dropping all of Gaalan's confederates before they could even react. Then he pointed the weapon at her as he slowly got back to his feet.

She stared back, her expression a mixture of surprise and delight. "I'm glad to see that you retained some of what I taught you... but a *t'jing*? Have you really sunk so low?"

"Have you forgotten our basic philosophy?"

"You mean the most effective weapon is always the one the enemy least expects?" She shrugged. "Well, that said, I certainly never expected the Hero of Cotopaxi to be carrying a *t'jing*."

The pulse suddenly sped up, stronger, now coming every two seconds.

"Neither did your friends," Khusaaq replied. "Pity that."

"But you won't kill an unarmed person—that was always one of your most glaring failings."

"Operative word is *was*. I got over it."

"Did you now. Well," she lifted her arms, "then shoot me. Go ahead."

"Like you, I find you are worth far more alive."

"Well, unfortunately, neither of us are going to be cashing in. I think your friend there," she jerked her chin towards Rukoobi as she slowly lowered her arms, "is on his last breaths. Not even your armor will save you—not this close even if you were wearing a helmet."

"Well, sadly for you, I have another unhappy surprise for you."

"Indeed, and what's that?"

Your jamming field—I must assume of Matarii design?"

"What if it is?"

"It's of rather limited scope."

Gaalan's smug grin stiffened.

"Not that there will be a next time for you, but you really should have gone with Gorm or Looper technology—but," he shrugged and sighed, feigning sadness, "you get what you pay for." He unclipped his tac-net with his free hand and brought it to his lips. "*Faridour?*"

Gaalan's grin vanished altogether.

At first he was answered by more electronic hash then a crackly voice replied, *"This is* Faridour, *Sha'ashahn. We read you. Ready to retrieve on your signal."*

"Have medical standing by, Rukoobi Kon'ta'aq is gravely injured—and scan around me. There's a third party present."

"Located and locked on—"

"Disable all weapons," he interrupted as he saw her start to reach behind her, "and flick the three of us outta here." He smiled at Gaalan and added, "You understand. Can't be too cautious these days," an instant before the flicker effect took hold.

Chapter 28

Isolation unit 2, sickbay, aboard the Baidarka, *2207.*

Sirin had kept time as she waited for word by counting how many cups of broth Pierson brought for Qar'qaah.

The medtech had just delivered mug number three and she plastered on yet another encouraging smile as she watched Qar'qaah cautiously sip at the less than tasty concoction.

Qar'qaah, blissfully ignorant of the nerve-racking turn of events, would every so often stop his single-minded analysis of the damaged fold-space generator to speculate on what was happening on the ground—as if he was truly beginning to accept that what he was experiencing was real—while she nodded and murmured her agreements. Perhaps he was just too tired to be scared any more—perhaps he was just trying to humor her.

Nihaal and Raudah were still seated on the deck but now they were leaning heavily against each other, heads nodding and data readers loosely held in their hands.

Sirin suspected Drakin was deliberately keeping Endooki and Laihiri away from the sickbay, away from Qar'qaah—thus keeping word about *Faridour* and her outriders' arrival from him as well. And the isolation unit was soundproofed, so even the klaxons and their warning dirge had been kept at bay—she only knew because Pierson had whispered the news to her while handing her the very first cup of the broth, which gave her renewed hope for Khusaaq's rescue. If anyone could find him, it would be his fellow Hahtooshans.

The ruse had worked. Qar'qaah, even with his acute hearing, clearly had no idea anything was amiss.

She looked back at him to find him intently watching her out of the corner of his eye. *Or do you?* Aloud she asked innocently, "Finished?"

He shook his head, brought the mug back to his lips and with a grimace, polished off the bland-tasting, vitamin and protein-packed liquid.

As he handed her the now empty mug, she responded with a genuine grin. He was trying his best and that deserved the real thing, despite the circumstances. "I'll let Doctor Amalfitano know you've kept everything down. So maybe tomorrow you can have something a little more appetizing—"

"Like chocolate milk?"

She smiled. "Yes, like chocolate milk."

He nodded then picked up the data reader and stared down at its display. By his rapid blinking, she could tell he was fighting the almost overwhelming urge to follow his friends into sleep.

"How 'bout you take a break?"

"But Lieutenant Perou—"

She plucked the reader from his hands. "Lieutenant Perou, and the foldspace generator, can wait 'til morning."

"But earlier you said—"

"I was joking." She placed the reader on the bedside table, then grabbed one of the folded up blankets Rosen had left on top of the nearby drug cart and drew it over him. "And you need some sleep."

By his expression, she could tell he was sorely tempted, but at the same time fearful of the terrors sleep might bring, fearful that everything he'd begun to believe might—*just might*—be real would disappear the instant he closed his eyes; that the game would start over, with new rules, new players but with the same goal.

"I'm not going anywhere, all right? *Relax,*" she soothed.

He tried. He honestly did. He closed his eyes, inhaled deeply then exhaled very slowly. His weakened, weary body readily embraced the idea, but the fear kept jolting him back to wakefulness.

"It's okay..."

He stared up at her, eyes already gone dull, unfocused, mind and body slipping, slipping into the dark—

"...you're safe, you can go to sleep..."

—but just to make sure, and with his last conscious impulse, he carefully, almost tentatively, wrapped his fingers around her hand—a lifeline, an anchor, to keep him from drifting too far away, back into the world of his nightmares.

"Shhhh..."

And he was gone.

She felt his entire body go limp. Breathing slowed and deepened—the relaxed cadence echoed by the muted, rhythmic *throb... throb... throb* of the over bed cardiac monitor.

She gave the empty mug a sidelong, suspicious glance, wondering if it hadn't been laced with a sedative—and equally suspicious this might be his way of testing her.

She waited a few minutes longer, then carefully eased her hand out from under his loosened grip. It would be hard to fool the monitors, but...

When he failed to react, when the readouts remained unchanged—not even the most minor of electronic twitches—and now satisfied he was truly fast asleep, she rose, picked up the other blanket, then walked over to Nihaal and Raudah and draped it over them.

Raudah barely stirred; Nihaal mumbled something unintelligible, then slowly slid down Raudah to end up with his head cradled in Raudah's lap.

She smiled then slipped back onto the fold-down chair, wrapped her fingers around Qar'qaah's wrist and with her free hand picked up her data reader, hoping she could lose herself in the romance novel she'd called up hours before, one that had come with Drakin's highest recommendation—five talons up on the steaminess scale—but hadn't, in fact, managed to read past the opening sentence.

Instead she again became aware of the sensation of being watched—only this time she knew it wasn't Qar'qaah.

Suspecting Amalfitano had come to check up on his charge, she lifted her gaze—and felt her breath catch in her throat.

A grim-faced Khusaaq stood in the doorway, his dust covered face and ghillie armor heavily smeared with blood.

His blood? Her initial, intense relief dissolved into a gut twisting, *Gods!* as she rose and hurried to him.

He backed up unsteadily, drawing her into the narrow corridor and then into the neighboring cubicle.

Once they were alone, she stared up at him as she cautiously wrapped her arms around him, fearful of concealed injuries despite the protection of his armor. He draped his left arm around her shoulders, then rested his cheek on the top of her head and for several minutes neither spoke.

Finally he lifted his head, said huskily, "Gaalan's in custody aboard *Faridour*."

She looked up at him, at his dirty, bloody face. "But something terrible's happened, hasn't it?"

"Rukoobi Kon'ta'aq is dead."

She instantly put a face—a handsome, youthful and smiling face to the name—and squeezed her eyes shut, muttered, *"Dammit."* Then, realizing Khusaaq was shaking, she carefully slipped from his one-armed embrace. "Come with me." She took his left hand in hers and led him out of the cubicle, down the short passageway and into the airlock.

As they waited for the small chamber to cycle she gave him a quick once over. He looked as if he was about to collapse— from fatigue, shock, injury, she couldn't tell. Then the outer door opened and she was intensely relieved to find Amalfitano, Rosen and the very imposing Tayya'shan waiting for them.

"This way." Amalfitano walked into the nearest triage bay.

Sirin and Khusaaq wordlessly followed as Tayya'shan and Rosen brought up the rear.

Once in the bay, Amalfitano angrily motioned to Khusaaq's armor. "Off—and don't either of you *dare* give me any crap about us having to leave for our personal safety—that our mere proximity while the armor was being removed would trigger it to detonate—"

Sirin flicked Khusaaq, then Tayya'shan a startled glance. *"What—"*

"—I never bought Murh'sooli's warnings anyway," Amalfitano continued crossly, "none of you can lie your way out of a damned soap bubble if you ask me—"

Tayya'shan and Khusaaq exchanged quick, baffled glances at that as Tayya'shan mouthed *'soap bubble?'*

"—but just to be on the safe side, I asked Hai'chellah the first chance I got, and she told me that was a bucket-load of *bullshit.* Narbrooi thought it was hilarious that we 'gullible Rimmers' as he put it, believed it for a nanosecond. So thank you for that. Thank you for the experience of hearing Hai'chellah and Narbrooi have a good *long* laugh at my expense. I suspect it's all over *Faridour* by now, likely the entire fleet."

That left absolutely no room to protest. Khusaaq nodded wordlessly, and with Tayya'shan's clearly annoyed assistance, quickly stripped down to just his form-fitting undershorts.

"Down." Amalfitano pointed at the narrow trauma bed and Khusaaq eased himself down on it. He was still shaking; muscles twitching uncontrollably.

Sirin edged around the bed and out of everyone's way, placing herself next to his left shoulder. Then, as Amalfitano and the others bustled around the bed, Khusaaq stared up at her with blood-shot eyes and managed a tight smile. She interlaced her fingers with his and as she kissed him on the forehead, he briefly closed his eyes and took a deep, ragged breath.

"Hai'chellah also warned me you'd refused treatment," Amalfitano grumbled as he gently pressed a signal suppressor against Khusaaq's bruised left shoulder, in the process drawing Khusaaq's pinched gaze. "I suppose asking you when the *hell* you'll ever learn is pointless at this point, isn't it?"

Khusaaq started to shrug then wisely thought better of it. "I didn't refuse. I just prefer your care."

Amalfitano wasn't swayed by the feeble attempt at a compliment. He exhaled explosively and shook his head as he slipped a small probe under the skin of Khusaaq's right wrist, affixed it then turned his narrowed stare on the over-bed monitor as it filled with data.

Sirin too looked up and was grateful by what she saw.

"Dislocated shoulder... fractured ankle... five cracked ribs—looks like you suffered some internal bleeding initially—not surprising—but its stopped now thanks to that armor of yours... a helluva lot of deep and superficial contusions, along with some cuts and scrapes." Amalfitano dropped his gaze to his patient. "You were *incredibly* fortunate—"

"If it hadn't been for Rukoobi, I'd be dead," Khusaaq replied flatly.

Amalfitano, his worry-fueled anger now visibly replaced by relief that Khusaaq's injuries were relatively minor, considering, gave him a commiserating pat on the arm and murmured, "I know, son. Hai'chellah told me what happened and we'll talk more later. For now let's get that shoulder back where it belongs." He turned to Rosen. "I'll need some muscle relaxant—"

"This is faster," Tayya'shan interrupted. Before Amalfitano could react, the medic placed the palm of his right hand on Khusaaq's upper right chest, grabbed Khusaaq's right hand with his left and at Khusaaq's curt nod, yanked hard on his arm.

Sirin visibly grimaced at the resulting audible *POP!*

Amalfitano fixed his deeply reproachful stare first on Tayya'shan and then Khusaaq. "You two just *couldn't* wait, could you?"

Tayya'shan replied with an unapologetic shrug. Khusaaq for his part rotated his right shoulder then nodded his appreciation to the medic.

"My damned sickbay—*my* damned rules, got it?" Amalfitano scowled at the burly medic. "And I'll be having none of *that*. This isn't some forward base camp!" He pointed to Khusaaq's injured ankle then again scowled at the medic. "Can I trust you to wrap it, rather than rip it off?"

"Yes... *ta'ahn,"* Tayya'shan replied with an equally annoyed sigh as he accepted an immobilizer from Rosen.

Amalfitano turned to Sirin. "I'm going to give him a painkiller—*no arguments from you!"* he snapped as Khusaaq started to open his mouth, "—then I want him to get some food and fluids into him and then I want him to lie down and *stay* down for a minimum of eight hours."

Sirin looked at the isolation unit then back at Amalfitano. "But what about Qar'qaah, what—"

"You let me and the nurses worry about Qar'qaah. Besides, he'll be sound sleep until morning."

So, the broth was laced. She smiled, then caught Amalfitano's sidelong, pointed glance. *And you're going to slip something to Khusaaq, too.*

While she didn't like the idea of giving Khusaaq something he'd refuse if asked—and knew Amalfitano didn't either—they also knew *him* too well: instead of getting rest, he'd instead spend the night rehashing all the details, looking to find fault—*his fault.*

She replied with an ever-so-slight nod.

Amalfitano accepted a ject-it from Rosen, pressed it against Khusaaq's left shoulder then handed it back to her. "Now, let's get those ribs taken care of." He offered him a hand up and Khusaaq rose awkwardly from the bed.

Once he was standing, Rosen and Tayya'shan made quick work of encasing his badly bruised torso in a lightweight compression dressing.

"Expect to be stiff and quite sore for a few days—absolutely *no* physical stuff, okay?"

Khusaaq flicked Sirin a meaningful look and she struggled not to laugh despite the situation; that wasn't what Amalfitano had meant—and in truth it wasn't a laughing matter. Perhaps he was serious; perhaps he desperately needed the reassurance only physical intimacy could offer.

Perhaps it was his attempt to ease her fears about him: *Don't worry, I'm okay.*

Perhaps it was a good bit of all of these.

"I don't want you to sprain, strain, bruise or break anything that has somehow, so far, miraculously escaped unscathed—while giving the parts of you that didn't a chance to recoup..."

She again met Khusaaq's unhappy gaze with a slightly wicked smile. *That just means I'll just have to do all the work.*

His mouth twitched and he quickly turned his attention back to Amalfitano as the doctor, seemingly oblivious to their silent conversation, continued, "...I'll order a tray from the galley—and you can use my cabin. It's closer than yours—don't want you hobbling around on that ankle any more than necessary. *Got it?*"

"Yes, ta'ahn. Once in bed I won't move more than a muscle—you have my word."

"Good," Amalfitano replied slowly, as if realizing that somewhere along the line, he'd missed something critical.

"Come on." Sirin carefully wrapped her arm around Khusaaq's waist and he draped his arm around her shoulder. Then, together, they started for Amalfitano's office.

The trip was slow as Khusaaq hobbled alongside. As soon as they reached the door of Amalfitano's private cabin, he released his hold on her, awkwardly hopped the last meter or so to the bed then cautiously eased himself down.

Sirin sat beside him and lightly grasped his knee as he dropped his head into his hands. Then, overhearing the sound of approaching steps, she looked up to find Rafe Pierson in the doorway, a tray held in his hands.

Pierson wordlessly handed it to her, and as the medtech retreated, closing and locking the door behind him, assuring them complete privacy, Sirin lifted the lid on the covered plate. "It's your favorite... mushroom frittata—with a side of chocolate cream pie."

"I'm not hungry." He ground the heels of his hands into his eye sockets, pressing, *pressing*, clearly trying to squeeze out the pain, the memory of Rukoobi's labored, gurgling breathing that just... *stopped*. After a moment he gave up.

Watching him, she realized he was no longer in the mood, had totally chilled down—had probably not been the mood to begin with, that his sidelong look had just been his way of trying to reassure *her*. But he was also trying not to retreat back into his Hahtooshan persona, trying very hard to stay with her. At that moment that was enough.

"You want to risk crossing Doctor Amalfitano again?"

He slowly lifted his head from its cradle to squint blearily at her as she placed the tray on his lap. "I guess I could eat something." He picked up the tall, frosty glass of ice water and downed its contents in several gulps, then picked up the fork and prodded the frittata with it. But that's as far as he got. The pie didn't even garner a glance. He tossed the fork onto the plate. "I'm really not hungry. Maybe later."

"All right." She rose and placed the tray on the cabin's small fold-down desk, then turned back to find that he'd sprawled back onto the bed and suddenly remembered the other silent conversation she'd had—the one with Amalfitano.

She pulled a spare blanket from the over-bed storage bin, but as she drew it over him, he opened his eyes.

"I thought you'd fallen asleep."

"No, just thinking."

"About Rukoobi?"

A muscle in his jaw twitched.

Answer enough... She sat beside his hip and wrapped her hands around his and murmured, "Tell me what you're thinking."

He fixed his gaze on the far wall, took a breath. "I suspected it was a trap from the outset. I *should* have gone alone—I should have insisted. It was *me* she wanted, no one else."

This time her only response was to tighten her hold on his hand.

He closed his eyes and for several minutes neither spoke— but she could tell by his breathing that he was still very much awake, still thinking, still tearing his actions apart, tearing himself apart, piece by piece.

Finally, unable to watch the private dissection any longer, she said, "Qar'qaah's improving by the hour. Doctor Amalfitano thinks he can even start on some limited physical therapy tomorrow."

Khusaaq opened his eyes; he wasn't fooled by her ploy but was willing to go along as he'd clearly run out of scenarios and had come to the same inevitable conclusion. "That's good news—"

"He's even been behaving himself."

"Are we talking about the same Qar'qaah?"

She smiled, hoping he wouldn't see her worries—he didn't need anything else heaped on top of him right now.

"Do you think he'll be strong enough to flick over to *Faridour* in a few days?"

"Uh... I don't know. That's something you'll have to ask Doctor Amalfitano, but why?"

"I wish to spare him the trauma of testifying in front of the Q'shaathrah. If he can positively identify Gaalan as the one who…" he paused, clenched his teeth, then continued stiffly, "who took him and the others prisoner, he won't have to return to the Orthodoxy, at least not until he's ready, and Narbrooi, understandably, is eager to return Gaalan for trial."

"Let's take things one step at a time, all right? And right now you need to get some sleep."

"But—"

She put her finger to his lips. "No buts. Doctor Amalfitano will have to give his permission for Qar'qaah to make the trip and he's not going to be very agreeable to anything if you don't do exactly as he told you. You've already said no to something to eat. Refuse to get some rest and your chances go out the airlock."

He reluctantly nodded and scooted over, making room for her on the narrow bunk.

She cuddled up against his chest and he wrapped his arm around her, tugging her even more tightly against him.

"How 'bout I help you get to sleep?" Her suggestion had been an innocent one; her intention had been to massage his taut shoulders, maybe his neck and temples.

He immediately released his hold and very carefully rolled onto his back.

She levered herself up onto one elbow and realizing that he'd warmed up fast—*real fast*—she grinned and murmured, "Now remember, let me do all the work… doctor's orders."

Chapter 29

Isolation unit, sickbay, aboard the Baidarka, *0632.*

"Mornin', Chief."

Amalfitano looked up from the isolation unit's bank of active monitors to find Pierson walking towards him, an overloaded meal tray in hand.

"Mornin', Kon'ta'aq." Pierson nodded to Jaa'qwah, who was seated beside Amalfitano at the small unit's horseshoe console. The medtech placed the heavily laden tray on the console, adding, "Ran into Nihaal and Raudah down in the galley and they mentioned you were both awake. So I thought I'd grab you some breakfast before Raudah snarfed up everything in sight—geez, that kid can *eat*, and Nihaal ain't no slouch." He placed a covered plate in front of each then removed the covers with a flourish. *"Voila!"*

Amalfitano couldn't help but grin as he saw what the man had brought.

It had quickly become common knowledge that Hahtooshans—at least the Hahtooshans they had on board, even the perpetually truculent Tayya'shan—all shared a *serious* sweet tooth. Cakes, puddings, pastries and cupcakes had vanished as quickly as the cooks could prepare them, much to the chagrin of the *Baidarka*'s resident dessert fanciers, chief among them Teague, Zayyad, Izraad and, most of all, Lesedi. But even Lesedi, who'd single-handedly kept a half-dozen thugs at bay in order to protect Tasende from their boss, an irate antiquities dealer who didn't appreciate being told he was selling blatant Dabih Negus fakes, wasn't foolish enough to get between a determined Hahtooshan and the last cream-puff on a dessert tray.

Amalfitano's nursing staff had even gone so far as to flick over a week's generous supply of double fudge brownies for Murh'sooli—the medic's personal favorite—to aid in his swift recovery, much to the puzzlement of the Hahtooshan flicker techs, not mention the *Faridour*'s medical staff. It had been left up to the medic if he shared, and going by the hourly updates Amalfitano was getting from Hai'chellah, the medic wasn't in a giving mood.

Pierson, tutored by the cooks as to Jaa'qwah's predilections, had brought him his favorite: a mountain of chocolate chip hotcakes smothered in chocolate syrup and whipped cream, along with a large mug of hot cocoa, also topped with whipped cream.

For Amalfitano there were from-scratch biscuits, jelly and a mound of scrambled eggs, along with a cup of coffee.

Jaa'qwah grinned his appreciation and immediately dug in while Amalfitano leaned back in his chair and took a leisurely sip of coffee.

Unable to retreat to the comforts of his private cabin, he'd instead spent the night seated at the isolation unit's console, with the intention of catching up on paperwork while keeping an eye on Qar'qaah.

Tayya'shan had dutifully accompanied him and then, an hour or so into the vigil, Jaa'qwah had arrived to relieve his fellow medic.

It didn't take long for Amalfitano to realize, much to his relief, that Jaa'qwah was the antithesis of standoffish and laconic Tayya'shan. Bar'ahani at least would engage in conversation, although she never instigated it. Even Murh'sooli and his mordant outlook on life had been a damned sight better company than Tayya'shan, who, Amalfitano had come to suspect, was physically incapable smiling and who found verbalizing more than five syllables at any given time an agonizing and utterly unnecessary chore. In comparison, Jaa'qwah was a veritable chatterbox.

Jaa'qwah and Amalfitano had spent the remainder of the night alternately making rounds and watching the bank of monitors while discussing their varied medical experiences, occasionally straying to personal anecdotes.

While separated by well over three decades in age, and having lived vastly different lives, they found common threads in their stories and by the time Pierson arrived with breakfast,

Amalfitano felt as if he'd known the affable Dakkeesh all of the young man's life.

He took another sip of coffee then said, "Thanks, Rafe."

"You're welcome, Chief." With a nod to the now bulging-cheeked and chocolate-lipped Jaa'qwah, Pierson turned on his heel and walked out of the unit.

Amalfitano had no sooner scooped up his first forkful of scrambled eggs when he noticed that Jaa'qwah was staring intently at something as the medic swallowed his substantial mouthful of hotcake with a loud, wincing gulp.

Amalfitano followed Jaa'qwah's startled stare and his own eyes widened. Qar'qaah stood in the open airlock that gave access to the isolation unit, clutching the frame with both hands.

"Cazzo!" Amalfitano tossed his fork onto his plate, rose and, following Jaa'qwah, hurried over to Qar'qaah.

Qar'qaah watched their approach with what looked to Amalfitano to be cautious relief at finding them instead of Cisne and her crew. Then it struck him that he hadn't been warned by the cubicle's monitors that Qar'qaah was not only awake, but up. Qar'qaah had somehow managed to override the bed's inbuilt alarm—perhaps for the very purpose of taking them by surprise, to test if they really were… real.

Jaa'qwah got a firm grip on Qar'qaah's elbow, steadying him, as Amalfitano carefully pried his tattooed fingers from their death grip on the airlock's frame. Much to his relief, Qar'qaah didn't fight, didn't try to avoid their touch beyond the normal Hahtooshan reluctance to physical contact—and most importantly, he didn't look too afraid. Wary, yes. That was to be expected—but not the fear that had been a constant in Qar'qaah's gaze, his body language. *That's a hopeful sign—a damned hopeful sign—*

"What are you doing up, Kon'ta'aq?" he asked in a mildly reproving tone.

In reply, Qar'qaah leaned close to Jaa'qwah and whispered into his ear.

Amalfitano turned his questioning gaze on the medic.

Jaa'qwah grinned. "You'll be pleased to know that his kidneys and gut are working."

Amalfitano stared at him for an instant. Then, grasping what Jaa'qwah was hinting at, he smiled at Qar'qaah and pointed to the nearby staff head. "Over there."

Jaa'qwah wrapped his arm around Qar'qaah's waist and as the two walked very slowly towards the door, Amalfitano studied Qar'qaah's gait and balance with a critical eye. Pleased by what he saw, he started back for the console—and his breakfast—when Aquila's voice crackled from a nearby speaker: *"Doctor Amalfitano... please respond."*

As he slipped back onto his chair, he squinted at the speaker, wondering what new disaster the man's page might herald, and thumbed the activator. "This is Amalfitano—"

"William," Aquila replied, *"just heard from Narbrooi—they've retrieved Beta team—"*

"Alive?"

"Yup. Narbrooi said none appeared to be seriously injured—a few broken bones, some cuts and scrapes from being roughed up by Gaalan and her hooligans—and of course more than just a little unnerved to find themselves aboard Faridour. The Hahtooshans are keeping the two Thalamians who'd been left to guard them... for questioning."

"I wouldn't want to be them, that's for sure. Thalamians don't seem to fair very well when they've gotten themselves on the wrong side of the Hahtooshans."

"No, they don't—then again, I think it's safe to say no one does. Narbrooi said he hoped they'd prove themselves valuable as far as implicating their leader, but said if the Coalition wants to press charges, we could file a request for extradition and he'd take it under consideration."

Amalfitano couldn't help but chuckle at that. "I say leave them with the Hahtooshans and good luck to them."

"Yeah, my thoughts too, but told him I'll pass along the offer to HQ. Narbrooi said once his medicos have checked Beta team out, they'll be flicked over to us."

Amalfitano exhaled as he slumped back into his chair then asked, "So, now what?"

"You mean what next with Gaalan?"

"Yeah."

"Now that everyone's accounted for, we're breaking orbit, along with the Hahtooshans and—"

"Good riddance to Poonda Five," Amalfitano muttered, realizing the planet's inhabitants undoubtedly felt the same way about them… and then some—a *lot* some.

"—Narbrooi's plan is to get into neutral space, then hold a preliminary hearing aboard Faridour, *maybe as early as the day after tomorrow to inform Gaalan of the charges against her—"*

"I *definitely* wouldn't want to be her, that's for certain." He couldn't help but give the closed door to the head a sidelong glance.

"Neither would I," Aquila continued, *"and who knows, maybe like Khusaaq suggested, the Hahtooshans have their own Senator Behardien—Narbrooi made no secret that this alliance has its doubters, not just among the rank and file, but while he didn't expressly say so, within the Q'shaathrah itself as well."*

"Let's hope they're more successful at rooting them out than our side has been."

"True, but if not handled carefully, Gaalan, just like Behardien, could turn into a rallying point for dissenters. She was at one time a hero among her people after all."

"But since then she's allied herself with the Matarrans, even sold out her own kind—"

"Never underestimate the power of a martyr, Will—or the ability of time to reshape history into something more to its liking." Aquila paused then asked, *"Uh, Will, Narbrooi wanted to know if Qar'qaah would be stable enough to attend the hearing."*

"Well, he's up and, believe it or not, walking around… with Jaa'qwah's help, but it's a little too soon to tell. I should have a better idea later today."

"Narbrooi did say he's willing to delay the hearing a day or more, if needed. He clearly wants Qar'qaah to appear, to give testimony, but he made it clear his attendance is voluntary—he will not order it."

"Good. I'd like Zarijan to have a crack at him first, assuming Khusaaq and Qar'qaah give consent. If she thinks he can handle it, psychologically, well, then I'll give a conditional medical go-ahead."

"I'll inform Narbrooi. And I'll let you know when our people are ready to flick over—Aquila out."

Amalfitano picked up his forgotten mug of coffee, took a deep gulp, and then another, chased down by one of the biscuits. Then, hearing the head door open, he turned.

Jaa'qwah's pleased grin chased away the last of his worries, about Qar'qaah's physical recovery. Instead of assisting him back to his cubicle, Jaa'qwah instead helped Qar'qaah over to the console.

Qar'qaah gratefully sank down onto the body-hugging chair next to Amalfitano, exhausted by the short walk.

Amalfitano gave him a moment to recover, then asked, "How are you feeling, Kon'ta'aq?"

"Tired," he breathed. Then, lightly touching his abdomen added, "a little sore—" His nostrils suddenly flared and he looked down at the plates of food.

"And hungry…?"

Qar'qaah flicked him another sidelong look and, after a moment's hesitation, nodded, albeit *very* reluctantly.

"That's a good sign—a really good sign." Amalfitano pushed his untouched plate of scrambled eggs and his fork towards Qar'qaah as Jaa'qwah seated himself to Qar'qaah's right and surreptitiously tugged his own plate closer to himself.

Amalfitano wanted to laugh out loud at Jaa'qwah's subtle refusal to share his breakfast, or Qar'qaah's furtive, almost acquisitive glance at the chocolate soaked hotcakes.

"Here," Amalfitano said, again drawing Qar'qaah's gaze. "This shouldn't be too much of shock for your new gut—and it's pure protein, something you need, but start out *slow*—let's see if your insides can handle it."

Qar'qaah, at Amalfitano's urging, cautiously picked up the fork, eyeing Jaa'qwah momentarily to see how he used the unfamiliar utensil. Then he scooped up a small mouthful of the eggs. He sniffed at the unfamiliar offering, then, with another glance at Amalfitano, slipped the food into his mouth. He chewed, cautiously, then finally, almost apprehensively, swallowed.

Once it was down, his eyes darted to Amalfitano then Jaa'qwah, and then back to Amalfitano as Amalfitano and Jaa'qwah stared back, waiting.

When a full minute elapsed, and nothing unpleasant happened, he scooped up another mouthful, this one a little larger, and then another and another. Before Amalfitano realized it, Qar'qaah had polished off not only the eggs but the remaining biscuit and jelly as well.

Amalfitano picked up the clean plate and set it aside, then turned back to him. Qar'qaah was staring down at the shiny surface of the console with an almost perplexed expression, as if not quite believing he'd just inhaled a large amount of food—very alien food at that—and had not promptly brought it back up.

"Full?"

Qar'qaah nodded.

Good, 'cuz I'm not sure you could hold any more without splitting open. Amalfitano rose and placed the plate in the nearby servo-door, then grabbed a blanket from the overhead storage bin and draped it around Qar'qaah's bare, bony shoulders. The young Hahtooshan hardly stirred and as Amalfitano resumed his seat, he saw why: Qar'qaah's intense gaze was now fixed on the bank of active monitors in front of him.

"Me?" He looked at Amalfitano.

"Yes." Amalfitano tapped the probe on Qar'qaah's wrist. "From here—it's actively sampling the chemistry of your blood and—"

"And this?" Qar'qaah touched the small disc attached to his upper chest, just below his all too prominent collarbone.

"It's a signal suppressor—it overrides the interference from your tattoos and provides other physiological data, like cardiac output, respiratory rate and depth—"

"Tah." Qar'qaah again studied the readouts, this time more skeptically, then before Amalfitano could stop him, he pried the signal suppressor from his chest, grabbed the knife off of

Jaa'qwah's plate and popped open the small device. "I can make this work much better—get rid of all the added 'noise'." He motioned to the monitors with the knife.

Amalfitano favored Jaa'qwah with a glance then looked back at the suppressor to find that Qar'qaah had completely eviscerated it and was now absorbed in studying each of its tiny parts.

"Doctor Amalfitano… you're needed triage bay two," came Fleming's voice from an overhead speaker.

He rose, then turned to Jaa'qwah as the medic said, "I think it best I remain here—make sure he doesn't take your entire sickbay apart..."

Amalfitano startled to chuckle before realizing the medic was deadly serious.

"I'll call Bar'ahani to accompany you." Jaa'qwah reached for his tac-net.

"No need—I'll just be 'round the corner." At Jaa'qwah's torn expression, Amalfitano added, "I promise I'll scream bloody murder if anyone even looks cross-eyed at me."

The medic hesitated, clearly baffled.

"I'll be *fine*."

Jaa'qwah, with an unhappy nod, reclipped the tac-net.

Amalfitano returned a short time later, after discharging all but one of the rescued search team and then briefly stopping by his cabin to check on Khusaaq and Sirin—both were still sound asleep—only to find Qar'qaah and Jaa'qwah exactly where he'd left them.

Jaa'qwah looked up from taking a sip from his cup of cocoa as Amalfitano approached and put his forefinger to his whip-cream rimed lips in a near universal signal for silence.

Amalfitano, realizing Qar'qaah was now fast asleep, nodded his understanding. Then, as he slipped back onto his chair he also noticed that the signal suppressor was again firmly attached to Qar'qaah's emaciated chest.

Amalfitano gave the monitors a quick scan and smiled; Qar'qaah had been good to his word.

Chapter 30

Amalfitano's office, aboard the Baidarka, *1005.*

Amalfitano, hearing the stirrings of life from within his private cabin, set his cup of extra strong coffee on his desk, next to a stack of flimsies, then looked expectantly at the nearby doorway as it slipped open.

Three hours before, he'd left Jaa'qwah to keep watch over the sleeping Qar'qaah and returned to his office. In that time, he'd caught up on a number of reports, sent a few memos, called up another plate of soft scrambled eggs—and he'd put in a large order with the galley staff for anything chocolate to be delivered to *Faridour*'s medical staff with his compliments— leaving it up to Hai'chellah whether *she* shared with Narbrooi or not. He'd even allowed himself the small luxury of nodding off for a few minutes.

Sirin was the first to appear, yawning, followed by Khusaaq. Both appeared rested, if a bit rumpled, and Khusaaq was walking awkwardly, favoring both right thigh and left ankle. More startling was that he looked prematurely aged, with his normally blue-black hair dust-grayed in streaks and his swarthy skin smeared in an ashen hue. Thankfully both were nothing more than the remnants of being trapped underground.

Realizing Amalfitano was seated at his desk, Sirin stopped in her tracks. Khusaaq, in the process of rubbing his eyes with his knuckles, bumped into her then he too turned his startled, rapidly turning to apprehensive stare on the doctor.

"'Bout time you two woke up—"

"Is everything okay?" Sirin interrupted before Khusaaq could voice his own fears.

"You mean is *Qar'qaah* okay? Yup, in fact he's already been up, ate a *solid* breakfast, performed a little of his engineering magic on one of Cyllo's signal suppressors and is now back asleep. And even more critical to his recovery is that he's starting to believe that everything is real—that he's not hallucinating." He grinned at Sirin. "Using your approach I might add."

Khusaaq turned a questioning gaze on her but before she could explain, Amalfitano continued:

"I also got an update on Murh'sooli and Shu'hah—both are stable and improving by the hour. Hai'chellah said Murh'sooli might even be cleared for light duty in a few days. Jenna and I asked if he could come back here to recuperate, assuming he's agreeable—"

Sirin grinned, "Softie."

"He's a damned fine medic," Amalfitano fired back. "You don't willing give up someone of his caliber..." Then, with a shrug and a smile, he added, "...and okay, okay, we've both grown quite fond of the ornery bastard—and besides he and Jenna make perfect bookends."

Khusaaq arched his brow and again looked at Sirin for translation.

"It means they make a good tag team—keeping the doctor here in line."

He replied with a perplexed, "Oh."

"And Matoosh is back aboard," Amalfitano continued. "Came over with our missing search team *Faridour* recovered a couple of hours ago. He also retrieved your duty uniform from *Jirah*, and brought over your weapons that were recovered from that mine." He motioned to the uniform and fully-stocked weapons belt, draped over a nearby chair. "He took your armor back to *Jirah*. Now he's helping Meerut keep an eye on Nihaal, Laihiri, Endooki and Raudah down in the galley."

Khusaaq blew out his cheeks and shook his head in astonishment as Sirin fixed her 'but you're not telling all' gaze on Amalfitano.

Amalfitano stared back then turned his attention to Khusaaq. "So, how're you feeling?"

Khusaaq shrugged, winced as he rotated his bruised shoulder, then glanced down at his ankle and said, "Stiff, still a bit sore. Hurts when I cough."

"Did you manage to get some sleep?"

He nodded.

"Did he eat?" Amalfitano asked, looking at Sirin.

"No."

Amalfitano scowled at him, then turned to the desk's servo-panel and tapped in an order.

"May I see Qar'qaah?" Khusaaq asked, his eyes flicking to the nearby doorway.

"Not until you eat. And take a shower. You look like hell. I won't have you worrying my patients—or me—unnecessarily."

"But—"

"No buts." He pointed to the chairs in front of his desk. "Sit!"

Khusaaq dutifully sat and Sirin slipped onto the chair next to him.

A moment later and hearing a familiar chime, Amalfitano turned to the wall-mounted servo-door behind his desk and withdrew a tray from the small dumbwaiter. He placed the tray, containing two covered plates and two cups of coffee, on his desk. "Here you go."

Khusaaq and Sirin each took a plate and a cup then began to eat while Amalfitano resumed his study of a report.

As Khusaaq took the last bite of frittata, Amalfitano rocked back in his chair and crossed his arms.

Khusaaq hurriedly swallowed his mouthful, chased it down with a gulp of coffee then wiped his chin with the back of his hand and met Amalfitano's steady gaze.

"Shower." Amalfitano pointed to his cabin. "Sirin—make sure he scrubs off at least the top three layers of dust. Don't even want to know the condition of my bed," he added with a grumble.

Sirin got to her feet and offered Khusaaq her hands for support. He unhappily rose, wincing as he did so.

"Don't worry about the dressings—they're waterproof." Amalfitano made shooing motions with his hands. "Go on."

The two vanished back into his cabin, Sirin gathering up Khusaaq's duty uniform as they went.

A few minutes later, they reappeared, Khusaaq looking much cleaner, if not happier, and fully clothed this time.

Amalfitano waited as Khusaaq donned the weapons belt, then again pointed to the chairs, and the two dutifully resumed their seats. "Narbrooi wants Qar'qaah to attend the preliminary hearing day after tomorrow," he continued, to which Khusaaq nodded. "He should be stable enough, physically, for a brief stay, but I want your permission for Zarijan to speak with him first. If she thinks he's psychologically strong enough, then I'll agree to let him go."

At Khusaaq's visible hesitation, Amalfitano added, "Listen, son, Zarijan is, among other things, an excellent psychiatrist. In fact the best I've ever worked with. Qar'qaah is going to need a lot of intense therapy to come to terms with what was done to him, not to mention overcome the host of issues he has with you..."

Khusaaq shifted uneasily as he flicked Sirin a sidelong glance.

"...and I truly believe she's his best bet. The fact that she knows exactly what happened to him, from his perspective, in fact experienced exactly what he experienced, is an added bonus of sorts—I think we should leave it up to her to decide whether to tell him or not." He paused, giving Khusaaq a moment to think about what he was proposing. Then, "So, do you give permission?"

"What if he refuses?"

"Then he refuses. He has that right—no one will force the issue, I promise you."

"I want to see him, now... please."

Amalfitano smiled. He'd pushed Khusaaq's patience and knew it. "Of course." He rose, said, "Come with me," and they walked out of his office.

Jaa'qwah looked up at the sound of approaching footsteps. Seeing who it was, he immediately rose from the console and came to rigid attention. Qar'qaah remained wrapped up in a blanket cocoon but as the three stopped nearby, his nose twitched as it picked up familiar scents.

He stirred, opened his sleepy eyes and blinked as he looked around, unsure what had awakened him.

Following Jaa'qwah's pointed stare, he glanced to his left then tossed off the blanket and managed to lurch unsteadily but unassisted to his feet as he gasped, *"Sha'ashahn...!"*

"I distinctly remember ordering you to remain aboard *Jirah*," Khusaaq growled in his best, menacing voice. "Do you have *any* idea the trouble you've caused?"

Qar'qaah nervously licked his lips as his eyes darted to Sirin, then Amalfitano before returning to Khusaaq. He dipped his head and mumbled, *"Paq, ta'ahn."*

Khusaaq pointed to the deck in front of him. "Quh!"

Qar'qaah did as he was told and stepped closer, and watching him, Amalfitano realized the young Hahtooshan was wide open, emotionally, physically, as open as anyone could possibly be—utterly vulnerable. Khusaaq could say or do anything and Qar'qaah wouldn't stop him—couldn't stop him.

He flicked Sirin a worried look; she stared back, equally apprehensive. Khusaaq's tone had been startlingly fierce, unexpectedly so. But instead of continuing with the expected verbal upbraiding and in front of others—Rimmers no less—Khusaaq instead wrapped his arms around Qar'qaah and drew him against him.

Qar'qaah reflexively stiffened, startled, both at the physical contact and the public display of emotion, then slowly, awkwardly, wrapped his arms around Khusaaq. Pressing his forehead into the older man's shoulder, he squeezed his eyes shut.

"I'm so sorry..." Khusaaq whispered, tightening his embrace, *"so, so terribly sorry... for everything."*

Amalfitano watched, worriedly, as Qar'qaah's knees wobbled and his breath started coming in short, sharp bursts.

With an explosive intake of air, he surrendered to the deluge of pent up emotions and he began to sob uncontrollably, violently, his body jerking and twitching with the soul-deep, gut-wrenching release.

Khusaaq held onto him, fully supporting him as Qar'qaah's legs buckled. He continued to hold onto Qar'qaah until he got himself back under control.

Only then did Amalfitano step forward, his concern for Qar'qaah temporarily outweighed by his concern for Khusaaq—the man looked as physically and emotionally drained as Qar'qaah. He lightly touched Qar'qaah's elbow. "I think you best sit down." He turned to Khusaaq. "You too."

Khusaaq reluctantly released his hold.

Qar'qaah sniffed, wiped his nose and cheeks with a shaky hand and allowed Amalfitano to guide him back a few steps to the chair.

Amalfitano motioned with his chin to another chair and Sirin helped Khusaaq over to it; he managed to sit down without wincing.

Only then did Qar'qaah realize Khusaaq's own strained expression, his awkward gait and the cuts and newly visible bruises on his face. "You've been injured."

"Nothing serious."

"But... what's happened?"

When Khusaaq didn't immediately answer, Qar'qaah looked at Sirin then Amalfitano. "Please, tell me what's—"

"Cisne's been apprehended," Khusaaq interrupted as he carefully shifted around into a more comfortable position in the chair.

"Apprehended...?"

This time Khusaaq only nodded.

"And you were injured—capturing her?"

"Yes. But we'll talk about that later—"

"Where's Matoosh?" He twisted in the chair and fixed his apprehensive gaze on Jaa'qwah. "I demand to know!"

Khusaaq leaned forward and lightly grasped Qar'qaah's shoulder, drawing his increasingly panicky gaze. "Matoosh is safe."

"Anyone else hurt?"

Khusaaq glanced at Amalfitano, then answered, "Shu'hah... Shu'hah was seriously hurt, and Rukoobi..."

"What about Rukoobi?"

"He was killed."

Qar'qaah stared at him for a moment in disbelief then whispered, *"It's all my fault—"*

"No, it's not. The blame falls squarely on Cisne's shoulders... and mine."

Qar'qaah shook his head. "If I hadn't disobeyed orders—"

"We likely wouldn't have captured her," Khusaaq interrupted softly but firmly.

"It's all my fault..."

Amalfitano favored Sirin with a sidelong look and murmured, *"Like father like son."* It wasn't exactly factual, but it certainly tripped more lightly off the tongue than *Like ta'katleh like doh'ha.*

Sirin replied with a resigned nod.

Oblivious to the whispered remark, Khusaaq tightened his hold on Qar'qaah's shoulder, painfully, enough to draw his watery gaze. "I said *no!* You are *not* at fault! None of this was your fault—*hear?"* He gave him a shake. *"Hear me?"*

"Yes," Qar'qaah mumbled unconvincingly.

"Cisne is an alias." Khusaaq paused, again looked up at Amalfitano and at the doctor's reluctant, nodding go-ahead, continued, "Her real name is Pashna'gaalan ket Tashar'anhi..."

Qar'qaah's eyes widened and his lips parted in instant, stunned comprehension. *"Ga... Gaalan...?"*

"...once Narbrooi Hahtra'tzrhi was notified of her true identity, he brought *Faridour*, along with a full assault force to Poonda Five to assist in your rescue."

Qar'qaah looked at Sirin, even more dumbfounded, before again fixing his wide eyes on Khusaaq.

"But before Hahtra'tzrhi returns her for trial, he has asked if you would be willing to attend a preliminary hearing, to establish her complicity in kidnapping you and the others."

Qar'qaah fixed his gaze on his bony knees and took several moments to gather his thoughts before asking in a voice barely above a hoarse whisper, *"When?"*

"It's entirely up to you," Khusaaq replied.

He squeezed his eyes shut and swallowed, hard.

"Hahtra'tzrhi is *not* ordering you to do this... and neither am I. It's strictly voluntary—no one will think the worse of you if you refuse, *understand?"*

Qar'qaah, his eyes still shut and jaws clenched, nodded.

"And you don't have to give me your answer now," Khusaaq continued. "In fact I want you to think about it. Doctor Amalfitano has also offered the expertise of Lieutenant Izraad to help you prepare, if you wish."

"Kon'ta'aq," Amalfitano began, drawing an uneasy, watery-eyed glance from Qar'qaah, "all we ask is that you think about it—no one is going to force you."

Qar'qaah took another shaky breath and shifted his gaze to Sirin. "Who is this Lieutenant Izraad?"

Sirin knelt beside him. "She's the *Baidarka*'s intelligence officer—" At his startled, rapidly turning to appalled look she added hastily, "—she's also an expert in treating people who've experienced severe psychological trauma. If you allow her, she can show you how you can limit the nightmares, the flashbacks." She flicked Khusaaq a quick, pointed look, then again fixed Qar'qaah with her gaze and wrapped her hands around his. *"She can help you."*

He bit his lip then after a moment, nodded.

Chapter 31

Isolation unit, sickbay, aboard the Baidarka, *1811.*

Izraad stepped out of the isolation airlock to find, not unexpectedly, Amalfitano, Khusaaq, Sirin and Aquila waiting for her. All wore varying degrees of the same intensely apprehensive expression.

She stared back, too tired to even muster a reassuring smile.

It had been a harrowing day: Qar'qaah's all too brief, all too intense life had been shattered into a million pieces. Together they'd taken the first very tentative steps in putting it back together, slowly, piece by puzzle piece. He'd even refused all but the briefest of breaks—desperate for the relief her therapy promised. He'd stopped only to gulp down another glass of chocolate milk from what seemed like a bottomless carafe Pierson delivered at the start of the session, to wash his face and collect himself, or walk or shake off the cramps that threatened his legs, his white-knuckled hands. Then he'd resume his seat on the edge of the bunk beside her chair, eagerly, and to Izraad surprisingly, reach out and wrap his fingers around hers and they'd start again.

Some pieces didn't fit; other pieces were missing altogether—*just gone.* In some cases it was only a matter of a few minutes, in others hours were lost. Izraad knew that Hahtooshans prided themselves on their astonishing memory for detail among other attributes and she had assured him, over and over, that memory loss was a *normal* response.

Despite her assertions, something as seemingly trivial as an unaccounted minute or two was a new and deeply upsetting experience and he'd asked her more than once what was so absolutely horrible that his mind refused to acknowledge it?

Those missing moments scared him. The knowledge that the missing pieces could resurface without warning scared him even more. Worse yet were the gaps—not holes—*gaps,* big, yawning gaps where his nightmares lived, where they multiplied and marshaled their forces. It was a seething darkness, packed full of shifting shapes, of the shivering sensation of being touched by ghostly fingers, of voices calling to him and laughter—Cisne's all too *human*, not Hahtooshan—sounding laughter, made all the more harrowing by his enhanced synesthesia.

Too many times during the hours-long session Izraad found him teetering on the edge, desperate not to look down and at the same time drawn in, feeling that nauseating sense of falling, of those same spectral fingers tugging at him, pulling him down into the smothering darkness.

Slowly he came to realize that she was living everything he was reliving—the terror, the searing pain, the raw humiliation, the sense of utter and complete helplessness—that she'd *volunteered* to do it; that no matter what she saw, what she felt, she refused to leave him, refused to abandon him—*refused to judge him.*

As a result, instead of pulling back from her, or shutting down completely as she feared he might once he understood just how truly immersed she was, he opened up even further, frantic in his need to find acceptance, find understanding... to find *some* meaning in what was done to him.

It had been a deeply traumatic experience—its impact lessened now only by being a shared experience.

She sat with him until he'd fallen into an exhausted sleep and found herself tempted to follow his example, to curl up in the chair beside him, her fingers intertwined with his. But the others were waiting for her, had in fact been waiting for hours, sequestered up in Amalfitano's office, and were now drawn to the isolation unit upon hearing the marathon session had ended.

So, she left Qar'qaah in the care of Meerut who'd promised her she wouldn't leave his bedside; she'd hoped to have a few minutes alone, to recoup, to collect herself, but—

"Well?" Amalfitano asked impatiently the instant she stepped out of the airlock.

"Perhaps the lieutenant would prefer to discuss this in your office?" Khusaaq said pointedly as he offered Izraad his arm, which she gladly accepted, not grasping the gesture's true significance until after the fact. He even waved off Aquila's silent offer to take over that duty, despite Khusaaq visibly limping.

"Oh, yes, of course," Amalfitano replied. "Sorry, Zarijan." He motioned for the others to follow him then he strode through the isolation unit, through the main sickbay and finally into his office. As he circled his desk, he motioned the others, who'd arrived at a slightly slower, Izraad-set pace, to seat themselves. "I'll call up some coffee—"

"And something for the lieutenant to eat, yes?" Khusaaq prompted, his worried eyes and supporting arm never leaving Izraad.

Izraad managed a feeble smile. She needed his strength more and more as her own failed. She was trembling, emotionally and physically done in.

"Yes." Amalfitano gave the woman another contrite glance.

Izraad gratefully sat down, clasped her hands in her lap and took a breath then exhaled slowly. She didn't need her heightened acuity to sense their mounting anxiety; it was palpable.

She had, after all, just spent almost six hours *alone* with Qar'qaah—far, far longer than she'd intended for their first session, far longer than the others had anticipated—giving them far too much time to assume the worst. Despite that, they had honored her request that she and Qar'qaah not be interrupted, that if either needed anything, it was up to them to ask for it.

She hadn't expected to come out of the grueling session whole, certainly hadn't expected Qar'qaah to come out whole. The young Hahtooshan's idea of self, of who and what he was had been shattered—bits and pieces flung everywhere, sharp, stabbing; they'd had sliced right through her gut and she still found herself wanting to check to see if she was bleeding.

Khusaaq was—she could feel it. He was hemorrhaging and had been the entire time and so she started off assuring him, assuring Amalfitano, Sirin and Aquila, that the time had been well spent.

She told them that, in truth, Qar'qaah didn't need to speak. She had, after all, seen what he'd seen, felt what he'd felt— she'd shared his *nonverbal* memories: "The memories you hold in your stomach," she said as she fixed her exhausted gaze on an equally haggard Khusaaq, "memories you hold in your knees, your shoulders, memories that give you that flutter in the belly, the wobble in the knees and tautness in the back that you can't control no matter how hard you try..."

He silently nodded his understanding.

"...worse, you have no warning when they appear, fully formed—they have *that* strong a grip on you. But he *wanted* to speak, Sha'ashahn, and by doing so, by putting names to each and every one of them, recognizing each memory for what it is—and perhaps even more importantly, what it is *not*—he's begun the slow, painful journey towards freeing himself of their vice-like power over him."

Khusaaq stared back, wide-eyed and unblinking, in the process—accidentally or intentionally, she couldn't tell—leaving himself every bit as open and vulnerable as Qar'qaah.

Up until that moment she hadn't liked the man. In fact she disliked him intensely and simply could not understand what Sirin or Amalfitano saw in him, what elicited such strong devotion. In large part, she now realized, her reaction to him had been due to her own unresolved feelings over the forcible mind-strip she'd conducted on him and its aftermath.

Without being aware of it, she'd carefully assembled a replica of him in her mind, bit by bit, using impressions grabbed here and there. Despite having seen his world from the inside out, she'd subconsciously picked the most unflattering, the least sympathetic, the ugliest memories upon which she'd constructed her facsimile Khusaaq, one she had every reason to dislike because she'd *made* him utterly dislikeable.

But now, as the two stared at each other, she saw him very differently: as someone thrust into the role of hero and father at a time in his life when he hadn't even figured out who he was— he had been barely more than a boy himself at the time, no older than Qar'qaah was now.

As she looked into his pale gray and decidedly bloodshot eyes, pieces of his mind-strip—bits that hadn't made any sense at the time, pieces she'd discarded in preference for more relevant information and yes, bits that fed into her two-

dimensional, loathsome doppelgänger—as well as fragments
from Qar'qaah's childhood recollections suddenly snapped
together, giving her a more complete and complex portrait of
this man. He'd done the best he could, had tried to do right and
had carried the tremendous burden of guilt over failing in both
roles, that of the son of an icon and an icon himself—roles he'd
never sought out, never volunteered for. Perhaps most
importantly, what had happened to Qar'qaah had been
Khusaaq's absolute worst fears realized, leaving him as
traumatized as Qar'qaah.

*It's time to forgive Ja'andai for abandoning you, my friend;
time to forgive yourself—and yes, time for me to forgive myself,
too.*

As if sensing her thoughts, Khusaaq briefly looked away,
then again met her gaze: his silent, steady, *'Go ahead'*.

"I can't provide details—patient confidentiality is critical
here. I've already told him that anything specific he says to me
is strictly between him and me—he can tell you what he wants
you to know later. He can tell you everything, or nothing—and
his choices must be respected—don't press him."

"Understood," Khusaaq replied.

Izraad settled back in her chair, and began, "Not
unexpectedly and despite of my repeated assurances, it took
some time to develop a rapport, for him to open up—I am, after
all, a complete stranger, worse, a woman, and a Rimmer to
boot. We talked about his interests—he showed me what he'd
been working on for Lieutenant Perou. I got quite a full lecture
on the differences between Hahtooshan and Coalition
engineering practices—must say, I didn't grasp most of what he
was saying except that the Coalition has a lot to learn..." she
cast a quick, smiling glance at Aquila, an engineer himself, who
smiled and shrugged good-naturedly in response. "But that
wasn't the point—he just needed to build up to what we were
really there to talk about. Once he did, he was startling in his
candor, Sha'ashahn, both about himself and others."

Khusaaq stared back but said nothing.

"I found him to be extraordinarily bright—remarkably
nimble in his thinking one might say, and he's unexpectedly

insightful for his age, at times single-mindedly intense when it comes to subjects that interest him, and, most critical to his recovery, he's *amazingly* resilient."

Khusaaq finally, visibly, exhaled, relieved; he even risked a very fleeting smile.

"Paradoxically," she continued, "he's also deeply insecure, hypercritical of himself and far too quick to dismiss his abilities." She favored Amalfitano with a sidelong look—*does this sound familiar?* to which he glanced at Khusaaq and nodded. Then she continued. "He combines these with a deep, long-standing resentment—no, let's be totally honest here, a deep and abiding hatred of *you*, Sha'ashahn."

Sirin gave Khusaaq's hand a squeeze, but his now watery gaze never wavered from Izraad.

"When I finally broached the matter of what happened to him aboard the *Huui'teh*, he at first focused on the sheer terror of being repeatedly put in a stasis pod awake, as if these experiences—magnified by the use of hallucinogenics—were the fountainhead of all the nightmares, the paralyzing flashbacks."

Suddenly Izraad found herself was awash in Khusaaq's deep anguish, his own helpless agony. She'd had to break the intense staring match, to give each some emotional distance from the other, to protect herself from his wholly unguarded reaction and him from the true depth of horror of what Qar'qaah had experienced, and which she had been subjected to.

She'd encouraged Qar'qaah to talk, to recall in his halting words what it felt like to be slowly suffocated, the burning pain of having the air sucked from his lungs while just enough oxygen to keep him alive was delivered directly to his bloodstream along with a cocktail of drugs; what it was like to scream and make no sound... to be utterly helpless, to crave death, or at least the temporary refuge of unconsciousness, only to be forcibly kept awake.

Despite reliving the experience just as Qar'qaah had lived it, she'd found his straightforward retelling to be so shocking, so terrifying, even she struggled to get her mind around how one individual could knowingly do such to another—and for what purpose? Gaalan *had* Qar'qaah. She only needed to wait for Khusaaq to come after him. But Gaalan wasn't sane, Izraad was sure of that now, and she hadn't been for a very, very long time.

Izraad had listened, kept her face an expressionless mask, painfully aware of just how hard it was for Qar'qaah to expose himself so completely to someone whom he barely knew, much less to himself.

With her help he relived the experience over and over, repeatedly confronting the terrorizing memories until finally their iron grip on his psyche began to loosen. With that came another unexpectedly sudden release: he began describing the deeply buried, soul-festering trauma of the rape, his words coming faster and faster, almost tripping over each other in their rush to emerge into the light.

She cleared her throat. Then again meeting Khusaaq's gaze, she continued. "We made a critical breakthrough when he confessed to a crushing sense of shame over his body's humiliating reactions to the sexual assault. He fears that meant he was not just a complete failure when it came to being your *doh'ha*, Sha'ashahn, but also when it came to being a true Elkanaghalli."

Khusaaq squeezed his eyes shut and muttered something in Hahtou. Then again he looked at her, eyes glistening anew, jaw muscles twitching under the veneer of tattoos and scarification.

"With my guidance, he's come to realize—and even more importantly has begun to accept—that he had no control over what transpired—and, even more importantly he had no control over his body's reaction, that it was, to be blunt, a drug and torture-driven *physiological* response. He is in no way responsible for his victimization—"

"Of course not," Khusaaq interrupted huskily.

"In some cultures," Izraad explained, "I'm sorry to say, the victims of such... *attacks* are often held up as the guilty party, not the culprit, so I wasn't sure—"

"Qar'qaah will not be blamed, but..." He shook his head, exhaled forcefully.

"But?" Izraad prompted with a sidelong glance at Sirin.

Khusaaq hesitated, then said, "My caste, my family... they are very strict when it comes to our vows. You either are or are not celibate. There are no shades of gray."

"So he will not be accepted by the Abhijit'tischinjgra—"

"Or Elkanaghalli'i. No."

"And Hahtooshans as a whole?" Izraad asked.

"Accepted, but because of the *turee* not fully welcomed."

"I'm very sorry to hear that," Izraad replied.

Khusaaq shrugged then added softly, "He always said he wanted to be free of what he called the Abhijit'tischinjgra curse, to find his own path. Perhaps a case of be careful what you ask for. He can overcome this... sigma of the *turee*, if he devotes himself to it. It *is* possible, at least in the eyes of the nonreligious castes, and our kith, the Kri'taaka, have been known, under certain conditions, to adopt those expelled by the Elkanaghalli'i over breaches in our religious codes, but I know of no Abhijit'tischinjgra who ever found himself or herself in predicament where the physical self was violated and they also suffered the *turee*."

Izraad settled back in her chair, cleared her throat then continued, "We'll just take one thing at a time then, one day at a time. The good news is that he's made huge progress, Sha'ashahn. Far more than I could have expected, and in an incredibly short period of time. Of course a lot of issues need to be confronted for him to put all of this in its proper place, but he's willing, and, as I said earlier, he's amazingly resilient. So I believe the overall prognosis is good for if not a full recovery, then a *livable* recovery, assuming you'll permit me to continue to work with him?"

"Of course," he replied.

For several awkward minutes no one spoke. Then Aquila, who, up to that moment had remained silent, said, "Will he be able to testify at the hearing? Sorry I have to ask, but Narbrooi is waiting to hear from us."

Khusaaq looked up as Izraad answered, "Yes. In fact he very much wants to testify, to confront Gaalan. Doing so will be integral to his eventual healing."

Aquila turned to Amalfitano. "Will?"

"I'll clear him for a medical pass for tomorrow evening." He turned to Khusaaq, "Twenty-four hours—give him a little more time to recuperate and to prepare. And he's only to testify—then I want him back here. Agreed?"

"Agreed," Khusaaq answered.

"I'll notify Narbrooi." Aquila got to his feet. "Tomorrow evening, say, eighteen hundred Standard?"

"And tell him he has him for no more than an hour," Amalfitano warned as Aquila turned for the doorway, "and *only* if I accompany him."

"I'll tell him—no guarantee he'll agree."

"Then he doesn't go," Amalfitano countered. "Simple."

Aquila blew out his cheeks, muttered, *"Simple... like hell,"* and strode out of the office.

Izraad looked back at Khusaaq to find him staring at her with weary eyes. "You have a truly remarkable *doh'ha*, Sha'ashahn."

"I've known it all along, Lieutenant." He paused, took a deep breath then added, "So much so, I often caught myself wondering if my efforts at protecting him were really more an attempt at protecting me."

"I don't follow," Izraad replied.

"Part of me worried if he was allowed to find his own way, seek his own contracts, he would demonstrate beyond all doubt that he was a far more worthy successor to Ja'andai than I proved to be, that he might even surpass Ja'andai's accomplishments." He smiled, ruefully. "Not a very flattering admission, is it? To be secretly jealous of your clone?"

"No, it isn't, but it's also not really surprising, considering. You are, after all, only... *human*."

He eyed her, then at her slight smile, shrugged. "Indeed." With that, he started to push himself to his feet.

"You can't shut it out, can you?" Izraad asked softly, stopping him in mid-rise.

Khusaaq glanced sidelong at her, at first confused and then with sudden understanding of what she meant. *"No,"* he answered tightly.

She dropped her gaze briefly, pointedly to his chair. To her surprise, he slowly resumed his seat.

Izraad looked first at Amalfitano and then Sirin to find both staring back at her, baffled and apprehensive. Getting the hint, Amalfitano hit the door release and it slipped closed, providing the four with complete privacy.

Izraad began: "Hahtooshans have truly remarkable memories—far better recall than non-Hahtooshan humans except for those rare few who have hyperthymesia, and those with hyperthymesia usually only retain incredible detail about themselves, not others. Hahtooshans, in essence, remember everything they are ever exposed to, down to the most insignificant minutiae. This is an amazing talent when it comes to say, learning even the most obscure dialect and accent or the at times mind-numbing intricacies of alien treaties—*and* perhaps even more critically, from the perspective, the biases of *each* signatory."

Everyone looked to Khusaaq. He replied with a slight, self-deprecating nod.

"On top of this," Izraad continued, "and almost from birth, your people are what we would call deliberately 'stress-inoculated', which does a remarkable job preparing Hahtooshans for what lies ahead. I think it's safe to say we can credit some of Qar'qaah's remarkable psychological resilience to this very technique."

She paused, again looked at Amalfitano and Sirin then met Khusaaq's gaze. "Your people also have the ability to compartmentalize, to lock away particularly painful memories when they choose and for as long as they choose, as well as temporarily switching off emotions such as empathy. It allows them to do what they do as mercenaries without individuals suffering the associated long-term psychological issues. It's a very reasonable survival tactic for a people who possess such an astonishing recall capacity, and one that has obvious benefits, both to the individual and the greater society. But you can't do that, can you? Never could."

This time he only shook his head.

"And add to the mix that you are a synesthete... the combination must be overwhelming."

He shrugged. "I know nothing else."

"And the same is true of Qar'qaah."

"And Ja'andai," he added quietly, "and Shushnua before him."

Izraad said, "Meaning it runs in your family—"

"Only through *doh'ha*, although not all *doh'ha* are so... blessed—those who do have the dominant gene are a minority of a minority. It makes those who carry this trait able to communicate directly with the Elkanasu and they with us at any time, without the need of an external conduit—"

"Like your dagger?" Amalfitano asked.

"Yes," Khusaaq nodded, "although having an external conduit nearby makes does make communication... clearer? More intense? And *undisputable*. All Elkanaghalli'i are capable of hearing the Elkanasu with the use of their daggers, although for most it only occurs when they are facing their own imminent deaths—call it a reassuring voice beckoning, guiding them home."

"So only Elkanaghallis are accepted back into the arms of the Elkanasu?" Amalfitano asked.

Khusaaq shook his head. "No. But only we receive a formal invitation."

Amalfitano squinted at him, clearly unsure if he was trying to be funny or not.

Not, Izraad determined just by the look in Khusaaq's eyes. To him it was still a point of immense pride.

"And one is not judged worthy based solely on one's last living act," Khusaaq continued. "The Elkanasu look at the sum of one's life to determine if one's memories are to be fully integrated into the collective, or discarded, in whole or in part."

"Meaning, technically, Gaalan could be accepted upon her death, despite the truly horrible things she's done?" Amalfitano pressed, leaving no doubt he was appalled by the concept.

"The *sum*, Doctor," Khusaaq repeated. "Gaalan was, at one time, a hero to my people, and more than deservedly so. It is not up to me to question this."

And definitely not up to us Rimmers, Izraad added to herself as she shot Amalfitano a pointed, cease and desist look; he surprised her when he took the hint and pressed his lips together in grudging agreement.

"Or so we are all raised to believe," Khusaaq continued, by his tone not offended by Amalfitano's questions. "A belief that can be confirmed only by those who are conveniently no longer in a position to corroborate it." He slowly shook his head, then added, "Elkanaghalli'i who do not carry this trait call it the *paas'nah...* the *gift,* but the tradeoff is that those who carry it cannot compartmentalize our memories, as you describe it, shutting out those which are particularly painful—"

"Back on Tuli," Izraad said, "right after the attempt on William and Xosé's life, Narbrooi mentioned this *paas'nah,* said some of your religious scholars believed your actions on Rasal Ghul were the result of this trait, as you call it, expressing itself in its purest form?"

Khusaaq chuckled bitterly, "Did he now?"

"I gathered he didn't accept that explanation," Izraad said.

"And he claims to be so devout," Khusaaq observed.

Izraad only shrugged. "When it suits him."

"Some gift," Amalfitano muttered irritably, drawing everyone's attention back to the original topic.

"It was, at one time," Khusaaq replied. "Those who carried it were considered to be the untainted voice of the Elkanasu. But these days... we are looked upon as potentially unstable, so those rare few of us who carry it hide the fact, deny it if asked, or risk the consequences." He chuckled again and shook his head. "But those who question us are right—it is difficult to be completely sane with the gods constantly tapping you on the shoulder or whispering in your ear."

Amalfitano, Izraad and Sirin exchanged worried looks.

"You have doubted my sanity, Lieutenant." Khusaaq fixed Izraad with a piercing, gray-eyed stare, "I was merely agreeing with you."

"All right, yes, I have. During your mind-strip," she said then visibly shivered, "I... I felt a collective presence, something utterly alien..."

Khusaaq said, "And you thought that was evidence of an underlying pathology—"

"I wasn't sure what it was to be honest—at the time it seemed a reasonable explanation." She glanced at Amalfitano, who nodded, then she turned back to Khusaaq. "I've dealt with dissociative identity disorder before, along with its associated conditions, but this... I've never experienced anything like it. Then again, I'd never mind-stripped a Hahtooshan before—"

"The Elkanasu—you sensed the Elkanasu, Lieutenant. They were there, observing."

"*Observing?*" Izraad repeated and couldn't help but glance sidelong at Amalfitano as she shivered again.

"For those of us who carry the *paas'nah*, the Elkanasu are always present," he lightly tapped his temple, "watching, listening."

Izraad couldn't help but catch Sirin's wide-eyed and rather appalled look.

"*All* the time?" Sirin asked.

"Yes," he replied. "However, in my case, they left when they set me free. So if you're worried that they were present while we were engaged in—"

"Oh, *good,*" Sirin interrupted hastily, her cheeks flushing as she glanced around at the others.

"That must have been truly frightening," Izraad continued— mercifully for Sirin who still looked like she wanted to withdraw into her chair.

"Frightening?" he asked, baffled.

"To be free of their... guidance, their presence. For the first time in your life, to be completely alone." She lightly tapped the side of her head.

He stared at her for a moment then replied, "It was the silence. It was as if suddenly I'd gone deaf."

"I can't even imagine," she replied.

"I'm getting used to it—with Sirin's help," he flicked the woman a sidelong glance and a small smile. "I don't feel alone anymore."

"But the *paas'nah* remains—the Elkanasu are gone, but it remains."

"Yes."

"And it's like a pebble in your shoe, isn't it?" Izraad continued. "It doesn't stop you from walking, running if need be, but it's always there, a constant, painful distraction." Her eyes briefly dropped to his right leg, the one he favored, then again met his gaze. "And that explains why Cotopaxi still has such a stranglehold on you—it's like it just happened. Something truly terrible transpired there, and it keeps playing in your mind, over and over."

"Yes."

"Which also explains, at least in part, why you shunned the 'honor' of being called the Hero of Cotopaxi, why you kept to your close kin, why you avoided any high-profile contracts."

"Yes. Although I didn't help myself, my family or my career at all by accidentally revealing, shortly after being extracted from Cotopaxi, that I carry the *paas'nah*. Shushnua had successfully hidden that he carried it—everyone assumed his public suicide was due to other... *issues*, and Ja'andai... well, there were rumors, but just that. Nothing proven. Sometimes it does skip generations, sometimes several generations—or so I've been told.

"Everyone who knew said I was a fluke, a throwback to a much earlier time, or that possibly the material used to clone me had been in some way adulterated or manipulated. No one wanted to consider that my clone-line carried the purest form of the gene, and always had—it had in fact been a very closely held secret among only a few of my very closest kin, the most deeply pious, who kept the gene alive because it was, after all, a direct link to the Elkanasu—the last direct link. That was part of the reason, a major part in fact, that my kin protested Gaalan demanding a new *doh'ha* be created. They knew he too would carry it, and if it somehow became known that one of us had the gene, then the other would be exposed as well, but unable to say why they were so opposed, they were overruled.

"The Q'shaathrah had high hopes of touting me as the living embodiment of what all A'tuu'shahn'i should aspire to be, and, in the process, endorsing their agenda. At the time we had just suffered a series of major... *setbacks*, had lost a goodly number of our own and in truth we were in as fragile a state as the Coalition and Matarii Empire, perhaps even more so. They were desperate for a living symbol of our collective determination to overcome the odds.

"The Elkanaghalli planned to hold me up as Ja'andai's more than worthy successor, having accomplished something they deemed heroic at an even younger age. But when I revealed that I carried the *paas'nah*, well... my family was fearful this might raise questions about my progenitors, cast their accomplishments into doubt—were they truly their own achievements or had they received direct guidance and yes, possibly even protection, from the Elkanasu? And of course by now the matter of Qar'qaah had been added to the mix. I honestly think some truly hoped he was the product of Ja'andai and Gaalan's rumored affair if only to avoid him inheriting the dominant gene for the *paas'nah*.

"The Q'shaathrah was more concerned how this... *gift* might express itself in me, fearful I might do something reckless if pressed too hard, or, even worse possibly draw the Elkanasu back into taking not just an active, but *proactive* part in our everyday lives, something that could have serious and long-lasting ramifications within the Orthodoxy at a time when it could least afford any disruption in the norm." He chuckled bitterly. "They never saw Rasal Ghul coming. Of course, neither did I. But the Elkanasu did."

That prompted another round of uneasy glances between Sirin, Izraad and Amalfitano.

"So Narbrooi was right—or, should I say the scholars were right," Izraad said.

To which Khusaaq replied simply, "Yes."

"Are you telling us," Amalfitano leaned forward in his chair, "that the Elkanasu knew ahead of time what was about to transpire on Rasal Ghul Seven?"

Khusaaq answered, "Yes. They told me as much, *here*, in this very office—the first time in my life they actually spoke to me. I'd felt their guidance before of course, many times, felt their hand on my shoulder, guiding me—in some cases giving me a not so gentle shove—" He chuckled at a private memory, but there was no mirth to it, then continued, "but I'd never actually heard their voices—never presumed I'd ever hear them, that I'd never be worthy enough. They told me many things."

"*Here?*" Now it was Amalfitano's turn to suppress a shiver as he glanced around.

Izraad sat up straighter in her chair, her intense gaze fixed on Khusaaq. "This was right after William told you about your people being infected—"

"Yes."

"And you ordered us out of this office."

He managed a small, almost embarrassed smile. "Yes, and rather forcefully too, if I recall."

"And when we returned, you..."

"Displayed a remarkable turnaround in my attitude?"

Izraad gave a slight snort. "If I remember correctly, I called it a miraculous transformation."

"Having an *exceedingly* candid conversation with the divine does tend to have that effect, Lieutenant."

"Yes, I... I rather imagine it would."

"But..." Amalfitano began, hesitated then started again, "how? I mean—"

"Your dagger," Izraad interrupted, her eyes widening. "You found your dagger—*William,*" she turned to him, "remember you put it in your desk drawer?"

Amalfitano stared at her then nodded, slowly. "Yes... we assumed when security came to collect your bandoleer, they took it as well, but thinking back, how would they have known to look in my desk?"

"Exactly." Izraad nodded. "So you found your dagger—"

"*Siah'ushu...* called to me. So one could say they found me, rather than the other way around. Up to that moment, I thought I was well and truly lost, even to the Elkanasu."

"And once you had it—"

"The Elkanasu spoke to me, told me I needed to fulfill my destiny."

"Which was?" Izraad asked.

"To cooperate fully with you, with the Coalition, thus saving my people from annihilation, and in return, they would set me free."

Amalfitano peered intensely at Khusaaq, "But why didn't they stop it before it even started?"

"Stop it?" Khusaaq repeated. "Stop what?"

"What happened on Rasal Ghul, and afterwards."

Khusaaq eyed him. "Why would they want to stop something they in fact had put into motion?"

"They put into motion?" Amalfitano repeated, incredulous.

"You think your ship picking up on the distress call that brought you to Rasal Ghul in the first place was pure happenstance?"

"You mean it wasn't?" Amalfitano said.

Khusaaq shook his head. "Hardly—the scout ship didn't have the range, even under the most ideal of conditions, and the Rasal Ghul system was far from the most ideal of conditions."

Amalfitano said, "So the Elkanasu made sure we received it—"

"But... we almost died on that planet," Sirin interrupted.

Amalfitano nodded vigorously. "And what about those two Hahtooshan ships, their crews—"

"They were..." Khusaaq's voice suddenly trailed off; his gaze turned inward for a moment and he winced, just a slight twitch around the eyes and the corners of his mouth, then he continued in a slightly more husky voice that sounded more like he was repeating verbatim something he'd been told rather than something he truly believed, "...they were a very small price to pay for the greater good." He glanced sidelong at Amalfitano and added in a stronger tone, "Can you deny that the alliance that has come out of this will save more lives, millions of lives, possibly even billions of lives?"

"Well, no, but... there had to have been another way."

"I trust the Elkanasu weighed all of the options carefully, Doctor. They have been around far longer than humans or even A'tuu'shahn'i after all, and have guided the fates of entire species before, in fact many, many times over for millions and millions of years. To use a Rimmer expression, they are 'old hands' at the game. *Very old.* Ancient in fact, even by the standards of the galaxy."

Amalfitano tapped the tip of his forefinger on his desk. "So you're saying they had this all planned out, that they were fully in control of events the entire time?" He glanced about his office as if fully expecting the Elkanasu to materialize out of nothingness and all around him, just like their Hahtooshan protégés. "That they're still in control?"

"I said nothing of the sort. I said they guided us— A'tuu'shahn'i *and* Rimmer. But guide is not the same as control."

"So things could have gone terribly awry."

"Yes. But they didn't."

"Only by matter of degree." Amalfitano leaned back in his chair, shook his head and exhaled forcefully.

"Or in the greater scheme of things," Khusaaq replied softly.

Izraad studied him for a moment, then said, "It pains you terribly that they spend your lives as easily as others do, doesn't it?"

He stared back at her, eyes suddenly glistening anew, jaw muscles bunching. Finally he replied stiffly, "I am not in a position to question their motives or their means, Lieutenant. I am only their obedient servant. And dutiful servants do what they are told."

Sirin wrapped her fingers around his knee, drawing his pinched stare. "Lieutenant Izraad meant no offense."

"Truly I didn't, Sha'ashahn," Izraad echoed. "I was merely making an observation—based solely on your facial expression, your change of voice," she added hastily, suspecting what he was thinking—that she'd been eavesdropping on his thoughts. "I'm sorry if I offended you. That was not my intention."

He looked down at the hold Sirin had on his knee and took a rattling breath. Then he again met Izraad's gaze. "You're right. It does... pain me *terribly*. For others to spend A'tuu'shahn'i lives like so much loose coin is hard enough—most of our clients do not think of us as anything more than a club with which they can bludgeon their enemies, and why not? To them we are faceless mercenaries, bodies and blood bought and paid for. But for the Elkanasu to do the same when they have known each and every one of us as individuals and from birth... it is, at times, *very* hard to accept. But," he shrugged, "as an A'tuu'shahn, accept I must, there is no other way."

"Things are going to change, Khusaaq," Sirin said, "you have to believe that. Now that your people and mine are allies, things are going to change."

He smiled sidelong at her, not very convincingly. "I hope so. For everyone's sake."

"And at the risk of offending you again..." Izraad began, and Khusaaq turned to her, "...you are positively terrified that Qar'qaah, who also shares this trait, this... *gift*, will end up like you, crippled by his memories of this truly awful event."

He only stared at her, startled by the underlying indictment of himself.

"He doesn't have to suffer as you have, Sha'ashahn, there are very effectively treatments for this sort of severe psychological trauma."

"Then please do whatever you need to do—with his permission of course. You need not ask me again, you have my absolute consent."

"On one condition."

He eyed Izraad. "And that is?"

"That you accept treatment as well—"

He jerked his eyes off her, fixed them on the floor.

"—because you're suffering too, Sha'ashahn, in fact far, far more than Qar'qaah because you've been suffering for years—almost your entire life—and in silence."

Khusaaq shrugged almost defensively, "Qharubi knew, Matoosh knows."

Sirin tightened her hold on his knee, drawing his wary gaze. "But they couldn't help you, all they could do is support you." She gave his knee a squeeze. *"Please*, Khusaaq, at least consider what the lieutenant is offering, she *can* help you."

He ran his fingers through his hair, combing it away from his face and as he did so, Izraad noticed that his hands were shaking.

"It can all be done very discretely," Izraad said. "Sha'ashahn, I promise you—no one outside of this room would know and anything you reveal would be held in the strictest confidence—just you and me."

He squeezed his eyes shut.

"If you'd prefer someone else, another psychiatrist, which is completely understandable, I can arrange that," Izraad offered.

"Please, Khusaaq," Sirin whispered, looking at his downturned face.

"I will... think about it." He rose suddenly and stiffly from his chair, the others reluctantly following suit. He gave his eyes a quick wipe, tugged his slowly morphing duty uniform into place and cleared his throat. "Right now my sole concern is Qar'qaah."

"Fair enough," Izraad replied.

He started for the door, but just as he reached the threshold, he stopped, looked at Izraad and said, "I am forever in your debt, Lieutenant."

"I'd rather think that all debts have been canceled, Sha'ashahn."

He held her gaze for a moment, murmured, *"Yes,"* and stepped through the doorway.

Chapter 32

Amalfitano's quarters, sickbay, aboard the Baidarka, *1750.*

Qar'qaah tossed the salve-coated wash cloth aside, then stared into the mirror, at the gaunt-faced, shadow-eyed stranger who gazed back at him—and now not even the burn cream to blame for his pallid tattoos. Up until that moment he hadn't seen his naked skin, had, up to that moment, tried to convince himself it wasn't the *turee*, it was just the thick burn salve. Now even that excuse had been cleanly wiped away for this much-anticipated and dreaded meeting. *This is who survived Rasal Ghul— survived Cisne. Not me. Not who I was. This.*

He was frightened, deeply disturbed and wasn't sure he could live with what he saw. He suddenly felt lost. Utterly and completely lost—abandoned even by his own body—

"Are you all right, son?"

Amalfitano's worried voice drew his uneasy stare. He licked his blister-cracked lips and managed a less than convincing nod. Then he very reluctantly turned back to the wall-mounted mirror, this time avoiding eye-contact with the stranger within by turning his full attention to his once form-fitting duty uniform.

He gave it an angry tug here and a yank there; the uniform dutifully responded to his mental and physical prompts and tightened snugly around him... in the process accentuating his emaciated body.

It was not exactly the image he wanted to project. *No!*

The freshly laundered uniform promptly returned to its earlier, baggy state, still making it painfully obvious that he was little more than a living skeleton.

He squeezed his eyes shut and tried not to scream. Instead he slowly counted to ten—the very peculiar but surprisingly effective Rimmer trick he'd learned from Sirin—then opened his eyes and fixed his stare on the nearby doorway. It seemed close enough to touch, and at the same time, so far away it might as well be on the far side of the Rim.

A soft but pointed cough drew his gaze back to Amalfitano. He very reluctantly reached out for the older man's arm, to steady himself.

"Ready?"

At Qar'qaah's nod, they walked slowly out of Amalfitano's private cabin, through the human's untidy office and into what he knew was going to be a lengthy emotional gauntlet that stretched from the *Baidarka*'s sickbay all the way to the *Faridour* and back. Just the thought left his knees aching and his stomach in knots.

He pointedly ignored the sympathetic stares of the sickbay staff that followed his progress. Instead his entire attention was fixed on the doorway as he willed his body not to fail him.

The task wasn't made any easier once they'd exited the sprawling sickbay. The corridor that led to the ship's main flicker chamber was not crowded by any means, but he couldn't help but notice the furtive glances of passing crew. Some, like the nurses and medtechs, were concerned, others curious, and still others covertly hostile or worse, carried a taint of pity.

By the time they reached the flicker chamber, his legs were wobbly, his breathing labored and his skin glossy with sweat. But with Amalfitano's help he managed to step across the threshold without stumbling.

Those within instantly stopped talking and turned to face him, and their range of expressions hit like a fist to his already rebellious stomach. There was no hiding here, no cover, no way to pretend not to notice their reactions as he had with passing crew.

Qar'qaah swept the small chamber with his eyes, briefly acknowledging Aquila, Izraad and Matoosh before his strained gaze fell on Khusaaq and the woman standing beside him.

Khusaaq favored him with a decidedly satisfied smile but before Qar'qaah could fully savor the man's response, Sirin hurried to him.

She stopped short then held out her arms. "May I?"

He nodded and as she hugged him tightly he had to fight the urge to collapse into her arms. He was suddenly so tired, so drained, and the worst was yet to come. *I can't do this, I can't—*

She kissed him on the cheek, startling him and breaking his train of thought.

His eyes darted back to Khusaaq, only to find the man's expression unchanged.

"Sir," the flicker tech said, also looking at Khusaaq, "the *Faridour* is requesting your ETA."

Khusaaq, his immensely proud gaze never wavering from Qar'qaah, said, "Kon'ta'aq?"

It was now totally up to Qar'qaah. Everyone had repeatedly assured him it was his decision, he could back out at any time; no one would think less of him if at the last instant he found he couldn't go through with it. Even Narbrooi had personally told him such.

But there was that look in Khusaaq's eye he'd never seen before. A look that said—

Now's your chance, a voice whispered in his ear—an all too familiar voice. The voice that haunted his sleep, tormented his conscience: Cisne. *Go on,* she urged, *just say 'I can't do this'. No one really expects you to go through with it, you know.*

Instead he slipped from Sirin's comforting embrace, said, "Tell them we are flicking over momentarily," and stepped, unassisted, into the flickerstage.

Matoosh stepped in behind him, followed by Amalfitano and Sirin, and lastly, Khusaaq. Qar'qaah knew Sirin and Amalfitano's welcome company was to be short-lived. Narbrooi had agreed to them flicking over, but the Rimmers were not attending the hearing. Instead they would be sequestered in a nearby anteroom.

He turned around to face the doorway and met Izraad's steady gaze.

"You can do this, Kon'ta'aq—you can," she said.

Looking at her, hearing her confidence in him, he could almost believe it. *Almost.*

He barely had a chance to nod to her before the door slipped closed. An instant later he felt the flicker effect wash over him and he squeezed his eyes shut.

There was no going back now.

Chapter 33

Main staging bay, Faridour, *start of Middle Watch.*

Qar'qaah stared at the two knives Matoosh held, each balanced on an outstretched, tattooed palm. The blade to his left glittered enticingly, bathed as it was in the bright, almost blinding light of *Faridour*'s massive main staging bay—Matoosh had told him the crew jokingly referred to it as the waiting room for war. And so it was. Countless battalions had formed up in this very chamber only to go forth and wreak havoc on a thousand worlds.

He shifted his full attention back to the knives, to the business at hand and couldn't help but smile, intensely pleased to see his dagger and mildly surprised. He'd assumed it was his no longer.

Tseih'sheh....

To his immense relief, the blade's sinuous design responded to his unspoken acknowledgement, slithering across its mirror-polished surface, towards the grip, eagerly and welcoming his familiar touch.

Below, the deck's glowing, snaking streamers mimicked the movement, in the process adding their own silent voices, their own opinions as the complex design writhed around his feet and Matoosh's like a host of iridescent serpents.

The other blade, devoid of all decoration, was nothing more than a ubiquitous utility knife, chosen purely at random from *Faridour*'s thirty-five thousand plus crew.

By choosing one over the other, Qar'qaah sealed Gaalan's ultimate fate: one returned her to the Elkanasu where her memories would merge with all those who had gone before her and all who would come after; the other consigned her to ignoble oblivion, her name, her earlier, irrefutably heroic deeds, her very existence wiped from all records.

He met Matoosh's keen gaze.

Matoosh's eyes darted to the utility knife, then back to Qar'qaah, making his own pick patently obvious.

Khusaaq had been painstaking in his instructions but with an added twist once they'd parted company with Sirin and Amalfitano: despite what the Rimmers had been told, this was no simple hearing to determine Gaalan's guilt. Her culpability was beyond question. The Q'shaathrah had in fact extended him an extraordinary privilege: to be the one to determine not just Gaalan's fate, but to mete out the punishment personally.

No one would question his decision, but in order for his choice to be binding every officer aboard *Faridour* had to be present, to witness the proceedings.

As an added and very unwelcome twist, Narbrooi had alerted them that Gaalan did in fact have an as yet unknown number of supporters among the *Faridour*'s crew—in particular officers who had benefited early on from her patronage. Officers and crew who now found themselves torn between their loyalty to Narbrooi, Gaalan's acknowledged successor and highly accomplished officer in his own right and Gaalan—with Qar'qaah, Khusaaq and the fledging alliance all caught squarely in the middle.

While Narbrooi hadn't explicitly stated that Qar'qaah, or Khusaaq for that matter were in danger from this faction, a six-man Chah'duu escort, explained as an 'honor guard' to the Rimmers, was waiting for them at the flicker chamber and chaperoned them to the staging bay. Amalfitano and Sirin too had their own Chah'duu guards, stationed discreetly outside of the anteroom, their presence explained away by Khusaaq as Narbrooi just wanting to guarantee his human guests didn't get bored and decide to go walkabout as the *Faridour* was off-limits to all but A'tuu'shahn'i. Amalfitano had grumbled about the 'lack of trust', and had even pointed out that Tasende had never mentioned such restraints—not that the pathologist had had time or for that matter the interest to stray beyond the ship's sprawling medical unit—but hadn't questioned the matter further; neither had Sirin.

When Qar'qaah first entered the huge oval chamber and felt the intense stares of over three thousand men and women come to rest on him, he felt as if the air had been sucked out of his lungs—*again*. Added to it was the stinging knowledge that within those silent ranks were individuals who still believed Gaalan was a hero, a martyr—and the *true* victim. But instead of succumbing to the suffocating fear, instead of grabbing hold of the rage and using that as a crutch to support him, he strode alone and purposefully into the chamber, through the only gap in the iridescent black, double ring-wall of silent officers, between Narbrooi and his imposing Quu'dahn second in command, Kaahn'deer, past Khusaaq and the *Faridour*'s CMO, Hai'chellah, who together stood slightly apart from the rest, and finally over to the person who stood at the very center of the expansive bay.

Matoosh had watched his approach, his face devoid of all expression. Such was protocol. In this very ancient, rarely performed ritual, only the accuser and the accused could to show emotion; only the accuser, when guilt was beyond question, could speak.

Qar'qaah wet his lips then, at Matoosh's signal, he overheard the soft shuffle of approaching footsteps come to a halt behind him.

He hadn't seen Gaalan when he first entered the chamber. He'd been too fixated on making it across the broad expanse without stumbling. But he had known from the start that she was there; he could smell her—hers was a scent he would *never* forget, despite it being only one of thousands that filled the bay, a slightly cloying and at the same time musty spoor—

Not that of a pure Elkanaghalli, more, he tried to humor himself, *like a sincerely dead Matarii.* It didn't work. He hadn't really expected it would.

He took a steadying breath and slowly turned around.

He'd anticipated a sense of gut-wrenching dread, of overwhelming fear, of aching bitterness. But the naked-faced woman who stood between two massive and grim-faced Chah'duu'i was anything but formidable. In fact in the harsh lighting of the chamber, she appeared haggard, old... and yes, even rather frail and bruise-eyed. It struck him that this might be yet another attempt to conceal her true self—perhaps even an attempt to play to his sympathy, not to mention her hidden loyalists.

Suddenly a Rimmer expression came to mind: *Hell if.*

He stared at her for a *very* long time—allowing her to do the same, and she did, her darting, mildly startled gaze taking in his faded tattoos—long enough for him to become aware of the uneasy shift of feet from the surrounding officers who stood, shoulder to armored shoulder, around the periphery of the huge chamber; long enough to sense Khusaaq's growing anxiety and Matoosh's bewildered frustration.

They all think I've lost my nerve.

Then he caught the quickly concealed trace of a smirk on Gaalan's lips. The same smirk he'd seen through the transparent wall of the stasis chamber as its paralyzing effect washed over him—

You think I've lost my nerve—or never had any?

Matoosh, at Narbrooi's ever-so-slight, impatient nod, stepped forward to stand beside him, to prompt him into action.

He flicked Matoosh a sidelong glance then began in a voice that was so calm and steady it even startled him: "Pashna'gaalan ket Tashar'anhi, first born of Tah'gynn Tashar'anhi-baalkhu… you knowingly took from me, A'uha-larkahn'qar'qaah Abhijit'tischinjgra, and by force, any right to claim that I am an untouched Elkanaghalli. Custom would say that is more than enough justification for me to take your life.

"The Q'shaathrah agree, as do all who are assembled here." If the rumors were true, that wasn't entirely accurate, but... it was the sentiment that counted, and the words, hastily rehearsed only moments before, flowed from his still swollen, blistered lips by rote as his gaze briefly swept the surrounding wall of expressionless faces before returning to Gaalan.

But from here on, the words were his, and his alone. He'd practiced them too, countless times and in private since being informed of this meeting, hoping by doing so, his voice wouldn't fail him. "But I am still A'tuu'shahn and always will be—that is one thing you can never take away from me, or, more importantly, from those who fought and died at Cotopaxi, carrying out your last orders, defending *your* honor, *your* memory.

"You, however, willingly turned your back on your crew, your people and the Elkanasu to live among those who would gladly see all A'tuu'shahn'i dead and in doing so, you've betrayed not just A'tuu'shahn'i but everything we believe in, everything we stand for." He paused, gave the two knives a pointed, sidelong glance, then again meeting her unblinking stare and bracing himself, continued, "Your fate, therefore, should be decided by our people, *not by me.*"

He couldn't help but overhear startled intakes of breath in the deathly silent staging bay—or spot the scattering of decidedly relieved smiles—smiles that vanished almost as quickly as they had appeared. Even Gaalan looked surprised. And out of the corner of his eye, he saw Khusaaq staring at him in slack-jawed shock.

He wanted to laugh—almost—as he slowly turned, his eyes again sweeping the entire chamber before they finally came to rest on an equally startled Narbrooi. "It was my decision, Hahtra'tzrhi—you said so yourself."

"Indeed I did, Kon'ta'aq," Narbrooi replied quietly.

And so is this. Qar'qaah took another breath, then again fixing his gaze on Gaalan, he snatched the utility knife from Matoosh's hand—causing a ripple of anticipation in the double-thick wall of officers—but instead of doing as everyone expected, he grabbed his own plait of hair and sliced the knife through it, just below the nape of his neck, to the collective gasp of those around him—even Gaalan.

He hurled the knife aside and it skittered, spinning, across the floor, then he thrust out the severed braid, his bony fist mere centimeters from Gaalan's face as he stared directly into her piercing blue eyes—as if he'd find all the answers there—desperate to find just *some* of the answers.

Realizing there were none—realizing that maybe *that's* what he needed to know, he released the braid to fall to the deck at her shackled feet. The deck's flowing design instantly coalesced around it, the luminescent ribbons curling and whipping in tighter and tighter knots.

He then pivoted on his heel and started for the imposing gauntlet of Narbrooi and the *Faridour*'s second in command, the two standing on either side of the airlock, bracketing his escape route.

Matoosh and Khusaaq, shaking off their own startled paralysis, had no sooner started after him than Gaalan sneered, "How very righteous," her commanding voice echoing in the chamber, breaking not only the strained silence but also the tradition of the ceremony and stopping the three in their tracks just short of the airlock. "When in truth you're a pathetic, sniveling coward, justly cursed by the *turee*, who doesn't have the stomach to kill me."

Qar'qaah met Narbrooi's unblinking stare, held it for several thudding heartbeats he could feel in his throat and behind his eyeballs, then he slowly turned around to face her.

"He does." Gaalan jerked her chin towards the fierce-eyed Matoosh then she looked past him to Narbrooi and Khusaaq who now stood together in stony silence. "So do they." She motioned expansively around her, to the ring of officers, adding, "They all do. But *not* you."

"You're right," Qar'qaah replied simply, "I don't." He grinned at her blink of astonishment.

"You're not fit to be Khusaaq's doh'ha—to be Ja'andai's ahathna'doh'ah!" Her heated response provoked a current of furious whispers within the wall of assembled officers. She then spat on the plait and the glowing streamers reacted, increasing their furious writhing under it.

"Again, you're right, I'm not—*you* made sure of that. But then again, I never asked for the 'honor'—quite the contrary..." Qar'qaah's voice trailed off as a snatch of conversation between Gaalan and her Matarii doctor, caught as he was being examined by the alien medic, suddenly bubbled to the surface unbidden. "But answer me this: what really happened to Ja'andai? He didn't die at Tindari, did he?"

The unexpected question, the startling suggestion of an account different than one everyone believed wholeheartedly to be truth hung in the air of the now deadly silent chamber; those present glanced at each other in unease.

Gaalan snorted, "Why should I tell you?"

"I thought you'd want an opportunity to explain your actions..." he gestured to the ring of assembled officers, to Narbrooi, Khusaaq and Matoosh, "...what drove you to this... *career choice*. Perhaps, just perhaps even save yourself."

She glared defiantly at him, then at all of those faces staring at her with expressions ranging from growing apprehension among the Elkanaghalli'i and Kri'taaka'i to anticipatory satisfaction among the Khighalli'i and their affiliated secular castes. To Qar'qaah it also appeared she was seeking out her loyalists while carefully avoiding acknowledging them by maintaining eye contact just a fraction of a second too long. A sidelong glance at Narbrooi and his second confirmed his suspicions: the officers were also closely watching her eye track. He had little doubt others too, carefully planted among the gathering, were doing the same.

Gaalan's gaze finally returned to Qar'qaah. She smiled an intensely smug smile and replied, "No, he didn't die at Tindari."

All eyes briefly shifted to a dumbfounded Khusaaq, then back to her.

"He faked his death, didn't he?" Qar'qaah continued. "Just like you did, later, at Cotopaxi. Why?"

"Because I *hated* being A'tuu'shahn, hated always being cast as Ja'andai's second, his shadow—*his lover*," she again looked all around her, this time her accusative glare picking out specific Khighalli officers among those present. "I am Tashar'anhi, a clan every bit as honorable *and* old as Ja'andai's, and I am a *first* born, not a *doh'ha*, yet no matter what I accomplished, I knew I'd never be perceived as being as worthy as him, the *doh'ha* of the always valiant, larger than life Shushnua. I could never surpass him, not in the eyes of the Q'shaathrah, and Ja'andai could never fail in the eyes of our people. It was untenable, for both of us, so yes, we plotted our deaths, left nothing to chance and just waited for an opportunity."

"Like Tindari," Qar'qaah prompted.

"Yes."

"But only he escaped."

"You mean, only he *succeeded*," she fired back. "Of course he would, he was Ja'andai—"

"And he left you behind."

"That was actually the plan—he'd go first, I'd follow, later. We believed that both of us dying in the same action might encourage a board of inquiry to dig deeper than it in fact did. But one surviving to testify, to heap more praise on the one who... *died*, to put the Q'shaathrah's incident investigators off the scent—"

"Only you never found the right opportunity to follow him, not until Cotopaxi."

"I was never given the right *opportunity*, as you so aptly call it. I was forced into a backwater position, effectively excluded from any high-paying but risky contracts—all due to the rumors... about you."

"So why did you insist I be created?" Suddenly it was just him and Gaalan, alone, the others forgotten. "I've always been curious. From what I've been told, or have been able to gather, demanding a second *doh'ha* be created only rekindled all the ugly whispers that had just started to die down—"

She laughed, a short, sharp bark of laughter. "I was following Ja'andai's directions, believe it or not—looking back, it was a stupid thing to do, and likely he knew doing so would make things harder for me, but..." She shrugged. "He wanted another *doh'ha*, one who would be raised properly, not as he was raised, or Khusaaq or even Shushnua. Raised the *ancient* way, with all the ancient rules. A suitable replacement, he said, because Khusaaq," her gaze shifted to the man, "could never measure up, and I must say, truer words have never been spoken."

Qar'qaah refused to look at Khusaaq, despite the almost overwhelming urge. "And you thought I would."

"No," she snorted. "But Ja'andai did. He was so full of himself, so full of the righteous nonsense the Q'shaathrah had pumped into him over the years he couldn't see he'd just be creating another him, another Khusaaq, a *doh'ha* who carried the *paas'nah* as a dominant gene, with all of its attendant... complications. But there was simply no saying no to him—

while he felt he could no longer live as an A'tuu'shahn, he also felt the Orthodoxy couldn't possibly survive without him, or, barring that, his clone. And since Khusaaq had proven himself... well, such a huge disappointment, another had to be created.

"He even refused to let me disable the gene, saying if properly raised, you'd know how to control it, to wield it, use it to communicate with the Elkanasu like no one had in generations—the ultimate legacy not only for himself, but Shushnua and for all Abhijit'tischinjgra, cementing their claim to being the most storied of all the clans, the most meritorious—the only family who still had direct contact with the Elkanasu. Matters didn't exactly play out as planned," she added with a chuckle as she looked him up and down. "I mean, look at you."

"So what happened?" Qar'qaah prompted.

"To you?"

"We all know what happened to me," he replied, somehow managing to keep the snap out of his voice. "To you."

"Me? I bided my time, waiting for the right, as you called it, *opportunity.*"

"And getting more and more embittered by the passing day."

She shrugged, nothing more than an irritable twitch of the shoulders as if all the years of waiting and hating wasn't worth mentioning.

"And Ja'andai?" he asked, knowing it was a question everyone present wanted answered.

She stared at him for a moment then replied simply, "He did, in fact, die."

"But not at Tindari, so... how?" he persisted.

"Precisely? How should I know? All I know is that he died shortly after Cotopaxi."

"Then how are you sure he's dead?"

"I trust my sources."

"Or maybe you murdered him?"

She snorted again. "And why would I have done that?"

"Maybe you resented him for leaving you behind, leaving you to deal with the rumors, the irreparable damage to your career—and oh yes, *me.*"

"You grossly overestimate your importance—a common but rather annoying Abhijit'tischinjgra flaw, I've come to realize. But so what if I did? I was finally free, able to go where I wanted, do what I wanted, be with whom I wanted—no thanks to Ja'andai."

Now it was Qar'qaah's turn to smile. "You discovered in your absence that he'd gone on to create quite a nice life for himself, quite a grand life in fact, one in which you wouldn't play a part. In fact his plan from the start was that you'd never play a part—true? He never planned on the two of you ever reuniting—he played you, just as you and he played the Q'shaathrah." He tapped his ear at her mildly surprised reaction. "Last thing to go, remember? You should've made sure I was unconscious, or you were out of earshot. So, when you finally caught up with him and he told you as much, you killed him, didn't you?

She stared back at him then smiled. "I didn't need to kill him. He'd made plenty of enemies; all I had to do was tell them where he was. But, as it turns out, I didn't even have to do that even though in truth I did—tell them where he was that is. And let's be clear, I did want him dead. Absence, paraphrasing the human saying, doesn't always make the heart grow fonder—" She glanced sidelong at Khusaaq. "Sometimes it gives you the perspective and detached clarity to see others for who and what they really are."

She then looked around her, to the wall of heavily tattooed faces who stared back with varying degrees of anxiety. "Do you all want to know how the Hero of Tindari *really* died? He died in a Korhugian brothel, so drunk he aspirated his own vomit." She turned back to Qar'qaah, again looked him up and down, leering as she did so. "Such an ignoble end for the Hero of Tindari, and now... the ignoble end to unrestrained Abhijit'tischinjgra aspirations."

"So why were you so desperate to entrap and kill Khusaaq?" Qar'qaah asked after a moment to give everyone a chance to absorb what she'd said. Ja'andai deserved that much, at least in his mind, despite the circumstances—assuming, of course, she was telling the truth.

She again fixed her piercing, cold blue gaze on the man in question, started to take a step closer but was restrained by the gauntleted hand of one her guards—a warning only. She twitched it off. "Ja'andai desperately wanted you to make something of yourself—not to overshadow his accomplishments, his career, oh no, but enough that you wouldn't in some way stain his exploits. He was solely responsible for your upbringing after all, your education, and knew he'd done a terrible job at it, too busy burnishing his own reputation to waste any valuable time on you. I suggested that I could mold you into something worthy of his legacy—we made a bet, but part of that bet was a backup, a fallback."

"Me," Qar'qaah offered helpfully.

She flicked him a sidelong and withering glare, replied with a curt, almost distracted nod, then turned back to Khusaaq, eyes flashing. "Unlike Ja'andai, I did see potential in you. I followed your early training—helped it along where I could—and despite the risks, the rumors, I requisitioned you. As it turns out, you *were* more like Ja'andai than I ever imagined."

Khusaaq raised his brows in genuine bafflement, started to open his mouth but she cut him off with a startlingly fierce: "*I should have been the Hero of Cotopaxi, the ultimate martyr, surpassing even Ja'andai—and I would have been had you died on that cursed planet as you were supposed to. But you didn't!*" She was suddenly breathing hard, shaking and unaware that the guards had stepped closer, ready for another quick grab. "Just like Ja'andai, you *betrayed* me, you took what was rightfully *mine*, what I'd so carefully worked for, for years, what had been denied me—"

"You abandoned the crew of the *Huui'teh*," Khusaaq replied stiffly, his quiet voice tightly controlled. "You abandoned the colonists, the planet... betrayed everything, everyone, for what?"

"For no longer having to be Elkanaghalli! For not having to live my life constrained by archaic, inane rules, to be seen as something other than a universally despised and feared A'tuu'shahn! To finally shake off the fetters of unquestioning servitude our *beloved* Elkanasu place on us at birth and only unlock upon our deaths... to be free to find my own path, to find pleasure..." her eyes briefly dropped to his bandoleer and the missing dagger sheath, added in a slightly calmer, more sneering voice, "just as you've done—"

"So, did you find pleasure in being a Matarii collaborator?"

"Do you find pleasure in being a Rimmer puppet?" she countered sweetly.

Before he could reply, Matoosh snarled, "Why do what you did to Qar'qaah?" as he withdrew his own utility knife. He was close enough that if he chose to hurl it he couldn't possibly miss.

She briefly shifted her gaze to him and to the white-knuckled hold he had on the knife and grinned maliciously, baitingly. Then she turned back to Khusaaq as Khusaaq grabbed Matoosh's hand and forced it back to his side. "You'd slipped through my grasp so many times... ironically, and I must say to my growing chagrin, each time your status as Hero of Cotopaxi grew—first there was Peshitta," she began, ticking the names off using her fingers, "and then the skirmishes of Elazig Rounds, the Battle of Massanhoyük Deep... the Chhotri and Tharus campaigns—"

"Get to the point," Khusaaq growled.

She grinned. "I was, but since you are *such* the reluctant hero, I'll skip over the glorious details you find *so* distressing to recount, I'll gloss over all the times you survived, largely unscathed, when so, *so* many others didn't, *yes?* Your astonishing habit of refusing to die only burnished your fame, didn't it? My, my, that must have haunted you. You were *so* underserving and you knew it, and those who were oh so deserving died all around you, but no one would listen, would they?"

"You didn't—I tried to tell you, but—"

"Oh, I knew, trust me, I *knew*. The moment I realized that you too carried the *paas'nah*, despite you desperately trying to hide it, just as Ja'andai tried but far more successfully I might add, and Shushnua before him, I *knew*—but once I was officially declared dead, there wasn't a damned thing I could do about it, at least not through the usual channels. There wasn't anything I could do to derail your career, even though I tried—believe me, I *tried*.

"And look at you now," she jerked her chin towards the impressive array of colorful medallions and campaign discs that decorated his ghillie uniform, "still referred to as the Hero of Cotopaxi by most, and held in such reverence by many, still admired even after all these years even though in truth you were, and remain, a complete failure in that role—a role anyone with even the slightest bit of acumen could have parlayed into a career and wealth beyond their wildest of imaginings. You only succeeded—no, *survived* because you carry the *paas'nah*—because the Elkanasu protected you, guided you, just as they guided and protected Ja'andai, and Shushnua before him! Their *precious* conduits! But you couldn't, or more accurately *wouldn't* take advantage of that, not like Ja'andai did."

She glanced around her, wild-eyed. "You think Ja'andai was solely responsible for his unrivaled success? *Think again!* He rationalized that this was his birthright, that he was one of the privileged few, chosen by the Elkanasu, so why should he question the massive advantages he'd been given? Not to profit from them, he said more times than I can remember, would be equivalent to slapping the Elkanasu in the face, so he parlayed the *paas'nah* in ways even I couldn't have foreseen, at first hiding his unquenchable avarice behind a façade of uncompromising fanaticism.

"But he became so greedy and so besotted with himself that he began to resent first the Q'shaathrah, and then even the Elkanasu, believing they were holding back, doling out little by little only a portion of what he deserved because they'd become jealous of him—yes, *him!*"

Then she fixed her stare on Khusaaq. "But you? Oh no—you were too naïve, too... *virtuous* to follow Ja'andai's lead even a little—more like Shushnua in that regard and we all know what happened to him! And just like with Shushnua, that refusal to cash in only added to your burgeoning reputation, didn't it?" She stopped, smiled at him. "So it would seem there is no way to avoid reaping the rewards of carrying the gift, is there? It's all just a matter of degree—unless of course you say enough and kill yourself. Does make you wonder what the Elkanasu thought of Shushnua doing just that. Talk about a slap in the face."

Khusaaq stared back, expressionless.

"Do you want to know why you are the object of such adoration or such pure hate? It's because unlike with Ja'andai, *everyone* knows you carry the *paas'nah*! The religious fanatics see you as the last of your kind, the last direct conduit to the Elkanasu. The haters see you as a fraud, who used that advantage to survive when others didn't, to trick—"

"I know," Khusaaq replied softly. "Or should I say I know now. One of my crew was kind enough to enlighten me to the fact that my status, which I'd always assumed was kept on a need to know basis," he couldn't help but glance at Narbrooi, "was in fact well-known. It explained a lot."

Gaalan chuckled, a harsh, barking chuckle—no longer human laughter but A'tuu'shahn. "I bet it did. I bet finding out it wasn't envy of your accomplishments that motivated the haters, it wasn't your reluctance to play hero that so angered your fellow A'tuu'shahn'i, but fear—that must've been a real blow."

"Not really, it just finally made sense—"

"As for me, well, this was all quite... *maddening*, so much so I found it difficult to think of anything else and to fully enjoy my new life—after Ja'andai's... tragic death I took over his business dealings you see, a very lucrative arms trade. I was doing very well, even better than he had because in truth I was far better at anything I put my mind to than he ever was—I wasn't used to relying on anyone or *anything* else but myself you see, unlike Ja'andai—who, I might add, suddenly found he wasn't so innately talented as he'd always assumed what with the Elkanasu unexpectedly and to him ungratefully withdrawing their patronage upon his... *death* at Tindari. But you remained, a constant, supremely frustrating reminder of what I could and should have been. Hero of Cotopaxi... indeed." She again spat on the floor.

"And worse," she continued, "your... *interference* at Rasal Ghul really annoyed my Matarii patrons—they'd spent a lot of time and effort there, and having you ruin everything—and yet *again*, come out a heroic figure, well... they were suddenly just as eager to rid the universe of you as I was. So I hatched what I reasonably felt was a fail-proof plan the moment I heard you'd accidentally left your precious *doh'ha* behind—I knew you'd come after him, knew it would be a far worse torment for you when you found out what I'd done to him—I felt that was just payment all the torment you'd handed me over the years, and besides, despite his *obvious* lack of experience, I found him to be quite... satisfying," she purred. "As did my *entire* crew."

Matoosh stiffened, his jaw muscles bunching in silent, murderous rage.

"But I didn't want him dead you see. He hadn't done anything to me, not yet at least, and besides, he *was* in fact the perfect payback, the perfect fallback." She smiled a very smug smile.

"I don't follow," Khusaaq replied coldly.

"I knew, once word got out as to his new... *status*, our dear caste would never accept him back, never permit him to claim kinship, much less parley his relationship to you or Ja'andai into anything meaningful. And neither would the Elkanasu welcome him. *Look at him!*"

All eyes reluctantly did as she commanded and turned to Qar'qaah, each and every one taking in his savagely cut hair, his pallid tattoos and the agonizing knowledge that the damage went far deeper.

"Your highly vaunted *doh'ha* line would end," she continued in a sneering voice, "so tainted no one would dare resurrect it. As I said, the perfect payback for what you and Ja'andai did to *me*—you destroyed me, I destroyed your lineage. In a strange way, I was doing the Elkanaghalli'i a huge favor by removing this unpredictable and highly undesirable *paas'nah* once and for all from its dwindling genetic pool— your *doh'ha* line is in fact the very last to carry it, you know that? You two are the last vestige of that genetic tether—or hangman's noose depending upon how you look at it—of our *beloved* Elkanasu. I had no need to kill the boy—now that he's served his purpose to me, he'll do it himself."

Qar'qaah slowly shook his head. He'd heard enough—
they'd all heard more than enough. With one last sidelong look
at Gaalan, he walked alone out of the chamber and started down
the passageway, towards the flicker chamber and its anteroom.

Behind him he heard a swell of voices, enraged voices,
everyone suddenly yelling at once, old enmities, long-held
grievances suddenly ripped from their hiding places by
Gaalan's ugly admissions, her stinging accusations—her very
presence. Then the airlock snapped shut, leaving only the sound
of his own footfalls to accompany him, along with the hammer
of his heart against his ribs.

Suddenly, all he wanted was to get as far away from Gaalan
as possible, away from the bitter truth of his bleak future, away
from the staging bay and the knowing, pitying stares of the
officers as fast as possible—back to Sirin and Amalfitano—
back to the relative anonymity of *Baidarka*, even to the honest,
undifferentiating hate of some of her crew.

His pace quickened, the hurried, shuffling walk turning to
an awkward trot, and then a loping, stumbling run.

He managed to reach the anteroom hatchway without
mishap but tripped on the raised threshold. Only the quick
thinking and well-placed grab by one of the Chah'duu guards
stopped him from falling to the deck.

Sirin too reached out to steady him then as the guard
released his hold, she wrapped her arms tightly around
Qar'qaah and whispered, "Are you all right?" Then she noticed
his hair. *"Gods, what happened? What the hell did they do to
you?"*

He didn't answer; instead he glanced back at the doorway,
gasping for breath, as they all heard the rapidly approaching
echo of feet.

Sirin tightened her protective embrace.

Amalfitano placed himself between Qar'qaah and the
hatchway, clearly thinking the worst as their Chah'duu guards
readied their weapons. A very grim-faced Matoosh and equally
upset Khusaaq appeared, followed by their bodyguards, and
wordlessly stepped into the room, leaving the Chah'duu'i to

take up a protective stance, blocking the doorway to any who might follow.

"What the hell happened?" Amalfitano demanded, looking first at Khusaaq, then Matoosh.

"We can talk about it once we're back aboard the *Baidarka,*" Sirin said pointedly, her arms still wrapped around Qar'qaah. "Come on." She gave him a tug. "Let's get out of here."

At her urging, and leaning heavily on her, Qar'qaah stumbled through the silent gauntlet of Chah'duu'i and into the corridor, then down the passageway to the flicker chamber, and finally into the flickerstage itself; Amalfitano, Matoosh and Khusaaq silently filed in behind them, again leaving the guards at the doorway.

Qar'qaah dropped his gaze to the grated floor and concentrated on slowing his panicky breathing, his heart's breakneck beat as he waited for the flicker effect to wash over him. Instead a hand grasped his shoulder.

Startled, he briefly looked at Khusaaq, realized tears were rolling down the man's cheeks and quickly fixed his pinched gaze on the floor.

"I'm so incredibly proud of you," Khusaaq murmured. "You managed to get Gaalan to admit everything, in front of—"

"May we go now... *please?"* he forced out, then clenched his teeth against an all too familiar sensation forming in his gut and back of his throat.

He retched, then, feeling Khusaaq's arms around him, supporting him as his knees gave way, he retched again, even more explosively, his entire body convulsing. He was dimly aware of Amalfitano barking orders, of Matoosh yelling at the tech not to initiate the flicker, while he continued to vomit.

Finally, having completely emptied his stomach, he hiccupped several times and closing his eyes, sagged against Khusaaq, exhausted and on the verge of blacking out.

"I think he's done," he heard Khusaaq say, followed by Amalfitano's angry, worried, "Then let's get the hell out of here."

And then to his relief, Qar'qaah felt the familiar tickle of the flicker effect, tugging at him, pulling him and the others back to the *Baidarka*.

Chapter 34

Flicker chamber, Baidarka.

"Sickbay," Amalfitano said the instant the flicker chamber's doors snapped open, depositing them back on the *Baidarka.*

Khusaaq nodded and scooped up the unresisting Qar'qaah into his arms then followed Amalfitano out of the chamber.

Amalfitano, keenly aware that Qar'qaah's eyes were closed and his breathing rapid and shallow, walked abreast of Khusaaq, his gaze fixed on his ashen-faced patient for the entire, hastily-made trip.

Matoosh and Sirin silently took up the rear.

It wasn't until Khusaaq placed Qar'qaah on a triage bed that Qar'qaah very reluctantly opened his eyes.

"Just want to run some tests," Amalfitano said as he pushed a small signal suppressor down the neck-slit of Qar'qaah's soiled duty uniform then pressed it firmly against the bare skin just below his collarbone.

Amalfitano then glanced around him to find Sirin, Matoosh and Khusaaq staring expectantly at the bank of over-bed monitors as they began to fill with data. Khusaaq's face, not to mention his hair and uniform were liberally splattered in vomit. The other two had somehow escaped.

"As I thought… just a delayed reaction," Amalfitano muttered, more to himself than his captive audience as he too studied the data that flowed across the monitors. "Shoulda known we were pushing you too hard—too much too soon." He dropped his very relieved gaze to Qar'qaah. "I want to get you back to your cubicle, keep a close eye on you for the next twenty four hours, all right?"

"Yes…"

"Think you can walk if I help you?" he asked, motioning for the others to back away.

Again Qar'qaah mumbled, "Yes." He cautiously levered himself up onto his elbows then very slowly eased himself off the bed and to his feet.

"You three," Amalfitano's eyes darted to Matoosh, Sirin and Khusaaq just as Meerut and Drakin entered the small bay. "Go get some rest, we'll take it from here."

Matoosh started to protest, but Meerut cut him off with, "Come on, Ruh'ta'aq, I know of a bed close by you can use."

Matoosh gave Qar'qaah one last worried look—to which Qar'qaah replied with a faint, almost embarrassed smile and he dutifully, grudgingly, followed the nurse.

Amalfitano turned to Sirin and Khusaaq. "You two as well—go on."

"Qar'qaah?" Khusaaq asked, not budging from beside the bed.

Qar'qaah managed a less than convincing, "I'm... I'm all right, ta'ahn."

"And I don't want to see hide nor hair of either of you until morning—*got it?*" Amalfitano added for good measure.

Sirin nodded. Taking Khusaaq's hand in hers, she led him away.

Amalfitano gave Qar'qaah a sidelong look only to find him staring back at him with sunken, blood-shot eyes. "Ready?"

Qar'qaah nodded and together they followed Drakin out of the bay, through the unusually quiet main sickbay and finally into the small isolation unit.

They reached his cubicle without mishap. Once inside, and with Amalfitano's help, Qar'qaah quickly stripped down to just his trousers as Drakin grabbed several washcloths from the over-bed bin and a basin from under the drug cart.

As she filled the basin with hot water, she glanced over her shoulder. "Lez get you cleaned up, all right?"

Qar'qaah nodded and sat on the edge of the bed.

She placed the basin beside him and handed him a soapy washcloth. "Here, wasssh your faz."

He took it and made a very cursory effort at cleaning himself, then handed the washcloth back to her.

Not satisfied with the result, Drakin took another cloth and without asking permission and without further ado grasped his chin in one hand and gave his face, then his throat and chest a thorough scrubbing while clicking her tongue. She then took his hands and gave them a good wash too.

Watching, Amalfitano noted the simple, but significant fact that Qar'qaah submitted without comment, without flinching and even more importantly, without tensing up—perhaps he was just too wrung out, physically and emotionally spent to put up a fight. At least Amalfitano hoped that's what it was.

"Much better," she said, drawing Amalfitano's gaze. "Now we need to reapply da sssalve, yez?"

Qar'qaah only nodded then closed his eyes as Drakin smeared the thick cream over his face, quickly moving on to his chest, arms and hands as Amalfitano did his part by applying the salve to Qar'qaah's bony and blister-pocked back.

"Dere, all done." Satisfied, she grabbed the basin and the soiled cloths and walked over to the cubicle's small sink.

Amalfitano stepped close and placed his hand on Qar'qaah's bare, salve-greasy shoulder. "Would you like to talk with Lieutenant Izraad, son?"

Qar'qaah shook his head then, as he began kneading his temples, whispered, *"Tomorrow..."*

"All right, but if you change your mind, she said to tell you she's on call, any hour of the day or night."

Qar'qaah only nodded this time.

Amalfitano shared a quick look with Drakin as he accepted a wash cloth to clean his hands of the cream, then continued, "Tell me this, it wasn't just a simple 'hearing' to determine Gaalan's guilt, was it? Narbrooi had already established that beyond any reasonable doubt, I'm sure."

Qar'qaah eased himself back onto the bunk. Then squeezing his eyes shut, he replied softly, "I... I really don't want to talk anymore."

"All right," Amalfitano said as Drakin drew a blanket over their patient.

Qar'qaah immediately rolled onto his left side, away from the two.

Amalfitano waited a moment, then asked, "Think you can get to sleep on your own or would you like me to give you something?"

Instead of replying, Qar'qaah tugged the blanket over his head.

Answer enough. Amalfitano shook his head, whispered to Drakin, "I'll stay with him," then pulled down the fold-down seat next to the bed and sat.

She answered with a nod of her own, then as she stepped out of the cubicle, he looked around him. *One of these nights I'm actually going to end up sleeping in my own bed—*

Overhearing what sounded to him like muffled sniffing, he glanced at Qar'qaah's blanket wrapped form, saw Qar'qaah's shoulders twitch. *But definitely not tonight.* He wriggled back into the chair then murmured, "Lights... off."

As his own very weary eyes stared at the flickering reflections of the over-bed monitors in the cubicle's semi-transparent wall, he let his mind wander, to his own future and whether to re-enlist, or do what he had threatened to do for so long: retire.

He'd always assumed he'd return to Earth, return to his ancestral village tucked away in the Dolomites—about as far away from deep space as one could get, unless you looked up at a crystal clear night sky. Then it seemed close enough to touch. Thinking about it now, he realized he had no one back there—at least no one he cared about.

He rose, pulled another blanket from the over-bed bin and wrapped it around himself. Then, reseating himself, he closed his eyes. *Just a catnap...* He exhaled slowly and his body responded by relaxing, but his mind refused to go along and instead continued to work.

His family was now here: Zarijan, of course, along with Sirin and Khusaaq, Jenna and his medical staff, Matoosh, and yes, now Qar'qaah, not to mention, at least temporarily, Endooki, Laihiri, Raudah, Nihaal and Jaa'qwah. He suddenly realized just how much they all meant to him—even the acerbic Murh'sooli—how he now felt responsible for them and how much he actually *enjoyed* the idea of feeling responsible—

Even if some of you might not be all that thrilled with the idea, he added as he forced open one sleepy eye and gave Qar'qaah a sidelong look.

By Qar'qaah's deep, even breaths, Amalfitano could tell that despite the tremendous emotional strain of the day's events—perhaps because of them—the young Hahtooshan had managed to slip into a natural, albeit exhausted sleep. *Another good sign...*

Turning back to his earlier thoughts, Amalfitano chuckled softly to himself as he wondered what his own family—his *real* family would think of his choice of surrogate kin. Thinking of his parents, his sister—doctors all—he realized they would fully understand.

Everyone needs a family, needs to feel responsible—the holo he'd kept with him, had refused to throw away, was proof enough of that. *A way to keep your place in the world—even if it's just a tenuous toehold.*

Now he *had* a real family—not a frozen image of people he'd never known—his new family might not be *his* flesh and blood family, but they *were* flesh and blood, not a holo purchased on the spur of the moment in a musty pawnshop for a measly credit. As for home... well, that was a matter for another time. Plenty of time to think about home—a new home perhaps, to go with his new family.

Still smiling, he felt himself start to drift off, his weary brain comfortably swaddled in cotton wool.

Then, overhearing a muffled groan and instantly awake—he turned to Qar'qaah as Qar'qaah began to mumble restlessly, his body twitching.

Amalfitano rose and started to reach out, to shake Qar'qaah awake, thinking he was in the throes of his nightmare... and froze.

Qar'qaah was indeed in the throes of something: his facial and neck tattoos had taken on an eerie bluish-green luminescence, visible if a little blurred through the salve and instantly reminding Amalfitano of the unsettling interior of the *Jirah*—or the sinuous, ever eeling walls, deck and ceiling of the corridors and anteroom of the *Faridour*.

Alarmed, but also intensely curious, he very carefully peeled back the blanket covering Qar'qaah and had his suspicions—his fears—confirmed.

The designs that snaked over Qar'qaah's bare arms, torso—feet—every bit of skin not covered by his trousers, and, Amalfitano had to assume every bit of skin period, had taken on the same odd glow. As he watched, to his growing amazement, new patterns began to emerge, like growing tendrils on a vine, rapidly filling in gaps on his right upper arm.

That's a hell of a thing...

Qar'qaah groaned again. Wincing, he breathed heavily as the fingers of his left hand tightly clutched his right shoulder.

Amalfitano had to fight the instinctual urge to touch him, suspecting that would be the worst thing he could do. Instead he fixed his worried gaze on the over-bed monitors and was relieved by what he saw. Whatever was happening was causing only moderate discomfort.

Then, noticing Qar'qaah had stopped moaning, he looked back at him to find that the tattoos had abruptly ceased glowing and as Qar'qaah's now relaxed fingers fell away, Amalfitano noted that the pattern on his right upper arm was now also far more complex.

A quick glance back at the monitors proved what he already knew: Qar'qaah had slipped back into a deep, peaceful sleep.

He gave himself a shake and rubbed his own goose-pimpled shoulders. *Cazzo.* Keeping a wary eye on his highly perplexing patient, he drew the blanket back over Qar'qaah then slowly resumed his seat.

Chapter 35

Amalfitano's office, sickbay, 2215.

Izraad entered Amalfitano's office intent on finding a critical report he'd vehemently insisted he'd returned to her days before but she knew he hadn't—and promptly stopped in her tracks.

Khusaaq sat in a chair in front of the doctor's report strewn desk, elbows on knees and head cradled in both hands. Sensing her arrival, he lifted his head and peered muzzily at her.

"Sha'ashahn... I wasn't expecting to find you here. I thought you were with Ensign Corsali—"

"I was," he replied in a very raspy voice as he straightened up, wincing as he did so.

"Then...?"

He cleared his throat, replied, "We... we had a disagreement."

"Oh. I'm really sorry to hear that."

He shrugged tiredly, replied, "She was right—she usually is. I just wasn't in the mood to admit it, so I felt... I decided it might be best if I slept aboard *Jirah* tonight." He started to rise unsteadily from the chair but she motioned him to remain where he was.

"No reason for you to leave," Izraad said as she walked over to the desk. "I won't be a moment."

He settled back and said by way of explanation, "I thought I'd come here first, get an update on Qar'qaah."

She began digging through a disheveled stack of reports on the desk. "William's with him. And they're both fast asleep."

"I know. The nurses told me, I just thought—"

"And knowing William, he'll stay there all night." Finding the flimsy she'd been looking for, Izraad smiled triumphantly and whispered, *"Hah! I knew it!"* Then she turned to face Khusaaq, only to find him staring up at her with very bleary eyes. "Why not go to *Jirah* as you planned, or better, back to Ensign Corsali's cabin—you look positively done in."

He gave his head a slight shake. "Not sleepy. I'll rather stay here, just in case... I'm needed."

She placed the flimsy back on the desk, realizing she had a far more immediate matter to deal with. "Sha'ashahn, Qar'qaah is *stable* and in the best hands possible—"

"I know, but—"

"—if there's any change, you'll be the first to know. Just tell the nurses where you'll be."

He again started to rise. "I'll leave then."

"Did you eat dinner?"

He slumped back in his chair, crossed his arms and grumbled, "Some."

She wasn't convinced, not that he'd made any effort to sound convincing. "Is that what you and Sirin argued about—if you don't mind me asking?"

"That's what started the argument. It went sideways from there."

She replied with a commiserating wince. "Well, somehow I missed my dinner completely—I was going to order up something while I looked over this report William so kindly left for me, marked urgent. How about you join me?"

He scowled at her. "You Rimmers are inordinately preoccupied with food. We A'tuu'shahn'i are not—for us food is a necessity, not a pleasure. We eat only when we are hungry."

"Sha'ashahn," Izraad replied calmly, "food is a huge part of our culture. Aside from its necessity, it offers comfort, comradery, a sense of belonging—to share what we have with others means a lot to us; it's a critical part of our social glue and always has been, as I'm sure it was with your distant forefathers. Are you telling me it isn't with your people?" He started to open his mouth, but she held up a finger, silencing him. "Before you say anything, I feel it is my duty to remind you that I've accompanied quite a few Hahtooshans to our galley and have seen with my very own eyes each and every one eat everything they can lay their hands on in truly staggering quantities and in a shockingly short period of time, with a decided preference for anything sweet—and then ask for more." She settled back, crossed her arms and smiled. "Now, you were about to say?"

He fixed his gaze on the floor. "I suddenly find I have no suitable rebuttal."

She responded with a startled burst of laughter, but all too quickly sobered. "You are running on empty, Sha'ashahn, and you're not going to do anyone, least of all Qar'qaah, any good if you collapse. We're all intensely worried about you, worried the truly profound effect all of the events of the past weeks have had on you. One of the ways you—the way most people—display extreme stress is by not eating, or at least not eating enough. You *need* to eat—whether you *feel* hungry or not. Otherwise you're going to end up in a sickbay bed and trust me, if that happens, William isn't going to ask nicely if you'd like a plate of his favorite frittata. He'll just order Drakin to shove a feeding tube down your throat and be done with it."

He surprised himself—he clearly surprised her, by nodding wearily. "Yes. You're right. Sirin was right—I already said so."

"Would you like to join me? Or I could have something sent to Sirin's cabin, or your ship if you'd prefer—"

"I'll... I'll join you."

She grinned, genuinely pleased. "So what sounds good?"

He shrugged, all the fight suddenly gone out of his voice, his body. "I'll have whatever you have."

"Excellent choice if I say so myself." She coded in the order into the wall-mounted dispenser then turned back to him. "Should be up in a jiffy."

He nodded again. Then as Izraad pretended to give the flimsy a cursory once-over, he glanced around at what was now the very familiar surroundings of Amalfitano's cluttered office, all the while trying to look fully at ease when he was clearly anything but—the fight might have left him, but not the fear of Izraad and what she was capable of doing, what she had already done.

The wall-dispenser chimed, breaking what was becoming a very awkward silence and he visibly flinched.

She rose, motioning for him to stay where he was, collected the two trays from the dispenser and offered him one.

He accepted it and placed the tray on his lap then gave its unfamiliar contents a worried look-over before looking up at her.

"Blueberry blintzes," she said in response to his quizzical and slightly skeptical expression. "With extra blueberries—"

He prodded at one, then replied less than enthusiastically, "Ah."

"—and warm milk, my grandmother's guaranteed recipe to cure a sleepless night."

He again lifted his gaze to meet hers with a blatant mixture of wariness and wish. "Guaranteed?"

"Never fails for me. William too, although he'd never admit it. He says it's nothing more than 'huujuu folk medicine'."

"What or who is this... *huujuu*?"

"It's a nonsense word for what he thinks is a nonsense belief."

Khusaaq responded with another noncommittal, "Ah," took a sniff of the milk, noting the odd mixture of scents with a slight wrinkling of his nose. At her encouraging smile, he took a very small, cautious sip. He swallowed with a grimace, placed the mug back on his tray and gave his lips a wipe with the back of his hand. Then he watched with mild interest Izraad's technique in attacking the blintzes. He cautiously followed suit, and before they both realized it he'd cleaned his plate.

A few minutes later Izraad pushed her own mostly empty plate to one side, leaned back and patted her belly as she sighed contentedly. "Full?"

He nodded, rose and gathered up their trays, said, "Thank you, Lieutenant—the food was... good," and placed them in the servo-dispenser.

"I'm glad you enjoyed it."

"The warm milk... not so much."

"I suppose it's an acquired taste," she replied, all the while sensing his concern that the milk had been drugged; she felt it prudent not to mention that if she'd wanted to drug anything, it would have been the less obvious blintzes—or both, just to cover every angle.

"I will leave you to your reports and I'll let the nurses know I'll be aboard *Jirah*—just in case." He started for the door.

She hesitated then asked, "Want to talk?"

His stopped in his tracks just short of the door, glanced back at her. "Perhaps... perhaps another time."

"Please? Just the two of us."

"What do you want to talk about?" he replied, remaining where he was. "You know everything about me."

"No, Sha'ashahn, rest assured I don't. A mind-strip doesn't reveal all, it can't. And we can talk about anything you want— no pressure. And whatever we talk about needn't go any further than these walls." She motioned around her. "I leave that entirely up to you, and I'll respect any areas you tell me are off limits. Please?" She motioned to the chair.

He hesitated just long enough for her to suspect this golden opportunity was going to slip through her fingers. Then in sudden and silent capitulation he limped resignedly back to his chair and eased himself down, clutching his thigh as he did so.

She tried not to look as pleased and relieved as she felt. "Leg's still really bothering you."

"Yes." He absently massaged it but it was clear to her that it was more a case of referred pain—a physical manifestation of a far deeper ache, his thigh a convenient repository.

She thumbed the door release and the outer door slipped closed with a soft *thump*.

Khusaaq jerked his eyes towards it then looked back at her, instantly on edge. With his Hahtooshan lack of body fat in combination with his already gaunt frame, the rapid pulse of blood in his neck veins was conspicuous as was his suddenly coiled spring-tight body.

"I'm sorry, I didn't mean to startle you—I just wanted to insure complete privacy, but, if you'd feel more at ease with the door open...?" she again reached for the hidden switch.

"No." He shook his head. "Leave it."

She smiled, "That's a good start, Sha'ashahn."

He shifted uneasily in the chair then he began toying with the cuff of his boot, his narrowed eyes fixed on his tattooed fingers' nervous busy-work. The fine tremor was back.

She gave him a moment to settle then asked quietly, "You don't trust me, do you?"

"I'd be lying if I said I did."

"Because of the mind-strip, because I'm with Intelligence... or both?"

"Both," he said, still refusing to make eye-contact.

"Fair enough—I have no doubt I'd feel the same way if our roles were reversed."

"And you dislike me," he replied as his fingers continued their now angry picking and tugging of the well-worn cuff. *"Intensely."*

"I *did*, I freely admit that. But over the past few days I've come to realize I'd greatly misjudged you—I was far too quick to assume the worst and I owe you an apology for that."

"Accepted, but you did have your reasons, and holding a knife to your throat and threatening to kill you every few seconds probably didn't help." He finally lifted his gray-eyed gaze to meet hers. "I owe you an apology for that. I would have killed you, you realize that."

"Yes, I do. But you had your reasons for the actions you took, and apology accepted." She leaned back, studied him for a moment then said, "Now we've got that out of the way, what would you like to talk about?"

He licked his lips, again shifted in his chair as his eyes darted to the closed door, then he promptly resumed his nervous tugging on the boot cuff. "I... I don't know."

"Yes, you do. I don't have to be a chempath to know what's on your mind, Sha'ashahn—what's always on your mind. So, why don't you start by telling me what happened to you on Cotopaxi?"

She'd gone right to the heart of the matter and in response she could literally feel him twitch both ways, desperately wanting to unload after years of waiting for this chance, desperately hoping for this chance, and at the same time fearful once he started, he wouldn't be able to stop—

"You're safe with me, Sha'ashahn. I fully appreciate that's extremely difficult for you to believe, but you are. Nothing you say will go any further. You have my word on that." She leaned back, careful not to cross her arms despite the urge. "We psychiatrists have a saying, 'you're only as sick as your secrets'. You *need* to talk—you need to get all this emotional baggage you carry off your shoulders or it *will* kill you."

He only nodded this time.

She rose, slowly, drawing his gaze, and started around the desk that to her was yet another barrier. "I want to offer something to you. You can say no and if you do, I will respect it."

"Go ahead," he replied warily.

"I can exude a pheromone—"

He jerked upright, hands on the arms of the chair, ready to rise in a hurry.

"Please, hear me out, Sha'ashahn. I'm not suggesting a mind-strip—gods not that. What I am offering just makes it easier for me to see exactly what you are remembering. If I could fully understand what you went through, what has caused these constant flashbacks, this near-crippling self-doubt, it will greatly assist in your therapy. All it will do is make your thoughts easier, clearer, for me to read—no entering your mind, no looking where I'm not welcome. But it *isn't* required. We can go the old-fashioned route: you talk, I listen. It's not quite as efficient, but it's almost as effective."

He stared at her, really stared at her, clearly desperate for the same relief she'd offered Qar'qaah, but also very, very fearful, the agonizing mind-strip suddenly at the fore of his thoughts, shoving aside everything else in his reflexive panic.

"Okay." She held up her hands and started back for her chair—on the opposite side of the desk. "It was just an offer— I'm sorry I even brought it up." And she was; the microscopically thin and nascent thread of trust between them, one that had taken her days to weave through her grueling work with Qar'qaah, was unraveling in a matter of a few thumping heartbeats.

"Like having a conduit—like... like *Siah'ushu*" he said, stopping her in her tracks. "Not completely necessary, but it aids tremendously in the... conveyance of thoughts."

She smiled, hesitantly and nodded. "Yes, exactly. Just as I did with Qar'qaah—to identify Gaalan. No mind-strip—you were there."

"But you made physical contact with him—"

"It was necessary with Qar'qaah. It was absolutely critical to see exactly what the person we knew as Cisne looked like in order to have any chance at apprehending her. In this instance precise detail isn't as important; overall recollection is, so I won't touch you, not without your express permission."

"And we can stop at any time."

"Just say stop—or think it—and I will."

He looked stared at her, chewing on his lower lip for what seemed like an inordinately long period of time, then, finally, he murmured, *"Proceed."*

She could feel *his* heart hammering rapidly in *her* chest; she could see sweat beading on *his* tattooed forehead and feel it trickle down *her* own skin. Thoughts, images already cartwheeled around her, the blurry vanguard of a confused and confusing juggernaut of pent up rage, bitterness and guilt, all unerringly headed her way like an avalanche. She braced herself as best she could against the oncoming onslaught.

She motioned to the chair next to his, and at his slight nod, eased herself down onto it. "Let's start by talking, all right? Nothing more. Just lay some groundwork." *And get you calmed down a bit.*

"Yes," he replied hoarsely.

She could almost feel him trying desperately to hold back the flood, to let it out in increments, clearly fearing a repeat of what happened when she'd done the same with Qar'qaah, the terrible effect it had had on her. But his efforts were to little avail against a combination of anguish, fear and exhaustion.

His sunken, blood-shot eyes fixed on her, pinpoint, while his ultra-sensitive nose sampled the air, clearly expecting the worst at any second and at the same time almost but not quite welcoming it by allowing himself the barest trace of hope that maybe, just maybe, this unassuming woman *could* provide him the release he'd futilely sought for so many years.

Izraad took a deep, slow breath of her own then held it as she absorbed and rapidly put in some semblance of order the initial surge of his chaotic memories combined with an Hahtooshan's potent blending of sights, smells, sounds and tastes—a veritable tangential tsunami.

Dealing with a synesthete's mishmash sensory take on the world around them would have been mind-boggling enough for a non-synesthete chempath under normal conditions. This situation, just as with Qar'qaah, was anything but normal. And unlike the mind-strip, which had a very distinct objective, to determine which planet and what organism, events that took place over a relatively short period of time, or when she eavesdropped on Qar'qaah's memories, where again, she had a very specific goal, this effort was far more diffuse, covering years of experience, decades of recollection, a lifetime that had been embellished upon by the imposed aspirations of others to the point that, despite his acute memory, it was difficult to always know what were his own, untainted recollections and what were false leads, little more than mnemonic echoes.

She exhaled just as slowly before stating in a calm voice, "You were very young at the time of Cotopaxi—about the same age Qar'qaah is now—and you were suddenly in command of a landing force of troops even younger and less experienced than yourself, without the benefit of any preparation and no idea if help was on the way."

"Yes..."

"You barely survived flicking down the surface..."

"Huui'teh was under attack—she'd sustained a number of direct hits. Many of the crew had been killed..."

She nodded as more images briefly flashed around her—everything suddenly bathed in a ruddy glow with glimpses of soldiers, fully armored, dashing past, leaving free-floating debris spinning wildly in their wake; curls of thick, oily smoke and the pervasive, nauseating stink of burnt wiring and flesh; the nonstop, undulating wail of klaxons accompanied by the high-pitched squeal of failing air scrubbers. Someone was standing beside him, speaking in a surprisingly unruffled voice, just loud enough to be heard over the din—no, not *someone*. Gaalan.

Izraad caught a glimpse of the woman's face—no longer the face of Cisne, pale skinned, aged and unadorned, but the face of a Hahtooshan in the prime of her life, a swarthy, heavily tattooed, scarified and blood-smeared face—as Khusaaq's mind's eye turned towards his commanding officer.

Izraad said, "And those still alive and able were ordered to evacuate to the surface—"

"By Gaalan, yes."

She felt his gut roiling in recalled panic, his skin drenched anew in sweat, the fine tremor now made audible in very youthful voice, far less timbre, a frightened voice that sounded eerily like Qar'qaah's. Izraad felt her body mirror the physical manifestations of his. Even without the pheromone, the two were beginning to merge, to become completely immersed in his memories. It was all happening far faster, far more easily than she'd anticipated. For a moment she grappled with the near-overwhelming sensory input, the sense of being sucked into the maelstrom before finally managing to reassume control.

And she *had* to maintain control. She had to guide him, forcibly if need be, step-by-step, through what had transpired on Cotopaxi, thus giving him the chance—and yes, the distance of years—to start the process of coming to terms with what had really happened. Not the revisionist history others had obliged him to believe and certainly not what his mind had slapped together in the heat, the terror of the moment or later, in a haphazard effort of trying to make sense of—or take the blame for it all. *Even perfect memories can make mistakes, my friend—even yours.*

He turned away from her silent assertion, not ready to hear it.

"And you were absolutely petrified."

He hesitated then answered softly, *"Yes."*

"Because you believed you were unfit to lead."

He forced a chuckle. "I *knew* I was unfit—"

"But you managed to keep the Matarrans at bay for over two weeks, a truly astonishing accomplishment in light of the resources at your disposal and what you and your troops were up against."

"Most of the colonists died in the first few days—most of my troops, too."

"And you blame yourself for that."

"Of course!"

Suddenly, and with his sharp intake of breath, they were *on* Cotopaxi, the two trapped together inside his form-fitting armor, staring out through his blast visor. A goodly portion of her visual field was now taken up by a mass of rapidly changing sensor readings, too complex, too alien for her to even attempt to comprehend. Beyond was a hellish, smoke- and flame-obscured landscape. The violent shift, from Amalfitano's untidy but familiar office to this, was enough to leave her briefly unbalanced, disoriented. She found it hard to adapt to what it felt like to wear Hahtooshan combat armor, to see such utter chaos through the mind of a synesthete, and was close to panic herself.

"What are you seeing?" she asked, then flinched as he unexpectedly grasped her hand and wrapped his fingers around it as one would do a lifeline, the direct contact bringing what had been a swirl of incoherent images into instant, razor-sharp focus.

"Are you sure?" she asked, not convinced the move had been completely voluntary—or cognizant, that it might have been more reflexive.

"Yes..." He confirmed it by tightening his grip, just a bit. *"Please,* don't let go."

"I won't."

Details he hadn't noticed at the time or had shoved aside as unimportant suddenly burst out into the light for both to see, adding to the tumult: the muffled sounds of a child crying somewhere nearby; the incessant, high-pitched whirr of Matarii blazer bombs arching high overhead; one of his troops muttering a prayer, another answering with a truly creative obscenity that had to do with Matarran reproduction; the distant, thundering boom of an explosion so powerful that it reverberated in his chest, momentarily making it impossible to breathe.

"W-w-where are... we?"

He sucked in air then answered huskily, "The colony's hospital... or what's left of it."

Before she could respond, Izraad was peppered with new images, memories no longer, but real-time reality, playing out all around and inside of her—horrific images of bodies ripped to pieces and blown skyward, followed by the flutter of tattered clothing and recognizable bits raining down like so much flotsam, the meatier oddments thumping against armor in a sickening cadence, of weapons blazing from all directions, little more than fleeting, brilliant streaks suspended within the murky pall, terrifying in their sheer destructiveness as the beams cut through unprotected flesh and plastacrete with equal ease, and everything enfolded in a cacophony of noise, from deep, guttural screams uttered by the mindlessly terrified and the wail of the dying, to the shrieking whistle of incoming rounds that vibrated deep in her very bones.

"My gods," she breathed.

A tremendous explosion shook the ground, nearly knocking Khusaaq off his feet. *"INCOMING!"* he yelled and dropped to a crouch, instinctively shielding his helmeted head with his armored hands as debris thrown up by the direct hit on the hospital now pelted down all around them.

Izraad cowered in response. She felt sizable pieces strike and clatter off his armor, the noise almost deafening and each hit a killing blow to anyone not similarly protected.

No sooner had the barrage stopped than he ordered, *"GO!"* as he lurched unsteadily to his feet. He ran into the hospital and down a sloping corridor that had somehow, so far, managed to withstand the onslaught. Bodies were everywhere, some moving, most not and over his labored breathing she heard voices, somewhere ahead but lost in the dust, the smoke, screaming for help. Out of the corner of his eye, she caught glimpses of trailing ribbons of color; soon they were all around him, keeping pace as he dashed deeper into the ruined building, towards the cries.

"What's... what's that?"

"Us," he replied. "That's what we look like to each other when camouflaged." He ducked under a fallen support, then stopped and breathing heavily, glanced around. "Recon! Go!"

The colored ribbons, which had just coalesced around him in a seething mass, immediately branched off, eeling into the smoky darkness to quickly vanish from sight.

All too quickly and one-by-one they returned, disembodied voices verifying the ruins were impassible, some warning it was about to collapse on top of them.

"OUT!—GATHER WHO YOU CAN AND GET OUT!" he bellowed then began his own retreat, covering them as he followed his troops towards the smoky gap of light, the only escape route, while the surrounding structure creaked and groaned ominously as upper floors began to slowly pancake onto themselves.

She couldn't help but cringe at the sheer horror felt by those they passed, hopelessly trapped and pleading for their lives, hands reaching desperately for the ghostly shimmers that raced by. "But you still held the colony, because those were your orders, Gaalan's orders," she continued as the images, the still-raw memories continued to tumble wildly around her as if caught in a whirlwind, tearing at her skin and stinging her eyes. "Orders she gave you that we now know she believed would assure your death and her escape."

It was a risk to bring him so suddenly forward in time, to recent, excruciating events when he was so fully absorbed in the equally harrowing past, but Izraad felt it was worth it, to help him put things in proper perspective—

They were again back in Amalfitano's office, seated together, Khusaaq's hand still grasping hers in a strong, not quite painful grip.

He squeezed his eyes shut and sucked in his breath as if someone had punched him in the gut.

"Matoosh told me what she'd said," Izraad added softly. "I can't even begin to imagine what it felt like to hear that... and from her own lips."

He replied with a curt dip of the head, afraid anything more would fully unleash the torrent of emotions that had been building up for years, the rage, the fear, the hurt, the utter bewilderment at it all. She could feel them, struggling to escape, and eerie, cord-whipping sensation at the edge of her awareness. It made her skin crawl.

"So the one parent figure you had was about to abandon you."

"I suppose you could say that."

"I just did."

He eyed her. "Elkanaghalli'i do not abandon their own. They do not betray their own."

"But she did. And now you find out she wanted you to die, has wanted you dead for a long time—was, in fact obsessed with your death out of some twisted concept of revenge—to the point that she was willing to destroy herself in order to destroy you. How does that make you feel?"

He squeezed his eyes shut, jaw muscles bunching.

"You need to confront this, Sha'ashahn, fully and head on or—"

"I should have been the Hero of Cotopaxi, the ultimate martyr, surpassing even Ja'andai... and I would have been had you died on that cursed planet as you were supposed to, but you didn't!" Gaalan's harsh voice echoed in Izraad's ears, just as they'd echoed in Khusaaq's only a few hours before. She felt the same stunned shock, the same rush of murderous hatred at the woman wash over her, flooding every part of her being.

She gave him a moment—gave them both a moment to collect themselves, then she cleared her throat and said, "And you were in command... of how many?"

"At first?" he replied, his voice a tight, husky whisper. "Forty-two."

"None of whom had ever had any ground combat experience."

"None but myself and Qharubi, no." He gave his head a sharp shake as he stared down at their joined hands. He carefully turned his wrist as if to get a better look at her hand, at the paleness of her skin, the bluish-purple blood vessels that were so obvious and the delicacy of the bone structure, a stark contrast to his much larger, darker, rougher and heavily tattooed hand.

She almost smiled at his seeming fascination, but she knew it was only a distraction. His mind was desperate to find something else to think about, to fall back into the old, well-worn paths of avoidance that had never in truth worked, and weren't working now.

"You were furious with Gaalan, weren't you? You wanted her to flick down, to command the landing party—"

"I'd never been in command—not like that." His shadowed eyes brimmed with tears as he lifted his gaze to hers and she had to stop herself from visibly flinching at the raw pain she saw there.

"I knew I wasn't cut out for it—I never understood why she hadn't realized that. Ja'andai knew—thought he could beat the skills into me, just as his progenitor, Shushnua, had successfully done with him—or so Ja'andai claimed. But then..." he looked away, gave his eyes a wipe with the shaky fingertips of his free hand.

"But then...?"

"Gaalan... aboard *Faridour*. She told me she did know. That the moment she realized that I carried the *paas'nah*—she *knew.*"

"So in other words, she sent you to the planet, knowing full well you felt you were unfit for command."

"She wanted us all to die there—she expected it, had planned on it—"

"And stacked the deck, so to speak, by leaving you in command."

"*Yes.* She could have named Qharubi. He wasn't that much younger than me after all, but was so much more adept at command. It came so naturally to him. I... I thought..."

She waited then prompted, "You thought what?"

"At the time, I thought she'd seen something in me that I hadn't. She even said so aboard *Faridour*. She said she saw potential in me that Ja'andai hadn't. Gaalan often told us that, told us she could see qualities in us that we hadn't even imagined—I... I kept telling myself that, hoping in doing so I could somehow conjure up those abilities in myself that everyone else was depending upon to survive. But it never happened and day by day I saw my troops die as a direct result of my orders, I saw the settlers die, I saw the Matarii take bite after bite of the colony and..." he shook his head violently then bit his lip until it bled, "...*there was nothing I could do to stop it—*"

"Forty-three of you, against... *how* many Matarrans?"

He looked fiercely at her as he angrily wiped his mouth, then his eyes with the same hand, and blinked rapidly at the sting of the blood. *"What does it matter?"*

"It matters a great deal. You were vastly outnumbered, going by Coalition Intelligence reports from the time the low estimate was a thousand troops to one—impossible odds for anyone, not to mention they had heavy ground artillery and orbital destroyers. You need to *internalize* that, Sha'ashahn, fully grasp that fact.

"I realize you've spent your entire life blaming yourself for what happened, for all those deaths," Izraad continued. "One cannot expect you to shift your deeply entrenched way of thinking in a matter of minutes, or days or possibly even weeks. You *can*, but only if you come to terms with the reality that your commanding officer *set you up to fail*, and fail you did— but not because of *anything* you did. You never had any chance at all to save the colony, the colonists or your troops."

"Then why did I survive?"

"And now we start to get to the heart of the matter. Why indeed. It's a good question, Sha'ashahn, and in truth I don't have an easy answer for you. In fact I don't have an answer at all, except of course the pat answer: it was pure, dumb luck."

"Luck indeed," he snorted softly. "I *would* have happily traded my life for any of those who died, willingly, eagerly, in fact, and now..." He squeezed his eyes shut and clenched his teeth.

"And now you find yourself in the unenviable position of being the last, the sole survivor of Cotopaxi," Izraad ended for him, gently, as she tightened her hold on his hand.

He flicked her a sidelong look. "But that was part of the Elkanasu's *plan*," he added with a slight sneer. "They told me as much, here," he motioned around them with his tattooed and now blood-smeared chin. "I didn't know or even think that at the time—had never even considered it. Now I know better. Other A'tuu'shahn'i, even Gaalan, had every right to hate me for the advantage, the... *protection* the *paas'nah* provided me."

Izraad couldn't help but visibly grimace.

"The Q'shaathrah called me a... a *hero*—they called all of us heroes. They gave us medals too, to prove it, along with a bump up in rank." He reached up, fingered one cobalt blue medallion just below his ghillie uniform's collar and colorful gorget, and next to the far plainer Coalition Battle Commendation, briefly drawing her gaze to the two awards. "At the time I so desperately wanted to believe them, I thought if I was able to do that, then maybe I could rationalize all those deaths as other A'tuu'shahn'i rationalize death, that I could accept that in the greater scheme of things, their deaths were necessary or even... *unimportant*, or there was a reason why they died and I survived. But... I knew the truth, or should I say I thought I knew."

"And what truth is that?" she asked.

"The medals, the awards... *everything*. It wasn't for what we'd done, as you say, keeping the Matarii at bay for as long as we did. It was for what we *found*. It was to keep us quiet, just as the Coalition bought off the Q'shaathrah—to keep them quiet— to keep everyone quiet, and to stop me from questioning everything, even our way of life."

"But—"

He inhaled sharply and as he did so, the true terrors started clawing their way to the surface, little tugs here and there, almost ghostly in their touch at first, but rapidly gaining strength. Khusaaq was too exhausted, too utterly wrung out to tamp them down... and in the process he'd again willingly opened himself completely to her.

"Seeing the colonists die," Izraad continued, drawing his watery gaze, "seeing your troops die... horrible enough, but for someone who carries the added burden of the *paas'nah...* you felt responsible for each and every one, didn't you?"

"I WAS RESPONSIBLE!" he snarled and tried to jerk his hand free of hers.

But she held fast, refusing to let go.

"You *felt* each death as if it was your own…" she continued, undeterred as she tightened her grip and was relieved when he abruptly stopped trying to pull away, "…but you couldn't tell anyone, you couldn't let anyone know just how much what was happening was affecting you, ripping you apart, inside. You just wanted it over with—the days and days of waiting to die, watching others die. It constantly gnawed at you, made you question everything you did, every order you gave. Why them, why not you—"

Another shift: they were now running pell-mell, leaping over debris, zig-zagging to dodge a hail of Matarran fire that chewed up the ground all around them. He was now carrying a colonist, the person's body draped over his shoulder, bouncing limply against him with each footfall, his full attention on making it across open, blasted ground and to the complex that suddenly loomed large in front of them. Others too, human and the eerie ribbons that marked individual Hahtooshans, were converging on the complex carved out of the face of a bluff, most carrying someone, a few of the colonists carrying useless possessions—a woman clutched a large ornamental vase to her chest, a man struggled under the awkward shape of a rocking chair, another carried an armload of what had clearly been very expensive clothing, their last tangible links to a dying dream— the absurdity of it almost laughable—and all were skirting around any injured, the dying, who lay in their path.

She heard and felt a soft, sickening *thump* and felt Khusaaq stagger sidewise, almost losing his balance. He took another couple of unsteady steps. Then he dropped to one knee, carefully pulled the human from his shoulder and placed her on the ground.

The woman had taken a Matarran projectile fragment to the head, leaving little but bits of skull, blood clotted hair and brain. He touched her lightly on her chest, murmured, "I'm sorry."

Then he rose and staggered over to another colonist whose right leg had been shattered by another fragment and was now desperately trying to drag himself towards the complex. He grabbed the man without making a sound, hoisted him onto his shoulder then again started off again, the colonist too shocked at his timely rescue to make more than a muffled *oooff*, as he landed on Khusaaq's camouflaged armor.

Then another violent shift in time and perspective: Khusaaq was just outside the complex, staring out at the smoking plain, at the massive Matarran emplacements.

A living torch ran into view, screaming. Izraad watched as their combined self took careful aim, listened as Khusaaq's inner voice kept repeating, *Wait... wait... wait... almost...* as the sensors in his visor tracked the target, constantly feeding him updates on distance, smoke and wind direction, even the human's vitals.... Most haunting of all, a name suddenly scrolled across their visual field: *Stoff, Charlene, hydrologist...*

She felt their finger start to squeeze the trigger, heard their silent voice order, *NOW!* and the woman's agonized cries were instantly swallowed up by a bright, silent flash.

Together they turned away then found themselves drawn to raised voices. A small group of colonists huddled just inside one of the complex's entryways, their expressions stunned then turning to horror as they stared at the invisible source of the maser beam. Someone was yelling but Izraad couldn't hear what they were saying over Khusaaq's labored breathing.

"What's happening?" Izraad asked.

"I... I just... killed a colonist—"

"I know."

"The others are screaming at me that I'm murderer—a yowie butcher—but there was nothing I could do to help. I... I thought I was doing the right thing..."

"What else do you see?"

He turned his head, again scanned the ruined plain for her to see for herself. Now it was from a vastly different angle, slightly higher and to the left. Time had clearly passed, days in fact. The colony had been utterly flattened; nothing remained that was even remotely recognizable. Here and there wisps of

smoke still rose from the rims of glass-walled craters into a sky
smeared with a greasy brown haze. Everywhere he looked, she
saw well-entrenched Matarran emplacements. But it quickly
dawned on her that Khusaaq's attention wasn't on the
Matarrans; they were only a cursory concern. His interest lay
with what edged the distant horizon, a range of snow-capped
mountains.

His intense longing bordered on an obsessive fixation that
welled up around her like a rising tide. But it wasn't a fixation
borne from a need to escape—the mountains were calling to
him, a chorus of soft, faint susurrations at the edge of her
hearing but slowly, ever-so-slowly, getting louder. The
sensation instantly reminded her of her experience with his
dagger, during his abortive escape attempt on Tuli when he'd
cast it aside in preference for Mladić's shocker as his suicide
weapon.

"Beautiful, aren't they?" he whispered, mesmerized by their
ethereal sirens' song.

She nodded while suppressing a shiver at the sudden
awareness that what he was hearing was in fact real, or real to
him—but how could mountains call to him?

"*Monnh'hayrhan...*"

She jerked her eyes towards him in instant recollection: this
was what Sirin had heard him mumble, repeatedly, in his sleep.
"Mon hah..."

"*Monnh'hayrhan...* the Night Mountains. The abode of the
Elkanasu."

"But—but on Cotopaxi?" she blurted out an instant before
she could stop herself.

Instead of being offended, he shrugged and smiled, "Why
not?" His smile soon faded as he shifted his gaze back to the
destroyed colony, back to grim reality. She realized he also
wasn't alone. Another Hahtooshan lay prone next to him, the
two crammed hip and shoulder together inside what appeared to
be a culvert or access tunnel. She felt the soldier's armored
body press against Khusaaq's, heard the other's breathing in an
off-cadence with Khusaaq's, filling his helmet with the

reassuring sounds of life while all around lay sheer destruction and death.

But before she could ask why they were here, why he'd recalled this particular memory, or who their companion was, someone—a colonist—walked out onto the blasted plain, towards the Matarrans. A name scrolled across the visor, *Lennox, John, quartermaster,* an instant before a ghostly voice—an intimately familiar voice to Khusaaq but a total stranger to her, whispered in her ear, *"Fool,"* as the soldier beside him shifted to get a better view—or, she amended as she realized he'd brought his maser rifle to bear, a better shot. *Telipinu*—the name just popped into her head unbidden and she gave him a nod of acknowledgement. *Nice to meet you.*

"He's my closest friend," Khusaaq added as he glanced sidelong at his companion.

All Izraad could see was a faint slither of orange, curling and twisting as if a ribbony pennant blown in the thick, smoky wind.

"Or was. He survived Cotopaxi only to die at the hands of the Coalition after the awards ceremony."

"Oh." Izraad didn't know what else to say. Instead she watched the scene play out: a human in once official and now grubby, tattered clothing slowly picked his way over clotted, smoking earth as Khusaaq provided the narrative: "He's walking out, hoping to negotiate with the Matarii. But they don't negotiate, they never negotiate. I told him that, I told all of the colonists that, repeatedly—*Gaalan...*"

"Gaalan what?"

"She told them." he whispered, then stronger: "She warned the colonists, they wouldn't listen to her, either." His mind replayed what happened next in graphic detail; he'd witnessed it so many times, over and over in his mind that everything seemed to be in slow-motion and in excruciating detail: Lennox walking, stumbling towards the Matarii firing platform, his footfalls stirring up smoke and embers from the still smoldering earth, leaving tiny, spinning tendrils in his wake, the ghostly voice of Telipinu counting softly, the platform rotating as the

crew within spotted him, Lennox withdrawing and then waving his dirty white flag—and an instant later a dazzling explosion.

Khusaaq shook his head, sighed. "I warned him..."

Then another shift: they were standing in a dimly and sporadically lit corridor. Chunks of ceiling debris lay everywhere and out of the corner of her eye, Izraad caught the palest glimmer of pure white light, sensed the presence of another Hahtooshan, and not Telipinu; she wasn't sure how she knew, but she was certain of it. "Who?"

"Qharubi." He turned his helmeted head, just so, and she saw the soldier as Khusaaq saw him: a column of scintillating white, like a faint, sparkling waterfall.

"Beautiful," she whispered.

"Don't let him hear you say that—he's vain enough as it is."

Izraad, taken off guard by the comment, almost chuckled. Instead she said, "Do you look like that to him?"

"Yes. But *I'm* not vain."

"Why the different colors?"

"Caste affiliation. White... Elkanaghalli; blue, Kri'taaka—" He suddenly shifted his attention back to the corridor, drawing her gaze along. A group of wary-eyed colonists stood not far away, all wrapped in a combined pale dusty gray aura sprinkled here and there with flashing of yellow. Suddenly his visual field was awash with names, professions, targeting information, types of weapons they carried—all concealed, or so the colonists thought—their pulses, respiratory rates, even skin conductivity based on perspiration.

Before she could fully absorb the deluge of raw data, he continued, "I decided to abandon the complex, take our chances in the mountains—I asked for a meeting to notify the colonists of these new plans, invite them to accompany us... or not, their choice. They weren't happy. They accused me of reneging on the contract. I told them the complex was indefensible, that we stood a better chance in the mountains—"

"And?"

"I gave them a choice—come with us or remain and fall on the mercies of the Matarii. But as we left, Qharubi noticed something—the walls of the corridor. They'd been bored out using Matarii equipment. It was then I realized that the Matarii were the rightful owners, that the Rimmer colony was illegal. I returned to question the colonists..."

Images fled past, frightened faces; a man the visor identified as Sergy Viehl, now little more than a seething mass of yellow sparks, was yelling, shaking his fist at Khusaaq, calling him a fucking yowie. Other colonists were backing away, telling Viehl to shut up.

"Why... why is he flashing yellow?"

"He's lying."

"Oh."

Izraad felt an odd tingle run down her spine, felt the armor that surrounded her begin to vibrate. The white shimmer beside them began to quiver violently and tiny sparks appeared in her visual field. *"What's happening...?"* she whispered, feeling her own rapidly thumping pulse match his.

"I'm about to teach the Rimmers a lesson that it's exceedingly unwise to lie to an A'tuu'shahn."

Izraad's mind barely formed a silent, 'O' when Khusaaq's much younger voice said, "My ship was destroyed, Mister Viehl, protecting you. Of those of us who managed to flick to the planet, almost half have died protecting you, defending a settlement that had no right to be here. So I give you one last chance. Tell. Me. The. Truth. Who among you *knew* ahead of time that this colony was illegal?"

"I am telling the truth! I don't know what the hell you're talking about!"

"Wrong answer, Mister Viehl...."

A brilliant flare... followed by another violent shift. Her eyes, still dazzled, couldn't make out anything but the blur of visual readouts that endlessly scrolled across the visor, then slowly details began to emerge beyond the deluge of the data stream: they were outside, she could make out the dark shapes of trees, of a rocky outcrop and she could hear something pelting against his armor—*no*, she realized, not something. *Rain. Heavy rain.*

"A strong electrical storm is passing over the colony and the surrounding mountains," Khusaaq explained a moment before their surroundings were lit up by a flash of lightning, "I used it to make good our escape from the complex."

She caught glimpses of colored ribbons slithering around him—white, orange, purple, four in all. "Where are we?"

"On the top of an outcrop, overlooking a gorge."

"You're cornered."

"Yes—the Matarii think they have us right where they want us—well away from the complex—they've been bombarding the gorge."

"And?"

"We've mined the rim—we're waiting for the majority of the Matarii to enter the gorge."

She studied his thoughts for a moment, the memories that flowed around her. "But something happened."

"I had a revelation—I suddenly realized the Elkanasu had brought me—brought all of us to this particular gorge, that it wasn't just a last minute, random choice on my part."

"Why did you think that?"

"I thought I felt the Elkanasu, I thought we'd reached *Monnh'hayrhan*, that they'd guided us here, that in doing so, they'd protect us—A'tuu'shahn'i and Rimmer alike."

"But...?"

He looked away, panting heavily, and she found it difficult to keep pace with the images that played across their shared visual field. The recollections of those final moments on the rain-drenched rim were coming fast now, a torrent of sights, smells... tastes, every sense heightened and frantically tumbling over each other as if in a panic to escape the inevitable. She could feel him being sucked in and down into the very heart of his deeply-rooted trauma, into the whirlpool of distorted voices, images warped into little more than blurs of light and color, all coming faster, faster...

"You're safe," she murmured calmly, drawing his panicky gaze as she tightened her hold on his very sweaty hand. "You're here, with me, on *Baidarka*—you're not *there*. Keep reminding yourself of that, but we're close, so very close to uncovering the core of all the flashbacks, of finding a way to if not stop them, then at least put them in proper context. And I can, with your

permission, stop what you are reliving at any time. Just say stop and they will, or I'll stop them if I think they are getting out of control. Agreed?"

They both knew what this meant, what she was offering—to actually enter his mind.

He hesitated, eyes wide and fixed on her. She felt his pulse jump as a fine tremor spread up his arm to engulf his entire body.

"You have to trust me, I know what I'm asking is incredibly hard, but we've come this far..."

He licked his blood-smeared lips and swallowed, hard, then tipped his head, ever-so-slightly.

"I have your permission?"

He nodded again, with a little more certainty.

"All right—now try to take some deep, *slow* breaths. This will feel odd, but the sensation only lasts a moment or two. And please, don't fight me this time."

He visibly braced himself, still struggling with the images of the storm- and fusillade-battered rim, of brilliant flashes, the ear-splitting and body-wracking concussions, the rain roaring and sluicing around his armor, the eerie glimmer of his companions, everything racing helter-skelter around him in a dizzying blur.

She cautiously slipped into his mind and his body instantly reacted like it had been given a mild shock, the very familiar sensation bringing with it a host of other, equally terrifying memories. Instead of waiting for him to fully to embrace the same pain, the same fear, she instantly surrounded him by a warm embrace and, *You're safe—you're with me. Come... let's go together.*

She had no idea how long they were gone—it seemed like his entire life; they'd walked its length and plumbed its depths after all, from his earliest memories right up to his fight with Sirin, accompanied by the echoing thump of his heart. He'd surprised her when she realized he'd laid everything bare for her to see, to pick up and turn over and examine it closely before moving on, with him a silent witness to it all, as if it was someone else's life, a total stranger's memories fully exposed as all the anger, the horror, the guilt played out anew, a seemingly endless flood until finally, mercifully it just... *stopped.*

They both sagged back into their chairs, still holding each other's hand but utterly exhausted and laboring for breath, eyes open but glazed. He didn't react when she slipped from his mind, or when she pressed a glass to his lips, but he respond when a voice told him to take a sip of water.

"Another," Izraad said and he took a deeper gulp. She then pressed her hand against his throat, his forehead. "Sha'ashahn?"

He rolled his eyes towards her.

Izraad smiled. "Welcome back."

He licked his lips, managed a nod.

"I want you to just sit there, don't try to move or speak, all right?"

Another nod.

"And I want to call Sirin, have her come here. I think... you could use her support right now."

Yet another hesitant nod, visibly taxing him to the last.

"Good." Izraad rose unsteadily from her chair, and walked very slowly over to the desk and pressed the com-unit. She cleared her throat, said in a strained, husky voice that didn't sound at all like her own, "C and C?"

The night shift com officer answered, *"Control here—"*

"This is Lieutenant Izraad... please... please have Ensign Corsali report to Doctor Amalfitano's office... tell her... it isn't an emergency, but to report as... as quickly as she can."

"Yes ma'am—ma'am, are you all right?"

She smiled tiredly as she wiped a lock of hair off her ashen face with a very shaky hand. "Yes... I'm fine, ensign, or I will be shortly. Izraad out." She slowly, very carefully, turned around to find Khusaaq still sprawled in the chair, eyes staring up at her but unfocused. She smiled again. "I can help you, Sha'ashahn... I can stop the flashbacks."

He suddenly he began to sob, huge, body-heaving sobs.

She staggered back to her chair, quickly gathered up his hand in hers, then held on until he finally got himself back under control. He wiped his face, his throat, with the back of his free hand then peered at her.

"I know the source," she said simply. She turned at a knock at the door. "Come."

The door slipped open and a breathless Sirin stepped in, clearly not sure what to expect. Then her gaze fell on Khusaaq, sprawled awkwardly in the chair, his body still wracked by the occasional gasping sob, his grayish face drawn and wet.

"Gods... what happened?" She ran over to him, wrapped her arms around him and pulled him, unresisting against her. Then she glanced, accusingly, at Izraad, only to realize the woman looked just as drained, just as awful and emotionally spent as Khusaaq.

"We just finished our first session," Izraad replied, her voice a little stronger.

Sirin hugged him even tighter, then looking back at Izraad said, "What can I do to help?"

"He needs to finish that glass of water," she replied, motioning to it.

"And you?"

"Maybe... maybe a warm blanket," Izraad replied, suddenly cold. And exhausted. She'd never felt so utterly exhausted, not even after her first session with Qar'qaah. But she also felt an incredible sense of relief and accomplishment.

Sirin grabbed the glass, pressed it into Khusaaq's hand, said, "Drink," then she hit the intercom. "Sickbay?"

"Sickbay here," a voice answered.

"This is Ensign Corsali. Bring some warm blankets to Doctor Amalfitano's office on the double."

"Uh, yes ma'am, right away."

"And some warm milk," Izraad said the moment the connection as cut as she rubbed her upper arms. "For all of us— my grandmother's recipe. The galley has it on file."

Sirin nodded, turned to the dispenser and quickly tapped in the order, hurried over to the door in response to a cautious knock and accepted an armload of folded blankets from a medtech. Then she returned, handed two to Izraad and draped one around Khusaaq's shoulders, the other across his lap. Finished, she stood back, crossed her arms and fixed Izraad and then Khusaaq with a firm, slightly reproachful stare. "Now, who wants to tell me exactly what's happened?"

Izraad began, "I offered and Sha'ashahn agreed—"

"Khusaaq," he interrupted, his voice still raspy, hollow, and *aged*. "Please... call me by my use name."

Izraad and Sirin smiled then Izraad said, "Only if you agree to call me Zarijan."

He nodded then at Sirin's pointed urging, dutifully gulped down the remains of the water.

"Well, as I was saying, I offered and Khusaaq agreed to talk. Just the two of us. It seemed as good a time as any, so we did."

"And...?" Sirin asked hopefully.

"We made some breakthroughs, significant breakthroughs, first and foremost we've established mutual trust, which will go a long way in your eventual healing," Izraad nodded to him. "And yes, I do believe you can fully heal, given time."

The dispenser chimed and Sirin retrieved three steaming mugs, then doled them out.

As Khusaaq accepted his, he gave the concoction an unhappy glance.

"This time I want you to drink it, Khusaaq, *all* of it," Izraad said.

He nodded then began sipping at it, making a face with each swallow, like a petulant child.

Sirin chuckled. "Trust me, Lieutenant, if he doesn't instantly like something, that's the best you're gonna get." She settled down on the arm of his chair, her own mug clutched in one hand, Khusaaq's free hand in the other.

"May I speak about what we just experienced in front of Sirin?" Izraad asked, to which Khusaaq looked up at Sirin.

"I want to understand," Sirin replied. "And to understand, I have to know."

"Are you absolutely sure?" he asked.

"Yes, absolutely," Sirin replied and with a firm nod, but to Izraad, she wasn't as confident as her tone and gesture implied.

He looked back at Izraad. "You said, 'you're only as sick as your secrets'."

"Yes, I did."

"Then no more secrets—not from Sirin, or you."

"Or you?"

He nodded, then added, "Go ahead."

Izraad took a gulp from her mug, then another, deeper one, as she put her thoughts in order. "You've spent your entire adult life holding all this guilt over what happened on Cotopaxi," she began. "Dissecting every order you gave, and most importantly, questioning your decision to make a last stand in that gorge, and what you later told yourself was a mistaken belief that the Elkanasu led you there, led you to your beloved *Monnh'hayrhan*, your Night Mountains..." Out of the corner of her eye, she caught Sirin's startled sidelong glance. "Led your troops and the colonists there, and in doing so, the Elkanasu would protect you."

"Yes."

"Instead all but five of you died on that mountainside."

He nodded unhappily.

"And when you later learned that the gorge was a Matarran munitions dump, you believed the Elkanasu sacrificed the others in order to alert the Orthodoxy and the Coalition. A small price to pay, one might say, in the greater scheme of things, a few hundred lives versus millions, possibly billions. Very small—or so you were reassured by your superiors and you desperately wanted to believe them. You desperately wanted to believe that exposing the Matarrans, exposing that Cotopaxi was in fact a gigantic weapons cache, was worth those lives."

He swallowed, hard, and started to put the mug down, but Sirin scooped up his wrist then held it and the mug close to his mouth. *"All of it*—you agreed."

He squinted up at her and took another annoyed gulp in reply.

"Isn't that true?" Izraad pressed.

He swallowed his mouthful, replied, *"Yes."*

"But no matter how hard you tried, no matter who reassured you and told you you were a hero, no amount of awards or accolades—nothing could reconcile your beliefs with all those deaths, of close friends, colleagues, even strangers. Every one of them had trusted you to protect them. And you didn't. So you not only suffered from the guilt that you'd failed even though Gaalan made sure you had no chance to succeed—not that you knew that at the time—you were compelled to take on the role of—"

"The Hero of Cotopaxi," he whispered bitterly, staring down at the mug he clutched in his hand.

"—and suffered even more than most because you carry the *paas'nah*. But you also suffered a major crisis of faith, one so deep, so soul-shattering you couldn't admit it, even to yourself. So instead you became even more fervently religious."

This time he only stared at her, gray eyes glistening.

"But it didn't help, did it?"

He slowly shook his head then said, "I thought... I thought maybe there was a greater reason for what happened, why the Elkanasu did what they did. That if I were only more devout, a more willing and unquestioning servant, they'd reveal it to me. An entire planet, a pristine planet..." He squeezed his eyes shut. *"Just... gone."*

Izraad took a sip from her own forgotten mug before setting it aside. "And there we have it."

He slowly reopened his eyes to stare at her as he arched a brow.

"You found you had to choose between blaming the Elkanasu for the utter destruction of Cotopaxi or blaming yourself and so you blamed yourself—you told yourself you were entirely responsible for the death of an entire planet, one that was so evocative of the ancient and mystical Earth of your distant forefathers that it even had its own Night Mountains. You convinced yourself that had you stayed at the complex, you and the others would have died, without a doubt, but the planet would have survived. True?"

He bit his lip instead of answering.

"I cannot tell you if the Elkanasu truly led you to that gorge, or if they did, if it was their intention to sacrifice your troops and the colonists in order to expose the Matarrans. But I sincerely doubt it was ever their intention to allow the planet to be wiped clean of all life, to be left a radioactive wasteland that it remains today and will remain for millions of years. What I've learned of them through you says they would have done everything to stop it if that had been possible. And if the Elkanasu couldn't stop what happened, any more than they could have stopped the Ufar'a from destroying that planet so many millions of years ago, using, by sad coincidence, the same method—"

"How... how do you know about the Ufar'a?" he asked, his voice cracking.

She reached out and lightly tapped his forehead, "You told me—you... *showed* me." Then she sank back into her own chair. "I was saying, if the Elkanasu couldn't stop what happened, why do you think you could have?"

"If we'd stayed—"

"NO!" She hit her fist on the arm of her chair for emphasis.

"If I'd surrendered the colony—"

"The moment the colony was established, the Matarrans knew it was only a matter of time before their secret was uncovered. When that happened the Coalition would more than likely attack, the Loopers and Thalamians and all the non-aligned systems, not to mention the Orthodoxy would pile on and the Matarran Empire would be reduced to cinders in a matter of months, if not weeks. To them the loss of one planet, even one as hauntingly beautiful and as rich in natural resources as Cotopaxi, was a very small price to pay for their secret remaining just that, a secret. Others might speculate on why they overreacted as they did, but with no evidence to prove anything, it would remain just that, speculation—"

"But—"

"You didn't kill Cotopaxi!" she blurted out and she felt him physically react like he'd been viciously punched in the stomach.

He doubled over, gasping for breath, the now empty mug falling from his grasp, then he began to sob again, deep, gut-wrenching sobs and Izraad couldn't help but wince at the soul-festering agony behind them.

Sirin leapt to her feet, started to grab his shoulders, but Izraad waved her off. "No!—this is good, he needs to fully embrace what I'm telling him."

Sirin reluctantly stepped back, her pained, helpless eyes darting between Khusaaq and Izraad as he continued to sob uncontrollably.

"That's the crux, isn't it?" Izraad pressed on, knowing it was now or never—he was still completely open, completely exposed, she could pound home her points and he couldn't stop her. "All these years you've blamed yourself for all those deaths, but even more, *the death of an entire world!*"

"It... it was so... beautiful—" Suddenly he began to wretch, his entire body spasming. He leaned forward and vomited on the blanket that was draped across his lap, then vomited again, and again, each time more violent and the moment he stopped, Izraad reached out, grasped his arm and continued,

"It was, Khusaaq. Cotopaxi was as close to paradise as anyone could ask for. *But you didn't kill it!* The Elkanasu didn't. The Matarrans *did*—they are totally responsible, not the Elkanasu and definitely not you!"

He fell back into the chair, squeezed his eyes shut as he gulped hungrily for air.

"And you've been struggling with the nagging fear that you were going to bring down the same fate on Tuli, haven't you?"

He peered at her.

"You left not just to rescue Qar'qaah, but—you believed—to save Tuli, to save Sirin."

"Oh, Khusaaq," Sirin whispered, wrapping her arms around him.

He buried his head in her stomach as his body continued to twitch but Izraad could feel what little reserves he had left bleeding out of him. One last chance to impress a thought on his mind, one that it would continue to work subconsciously, poking and prodding without his conscious knowledge.

"You've spent your life seeking absolution... " She waited until he slowly lifted his head and met her even stare, then added, "Or...?"

"Or?" he asked, his voice raspy.

"You tell me."

He gave himself a shake, freeing himself of Sirin's protective embrace.

"Or a way to seek revenge," Izraad continued.

He wiped his mouth with his hand, replied, "Revenge against whom?"

"You tell me."

Another shake; she wasn't even sure if he was consciously aware of doing it.

"Those who forced you to be something you didn't want to be, and without realizing it, forcing you to take credit for the death of Cotopaxi, the deaths of your soldiers and the colonists?" she asked.

He fixed his bruised eyes on nothing in particular, muttered huskily, "That's a long list—*very* long."

"Indeed it is. But I'd wager it starts with the Elkanasu and ends with Gaalan. And now you're finally free of both—you *survived* both," she added, using the most emotionally charged word she could pick.

He fixed his gaze on her and exhaled forcefully, wearily and as he did so she noticed that the fine tremor, so obvious only moments before, so obvious each time she'd watched him confront something ugly, something that dredged up all the horrific memories, was gone.

She smiled a private smile and rose, still more than little wobbly herself. Then, looking at Sirin, she motioned to Amalfitano's cabin. "William's in with Qar'qaah—they're both asleep and likely will be until morning. So let's get him to bed while he can still move under his own power."

Sirin nodded, carefully gathered up the vomit-splattered blanket from his lap, rolled it into a ball and placed it on the floor, then said, "Khusaaq? Come with us." When he remained where he was, she followed up with a tug on his arm and a stern, "Up!"

He dutifully lurched to his feet.

They each grabbed an arm to steady him then slowly maneuvered him, stumbling and staggering, into the darkened cabin and over to the bed.

"I'll step outside while you help him get undressed," Izraad said.

Once assured Khusaaq was able to stay on his feet without her support, she withdrew, gathered up the soiled blanket and walked out of Amalfitano's office only to hand it off to a passing medtech with a smiling apology. Then she returned just in time for Sirin to appear in the doorway and motion to her.

Izraad walked back into the cabin to find Khusaaq sprawled on the bed, covered in several blankets, his duty uniform mounded haphazardly on the fold-down chair, his boots below. She eased herself onto the edge of the bed, next to his hip then took his hand in hers. "How are you feeling?"

He thought about it for a moment then mumbled, *"Tired...."*

She smiled, "I bet. Must say I've felt more chipper. Now," she gave his hand a squeeze, "you need to sleep, and sleep as long as possible. And since you rudely barfed up my grandmother's wonderful warm milk, not to mention my blintzes—thank you for that visual, I'll be off them for quite a while I think—I want to offer you an alternative."

He blinked, slowly, and asked, "Will I sleep?"

"Guaranteed."

"No... huujuu?"

She chuckled, surprised he'd remembered. "No. And no dreams—at least *no* nightmares. Do I have your permission?"

He glanced up at Sirin, who stood behind Izraad, and at her pleading nod, said, "Yes."

Izraad reached out with her other hand and ever-so-lightly ran her fingers across his forehead and down his cheek. His hollow, blood-shot eyes followed, and as her fingertips reached his chin his eyelids fluttered. He took a deep, ragged breath, another, and then, without further ado, seemed to go completely lifeless, his head lolling to one side, his mouth agape.

Izraad gave his hand another squeeze then slipped it under the blankets. As she rose, she said, "He should sleep for at least ten, maybe twelve hours—hopefully longer."

"Can I...?" Sirin motioned to the narrow gap between the now deeply asleep Khusaaq and the wall.

"Yes. In fact he needs to feel your presence."

"Saying thank you doesn't seem to be enough." Sirin stared down at Khusaaq, smiled wearily herself, then turned to Izraad.

Izraad tried not to look as utterly done in as she felt. "It's enough. Trust me. If what we accomplished tonight in any way lessens his emotional torment, and I truly think it will, then that's all the thanks I need."

Sirin suddenly grabbed her and hugged her tightly.

Izraad responded, wrapping her arms around her and for a moment the two women held each other and then let go with slightly embarrassed smiles as each blinked away tears.

"He's a good man, Sirin. A decent man—just badly broken. He needs time to heal, but he will, given time and your support."

Sirin stared down at him for a moment then looked back at her. "You didn't do so badly yourself, if you don't mind me saying so."

Izraad grinned. "Yup, William is definitely a keeper."

"I bet you never, in your wildest dreams, thought you'd end up being a therapist for not one Hahtooshan, but two."

"Can't say I did, but... I'm not complaining." She lowered her voice, added, "Just don't tell anyone or I might have more Hahtooshan business than I can deal with—something tells me they could all do with a session or ten on a psychiatrist's couch."

Sirin grinned. "Mum's the word."

"Now, get to bed and get some sleep yourself. I'll let the nurses know you two are in here, so no one disturbs you." She backed away, and with one last glance down at the utterly relaxed Khusaaq, she stepped out of the office, tapping the door release as she went.

She walked over to Amalfitano's desk, and with a very weary sigh, snatched up the flimsy he'd marked urgent and gave it a glance. *"Damn..."* With that she sank down into his chair, and began reading—then had a thought. And not just any thought, but a most excellent thought.

She glanced back at the closed door of Amalfitano's private cabin, grinned then hit the intercom toggle. "C and C?"

"C and C—"

"Ensign, what time is it on Tuli, specifically Girsu."

There was a pause, then the com-op replied, *"Late afternoon, ma'am."*

"I need to speak with President Seitakap urgently."

"Yes, ma'am." There was another pause, this one longer, then the com-op said, *"I'm sorry, ma'am, he's in transit between Alhajoth and Girsu and won't be arriving for another three hours, however, I can leave a message with his secretary, which will be given to him immediately upon his arrival."*

She exhaled, said, "Then please pass along this message, *verbatim;* 'President Seitakap, in reference to an earlier conversation we had—I think I have a potential buyer and I would greatly appreciate it if you would contact me as soon as possible to discuss the matter further'."

"Yes, ma'am," he replied, clearly a little confused, *"transmitting your message—verbatim—now."*

"Thank you." She cut the connection, then settled back in the chair and allowed herself the luxury of a satisfied, if very tired chuckle but was cut off by Fleming's familiar voice:

"Lieutenant Izraad?"

She thumbed the toggle. "Yes?"

"I'm really sorry to bother you, but Qar'qaah is awake and asking for you."

She sighed, "Tell him I'll be right there," and rubbing her eyes, rose wearily from the chair.

Chapter 36

Aboard the Baidarka, *0556.*

"Better?"

Qar'qaah ran his fingers through his neatly clipped hair and smiled, almost bashfully, at Izraad.

She grinned back then nodded appreciatively to the ship's barber whom she'd rousted out of bed an hour before his shift started and silently mouthed, "I owe you one."

The man had been startled and deeply aggrieved both by the early wake up and then by his surprising client. Yet despite that, despite Qar'qaah's constant fidgeting and the barber's occasional yawning, he'd managed to turn Qar'qaah's unruly, raggedly cut mop of blue-black hair into something quite stylish.

While Izraad had come to accept the Elkanaghalli custom, she'd never been one who found long hair on men attractive. Khusaaq and Narbrooi had been the notable exceptions, where their below-the-waist length hair enhanced their exotic—not to mention blatantly erotic—allure.

She shifted uncomfortably at thinking such thoughts and turned back to her charge, who with her assistance, had grabbed the bare essentials of his duty uniform, boots, trousers and sleeveless undertunic, then escaped from his isolation cubicle without awakening the snoring Amalfitano. Qar'qaah had said he'd wanted to talk some more and despite her own exhaustion she was loathe to refuse. But the impromptu therapy session soon turned into a stop at the barber when Qar'qaah would not stop his distracted fiddling with his hair, the true depth of his spur-of-the-moment decision only now starting to hit home.

So she'd suggested a *proper* haircut—her treat—and Qar'qaah, as far as she was concerned, looked much better with the short, layered haircut that was popular among the younger crew, although she could have done without the thick lock of hair that kept falling across his eyes. But that was the fashion, too.

She had to forcibly stop herself from stating what was patently obvious, but not likely welcome news to the young Elkanaghalli: he was going to be the hot topic of conversation among the unattached crew—now that most onboard had overcome their initial consternation at finding Hahtooshans in their midst. Despite the lingering effects of his poisoning, Qar'qaah was, like Khusaaq, strikingly handsome—except in Qar'qaah's case he was naïvely unaware of it, which, paradoxically, made him even *more* attractive.

She gave him another appraising look as he rose from the barber's chair. In spite of everything he'd been through, despite a formidable reputation—confirmed by Sirin and Drakin—as a handful, prone to tremendous fits of pique and willful stubbornness of epic proportions, he had an aura of innocence that his brutal profession—and recent experiences—had failed to destroy.

As if sensing her thoughts, he looked back at her. Tucking the wayward lock of hair behind his right ear, he smiled sheepishly again. Then he turned to the barber and extending his tattooed hand in a very non-Hahtooshan gesture, said, "Thank you, sir."

The man hesitated then, with a prodding stare from Izraad, replied with a reluctant handshake. "Uh, yeah, well... anytime, kid."

"Now," Izraad said, "how about that breakfast?" *And an infusion of strong, hot coffee*, she added to herself as she fought back a watery-eyed yawn.

Qar'qaah nodded.

"Come on then."

It was early—barely past oh-six hundred as they walked together down the passageway and towards the ship's main galley. Few crew were about—either they were still at their posts, in the rec rooms, in the galley or asleep. Change of watch was not for fifty minutes and her young charge looked around him with eager eyes, only occasionally glancing at her once he realized they were not returning to sickbay, but headed some place new.

She smiled back then fixed her hard, extremely displeased scowl on any passing crew who did not respond to his curious stare with an affable nod or, better yet, a pleasant, "Good morning".

Once they reached the galley, she guided him over to a corner table, not far from the main doors, with a clear view of the comings and goings. It was the same table favored by Matoosh, Laihiri, Nihaal, Raudah and Endooki, along with the Hahtooshan medics. She strongly suspected their choice had been based on a need to place themselves where they felt the least vulnerable: their backs against the wall, an escape route close at hand and a complete, unobstructed view of the spacious dining hall.

As Qar'qaah slipped onto a chair, Izraad caught the eye of one of the galley staff. The crewman, having learned from prior experience with the other Hahtooshans, immediately brought her a welcome cup of coffee and Qar'qaah a large mug of hot chocolate.

While the hot variety was new, the basic ingredient wasn't. Qar'qaah stared at the mug, his nose twitching at its familiar, enticing and now warmed scent as he shifted in the chair, painfully aware of the covert stares of crew already seated nearby or walking well around their table.

It hadn't helped that conversation ceased the instant the two had arrived. The other Hahtooshans had garnered the same cool, bordering on hostile reception, but they in turn had pointedly ignored the less than friendly welcome as a matter of pride—or Hahtooshan arrogance—while focusing their interest on something more worthy of their undivided attention: the endless supply of exotic food.

But Qar'qaah was alone, deserted even by his Hahtooshan façade of aloof superiority and surrounded by Rimmers—worse yet, knowingly *dependent* on Rimmers.

On Rasal Ghul the others had looked to him for their very survival, for guidance and encouragement and he in turn had never let them see that he was just as afraid as they were; never let them see that he was even sicker than they were. And the ruse had worked.

On Poonda Five he was again the one in control—at least he'd convinced himself that he was—over his fate, over his two Rimmer charges, and as a result he had delivered Sirin and Drakin unharmed into safe hands, again, to the determent of his own, now extremely precarious health.

But once aboard the *Baidarka*, everything changed. All pretense that he had control over anything—even his own body—evaporated as he was stripped not only of his veneer of superiority, of his sense of invulnerability, of his belief in himself, but his very sense *of* self. He no longer knew who and what he was and it left him feeling utterly exposed, lost. *Abandoned.*

The result was an intensely shy, scared-stiff adolescent. Worse yet, it was obvious to everyone—possibly the first time in his life that he had *scared* written all over him. And just as clearly, there were crew nearby who delighted in seeing a Hahtooshan frightened of them instead of the reverse. The perfect payback.

"What would you like for breakfast?" Izraad asked softly.

He pulled his sidelong gaze off the surrounding, silent wall of faces, fixed it on the shiny surface of the table and as the lock of hair fell across his eyes, he mumbled, "I'm really not hungry."

Damn. She swept the room with her rarely used but when employed truly ferocious glare. Everyone immediately returned to their own meals while conversation—albeit clearly forced—resumed.

"May we go?"

She looked back at him to find him watching her intently through the veil of hair as if it was his last bastion.

"No. Not until you eat." She motioned to the mug. "Why don't you start by drinking your hot chocolate?"

He dutifully, albeit very reluctantly did as he was told, and as she took a sip of her coffee, he drained the contents of the cup in four loud gulps. He placed the mug on the table, burped softly, then wiped his mouth and asked again, "Now may we go? *Please?*"

She sighed. It was cruel to force him to stay—it had been a stupid mistake to bring him here where there was just too much input, too much focus—more than someone this emotionally fragile could handle and she should have known that—would have known it had she not been so dog-tired—but before she could agree, before they could make good their escape, Perou, along with three of his engineering techs arrived, entering through the door at the opposite end of the galley, a boisterous foursome who couldn't help but draw the eye.

Perou immediately spotted them in the sparsely populated galley and motioning for his techs to follow, made a bee-line for their table, dodging wait staff and crew in his haste. *"There you are!"*

Qar'qaah glanced at Izraad then back at the approaching Perou; now he was really spooked, despite Perou's broad grin.

"It's okay," she whispered. "You remember Lieutenant Perou, don't you?"

Qar'qaah wet his lips as his eyes flicked to the nearby doorway, assuring himself of an escape route, before looking back at her with a panicky stare.

"He's the chief engineer," she explained hastily; by the look on Qar'qaah's face and the tension in his body, he was clearly planning to bolt. "He gave you the specs on the foldspace generators—*remember?"*

He stared at her then squinted intensely at the approaching Perou and sudden recollection flooded into his eyes and he breathed, "Yes…"

And not a moment too soon. Izraad smiled up at Perou as he stopped in front of them, his companions crowding around him. "Mornin' Alain."

"Good morning, Zarijan, and good morning Kon'ta'aq— didn't recognize you at first with the new look. Suits you."

Qar'qaah flashed him a quick, uneasy glance as he self-consciously tucked the lock of hair behind his ear. Then one by one, he met the stares of the three techs, clearly expecting hostility.

They, however, responded with nodding, intensely curious smiles.

"Mind if we join you?" Perou, not waiting for a reply, pulled out a chair and sat down at the small table designed to comfortably sit four, not six.

"Uh, I suppose not," Izraad replied, painfully aware of Qar'qaah's tightly controlled reaction as two of the techs immediately seated themselves on either side of him, boxing him in, while the third had to grab a chair from a nearby table and squeeze in between Izraad and Perou.

A quick getaway was now impossible and by the look on Qar'qaah's face, he clearly realized it.

"Ordered yet?" Perou asked, still seemingly oblivious to Qar'qaah's growing panic. He glanced over his shoulder and motioned to one of the cooks.

"We were just about to, weren't we, Qar'qaah?" Izraad replied.

His eyes darted to her, then to Perou but didn't say a word.

"I was hoping to catch you early, Kon'ta'aq," Perou continued. "Wanted a chance to go over those modifications you came up with—the patch worked perfectly by the way. Don't know if you were told. The generator's up and running like new." He looked up as the cook set a tray containing a large decanter of coffee, four cups and another mug of hot chocolate on the table.

"Here you go." The cook placed the full mug in front of Qar'qaah and picked up the empty one. "And how 'bout some chocolate chip hotcakes to go with that?"

Qar'qaah only stared up at him.

"I'll take that as a yes." Izraad smiled her thanks to the cook, who winked back at her then he looked around the table. "And the regular for the rest of you?"

The four from engineering nodded.

Izraad said, "Uh, I'll pass on the blintzes today, Jerry— maybe a muffin—anything but blueberry?"

"You got it. Just made a fresh batch." He hurried off.

"I'm Jakson," one of the techs said, the one seated to Qar'qaah's left. He started to offer him his hand then quickly thought better of it. The entire crew had been briefed: a non-Hahtooshan was *never* to touch a Hahtooshan without the

Hahtooshan's permission. He deftly concealed the near gaffe by grabbing a cup of coffee instead. "Paul Jakson. Pleased to finally meet you."

The tech seated to his right smiled. "I'm Nobia Zendejas."

"And I'm Ben Dekker," said the third, the one seated next to Izraad. "We've heard all about you—"

Qar'qaah fixed his startled eyes on Izraad and she privately winced, painfully aware of how he'd taken the remark.

"—the lieutenant here hasn't stopped talking about what an amazing engineer you are to the point we were all beginning to think you were just a figment of Mister Perou's overly active imagination." Still oblivious of the effect of his words, Dekker laughed then took a deep gulp from his mug.

Zendejas and Jakson were a little more perceptive, as was Perou.

"Kon'ta'aq," Perou said quietly, drawing his anxious gaze, "I'd really like the chance to show you around Engineering—"

Izraad coughed softly.

"—assuming Doc and the lieutenant here give the okay," he added quickly.

Jakson leaned close—but not *too* close—and despite Qar'qaah's muscle twitch and wary sidelong stare, whispered loud enough for everyone at the table to hear, *"In other words, he wants to put you to work."*

Qar'qaah, who up to that moment hadn't spoken, who had looked about as intensely ill at ease as a person could look, turned to Perou, his face suddenly brightening. *"Really?"*

Perou, in the process of taking a sip of coffee, nodded, then, seeing Qar'qaah's hopeful expression, nodded again, this time eagerly. "Damned straight."

Izraad sighed and slumped back into her chair, feigning frustration.

"That is if Doctor Amalfitano says I can," Qar'qaah added with a sidelong glance at her. "And if it's all right with Lieutenant Izraad."

"Eat your breakfast—*all of it*—then we'll talk," Izraad replied and not a moment too soon as the cook reappeared with a large tray laden with plates heaped with food.

Once everyone was served, the others wasted no time in tucking in. Qar'qaah hesitated as he poked at the unfamiliar plate of hotcakes. His eyes slid to Zendejas' more familiar scrambled eggs, then back to his own plate.

"Wanna switch?" she muffled through a mouthful of eggs.

He was clearly tempted.

"Here." She placed her plate in front of him while sliding his in front of her but not before Dekker reached across the table and skillfully forked a hotcake off the moving plate and onto his.

Qar'qaah looked around, clearly taken aback by the rapid exchange.

"Better get used to it," Jakson said, "in Engineering, its share and share alike."

"More like grab what you can while you can," Zendejas added as she lightly smacked Dekker's hand as he tried to snag another hotcake.

Then, with a prodding grin from Jakson, and a sidelong smile from Zendejas, Qar'qaah began to eat, much to Izraad's intense relief. She flicked Perou a quick glance, to which he grinned and winked then he took a deep gulp from his mug.

The mealtime small talk all too quickly progressed to a very animated conversation about of fold generators. Napkins became schematics once Perou produced a stylus; knives and forks turned into surrogates for recalcitrant fold generators; cups and saucers became engineering work pods.

Soon the tabletop was a miniature mock-up of engineering, and after a few minutes Izraad gave up trying to follow the discussion and settled back in her chair with her cup of coffee to watch in silent amazement as Qar'qaah blossomed under the rapid-fire back and forth among the engineers.

The lively discussion soon drew a modest crowd of onlookers who listened attentively, all reservations about a Hahtooshan in their midst having been replaced by genuine curiosity at his startling expertise.

Even without a detailed understanding of engineering, it was obvious to Izraad that Qar'qaah was in his element, talking with peers about their shared passion. He was no longer the scared teenager, painfully aware that he was an unwelcome outsider. He was no longer a Hahtooshan surrounded by Rimmers. He was now a fully accepted and greatly admired member of a very tight-knit group.

Izraad briefly caught his eye during a brief lull in the lively roundtable while Dekker refilled their cups and Qar'qaah gulped down the remains of his third mug of hot chocolate.

He wiped his lips with the back of his hand, grinned at her then dove back into the debate while she smiled a private smile and took a leisurely, if sleepy-eyed sip of her coffee.

Chapter 37

Amalfitano's office, sickbay, 0848.

"I was beginning to wonder where you two had gone off to," Amalfitano grumbled as he rose from behind his office desk. "Sneaking off like that without even leaving a note."

"We weren't gone that long, and you were sound asleep when we left, if I remember correctly," Izraad replied. "Isn't that right, Kon'ta'aq?"

Before Qar'qaah could answer—not that he looked like he wanted to answer and risk the appearance of taking sides—Amalfitano said, "Well, it's not like I could sleep in my own bed now, is it?" and motioned to the closed door of his private cabin.

Qar'qaah glanced sidelong at Izraad.

"Khusaaq and Sirin are in there."

Qar'qaah's mouth formed a silent, albeit mildly confused, 'O'.

"And I might as well tell you both now," Izraad said, "while I have the chance. Khusaaq and I talked last night—in fact we talked *most* of the night."

"Talked?" Qar'qaah asked, even more bewildered. "About what?"

"How'd it go?" Amalfitano said a second later, knowing exactly what she meant and clearly worried.

She answered Qar'qaah first: "About what happened on Cotopaxi... and after. He's going to need a lot of therapy, just like you, Kon'ta'aq, to overcome what he's been through." She then turned to Amalfitano. "But we took the first step, and that's a good sign, a *very* good sign."

Amalfitano audibly sighed in relief then turned to Qar'qaah. He had suddenly noticed Qar'qaah's new look. He slid his eyes back to Izraad and raised his brows. "What the—"

"Treated him to a proper haircut then ran into Perou and some of his gang in the galley and stayed to eat breakfast."

Izraad smiled at Qar'qaah. "Our boy here has developed quite a fan club. I had a hard time prying him from their grasp."

Amalfitano turned back to Qar'qaah to find the young Hahtooshan fighting back a decidedly pleased grin. But behind the grin was a drawn face and very tired eyes.

"Looks like they wore you out—I don't want you exhausting yourself, understood?" He belatedly motioned to a nearby chair, realizing Qar'qaah wasn't going to sit without being given permission, and Qar'qaah gratefully sat down. "You need to build up your stamina, slowly, or risk a serious relapse."

"But ta'ahn, Lieutenant Perou asked if I'd—"

"Later, okay? There will be plenty of time, *later*. Get this in your head right now, to Lieutenant Perou, there's not one thing in engineering that isn't in desperate need of being upgraded or replaced or refitted, and it should have been done yesterday, or better, the day before that..."

Qar'qaah replied with a perplexed stare. "But, I don't—"

"But it's rarely the case—he's always playing the crisis card—and right now *you* need to get some rest. Or do I have to make *that* an order?"

"No, ta'*aaaaah*—" he cut himself off with a yawn. Qar'qaah knuckled rubbed his watering eyes and yawned again. He blinked then fixed his suddenly very heavy-lidded eyes on Amalfitano.

"You can stay here with me if you'd like."

Izraad gathered up one of the discarded blankets from the chair she'd been seated in earlier, and draped it around Qar'qaah.

Qar'qaah responded by snuggling into the covers while murmuring wearily, *"Jaas-nhe."*

Izraad picked up the remaining blanket, wrapped it around her own shoulders and seated herself beside him.

Amalfitano grinned, jerked his chin towards Qar'qaah and Izraad followed his amused stare. He'd already slipped effortlessly into a sound sleep.

Amalfitano shook his head, looked at Izraad and said softly, "Did he eat?"

"Not a lot but enough—four mugs of hot chocolate and a half a plate of scrambled eggs—*and* he kept everything down."

"Need to watch him—don't let him exhaust himself. He simply has *no* reserves to pull from."

"I know, but you should have seen him, William. He was really enjoying himself—it was a pure pleasure to watch and I figured he'd earned a little fun."

He motioned for her to lean close and keeping his eyes on Qar'qaah, whispered, "Did you notice his tattoos?"

"His... *tattoos?*"

"They're darker. I swear they are—didn't you notice?"

Izraad eyed him with a decidedly bleary eye. Point made, she gave their charge a sidelong, appraising stare. "But, how's that possible? According to Murh'sooli—"

"Last night, I... well, I'm really not sure what I witnessed—but I saw them... well, I saw them *change*. Didn't realize until just now that they're much darker, too—not as dark as the others, but much darker than they were."

Izraad arched a brow as she slowly eased herself back into her own chair.

"And on his right upper arm. I watched as they *grew?*—maybe better to say the designs were embellished upon, ending up slightly more complex? More ornate?" He gave himself a shake. *"Hell of a thing."*

"But... how?"

"Damned if I know that, either, but I *know* what I saw. Take a look."

Izraad, with a shrug, reached over and carefully lifted the blanket, exposing Qar'qaah's right arm, which, like his face and throat, was still coated in a film of burn cream. The tattoos did appear more complex, even to her tired eyes.

"See what I mean?"

She nodded distractedly, carefully recovered Qar'qaah and turned back to Amalfitano. "Curiouser and curiouser."

"You can say that—" His eyes suddenly narrowed at a fleeting memory. *"Wait a minute..."* He knit his brows in concentration—then it came to him. "Same was true of Khusaaq—"

"I beg your pardon?"

"When I saw him for the first time on Tuli—when I flicked down first, to see how he was, before you and Robert told him about the kidnappings—I noticed something different about his physical appearance. Couldn't place what it was at the time, but now... *it was his tattoos*. They were different—not darker in Khusaaq's case, just more intricate. *And* it was the same damned right arm."

Izraad pursed her lips then said, "We could wait until Khusaaq wakes up—or we could contact Narbrooi. I'm sure he could explain it."

"I'm sure he could, I'm just not sure he's the one who should." Amalfitano jerked his chin towards his cabin door. "Let's wait."

"Agreed," she replied and snuggled down in her own blanket.

"Ah... just a moment, before you drift off to dreamland yourself. I have a message for you."

"Not again," she groaned softly, then elbowed her way back to a more upright and marginally more alert position.

"From President Seitakap no less."

"Oh." Then her face brightened. "Oh!"

"Came in while you two were off gallivanting around the ship. I told him I'd have you contact him as soon as you were free, but the president said he didn't think you considered the matter confidential—although if you ask me it does sound deliberately ambiguous—so he told me to tell you the following: 'The buyer is exceedingly motivated and I can arrange a meeting as soon as you return to Tuli'."

She grinned, a very pleased if weary grin and again settled back in her chair. "Excellent."

Amalfitano scowled at her. "So are you going to enlighten me?"

"Can't it wait?"

"What do you think?"

"I think it can."

"I don't. My office, my rules."

"Fine." Izraad yawned, then said sleepily, "Remember that welcoming dinner—our first night on Tuli?"

"Of course."

"Well, the president and I spent a lot of time talking—"

"I recall that as well. So much so, I thought I might have some serious competition."

"—he spoke of his heritage, where his family came from—the Marshall Islands, originally—then asked about us, asked where we were from, originally. I told him the Meridiani Planum colony on Mars for me, the Italian Dolomites for you and—"

"Cortina d'Ampezzo to be specific."

She grinned; that had always been a tremendous point of pride for him. "And a mining conglomerate in the Outer Belt for Robert." She shrugged, added, "He asked when we'd last been home, if we ever returned home on leave, or planned to, once we retired. I told him neither Robert or I had any desire, that we were both so damned eager to leave that life behind we had never been back, never planned on going back, but that you'd very recently threatened to retire and go back to Earth, presumably to your ancestral and much beloved Cortina d'Ampezzo because I know you still have some distant family there, but..."

"But?"

"He mentioned that one of the privately owned provinces, the northernmost, Havilah, is sometimes referred to as Nuevo Europa, although he says it's far more rugged that most of Europe, more like—"

"The Dolomites."

"Yeah."

"And?"

"He suggested that maybe we plan a trip there, that the mountains are truly spectacular and you'd likely really enjoy it."

"As much as a sun-drenched and secluded beach?"

She shrugged again. "Who says we can't do both?"

"Do you have any idea just how much work the two of us are facing when we return? I doubt we'll have time to take a prolonged and private piss, much less take a tour of the natural wonders of Tuli."

"I know, but—"

"And what's with the motivated buyer? Don't tell me you gave him the impression I might want to buy myself a mountain? Did you mention I'm afraid of heights?"

She managed a tired chuckle. "Not for you..."

He arched a brow. "Then who?"

"Remember Sirin said that Khusaaq kept repeating a word? But when questioned, he got evasive?"

Amalfitano scratched the side of his head. "Vaguely."

"Monnh'hayrhan."

"Yeah," Amalfitano pointed at her, "that's it."

"It means night mountains, but not just any nighttime mountains. It's the mythical home of the Elkanasu—"

Qar'qaah briefly stirred, drawing their gazes, smacked his lips and mumbled something, then promptly went limp again.

Once satisfied he was indeed still fast asleep, Amalfitano continued, but in a slightly lower voice: "Oh. Well, one mystery solved, but I don't—"

"As I mentioned earlier, Khusaaq and I had our first... session last evening. I came here looking for that oh-so critical flimsy you swore you'd given to me, and I knew you hadn't— and, oh, by the way I found it on your desk—and who did I find sitting in that chair?" she jerked her chin towards the sleeping Qar'qaah.

"Khusaaq."

"In the flesh. He and Sirin had had an argument; he decided to sleep aboard *Jirah* but stopped here first to check on Qar'qaah. I managed to convince him to eat something, and then, to my shock, he agreed to talk—just the two of us. Now I can't discuss exactly what we talked about, I can tell you that these Night Mountains are a huge part of the Hahtooshan belief system, and played a key role in what transpired on Cotopaxi. We had a breakthrough—I now know what happened, why he suffers from these flashbacks, and I think he can be successfully rehabilitated, given some time and a lot of therapy. Afterwards, I called Sirin, felt he really needed her, but he was so wobbly and in truth so was I, we didn't think he could make it back to her quarters—"

"So yet again my private quarters were appropriated—"

"You were in with Qar'qaah and the two of you were sound asleep. What was I supposed to do? Let him sleep in the corridor where he dropped? Or maybe a stairwell? Or maybe there," she pointed to the nearby chair.

"Qar'qaah seems comfy," Amalfitano muttered.

She laughed softly. "Be that as it may... once we got him tucked into bed, I sat down at your desk, started to look at that flimsy when I had a brilliant thought, which, considering how tired I was at the time, is truly remarkable."

"And that brilliant thought has to do with these Night Mountains of the Hahtooshans and Tuli's version of the Dolomites."

"Yeah. I can't explain it, because Khusaaq never said so, but I sense these Night Mountains of the Elkanasu might in fact be some remnant Neanderthal memory of a mountainous area on Earth. From what I learned about Neanderthals, their last strongholds were mountainous regions, and Khusaaq's ancestors did in fact come from an area called the Altai—a very rugged region of Siberia that even today is sparsely populated. And the Elkanaghalli are the oldest clan, so... perhaps these Night Mountains of their mythos are, or should I say were, the Altai. I thought maybe, just maybe the Hahtooshans themselves might be interested in possibly setting up... well, for lack of a better description, a holiday camp there—"

Amalfitano couldn't help but chuckle at the mental image that conjured up.

"—I mean it's not like they can go just anywhere for R and R, or at least they couldn't, and I doubt they'd be welcome, even with their new ally status, in most of your usual holiday destinations. If my experience with the Hahtooshans I've met so far is any guide, I can say with some certainty that they could all use some serious R and R, or, perhaps more to the point, some very serious *non*-serious R and R."

"Yeah," Amalfitano replied, rubbing the back of his neck then chuckled again. "I dunno... I just cannot imagine Narbrooi soaking in a mineral pool, sipping a martini after having a steam and massage, can you?"

She grinned at the image. "No, but I can see him running barefoot through a forest, spear in hand, chasing game, or tackling an especially steep cliff face. I'd imagine that would be close to heaven for a Hahtooshan—in more ways than one."

Amalfitano nodded in grudging agreement.

"Clearly Khusaaq feels a deep connection to his ancient past and likely most Hahtooshans do, even the secular castes, whether they want to admit it or not. And according to President Seitakap, the private owners of Havilah have been talking about selling for years, but couldn't find a single buyer willing to even come close to their asking price. Only a fraction of Havilah is arable, with a little more being classified as pasturable. The vast majority of the province, which is actually a continent a little smaller than Australia, is just too rugged and cold and so has remained virtually untouched.

"The original colonists, when they realized the province's hinterlands didn't contain the mineral wealth they'd been promised, hoped to turn the area into some vast game park, for hunting and also to build up the numbers of species that no longer exist in the wild on Earth. Since Havilah has no large herbivores or carnivores of its own, there was no ban on them importing stock from Earth, like elk, bison, wild boar, even tigers, leopards and wolves.

"They even tried—according to President Seitakap—to buy some cloned mammoths and wooly rhinos from that crazy multi-trillionaire... what was his name? The one who made all his money cloning people's pets and then branched out into cloning their deceased loved ones, until someone got wind of it and he fled to the planet he owns to avoid being prosecuted under any number of planetary laws?"

"Johnathon Izaki." The name came just a little too quickly to Amalfitano's tongue, and with a decidedly bitter tang.

Izraad glanced at the small holo cube and its suspended image of the small black dog, a beloved pet that he still spoke about, decades after its death. "Were you ever tempted?"

He squinted at her, clearly unsure how far she meant and answered emphatically, "No."

She shrugged, then continued, "They thought people would come in droves just to see mammoths and rhinos and the like, since Izaki's planetary game preserve is for his eyes only, but he refused to sell even genetic material, much less a whole animal or two, and in the end few tourists came—it's a hell of a long way to come to bag yourself a trophy elk or moose or tiger when you can just buy a perfectly realistic fake to hang on your wall, if that's your idea of décor. Plus there are hunting parks on planets that aren't as far off the beaten track as Tuli and with a lot more exotic, alien animals to kill—and with no place to reintroduce these species back on Earth... well, they soon found they had an overabundance of animals but no one to buy or shoot them, so their plans failed on all counts and they've been in desperate financial shape for years.

"Plus, I'd heard rumors among the Tulians that the Havilahians weren't too happy with the Hahtooshan 'occupation' of their planet even though not a single Hahtooshan has stepped foot on Havilahian soil, the Havilahians figuring that that would be the last nail in the coffin of their now rather tattered grand plans for their province being a big-game tourist hot spot."

"But you think they'd sell some of their land to those very same Hahtooshans, assuming the Hahtooshans are in fact interested?"

"I guess we'll find out. But in my experience, most people find ways of overcoming their moral reluctance when large sums of money are involved, and let's just say the Hahtooshans aren't short on cash—I suspect they could buy the entire continent without making a dent in their piggybank. Who knows? In a few years, Havilah could be the Hahtooshan tourist trap the original colonists could have only dreamed of."

Amalfitano shook his head. "I still cannot picture Hahtooshans as tourists."

"Not so much tourists." She burrowed down into the folds of the blanket, then smiling, added, "More... reliving their childhood."

Amalfitano thought about that for a moment, nodded his agreement.

"And that prompted another idea..."

Amalfitano braced himself. "And that is?"

"We never got Sirin and Khusaaq a wedding gift."

Amalfitano thought about it then nodded. "You're right, we didn't. Of course they technically never had a wedding—"

"I thought maybe a pristine mountain range and its surrounds might be about as perfect as perfect can be—"

"The perfect backdrop for an honest to goodness and... rather *overdue* wedding?" he added then at her sidelong look, winked.

She stared at him for a moment, not sure he was suggesting what he seemed to be suggesting then she grinned and said, "In fact, yes—very much *yes,"* she added with a vigorous nod, or as vigorous a nod as she could manage. "And I bet we can get the best of the best without breaking either your piggybank or mine."

"Do it."

She lifted her head and looked around her, then fixed her blood-shot eyes on him. "Now?"

"No, not this minute, but the first chance you get. Once the rest of the Hahtooshans get wind of this, and the Havilahians realize they might have a buyer with *huge* pockets, I suspect prices will rise dramatically—I want to get in on the bottom floor, so to speak, and grab the best bunch of damned mountains we can get—tell the Havilahians it's for me, for *us*—a reminder of home, a place to retire... eventually. Who knows, it might just be the truth—hell, maybe the Havilahians will sell us the choicest spot at a rock bottom price, so to speak, their way of thanking us for saving them."

"You're wicked."

"I thought that was what you found most loveable about me."

"One of many qualities, William, one of many."

"Besides, I see nothing wicked in hoping for something more substantive than a thank you dinner for saving an entire planet."

"But technically you didn't. As you pointed out to the Tulians, it was Tasende—"

"Let's not quibble over the details, okay? There's more than enough credit to go around."

She grinned, "Agreed... and as soon as I wake up I'll contact Varron of Havilah first thing. Promise." She snuggled down, yawned, then knuckle-rubbed her eyes.

"Why not go back to your cabin and get some sleep?"

"This is clearly the place to be. Besides, I'm comfy too."

He eyed her. "If either Khusaaq or Qar'qaah need you, I'll call you."

"I'm right where I need to be—now shut the hell up and let me get some shut-eye." With that she covered her head with the blanket.

Chapter 38

Conference room aboard Baidarka, *1638.*

Aquila looked up as the conference room door opened, acknowledged the belated arrival of a rather harried Izraad, then turned his full attention back to Narbrooi, who was seated to his left at the elliptical table, the Hahtooshan admiral in the process of bringing a steaming cup to his lips.

"Lieutenant." Narbrooi smiled and, placing the mug on the desk, rose.

Aquila, Izraad noticed, took the hint and not to be outdone in the courtly department also got to his feet.

"Hahtra'tzrhi," Izraad replied with a quick duck of her chin to Narbrooi, followed by a glance at Aquila. "Commander. I apologize for the late arrival, but I was just wrapping another session with Kon'ta'aq when—"

"No need for apologies," Narbrooi interrupted. "This meeting was rather last minute, and Kon'ta'aq's needs certainly have priority. Please." He motioned to the chair next to his, and as she seated herself, Narbrooi and Aquila following suit, he continued, "As I was just informing Commander Aquila, Gaalan is already on her way back to the Orthodoxy to stand trial."

"Kon'ta'aq will be pleased to hear that," Izraad said.

"Relieved is closer to the mark, yes?"

Izraad chuckled. "Much closer to the mark."

"Care to join us?" Aquila offered, holding up a decanter and an extra cup and she nodded, but when he handed her the mug, she realized it wasn't the hoped for coffee, but instead hot chocolate. She flicked Narbrooi a sidelong look to see him clearly savoring the contents of his own mug.

Aquila chuckled, said, "I've already had the galley send over a chemical ingredients list so their cooks can recreate it."

"Most delicious," Narbrooi said as he settled back in his chair. Izraad couldn't help but marvel that he was totally relaxed, and it wasn't just pretense—his ferocious persona had inexplicably been replaced by a man fully contented by something so mundane as a cup of cocoa. In fact she'd never seen a Hahtooshan so laidback—and Narbrooi of all people? She'd come away from their first meeting with the impression that the officer was the sort who slept in his ghillie armor, and subsequent interactions had done nothing to dissuade her from that view. Yet here he was, in his coppery duty uniform no less, loose-limbed and thoroughly enjoying a cup of cocoa. *If everything could be so easily defused...*

Narbrooi took another slow sip then continued, "But before she left, she and I had a long, brother sister... *chat*."

Izraad couldn't help but share a look with Aquila as images of the Hahtooshans' interrogation of Amalfitano and Tasende's Thalamian would-be assassin suddenly came to mind.

Narbrooi noticed, smiled and said, "It was most enlightening. She proved, and will continue to prove to be a veritable treasure trove of intelligence, not only on the Matarii, but others who pose a threat to our alliance—inside and outside—I've already forwarded a transcript to your HQ," he motioned to a data disc that sat in front of Aquila, "and brought one for you to read over at your leisure."

Izraad glanced at the disc. Narbrooi could have transmitted it, ship to ship. It certainly would have been faster, but the fact that he elected to bring a disc personally spoke volumes.

The Hahtooshan admiral took a less measured gulp, wiped his lips with the back of his tattooed hand then continued, *"Faridour* and her outriders will accompany *Baidarka* back to Tuli." He nodded to Aquila as he toyed with the mug's handle. "My crew, like yours, Commander, has more than earned some shore leave and the planet's governing body has extended an offer to stay as long as we would like—a truly unique gesture as I cannot remember when any planet *willingly* offered A'tuu'shahn'i shore leave. But..." he smiled, his pale eyes holding a certain mischievous sparkle, "with tensions rising along the border, it's *remotely* possible that this surprisingly generous proposition is not entirely without strings."

Aquila chuckled.

"If so," Narbrooi briefly met Aquila's amused stare with a casual shrug, "then so be it. I for one am just grateful my troops will be welcomed, if not entirely warmly then at least without obvious panic or blatant hostility. It will be a novel experience for all of them to be sure."

"And you?" Izraad prompted as she brought her cup to her lips.

He smiled, "A novel experience for me as well, Lieutenant. I've never spent any time on a planet that wasn't an active war zone."

"And hopefully this is just the beginning," Aquila said. But all knew it would be a very long time before Hahtooshans would be able to travel openly and freely within the Coalition itself.

"One step at a time, Commander, for all of us. Trust is not earned quickly—it will take time for both sides to fully embrace the other, and in truth that might never happen..."

As Narbrooi spoke, Izraad suddenly realized that he'd come alone to the *Baidarka*, no escort, at least none visible and invisible would have been a breach of protocol—only Amalfitano's guards were permitted such—and aside from his ritual dagger, he was unarmed, a not-so-subtle message on his part on the crucial matter of trust, and a personal risk, however small.

"...the alliance may always remain a fragile construct, one that takes constant work to maintain." Narbrooi polished off the contents of his mug, set it on the desk then stared at it with an expression that bordered on melancholy. "It's ironic, Gaalan claims she despised our way of life, the very strict and at times the suffocating anachronistic religious restrictions of being Elkanaghalli, of A'tuu'shahn'i being treated as little more than blood currency for greedy, cowardly and ungrateful aliens with the willing complicity of the Q'shaathrah *and* the Elkanasu. And yet she also desperately craved being a hero in the eyes of our people and was enraged beyond measure when that honor was bestowed, instead, upon Khusaaq Sha'ashahn."

He shook his head, reached for the decanter and offered Izraad and Aquila a refill and at their wave-offs, poured himself another cup. "Her desire to see him dead as punishment for usurping her glory, in combination with her entrenched bitterness over Ja'andai's faithlessness quickly blossomed into a single-minded obsession to destroy not just Khusaaq Sha'ashahn, but discredit his lineage. And as you might have come to realize, lineage is very important to us A'tuu'shahn'i.

"Worse for her, one attempt on Sha'ashahn's life after another failed—in truth they were all so heavily reliant on unreliable alien confederates none really had a chance at success. But she saw it differently." He paused, took a gulp from his mug, exhaled, then continued:

"Gaalan became convinced that the Q'shaathrah had somehow learned of her treachery and that she was in fact still very much alive, and they were using Khusaaq Sha'ashahn to lure her out of hiding, much as she hoped to use Kon'ta'aq to lure Khusaaq into her trap. She was equally consumed with the fear that her carefully manicured status as the *true* hero of Cotopaxi, the ultimate martyr for the cause, even among her diehard loyalists, was rapidly dwindling from the collective consciousness—she'd forgotten, somewhere along the line, that dead heroes all too quickly fade from the public eye, and being that she was officially dead, there wasn't anything she could do about it.

"The Q'shaathrah *hadn't* forgotten this truism, which is why they named Khusaaq Hero of Cotopaxi—A'tuu'shahn'i desperately needed a living hero, a vibrant reminder of who and what we are when we are at our best, to keep us focused on that during what was an otherwise very dark, very bleak period."

Narbrooi took another sip, swallowed, then toying with the cup's handle said, "I must admit that I, albeit unwittingly, played into her plans by actively promoting her as the true hero of Cotopaxi, keeping her memory alive, while doing all I could to derail Khusaaq Sha'ashahn's career. I truly believed, *bitterly* believed he was a usurper, worse, a derisory copy of Ja'andai, utterly undeserving of the honors—honors that should have gone to her, and therefore my family and yes, to me.

"Our families, the Tashar'anhi and the Abhijit'tischinjgra, have long been rivals in that regard—equally old, equally storied, equally stubborn and discriminatory. And my kin and I truly felt Khusaaq being named hero rather than Gaalan was the final snub from the Q'shaathrah, one last swipe at Gaalan and Ja'andai for their rumored union, but one that tarred only *my* family, not Khusaaq's and one that would, and did, influence my career and those of my kinsmen."

"If you don't mind me saying so, Hahtra'tzrhi," Izraad said, "you appear to have vastly overcome any hindrances."

"You mean I've overcompensated—true enough." He chuckled, settled back in his chair and stared at the mug he now clutched in both hands, and for a moment remained silent. Then he shifted around, suddenly and visibly uncomfortable. "Early on, long before Cotopaxi, I was in fact deeply suspicious of Gaalan, of her motives, her blind ambitions. Simply put, I hated her, always have, and as it turns out, she's always felt the same way about me only more so."

As Izraad listened, she realized his deep voice was now suddenly devoid of pretense; he was keenly aware that he was about to bare his soul to two Rimmers of all people, and clearly had no idea how Izraad and Aquila were going to react. *Understanding? Empathy? Disgust?* Even more surprising to Izraad, it was important to Narbrooi how they reacted, unexpectedly and deeply so, as if he was fearful that the nascent trust he'd spoken of, and which he'd eloquently demonstrated by coming alone and essentially unarmed, was about to be tested in the most personal of ways.

"...I voiced my concerns to my kinsmen and to the Q'shaathrah," he continued, his eyes fixed on the mug he held. "But my fears were brushed aside, chalked up to my own selfish and patently grandiose aspirations, to my youthful envy of Gaalan's accomplishments—and, yes, a deep resentment that my promising career had been damaged in its earliest stages, possibly irrevocably, by the rumors about her and Ja'andai—all of which, I readily admit, were entirely true.

"So I tried very hard to believe those older and wiser than me, tried desperately to believe her. I so *wanted* to believe—" He took another, hasty gulp of the cocoa. "When I was told she'd died at Cotopaxi, I wasn't sure whether I should mourn or be relieved—I was given no choice but to publicly play the role of grieving younger brother, pledging to avenge her death and the deaths of her crew and heap more than equal misery on the Matarii, to live up to her legacy. But privately I still had these nagging doubts not to mention a sense of overwhelming relief that I'd no longer have to play nice to her, to act unfazed when she made one of her many deliberately demeaning remarks about me or my accomplishments which she did at every opportunity—sounds childish, doesn't it?"

Aquila said, "I can't speak for Lieutenant Izraad, but I do have some inkling of what it's like to have an overbearing older sibling, although I freely admit my brother pales in comparison to your sister—no offense."

"None taken." Narbrooi smiled, briefly. "It took me years to convince myself that I'd been wrong about her, that everyone else was right, that what she'd told me about her and Ja'andai was the truth—a sense of guilt, perhaps, over my less than pious personal reaction to the news of her death. In the process I displaced all of my anger, all of my frustrations on Khusaaq Sha'ashahn. I blamed *him*, just as Gaalan did." He paused again and managed a crooked smile.

"The irony is that had I had the chance," Narbrooi added, the smile now gone, "I would've killed Khusaaq, with my bare hands if need be—and in doing so, I would have unwittingly fulfilled her ultimate desire. Fortunately, I was never given that chance. Looking back, I now suspect the Q'shaathrah went to great lengths to keep him well away from me, at opposite ends of the arm as they say and in fact, knowing if I was ever successful, the repercussions of such an act would cause widespread chaos within the ranks of the Elkanaghalli, with ripples reaching even the lowliest castes, at a time when we were least able to cope."

He ran his finger around the rim of the now empty mug. "Gaalan admitted to me that she had been impatiently waiting for me to do just that, murder him, no matter the consequences to our lineage or to the Orthodoxy as a whole—so it came as a great shock to her that of *all* people, I was the one who came to Sha'ashahn's rescue, came to the rescue of his *doh'ha*." He flicked Izraad another sidelong, bordering on woeful look. "Had I *listened* to my own instincts from the start, Lieutenant, had I *acted* upon them, forced the Q'shaathrah to revisit my suspicions, *none* of this would have happened."

"You don't know that, Hahtra'tzrhi," Izraad found herself obligated to say, but in truth she didn't know if anything he could have done would have changed the outcome, one way or another, and she knew he knew she didn't.

He managed a smile. "Perhaps. Gaalan was—*is*—quite mad, perhaps driven to madness by the guilt of her actions, of the tens of thousands of lives her pride, her ambitions have consumed... or perhaps she was mad from the very beginning and it somehow went undetected, even on a genetic level. It would certainly explain her hatred of our lifestyle and our deeply held beliefs—and her blind fixation on Khusaaq Sha'ashahn as the cause of all her problems."

His stare turned inward, long enough for Izraad and Aquila to share a look, then he lifted his head, met Aquila's curious gaze. "Now, Commander, perhaps we should set course for Tuli?" He rubbed his hands together and smiled. Granted, a forced smile, but a smile nonetheless. "I know I speak for my crew when I say that we are all quite eager to experience what Tuli has to offer."

"Of course, Hahtra'tzrhi—I was about to suggest the same thing."

"If I might be so bold," Izraad said, "may I suggest the province of Havilah? I believe you and your crew will find it well worth a visit." She noticed Aquila's quizzical, prompting look, but ignored it.

"*Havilah,*" Narbrooi repeated, then nodded to her, "Thank you, Lieutenant, your recommendation is most appreciated." He rose. "Thank you both, for the hot chocolate... and your willingness to listen."

"Anytime, Hahtra'tzrhi—and I truly mean that," Aquila replied, then tapped the door release.

As it slipped open, Narbrooi turned to Izraad. "I am as much in your debt as I am Doctor Amalfitano and Crewman Tasende,

Lieutenant. Understand, if you ever need anything, and if it is within my power to grant or give it, it's yours."

Izraad suddenly found herself blushing. "Thank you, Hahtra'tzrhi, but William, Xosé and I are just doing our jobs."

"Indeed. As we all are." He nodded to Aquila. "We will see you again on Tuli, Commander."

"Allow me to walk you to the flickerstage," Izraad offered, surprising not only Narbrooi but Aquila.

Narbrooi grinned, genuinely pleased. "Thank you, Lieutenant, I'd like that very much."

Chapter 39

Isolation unit 2, sickbay, aboard Baidarka. *1911.*

"Mind if I join you?"

Khusaaq looked up to find Amalfitano standing in the narrow doorway of Qar'qaah's isolation cubicle. He managed a tired smile and wordlessly motioned to the fold down seat on the opposite side of Qar'qaah's bed.

Amalfitano gave the over-bed monitors a quick scan, nodded and slipped onto the chair. He glanced at the soundly sleeping Qar'qaah, then met Khusaaq's weary gaze.

"The nurses can keep an eye on him—if previous sessions are any guide, he'll sleep soundly until morning. Why don't you go back to Sirin's cabin and get some sleep yourself?"

Khusaaq dropped his gaze to Qar'qaah. "Sirin's with Lieutenant Drakin and Doctor Fleming—they took Endooki, Laihiri, Raudah, Nihaal and Matoosh to the galley. Sirin said the cooks had prepared something special for them."

Amalfitano stared at him; he knew Khusaaq was not telling all. "Qar'qaah's gonna be okay, son—Zarijan's incredibly pleased with the progress he's made so far, and once we're back on Tuli…" his voice trailed off as he realized Khusaaq was now staring at the deck. He rose. "Come with me."

Khusaaq glanced up at him.

"I said come with me."

Khusaaq reluctantly rose and together they walked down the short corridor and into the airlock. The interior door closed behind them with a soft sigh.

A moment later the exterior door snapped open; Amalfitano stepped out, nodded to the barely visible distortion of his ever-present bodyguard—Jaa'qwah this time, at least as far as the duty roster he'd been given was concerned—and headed for his office.

As he entered the untidy heart of the *Baidarka*'s sickbay, not looking to see if the two Hahtooshans followed, he gestured to a chair. "Take a seat." He circled his desk then fixed his eyes on the doorway, on the slight distortion, as Khusaaq dutifully sat. "Private meeting—sorry, Kon'ta'aq, but I'm going to have to ask for you to remain outside."

The distortion withdrew and he hit the door release. It slid closed.

He then fixed his gaze on Khusaaq. "Did you eat dinner?"

"No and it's pointless to say I'm not hungry, isn't it?"

"Yup. So I'll order us up something." Amalfitano tapped in a request then reached down and withdrew the decanter of his very best whisky and two glasses from the bottom drawer of his desk. He placed the mismatched glasses in front of him and poured them each a healthy dose then slid one of the glasses across his desk towards Khusaaq.

He waited until Khusaaq had taken a sip then said, "Zarijan told me you two had talked. She, of course, didn't give any specifics and I didn't ask for any—it's none of my business, but said she was every bit as pleased by the progress you've made as she is by Qar'qaah."

"Yes." Khusaaq took another, more generous gulp from his glass.

"That's not what's troubling you, is it?"

"No."

"Wanna talk about what is?"

Khusaaq stared down at his glass and without preamble said, "Matoosh was offered a helmsman's posting on *Faridour*. The others too have been offered postings aboard her." He took another sip, exhaled then added, "I released all of them from any obligation to me—"

"Have they accepted?"

"Our Rasharawan'tischinjgra kinsmen were very persuasive, and to be asked to serve aboard *Faridour* by Narbrooi Hahtra'tzrhi personally is an honor beyond measure. They've all accepted—and will flick aboard once we reach Tuli. That's why they went to the galley—for a farewell meal of sorts. All of their favorites."

Amalfitano felt an all too familiar, commiserating pang in his gut. He'd known Raudah, Laihiri, Nihaal and Endooki only a few days—too brief to form more than a casual attachment—and one he could easily rationalize as being purely of a medical concern, but Matoosh was another matter, despite their rocky start. Plus Matoosh and Khusaaq had seemed inseparable—*had been* inseparable, according to Matoosh, since he'd been old enough to accompany Khusaaq.

Amalfitano took a sip, savored the whisky's rich and familiar blend of burnt toast and molasses taste then swallowed the liquor. "After I got over the initial shock of losing my entire family at Raumalle, I realized I had no idea what I was going to do with the rest of my life."

Khusaaq, in the process of taking another sip himself, flicked him a cautious, sidelong glance.

"I'd had everything planned out you see." He chuckled softly. "I thought I'd covered every contingency… except them being killed." He exhaled, and settled back into his chair. Cradling the glass of whisky in his hands, he continued softly. "My father once said you never lose your place in the world as long as you have your family—" He flicked Khusaaq a glance to find him intently studying his own glass of whisky, "—and I thought, 'Yeah, nice to think so.' I mean, who plans to lose their entire family? It's not something you'd do intentionally, any more than deliberately losing your place in the world."

He paused again, this time long enough to draw Khusaaq's sidelong, and this time fixed stare. He knew he was cutting very close to the bone—for both of them—and waited until Khusaaq responded with a slight tip of the head, his silent 'go ahead'.

"A few months later I found out he was right—in the time it took me to read one sentence in a fold net message telling me they'd all been killed, I lost *everything*." He took another sip to loosen the knot that had suddenly formed in his throat then he continued. "I bounced around for years, from this ship to that—no plans, no idea where I was going—didn't care, to be honest. With the war and all, I figured eventually I'd get myself killed too, so why think about a future?" He paused and met

Khusaaq's stare as they each took a deep, bracing gulp of whisky.

"Then I met this woman in a bar on Mirfak…"

Khusaaq raised an eyebrow.

"She'd just been promoted to commander and had been given her own ship. As it turned out, she was looking for a medical officer—thought the one she was going to be assigned was a flaming idiot better suited to be a second tier sewage line inspector on some mined-out asteroid, or so she said. She was funny, incredibly bright, and it didn't hurt that she was damned gorgeous… of course I fell madly in love with her. Calling in all my debts, and her doing some backroom bargaining, we managed to wangle me a transfer—ditto the medical officer originally assigned to her ship... and to an asteroid no less." He chuckled. "Her idea of a joke."

Khusaaq swallowed his mouthful of liquor then asked huskily, "What happened?"

"I quickly found out she wasn't madly in love with me."

Khusaaq quirked the same eyebrow but said nothing.

"I mistook her interest in me as a damned good doctor for interest in me as a man. Silly mistake. Looking back, I realized she'd never done anything to suggest her interest in me was anything but professional." He shrugged, added, "But by the time I realized this, it was too late; I was aboard the *Baidarka* and we'd shipped out. So, I figured I'd make the best of the situation—not that there was much else I could do. I felt like a complete fool—*was a complete fool*. But you know it didn't take long for me to realize that that transfer was the best thing that had ever happened to me. Because while Gildun Vildur didn't share my affections, she turned out to be a great friend—the closest friend I've ever had.

"And before I knew it, this ship had become my home and this crew had become my family—I also found the love of my life—the *true* love of my life, Zarijan." He stared down at his glass for a moment, added softly, "Gildun was killed shortly before I met you—in a Matarran ambush. Most of the damage..." he waved his hand around.

Khusaaq nodded his understanding. "I'm very sorry."

To Amalfitano, he did sound sorry—and not a little relieved, as if fully expecting Amalfitano to tell him he'd lost yet another loved one to Hahtooshans.

Amalfitano twitched off the comment. "Death comes to us all, son—and she was doing what she loved best—captaining her own ship, protecting the Coalition... probably didn't even know what hit her... a Matarran mine holed the conference room, killed twenty eight crew—it was her fiftieth birthday party and from what I heard afterwards, she was having the time of her life, so were all the crew present. I was running late, furious a damned moron of a rail gunner had smashed his finger—" He paused to take a deep, ragged breath then he looked squarely at Khusaaq. "Nothing stays constant, son, no matter how much we'd wish it were so."

Khusaaq took a wincing gulp of the potent liquor then admitted softly, "I... I don't know what I am going to do with the rest of my life." He then took another, smaller sip and swallowed. "I never thought about my future—never had any reason to, until I met Sirin. I *want* a future with her, I want to grow old with her, but..."

"You can't return to the Orthodoxy, even briefly."

He shook his head.

"Which means you cannot serve aboard any Orthodoxy vessel."

This time Khusaaq nodded before tossing back the rest of the liquor.

"Maybe things will change—Commander Aquila told me that Narbrooi admits you were blameless—"

"*Before*. But we're not talking about *before*. We're not talking about Cotopaxi and Gaalan. We're talking about *now*, about my decision to ally myself with the Coalition... *before* the Orthodoxy decided to ally itself with the Coalition."

"So *this* before, not *that* before."

"Yes."

"But you did what you did not out of some selfish need, but to *save* your people—and you were encouraged, one could even say *compelled* to do so by your Elkanasu—you told me so yourself, and I assume you got a chance to tell Narbrooi that, too."

"Yes." He nodded. "But A'tuu'shahn'i, as you might have noticed, aren't prone to seeing the world around them in shades of gray—unless they're around humans," he added as if it was some sort of private joke, "any more than they welcome freethinkers. Everything is black and white—in our line of work it has to be, otherwise we'd be constantly questioning ourselves and everything we do. And ironically, the more devout the A'tuu'shahn claims to be, the less likely he or she will accept the 'Elkanasu made me do it' rationale."

"So you don't think you'll *ever* be forgiven for averting the intentional genocide of your people."

"Officially? Perhaps. According to Hahtra'tzrhi, some sort of amnesty is in the works, but again according to him, *unofficially?* No."

Amalfitano blew out his cheeks and shook his head, then decided to change tack. "You have a skill Tuli direly needs, son. You'll never want for work—in fact I think you'll have more offers than you'll know what to do with."

Khusaaq nodded again but there was a crease in his brow that spoke more eloquently than any words: he was far from convinced.

"And you'll have other things to keep you occupied."

Khusaaq gave him an almost wary look.

"For one, Zarijan and I have a wedding gift for you."

He arched a brow.

"She swore me to secrecy until we all get back to Tuli, but trust me, you're gonna really love it. Picked it out myself."

The brow remained fixed where it was.

"And then there's Qar'qaah—"

"Yes," he sighed, "Qar'qaah. He can't return either, you realize that—even without the matter of what Gaalan did to him... well, he's my *doh'ha*. On top of that, he's undergone the *turee*."

"I... sort of figured that might be the case. I'm sorry."

Khusaaq shrugged.

"Wait—speaking of the *turee,* I've been meaning to ask you—about your tattoos, and his."

"What about them?"

"I saw his change... darken a little bit, after we returned from the *Faridour.* And yours are more complex than they were, I swear they are—his too."

Khusaaq lightly touched his right arm with his left hand. "The Elkanasu... call it our... reward for being their faithful servants."

"Reward? I don't—"

"My reward for saving my people, and Qar'qaah's... he was given the opportunity to execute Gaalan—did he tell you that?"

Amalfitano shook his head.

"He refused, said her fate wasn't up to him. And in not allowing himself to seek revenge, as richly deserved as it was, Gaalan will now answer to the Q'shaathrah. You could say each was a test of our true selves—our true devotion to our people and the greater good, no matter the personal cost." He shrugged, as if it meant nothing when it was obvious to Amalfitano it meant everything—had in fact cost both of them dearly and almost beyond imagining. "We both passed," he again fingered his right arm, "as you Rimmers would say, with flying colors."

"Robert said that Narbrooi said Gaalan will be a treasure trove of intelligence."

"Indeed she will—she already has. Assuming she makes it back to the Q'shaathrah."

"You think someone will assassinate her to keep her quiet?"

"Or engineer her escape."

Amalfitano sat back in his chair; that was a scenario that hadn't occurred to him.

"She still has her followers, *husahn,* and her unexpected resurrection from the dead as stirred old passions, old enmities. This alliance with your Coalition is not popular among the rank and file, as I think you know."

"Narbrooi told the commander and Lieutenants Izraad and Teague as much, so yes—"

"The dead should stay dead," Khusaaq muttered as he stared down at his empty glass, "where their ability to create mischief is limited to haunting one's dreams."

"Indeed," Amalfitano replied, waited a moment then said, "So the Elkanasu somehow *embroidered* on your existing tattoos as a way of saying thanks, job well done."

"Yes. You could say that."

"And what about Qar'qaah's—they not just more complex, they *are* darker, aren't they? Murh'sooli gave me the impression that once you've begun the *turee* there's no going back. It might stop, but it doesn't reverse."

"The Elkanasu can largely reverse it—in rare cases."

"Oh," Amalfitano replied, confused.

"It seems there is some benefit to carrying the *paas'nah* after all," Khusaaq added, then smiled thinly at him.

"Oh... *oh!"* Amalfitano said and suddenly grinned. "I'll be damned."

"They'll never be as dark as they were, but dark enough other A'tuu'shahn'i won't dare treat him as a pariah—how can you be an outcast when you've been so visibly extolled by the Elkanasu?"

"Indeed not." Amalfitano chuckled then picked up the decanter. "I think you need another drink—we both do."

Khusaaq immediately held out his glass and Amalfitano filled it to the rim then quickly filled his own. "Bottom's up." He drained the glass in several loud quaffs.

After a moment's hesitation, Khusaaq followed suit, hastily gulping down the contents of his own.

Amalfitano gave the potent alcohol enough time to hit Khusaaq's bloodstream—and his—by muttering irritably about their delayed dinner. In fact he *had* put a delay on it, hoping to use the time to get Khusaaq just a little drunk, a little loosened up by taking advantage of his empty stomach.

"There's something else I've been meaning to talk to you about—"

"And that is?" Khusaaq was instantly *on*—adrenaline trumped alcohol, every muscle in his body had tightened, startled, his mind clearly running through all the possibilities—none of them good, warned by Amalfitano's change in tone—

"Sirin's pregnant."

A couple of thumping heartbeats followed.

"I know," Khusaaq replied simply and brought the glass to his lips, too late realizing it was empty.

Amalfitano stared at him, stunned and at the same time, deflated. "But... but how the hell could you possibly know? She's only a couple of weeks along—" He held up his hand. "And please don't tell me it's because you're A'tuu'shahn."

Khusaaq replied with a cryptic, "I was able to induce her cycle—your Lieutenant Izraad isn't the only one who can generate *very* specific pheromones—then all it took was some mutually agreed upon physical effort, quite a lot in fact, just to make sure." He paused to grin a very pleased grin. "Sirin had said she'd always wanted children, in fact wanted to get started on a family as soon as possible... and I thought if something happened to me..." He chuckled, "*A son.* I'm going to have a son... and you're going to be a grandfather."

"A... a *boy?*" Amalfitano slumped back in his chair, stunned. Once the lab had notified him of the startling results of Sirin's physical and that the hybrid embryo was viable, he swore the techs involved to secrecy. He'd gone no further, too preoccupied treating Qar'qaah. Then the full impact of what Khusaaq had said hit him and he started to laugh.

Khusaaq grinned, grabbed the decanter and topped off their glasses.

Amalfitano eagerly reached for his. "Have you told Sirin?"

Khusaaq's grin dissolved. "No... have you?"

Amalfitano suddenly sobered as he realized that somewhere along the line a very important part of the equation had been left out. "I'd planned on telling you together, but things kept happening..." He paused, looking a little sheepish. "I suppose we should."

"Well, if we don't, I suspect she'll figure it out... eventually."

Amalfitano chuckled and rose from his desk. "Come on, we have some good news to deliver... along with a grandson!"

We hope you've enjoyed OUT OF THE EMBERS OF HELL by J. E. Bruce. Be sure to check out all of the novels in the Coalition/Orthodoxy Universe series as well as the author's other tales of speculative fiction.

Books by J. E. Bruce

Redoubt of Ghosts
Stalking the Apocalypse*
Path to the Night Mountains*
Out of the Embers of Hell*
Snakestone and Sword**
Hide and Sidhe**

* Coalition/Orthodoxy Universe
** Centurion in the Land of Fae

www.ingramcontent.com/pod-product-compliance
Lightning Source LLC
Chambersburg PA
CBHW060342260626
47160CB00006B/2182